The Collected Supernatural and Weird Fiction of Malden & Pater

The Collected Supernatural and Weird Fiction of Malden & Pater

Twenty-Three Short Tales to Chill the Blood
Including 'The Dining-Room Fireplace',
'Between Sunset and Moonrise', 'The Coxswain
of the Lifeboat', 'The Warnings', 'The Treasure of
the Blue Nuns' and 'The Scapegoat'

R. H. Malden
Nine Ghost Stories

&

Roger Pater
Mystic Voices

LEONAUR

The Collected
Supernatural and Weird
Fiction of
Malden & Pater
Twenty-Three Short Tales to Chill the Blood Including 'The Dining-Room Fireplace', 'Between Sunset and Moonrise', 'The Coxswain of the Lifeboat', 'The Warnings', 'The Treasure of the Blue Nuns' and 'The Scapegoat'
R. H. Malden
&
Roger Pater

FIRST EDITION

First published under the titles
Nine Ghost Stories
and
Mystic Voices

Leonaur is an imprint of Oakpast Ltd

Copyright in this form © 2025 Oakpast Ltd

ISBN: 978-1-917666-38-1 (hardcover)
ISBN: 978-1-917666-39-8 (softcover)

http://www.leonaur.com

Publisher's Notes

Contents

Nine Ghost Stories

R. H. Malden

Contents

A Collector's Company

The story which follows was told to me rather more than thirty years ago. The narrator was elderly then. He died very soon after the end of the last war with Germany, so there can be no harm in repeating it now. His name, if you want to know, was Arthur Harberton. As he was a young man when it happened to him, I suppose it must be dated not long after the year 1870. I made notes of it at the time, and reproduce it now as nearly as I can in his own words.

'Three years after my ordination I was offered a post as a college lecturer at Cambridge. That was the kind of work which I had always thought that I should like, at any rate for a few years, so I accepted the offer very gladly. I have never regretted that I did so; nor that I did not devote the rest of my life to academic work.

'I was not dean of the college, and as in those days the number of Fellows in Holy Order was much larger than it is now it was very seldom necessary for me to be in the Chapel on a Sunday. Accordingly, I used to go about the diocese a good deal, visiting the country churches. I don't think that I was under any illusion as to my powers as a preacher, even then. But I thought, without, I hope, undue vanity, that it might be good for village congregations to hear a fresh voice occasionally, and even for the incumbent if he were present. That was not always the case, for I was always willing to take the whole duty of the day if I were asked, so that the incumbent might secure a short holiday.

'As a rule, I enjoyed these expeditions thoroughly. They began with a short train journey, followed by a drive from the station, sometimes of as much as ten miles. Country lanes were country lanes then. They had not been blackened with tarmacadam and motor-cars were, of course, unknown. An occasional traction engine, preceded by a man on foot carrying a red flag, was the only disagreeable object likely to be encountered. From a dog-cart, which was usually the vehicle

11

which came to meet me, it was possible to see over the hedges and to get a very fair idea of the country as you went along at eight to ten miles an hour.

'My hosts were generally interesting. For the most part they were country-bred men who belonged naturally to their surroundings. Many of them had a wide variety of interests (and sometimes a store of real knowledge) on which they were ready to discourse to a stranger. When I had the house to myself it was amusing to try to deduce what manner of man the owner might be from his books and pictures.

'Most of the churches and a good many of the houses presented features of architectural interest, which appealed to me strongly. Besides, I used to enjoy such conversations as I might have with rural churchwardens, sextons and other parish officials. I remember one churchwarden (a farmer, I think) who had heard that Huntingdon was a fine town. Personally, he had never penetrated farther than St. Neots. When I told him that I lived at Cambridge I might as well have said Pekin, or Timbuctoo.

'In another place the village school-master was opposed to elementary education in the abstract: not merely to the particular form of it which he was required to administer. He thought it unsettled children and took them off the land. There was, no doubt, something to be said on behalf of his views; but I couldn't help wondering whether he were *quite* the right man in the right place. Well—no doubt the countryside is more sophisticated now, and I won't bore you with speculations as to whether the gains outweigh the losses or not.

'So, as you see, I had good reason to look forward to these excursions. In fact, I only once got to a place which I should not care to visit again, and that is the one which I am going to tell you about now. All the same, I don't entirely regret that I did go there. Anyhow, it was a unique experience.

'Towards the end of one October term, I got a letter from the bishop's chaplain, asking me if I could preach twice on the following Sunday at a village about twenty-five miles from Cambridge—I don't think I will tell you in what direction. The incumbent, it appeared, was not very well, and having no curate was doubtful of his ability to get through the day single-handed. As it would be the second Sunday in Advent it would not be difficult for me to preach at short notice. The collect and epistle for the day provided me with a subject ready-made: a subject, moreover, which I have always found particularly congenial.

'I discovered that there was a convenient train to the nearest station on the Saturday afternoon and from it on the Monday morning, so I telegraphed Yes, and wrote to my prospective host to say when I might be expected.

'It was a little after three when I got out at a wayside station. I was met by a groom with a dog-cart who brought a note from his master apologising for not having come in person. As I had understood that he wasn't well I hadn't expected him. I will call him Melrose.

'As we drove away from the station I said to the groom, "I hope Mr. Melrose has nothing serious the matter with him?"

'"No," he replied, "but he *du* come over all queer-like at times—so he du. When he have one of his turns—well, it's not for me to be explaining of it, if you take my meaning, Sir."

'I was not at all sure that I did, but thought it would be ill-bred on my part to ask for details. Also, I was inclined to suspect that they might be copious rather than enlightening. However, as my companion seemed inclined to talk, I did not feel bound to try to suppress him.

'I gathered that Mr. Melrose was wealthy and a bachelor. He had "travelled furren," which was regarded locally as a hazardous proceeding, on the ground that all foreigners are well known to be black, and that they blackamoors might be up to anything. He was much took up with reading: also in my companion's opinion a dubious proceeding. For if there was good in some books there was bad in others, and how'd you know which till arterwards, and then it was done.

'The general impression left on my mind was that while Mr. Melrose might be loved by his parishioners he was certainly feared. I thought that I might look forward to an unusually interesting weekend. As it turned out this expectation was not unduly sanguine, as I think you will agree when you have heard the rest of my story.

'After a drive of about seven miles we arrived. The light was failing, but I could see that the house was an old one. It was rather larger than the average, and I judged that there was probably a considerable garden behind it. I looked forward to examining both more closely between services on Sunday.

'Mr. Melrose made me very welcome. He was a tall man who stooped a little. I set him down as about seventy; probably over rather than under. He had abundant white hair and very prominent white eyebrows. His eyes were dark and his nose aquiline. The general effect was scholarly and striking. He would have been noticeable in

13

any company, and once seen would always be remembered. My first impression was that he was very handsome.'

Here Mr. Harberton paused for a minute or two and then said rather abruptly, 'Did you ever see Thompson (W. H. Thompson, 1866-86.), the Master of Trinity?'

'No,' I said. 'He was some years before my time. But I know the portrait; by Richmond, I think.'

'No, of course you didn't,' he went on. 'Stupid of me. But one forgets how time passes. I don't think the portrait really does him justice. However, if you know it, you'll understand what I am going to say.

'I knew him very well by sight and he was one of the most distinguished-looking men I have ever seen. He was handsome if you like, and you couldn't doubt his ability or force of character. You had only to look at him to see that he was a great man. Yet somehow, I never could think his face a pleasing one. It always seemed to me to contain great possibilities of evil. I could believe him to be capable of absolutely diabolical conduct.'

'Well,' I said, 'I believe that when Richmond painted Lightfoot, he declared that he had never had a sitter whose jaw was so obviously and unmistakably that of a murderer. And I have been told by people who knew the bishop well that they could believe that he had a naturally violent temper, and that his complete mastery of it was part of his greatness. The same may have been true of Thompson.'

'Yes,' said Mr. Harberton, 'it may. Anyhow, this was the effect which Mr. Melrose produced on me. However, I tried to dismiss it from my mind as foolishness.

'After tea, which we had in a square hall by a log fire, Mr. Melrose asked me to excuse him until dinner-time as he had some letters to write and the post went out at six-thirty. He had a small study on the first floor opening out of his bedroom to which he proposed to betake himself. The library, which was on the ground floor and opened out of the hall, was at my disposal and there were writing materials there if I wanted them.

'The library was a large room, completely lined with bookcases. A cursory inspection of these showed that my host was a man of wide and miscellaneous reading. He seemed to be particularly interested in the later Neoplatonists and to be well supplied with Orphic literature. On a glass-topped table by the window was a collection of Gnostic gems. An Egyptian mummy-case stood upright in a corner. On a table by the fire was a book which he had presumably been reading when I

14

arrived. I picked it up and found that it was Philostratus' *Life of Apollonius of Tyana*. It had been interleaved and was copiously annotated. I should have liked to read some of the notes, but thought that would be impertinent.

'Evidently I was in the house of a scholar whose interests were out of the common run, and the possessor of means which enabled him to indulge them freely.'

'At dinner he proved very good company. He had travelled widely and had visited places which were then very much off the beaten track, such as Sicily and Transylvania. He had spent some considerable time in the latter country and had made a careful study of its grim folklore.

'The dinner was good, and my host exerted himself to be pleasant. Interesting he undoubtedly was, but I was not at all sure how much I liked him. I had a vague feeling that in some way he was playing a part. But I could find no rational ground for my suspicion. And, after all, why should he think it worthwhile to try to impress anyone so much younger than himself?

'It struck me as curious that a man of his calibre should be content to bury himself in so obscure a place. Of course, the country was much more prosperous then than it is now and rural life offered more interests than I fear it does today. But this particular neighbourhood was not specially attractive in any way. Most of the land had belonged to the See of Ely and was now administered by the Ecclesiastical Commissioners. I believe that they are always considered to be good landlords, but naturally there are seldom any country-houses other than farms on their estates. I could hardly see my host at ease in the society of farmers, nor could I imagine that they would be able to make much of him. (I had discovered that he did not shoot or hunt, and in those days a man who did neither was very much out of it in the country.)

'When he told me that he had been rector of the parish for more than thirty years I could not help expressing surprise—rather clumsily, I fear, and perhaps not too politely, but I was very young then—and saying something about the solitariness of the life which he led.

'"Yes," he said; "I don't wonder that it strikes you like that. The road from the station is rather desolate. But I have plenty of occupation and interests here; and do you know I find some of my neighbours more companionable than you would expect."

'The last sentence struck me as rather odd, not only in itself but in the way he said it. I felt that there was more behind the remark than I was meant to understand, and did not like the feeling. I liked the laugh which followed it even less. However, there was obviously no more to be said about that. Perhaps he thought I had been rather impertinent, and perhaps he was right.

'After dinner we went into the library for coffee, and somehow our talk drifted to witchcraft, necromancy and kindred topics. I had always taken an interest in such matters, if not a very serious one, and have often wondered what foundation, if any, there is or was for the belief that the powers to which witches lay claim have any real existence.

'At this distance of time I do not mind admitting that as an undergraduate I had once made an essay in Invultuadon. The object was the Vice-Chancellor of the day, whom I did not know by sight. He had annoyed me by refusing to allow a play which I had written to be acted publicly by the A.D.C., on the ground that it was disrespectful to authority. I adopted the only method of retaliation which seemed to be open. I made a waxen image and placed it on my mantelpiece. After some incantations which I thought appropriate (*Flectere si nequeo superos Acheronta movebo* (*Aeneid*, vii. 12.) is the only line which I remember now) I inserted a pin into one leg. The very next day I heard that the Vice-Chancellor had slipped going downstairs in his lodge and had sprained one of his ankles. I felt that my cause had been vindicated and took no further steps. But, as you will understand, I had not been serious in the matter. I never pretended to think that the accident had been more than a coincidence for which I need not reproach myself. The story leaked out somehow, and one comment on it which came to my ears was "Whole religions have been founded upon less evidence." I will not name the author, but I still think he ought to have known better.

'Mr. Melrose's discourse seemed to me to be a very different story. I could not help thinking that he knew more than he ought about a great deal which was very undesirable. And he spoke with an air of inside knowledge which I found disquieting. His tone was that of a lecturer on a subject which he had really made his own, and he gave the impression of having verified at least some of his knowledge by experiment. I felt that there was something malign about him, as well as creepy.

'Finally, I came to the conclusion that he was like an evil caricature of Dr. Hans Emmanuel Bryerley, the Swedenborgian teacher in *Uncle*

16

Silas. (By Joseph Sheridan Le Fanu.) Altogether I was extremely glad when he suggested a move bedwards, and was at pains to lock the door of my room. Perhaps that would not avail much if it came to the point. But the illusion of security which it produced was comforting.

'I do not know how long I had been asleep when I awoke with the impression which one sometimes has of having been disturbed by a loud and sudden noise. Probably the church clock, I thought, though I had not noticed its strike earlier in the evening. I was just disposing myself for a renewed period of slumber when it struck me that although my fire had burned low the room was curiously light; not with firelight either. I had drawn back the window curtains before going to bed, as I usually did, and the light was coming from the window.

'"Moonlight," you will say. 'But I knew that it was not. In the first place, the moon was several days short of full, and in the second, the light was not coming from a particular point. It was evenly diffused, like daylight on a cloudy day; and no moon could have produced so much light from behind clouds. It seemed to me to have a bluish tinge which was unnatural and unpleasant. I went to the window and looked out. It commanded a view of a good-sized lawn flanked by dark shrubberies of some sort—rhododendrons; I found out subsequently.

'This lawn sloped slightly upwards away from the house, and at the farther end was a low wall with a gateway in it leading to the churchyard. This and the church itself were as plainly visible as if it had been midday instead of just after midnight in December. But everything to right and left was in darkness. I felt as if I were looking down an illuminated tunnel, and it seemed obvious that something would appear at the upper end. I took my courage in both hands and waited. I did not have to wait long. Through the gate in the churchyard wall came my host. He seemed to be wearing a cassock with a long black cloak over it. On his head was a high-pointed cap, something like a mitre, and he carried a short rod in his right hand. He came straight down the lawn towards the house. I wondered whether I was as visible to him as he was to me; and hoped not. Anyhow I felt bound to see the performance through. He was followed by a number of figures: I think about twelve, but I could not be sure.

'Although there seemed to be plenty of light, they were somehow curiously indistinct. They may have dodged behind each other from time to time in some odd fashion. Anyhow I found that it was no use to try to count them. They were dressed in long black cloaks with

17

hoods, which prevented their faces from being seen. On the whole I felt glad of that. They moved rather stiffly, like marionettes. Of course, their feet made no sound upon the grass. But I was conscious of a faint creaking, the source of which was not easy to determine. It might have been produced by the breeze in the shrubbery; but I did not think that it was.

'The procession advanced until it had reached the middle of the lawn. Then the leader stopped and the others formed a circle round him. Still, I could not be sure how many they were. Every time I tried to count them, I became confused and arrived at a different result.

'Then they began to dance while he beat time or conducted, how-ever you like to put it, with his wand. They moved more quickly than I should have expected, though they still suggested marionettes. The faint creaking which I had heard before was more audible. There could be no doubt now that it came from the dancing figures.

'Do you remember a story told by one of the minor characters in Stevenson's *Catriona*? About Tod Lapraik, the warlock weaver of Leith. He used to fall into a dwam in his house and once while he was in that state, he, or something in his likeness, was seen dancing alone on the Bass Rock "in the black glory of his heart." Those words rose in my mind now. The performance which I was watching seemed to be inspired by an unholy—well, *joie de vivre* I suppose I must call it, though I don't know how far the dancers could be considered to be alive. The whole effect was abominably, indescribably evil. Yet, curi-ously enough, I did not feel afraid. I have never considered myself a particularly courageous person, and have not had many opportunities of discovering whether I am or not. But anyhow I was not conscious of any fear then. Partly perhaps I was too deeply interested in what I was watching to think of anything else. Also, youth and a good diges-tion will carry their possessor securely through many of the changes and chances of this mortal life.

'The dance grew faster, and the ring of dancers contracted. As it did so the mysterious light contracted too. I could no longer see the church, or the greater part of the lawn. Only the tall stationary figure with his black-shrouded companions whirling—it had come to that now—whirling round him. The group was illuminated as a particular figure sometimes is upon the stage (spotlight, I think they call it), but as before the light did not seem to be coming from any particular direction. Perhaps this was why I could see no shadow upon the grass.

'In another minute the dancers seemed to have closed in and then (as was perhaps to be expected) the light went out. I could neither see nor hear anything. The garden seemed to be as dark and deserted as you might expect between midnight and 1 a.m. on a moonless night in December. As I turned away from the window I heard the discordant cry of a night-jar (at least that was what I thought it sounded like) very loud and apparently very close to my window. Immediately afterwards I heard a low chuckle. It was not a pleasant one. I felt pretty sure that whatever the joke might be I should prefer not to meet the author of it. I made certain that my door was locked, made up my fire to last until daylight, got into bed and rather to my surprise fell asleep almost immediately.

'It was getting light when I woke. I got out of bed and unlocked my door. As I waited to be called, I naturally thought of my experience of a few hours earlier. The more I considered it the less confident did I become that I had not dreamed the whole thing. I have always been an active and vivid dreamer, but have never had a vision of my head upon my bed worth taking seriously; even by the most nasty-minded psycho-analyst who ever came out of Vienna or anywhere else.

'At eight o'clock the butler brought me tea and hot water. On the tray was a note from Mr. Melrose saying that he regretted that he was unable to leave his room. The clerk would show me where everything was in the church. Would I make myself at home in the house and ask for anything I wanted, etc. etc.'

'"Is your master seriously ill?" I asked the man. "Ought a doctor to be sent for, or can you look after him?"

'"No, Sir, not serious. But he don't come down as a rule, after one of his nights, not for a day or two."

'For a moment I thought he was going to say more, but he turned away and began laying out my clothes. So, I said something to the effect that old people often slept badly and that no doubt a wakeful night was very exhausting.

'To this he merely replied, "Yes, Sir," and left the room.

'While I was drinking my tea, I thought I would look at the lessons for the day, as I should probably have to read them myself. There was a Bible beside my bed and I opened it at Isaiah (the first lesson was Chapter 5, as you probably remember), and it so happened that the first words which caught my eye were from Chapter 8, verse 19, *Seek unto them that have familiar spirits and unto the wizards that peep and that mutter.*

'No doubt a coincidence. But as I dressed, I became more and more inclined to think that I had not been dreaming.

'The day passed uneventfully. Evensong was at three, as was not unusual in the country then during the winter months; I must confess that I was glad of this as I did not relish the prospect of coming down the lawn from the church in the dark. Of course it was getting dark by the time service was over, and as I went through the gate leading from the churchyard, I had an uncomfortable feeling that my movements were being watched by some person or persons whom I could not see—and not with any amiable solicitude for my welfare.

'However, nothing untoward happened then or during the evening. I went to bed early and slept soundly all night. Next morning the butler brought another note from my host, expressing his regret that he would be unable to see me before I left, the disappointment which he felt at having had so little of my society, and a hope that I had been made comfortable.

'I replied to the first two heads of this communication as politely as was consistent with the truth. As regards the third I could reassure him honestly. I left the house soon after breakfast. The butler had not seemed disposed to be communicative, nor was the groom who drove me to the station. Three days later I went down for the Christmas vacation.'

'Mr. Harberton was silent for a minute or two, so I asked—I must admit with a feeling of disappointment—'Is that all?'

'Not quite,' he replied. 'But for the conclusion of the story you had better read this.'

He handed me a cutting from a newspaper, probably a local weekly, which he took from a large old-fashioned pocket-book. I had seen the book before, as it was his practice to carry it with him. The cutting was from the bottom of a column, so no date was visible. I judged it to be about thirty years old. It ran as follows:

'Rector's Strange Death
'A painful sensation was produced at (the name of the place was carefully erased) on Christmas morning.
'As soon as it was light the sexton (Mr. Jonas Day) had gone to the church to make up the fire in the stove. As he approached the south door, he was horrified to observe the body of the rector lying face downwards on a flight of four steps leading from the churchyard to the rectory garden. He went at once to the house and summoned the butler (Mr. Thomas Blogg) and the

20

groom (Mr. Henry Meekin). They carried the Rev. gentleman to his room, but it was all too evident that the vital spark had ceased to pulsate. Dr. Horridge was sent for and arrived a little before ten o'clock. He reported that the neck of the deceased was broken and that death must have intervened some hours before.

'It may be presumed that the unfortunate gentleman had gone to the church at a late hour to satisfy himself that everything was in order for the morrow. The steps were slippery with frost and he did not appear to have taken a lantern.

'The Rev. (name erased) had held the rectory for thirty-two years and the sad occurrence cast a deep aroma of gloom over the festivities naturally incidental to the day.

'The inquest was held at the Fox and Grapes on the 30th ult., Dr. Horridge presiding as Coroner. Mr. Blogg deposed that his master not infrequently went to the church late at night. When asked by one of the Jury if he knew for what purpose, he replied that he had never demeaned himself to curiosity in his master's business. He was warmly commended by the coroner for his reply.

'Mr. Day deposed that when he approached the body, he saw some curious marks on the back of the coat. When pressed to describe them he said "Like muddy claws." Neither Mr. Blogg nor Mr. Meekin had noticed these. The coat was sent for, but it had been brushed. The coroner thought that they might easily have been made by an owl or some other bird of the night perching upon the body after life was extinct, and by his direction the Jury returned a verdict of *Death by Misadventure*.

'The funereal obsequies were celebrated on the and instant.'

'May I take a copy of this?' I asked.
'Yes, if you like,' said Mr. Harberton. And I did.

The Dining-Room Fireplace

Anyone who knows the neighbourhood of Dublin will remember the good-sized country-houses in which it abounds. Most of them date from the eighteenth century, when Irish landowners were prosperous and labour was cheap. Some of them incorporate bits of older buildings which may have begun life as castles of the Pale. Most of them are now in a state of dilapidation which is not unpicturesque, though it would be out of place in England.

Perhaps I ought to have used the past tense. I do not know how many of them have survived the establishment of Eire—or whatever that part of Ireland chooses to call itself nowadays—and I do not feel tempted to go and see.

I am writing of things as they were during the closing years of the reign of Queen Victoria.

It was during a visit to one of them in the autumn of the year 1899 that the experience, I can hardly dignify it by the name of adventure, which I am about to relate befell me.

It belonged to a family named Moore who had inhabited it for several generations. The present owner was a young man, unmarried and in the army. Naturally he could not spend much of his time there and was glad to let it when he could. It had been taken for one summer by some cousins of mine who lived in Dublin, and it was on their invitation that I was there.

I need not try your patience by attempting to describe it in detail. There was nothing very noteworthy about it except an almost ruinous tower at the north-west angle. This was obviously much older than the rest of the house, and we young people thought it ought to contain a ghost. We could not, however, hear of any story to that effect. We explored it pretty thoroughly, but found nothing more exciting than a very large quantity of dust and a few bats. We went there once late on a moonlight evening, but even then, could not pretend that we saw or heard anything unusual.

The south side of the house consisted of three large rooms: a drawing-room at the western end, then a dining-room opening out of it and lastly a billiard-room which was also used as a gun-room. Probably, in fact, it had been built as a gun-room and the billiard-table had been added afterwards. It had a door leading into the garden, but there was no access to it from the house except from the dining-room.

The dining-room was hung with portraits of bygone Moores, who had no doubt played their several parts adequately in their generation. But none of them had reached fame and the pictures were of no outstanding artistic merit. The collection as a whole looked well enough, but was not likely to be of much interest, except to members of the family.

One picture there was, however, which did arouse our curiosity. It represented a man of about thirty. There was no name or date upon the frame, but the dress was that of the closing years of the eighteenth century. The most remarkable thing about it was the attitude which the sitter had chosen to adopt. He was astride of a chair with his arms folded and resting on the top rail. His back was towards the spectator, so that his features would have been invisible if he had not been looking over his left shoulder. His face, so far as it could be seen, did not resemble a Moore. The upper part suggested considerable intellectual power; the lower part was not pleasant. The whole effect was formidable and bespoke a man who would be a very dangerous enemy.

The execution was not particularly good; in fact, the technique suggested an amateur. But it was impossible not to feel that the artist had caught the likeness of his original well; and difficult not to regret that he had done so. We wondered why such a curious picture, which did not look like a family portrait, should be displayed so conspicuously. It looked as if there must be a story of some sort about it.

A few days later Captain Moore called. He was stationed at the Curragh, and having some business to transact in Dublin very civilly looked in to ask after his tenants' comfort. We ventured to put a question about the curious portrait.

'Yes,' he said, 'it's a fantastic thing, isn't it? Clever in a way though, and I should think a good likeness. But I don't know who it is any more than you do. It isn't one of the family—you'd guess that, I hope, by looking at it. All I know about it is that my great-grandfather—the old boy over there (here he pointed to a portrait of the same period which hung exactly opposite on the other side of the room)—stuck it up about the time of the Union. I rather think he painted it himself. Anyhow he was so keen about it that he left directions in his will that it was never to be moved. So, there it's been ever since. I expect there is a story, if I knew what it was. I believe my great-grandfather had been pretty wild in his young days. A lot of his generation were dazzled by the French Revolution, y'know.

'I dare say it looked better at a distance than at close quarters. But while he was still pretty young—about the turn of the century, I think—he turned over a new leaf, Model Country Gentleman, Magistrate, Churchwarden, all that sort of thing, y'know, and I believe a really good man into the bargain. Very charitable and so on. Not very hospitable though, by all accounts. In fact, during the last years of his life when he was a widower, he would hardly see anybody, and I believe was nicknamed The Hermit. I remember once when I was a little chap, about six, I think, I was playing in the dining-room on a winter afternoon. I think the nursery chimney was being swept; anyhow I had been sent downstairs for some reason. It was getting dark—and something gave me a terrible fright. The funny thing was that I couldn't say what it was and I don't know now.

'But I think it was something to do with that picture. I ran screaming into the drawing-room where my mother was and though I couldn't tell her what was the matter, I am sure that she thought it was that. When I had been comforted my father came in (he had been out shooting, I think) and she began to talk to him very earnestly. I wasn't meant to hear and don't suppose I should have understood much if I had, but I do recollect that she said something to the effect that it couldn't go on and that it wasn't as if this were the first time. And he said that he couldn't do—whatever it was she wanted him to do. I suppose now she was asking him to have the picture moved, or perhaps to get rid of it outright and he was reminding her of the clause in his grandfather's will. Of course, ninety-nine women out of a hundred would see no reason why the wishes of someone who had been dead for more than fifty years should be allowed to interfere with their own. Anyhow, that was the nearest approach to a quarrel which my father and mother ever had, that I can remember. And the picture stopped in its place, as you see.

'I once asked him about it. He looked very grave and was silent for a minute or two, as if he were making up his mind about something. Then he said, "I'll tell you what I know about it someday, but not just now. You must wait until you are older," and I had to be content with that.

'Both he and my mother died soon afterwards, and I went to live with an uncle on her side (my father had been an only son), and the house was shut up for several years. So, I never heard the story, whatever it may be. I expect old Barton at the lodge knows something about it. He's been on the place all his life, and his father and grandfather before him. But I'm pretty sure he wouldn't tell anybody if he did know.'

After Captain Moore had gone, I went and examined the picture more closely than I had ever done before. I came to the conclusion that it was a cleverer thing, and a more repulsive subject, than I had thought at first. One thing perplexed me very much. I tried to put myself into the position of the sitter and found that I could not twist my head round as far as his. His chin was almost on his left shoulder. Why had he chosen to be painted in such an unnatural and indeed, as it seemed, impossible attitude? And how had he contrived to sit for it?

I don't think the expression Rubber-neck (which I believe to be American for Sightseer) had been coined then. Or if it had it hadn't crossed the Atlantic. But I can think of no one to whom it would be more appropriate.

A day or two afterwards I happened to see Barton in his garden and thought I would try whether there was anything to be got out of him. Like all his kind his conversational powers were remarkable and he was never unwilling to exercise them. Eventually, I got him on to the pictures in the house, and I thought that he seemed to feel that he was being drawn towards thin ice. How would the like of him know anything about them, or photygrafts either? Sure, I must ask the young master about them, and wasn't he in the house only last week?

I recognised that Captain Moore's estimate of him as a source of information on this point had been accurate.

A few nights afterwards when we were all in the drawing-room after dinner I had occasion to go to the billiard-room to fetch a book which I had left there. Dinner had been cleared away, so I took a candle to light me through the deserted dining-room. Just as I was passing the fireplace I was conscious of so strong a draught that my candle guttered and was nearly blown out. I supposed it was a down-draught, due to the large size of the chimney and to the fact that there was no fire in the grate, and rather wondered that we had never noticed it before. It was not a windy night, so that if there were a strong draught now one would suppose that it was a permanent feature of the room, and that whoever sat on that side of the table would want a screen behind his chair. But hitherto no one had made any complaint.

On my way back I was surprised to find the draught equally strong in the opposite direction. It was now sucking inwards towards the fireplace. I held my candle high, shielding it with the other hand, and looked round to see if there were an open window. But the windows were all securely shuttered, and the doors at each end of the room were shut. I could not account for any draught, much less for one which apparently changed its direction, almost as if it were due to the slow breathing of some gigantic creature crouching in the fireplace. While I stood there the inward draught suddenly ceased.

After a moment's stillness there came an outward puff—really strong enough to be called a gust—which blew my candle out. This was too much. I groped my way to the end of the room as quickly as I could without stopping to light a match. Once out of the room I felt rather ashamed of myself for having been so easily scared. I suppose that was why I did not feel inclined to say anything about what had happened. Probably I said to myself there was really more wind outside than I had imagined, and of course a rambling old house was likely to be full of unaccountable draughts. Most likely this one depended upon the wind being exactly in one quarter, which was why we had not noticed it before, and more to the same effect, But I did not find this cogent reasoning convincing.

When I went to bed I looked out and everything seemed to be perfectly still. This, I was bound to admit, was as I had expected. Three nights later I had a curious dream. I dreamed that I was in the dining-room, and that the figure over the mantelpiece had come down from his frame. He was seated astride of a chair as he was painted, almost in the fireplace. His back was turned to the room, but instead of having his head upon his shoulder, it was turned away so that nothing could be seen of his features. He appeared to be speaking with great earnestness to an invisible personage who must have been stationed a few feet up the chimney. I could not catch what he was saying, for he spoke very rapidly. But his tones were those of a person in deep distress.

When he had finished speaking there came a rumbling, moaning noise in the chimney, such as is made by the wind on stormy nights. This presently began to shape itself into words. At first, they were not at all distinct, but gradually they became clearer, though they seemed to be in a language unknown to me. I wondered whether it could be Irish. The voice spoke very deliberately with a cold malignity of tone which made me feel very thankful that I could not follow what it was saying. There was something indescribably evil about it. It was the most unpleasant sound to which I have ever listened, asleep or awake. If fear can make the hair stand on end, I must have resembled a clothes-brush.

At this point I woke, and it was more in obedience to some automatic instinct than to any reasoned courage that I decided to visit the dining-room. I do not know what, if anything, I expected to see. As I opened the door there was a grating sound, as if a chair were being hastily dragged across the uncarpeted part of the floor. But I told myself that that was caused by rats. The house abounded in them and everyone knows that they can make extraordinary noises. I suspect that they are at the bottom of a great many ghost stories.

I advanced to the fireplace, but beyond the fact that the hearthrug was curiously bundled up into a heap—a circumstance which did not for some reason strike me at the moment, though I wondered about it afterwards—there was nothing in the least unusual to be seen. My candle burned quite steadily as I held it high and looked round the silent empty room. I stared up at the odd, forbidding picture above the mantelpiece, but there did not seem to be anything to be got out of him. Upon the whole I was glad of that, for he did not look like the sort of person I should have chosen for a midnight *tête-à-tête*.

'Well,' I said aloud, addressing the portrait, 'I wish I knew rather more about you. But as you aren't in a position to explain yourself, I shall go back to bed.'

I did so; and slept soundly for the rest of the night.

Next morning I did not mention my dream to anyone else. Perhaps I was a little ashamed of it. Also, the walls of Irish houses have even acuter ears than those elsewhere and I did not wish to be responsible for an outbreak of hysteria among the servants.

It so happened that I had no occasion to be in the dining-room alone after dark during the next day or two. Perhaps I was at pains not to be. No one commented upon the curious draught which I had noticed. Indeed, I do not think it was perceptible in the daytime. My dreams, when I had any, were, as usual, entirely commonplace.

One evening, when my visit was nearly at an end, one of my cousins and I were sitting talking in the billiard-room after the rest of the family had gone to bed. Our conversation turned on ghosts and apparitions of various kinds; a subject in which we both took a keen if sceptical interest. Dreams and their value (this was before the days of psychoanalysis) and the possibility of their coming true were also discussed and it was past midnight when we got up to go to bed. We then found that there were no bedroom candles for us. Presumably they had been left in the dining-room or in the hall beyond it. The oil lamp by which we were sitting was too big and heavy to take with us. As it was past the middle of September and the day had been wet, we had had fires in the sitting-rooms. The dining-room fire had been burning brightly when we finished dinner, so that it was probable that there would still be enough of it left to prevent our passage through the room from offering any insurmountable obstacles. So, we put the lamp out and prepared to go.

As soon as we opened the door, we saw that our surmise had been correct. There was a sufficient glow in the fireplace to light us down the room. But we had hardly taken a step before we were startled by a rapid thudding sound, such as might be produced by a big dog beating his tail upon the floor. There was a dog about the place, but at night he had his own quarters in the stable-yard. Even if he had not been put to bed then properly—as might very well be the case in a household of Irish servants—he had certainly not been in the dining-room during dinner and could hardly have got there since.

The thudding ceased as suddenly as it had begun. But next moment we were even more startled by seeing the fire beginning to disappear. I remembered a story which I had once read—by H. G. Wells, I think. In it the lights in a haunted room go out one by one and as the occupant rushes to the fire to rekindle them that too dies away into absolute blackness.

But we soon saw that our fire was not going out like that. It was being obscured by some large dark object which was rising from the ground between ourselves and it. It was as if the hearthrug were slowly humping itself into the form of an animal of some kind. It rose and rose without a sound.

Soon it was larger than any dog and its movement had somehow an uncanny suggestion of deliberate and malign purpose. Its bulk and outline, so far as we could make them out, suggested a bear more than anything else. But the head was not shaped like that of a bear. There was something more than half-human about the outline which made it peculiarly horrible. There seemed to be a nose not in the least like the snout of any animal. Presently no vestige of the fire was to be seen. Then it suddenly reappeared. The creature, whatever it was, had gone up the chimney.

We felt that the longer we waited there the less we should like

29

it, so as soon as the coast was clear we ran down the room as hard as we could go, keeping as close as possible to the side away from the fireplace.

There was plenty of firelight in the drawing-room and we soon laid hands on our candles and made our way upstairs. Our bedrooms opened into each other and we left the door standing wide. I do not think either of us slept well, but there was nothing to disturb us except the owls, who (we both thought) were noisier than usual.

Next day we told our story to the rest of the family and I added what I had to say about the mysterious draught and my dream. Of course there was only one thing to be done. The whole thing must be laid before Captain Moore as soon as possible.

Meanwhile the doors of the dining-room must be kept locked and meals served in another room, which a house-agent would probably have called The Breakfast Parlour. I was obliged to return to England on the following day, so it was some weeks before I heard the sequel.

In response to an urgent if guarded letter Captain Moore came over from the Curragh as soon as he could get a few days' leave. He soon knew all that there was to tell. His first step was to pay a visit to the lodge, but unfortunately the day before his arrival Barton had had a stroke from which he never recovered. He seemed to recognise his master and to be glad to see him. But he was in no state to be questioned. He died that night. Next day his daughter, who lived with him, told us that after Captain Moore's visit her father seemed to have something on his mind. Just after midnight he sat up and made an effort to say something. The only words she could make out sounded like 'trouble' and 'back of the picture.' Immediately afterwards he fell back on his pillow and expired.

This was something to go upon. The queer portrait must be meant. A step-ladder was procured and Captain Moore and my cousins set to work. It took them longer than they had expected, as the picture was not hung in the usual way. A number of long screws had been driven through the frame, which was very solid, into the panelling of the wall behind. At last they were all got out; not without difficulty, though they did not seem to be particularly rusty. The immediate result was disappointing. There was nothing to be seen either on the back of the picture or the surface of the wall.

Then somebody noticed what looked like a fine crack running across the top of one panel just below the raised frame containing it. Closer examination showed that the wood had been cut through on all four sides with a very sharp knife. A little picking at the top and out it came, disclosing a cavity, obviously the work of an amateur mason, in the thickness of the wall. In it reposed a small book, about nine inches long by five broad. At the top of the title-page were the two words

The Club

. . . .and underneath was a list of twelve names; presumably those of the members. Several of them belonged to families still represented in the neighbourhood. The last was Robert Moore, Captain Moore's great-grandfather.

By this time lunch was ready, so further research was postponed.

When the party returned reinvigorated to their task they discovered, as was not unexpected, that what they had found was an informal minute-book.

It was apparently the custom of the Club to dine once each month with one of the members and discuss topics of general interest. The first dinner was held on 14 July 1778. There were notes as to the amount of wine consumed, which need not be recorded here. One would imagine that the members of the Club must have acted on the principle which was adopted subsequently by Mr. Jorrocks—'Where I dines I sleeps and where I sleeps I breakfasts.'

There were also notes of the discussions. These were more interesting. At first, they were principally political. The recent revolt of the American colonies appeared more than once, and though no formal vote was ever taken, it was obvious that opinion was divided as to the character of George Washington. Some members regarded him as a high-minded patriot; others as a sordid tobacco-planter who did not want to make any contribution to the cost of the campaigns to which he and his like owed their security and prosperity.

The revolution in France also aroused much interest. General opinion seemed to have been more favourable to it than most people—at any rate in England—would have approved. But the members of the Club were probably all young enough to feel it their duty as well as their pleasure to ventilate opinions which would have shocked their elders could they have heard them.

As time went on the tone of the meetings became less innocent. A certain amount of profanity began to appear, and once or twice some rather vague entries suggested some dabbling in black magic. At one dinner, held in the year 1797, there was a note—'The President's Health was drunk in bumpers with (probably acclamation,' but the fact that the writer had changed his mind more than once as to the proper spelling of the word, added to two considerable blots, had made it indecipherable). On the next page was a plan of the table with the name of each member against his place. There were six on each side; no one at top or bottom. The top was, however, marked with an X. From this time onwards there were frequent references to The President, but curiously his name was never given. The minutes were usually initialled J.B. James Butler was the first name in the original list, so was presumably that of the senior member. It was not, however, clear whether he was to be identified with the President. Near the end of the book was an entry in a different hand. It ran:

'The Club is dissolved. Lord have mercy upon us.'

It was signed Robt. Moore and dated 23 September, 1799. My odd experiences had culminated on 23 September, 1899. There was nothing else in the cavity in the wall except two small scraps of paper. They had obviously been part of a larger sheet which had been torn up. What had become of the rest it was impossible to say. On one appeared the words like a bear, on the other *clean broak*. That was all.

Despite his ancestor's wishes Captain Moore felt justified in destroying the portrait. It was soon hacked to pieces and the bonfire which it made in the garden consumed the minute-book of the Club as well. The panel was replaced and another picture hung over it. As far as I know there were no further disturbances. Perhaps a century is a kind of statute of limitations in such matters. We do not understand them sufficiently to be able to speak positively about them.

It seems pretty clear that at its last meeting the Club somehow got more than it had bargained for. But it is impossible to reconstruct exactly what had happened. Who was the President, and was the last meeting the first at which he was actually present? Was the queer portrait, which was presumably Robert Moore's work, intended to operate as a warning, like the public executions which were then in vogue?

Some years afterwards I happened to find myself sitting next to an Irish clergyman at a public dinner. He was incumbent of a parish near Dublin, he told me. As the evening wore on, and the tide of speech-making flowed strongly, our talk, in the intervals, turned on superstitions.

'It's queer,' he said, 'the way they lay hold of people for no reason that anyone can see. Now there is one grave in my churchyard that the people won't go near. And when we turn in sheep to keep the grass down the farmer always sends a boy to see that they don't graze by it. It's a nuisance, because we always have to scythe that bit—and the sexton doesn't like doing it either. It's an ugly, pompous thing to a member of a family that used to be well known there, I believe, though there's not been any of them about these fifty years. But why there should be anything unlucky or wrong about it I don't know. I'm not sure that the people do. Anyhow, if they do you won't get it out of them.'

'I wonder,' I said, 'whether the occupant is named James Butler and whether he died on 23 September, 1799?'

'Why, yes,' he said. 'But how in the world do you know anything about it?'

'Oh, I used to have relations with whom I sometimes stayed in that neighbourhood.'

I thought that was as much as I need tell him.

Stivinghoe Bank

The coast-line of Norfolk is one of those which have altered considerably in historic times. Along some stretches the sea has encroached. At low water traces of lost villages can still be seen, and in stormy weather pieces of wood from drowned forests are sometimes washed ashore. At Cromer a lighthouse which I remember has disappeared long since, though it was not very near the edge of the cliff when I knew it. A new one has been built at some distance inland.

Along other stretches the sea has receded and towns which were once thriving ports are separated from it by a wide expanse of marsh, where cattle graze and abundant mushrooms can be found in early autumn. These marshes are intersected by deep and muddy channels up which the tide creeps sluggishly. But even at high water nothing larger than an open boat can use them. The harbours whence the cloth was shipped in the great days of East Anglia, when Norwich was the third city in the kingdom and nearly wrested the second place from Bristol, are almost useless now. The towns which lived by them have dwindled to small villages. Here and there a fine old house may still be seen on the water-front. But for the most part the large and magnificent churches are all that remain of their former glories.

Melancholy as these villages are they have a beauty and dignity of their own. The wide horizon of marsh, beach and sea beyond gives a sense of spaciousness which can hardly be found elsewhere. Anyone who knows them will understand why a Norfolk nurserymaid when taken to Grasmere complained that she felt unable to breathe and that the mountains spoilt the view.

They have always been well known to sportsmen as the marshes teem with wild-fowl in winter.

Of late years artists have begun to discover them. But I must admit that I hope they will never become popular resorts.

It was at one of them, which I will call Stivinghoe, that the experience (it hardly deserves to be called an adventure) which is set down here, befell me some years ago. If, when you have heard the story, you think it rather pointless, that is not my fault. I do not think that I should have admired Mr. Chadband (See *Bleak House*.) had I met him. But his insistence on what he called *The Terewth* always seemed to me worthy of imitation. And I could not make the story more exciting without departing from the standard set by that eloquent divine.

Stivinghoe differs from its neighbours in the possession of a bank; that is to say a causeway some eight feet high running across the marsh land and projecting beyond it into the sea. I suppose it is natural, as it is not easy to see why anyone should have taken the trouble to construct it. There is a rough track along the top. At the shoreward end the sides are clothed with coarse grass where sea-pinks and yellow horned poppies grow. The last half-mile is sand and shingle.

At high water the sea comes up to it on both sides. When the tide is out it is flanked by a wide expanse of wet sand. At the far end there is a little hillock on which are the remains of a ruined chapel. It is as lonely and desolate a spot as can well be imagined. I suppose the chapel had escaped demolition because it had never been worth anyone's while to pull the walls down and cart the material away. It was a cell of the great house of Walsingham and had been established as a place where prayer might be offered continually for fishermen along the coast and all who got their living from the sea.

After the dissolution of the monasteries a large part of the lands of Walsingham had gone to the Earl of W., whose descendant is still one of the magnates of Norfolk. I had reason to believe that some books from the library had made their way to his great house at Folkham. There was no adequate catalogue of them and as I had known Lord W.'s son at Cambridge I ventured to write and ask whether I might come and look at them. His reply was very cordial. He regretted that he could not ask me to stay as the family was away and the house shut up. He had written to the housekeeper telling her to let me see anything I wanted, and added that while the only inn in the village was not to be recommended, I should be sufficiently comfortable at the Fishmongers' Arms at Stivinghoe.

The map showed me that the distance from Stivinghoe to Folkham House was only about three miles. A bicycle would solve the question of transport. I had never slept at the Fishmongers' Arms, but had had tea there more than once when exploring the neighbourhood, and my recollection of it confirmed Lord W.'s opinion.

36

Accordingly, I wrote engaging a bedroom (if possible, with a table at which I could write) for a week and established myself there one fine afternoon in the middle of September.

The greater part of the next three days was spent in the library at Folkham. The result was, however, rather disappointing. The manuscripts were not many. Neither contents nor workmanship were of outstanding interest. I thought I had got to the end of them when I came upon a bundle of papers tied up with tape and docketed, in a modern hand, Stivinghoe Chapel.

The housekeeper had just come into the room with some tea and I noticed that she seemed to be disconcerted when she saw the bundle in my hand.

'Are these private papers, do you suppose?' I said. 'They were on the same shelf as the other manuscripts. Is there any, reason why I shouldn't read them? I see that somebody had them out not very long ago.'

'Yes, Sir,' she said. 'That were His Lordship's father, that were. The day before the great storm, not that that had anything to do with it, I do suppose. No, I don't see there'd be no harm—if so be as you're careful, Sir.'

Of course, I told her that I would take great care of them, that I was accustomed to handling old books and papers and so forth. But I couldn't help thinking that that was not quite what she meant.

It was too late to do any more that day. So, I said I would come back and go through them tomorrow morning.

I mounted my bicycle at the front door expecting to enjoy the ride home as it was a beautiful evening. But somehow, I did not. For some reason I felt uncomfortable and could not get rid of the idea that there was someone following me. Though after all why shouldn't there be on a public highroad? And what harm could he do me in broad daylight if he were evilly disposed? All the same so strong was the feeling that I looked behind me more than once. But I had the road to myself. All the same I rode faster than usual and was glad when I found myself at the Fishmongers' Arms.

After dinner I went into the bar-parlour as usual and got into conversation with its frequenters. The talk was of the usual description in such places. Interesting enough to anyone who, like myself, can find pleasure in listening to reminiscences of past harvests, speculations as to quality of the next one, the market prices of beasts and local affairs generally. But not worth attempting to set down here.

The company broke up early and I went early to bed. Contrary to my usual custom I did not sleep very well. I was troubled by a recurrent dream, the details of which eluded me, try as I would to recall them. The general sense was that I was going somewhere where I expected to meet, or at least feared that I might meet, somebody whom I did not want to see, Just as I was on the point of coming face to face with him, I always woke up. This performance was repeated with monotonous regularity four or five times between midnight (which I heard on the church clock) and dawn. As soon as it was light I gave up trying to go to sleep and read until it was time to get up.

After breakfast I bicycled to Folkham House as usual and got out the bundle of papers.

They proved more interesting than I had expected. They belonged to the years 1531-2 and appeared to relate to the incumbent of the chapel at the end of the bank. John of Costessey was his name.

The first document was brief. It was addressed to the Prior and Convent of Walsingham and was a request bearing about a dozen signatures, of which three seemed to be those of the rectors of Stivinghoe and two neighbouring villages, that John might be recalled to Walsingham and someone else despatched to take his place.

Presumably the prior wrote, as he was bound to do, to ask the reason for this request, for the next letter was considerably longer. It appeared that John was suspected of having entered into a compact with the powers of evil. He was a man of violent and vindictive temper and it was noticeable that those who offended him were dogged by persistent and inexplicable misfortune. Next time they went to sea they met with no fish; or nets broke mysteriously as a catch was being brought on board. Unaccountable accidents, some fatal, occurred on board their boats. More than once a boat had been lost with all hands in a sudden and very violent storm, which had not been foreseen by the most weather-wise seamen along the coast.

More than once, he had been seen from boats rounding the end of the bank close inshore to make the harbour, standing at the water's edge with an imp seated on his shoulder. The said imp had screamed and waved its arms (here followed an illegible word which I guessed to be meant for *devilishly*).

More than once at night-time the window of the chapel had been seen, to be brightly lighted, and bursts of song were heard proceeding from it. These melodies did not suggest the familiar offices of the Church and more than one voice seemed to be taking part.

Next came a letter from John himself, obviously in answer to a communication from the Prior. He protested that he could not be expected to reply in detail to such malicious and unfounded charges (*crimina tam perfida ac dolosa et omnino nugatoria*) and hinted that if his nocturnal vigils had been solaced by celestial company no fault could be found with him on that score (*quid in hoc improperii vel quae increpationis causa?*).

The prior's answer to this may be inferred to have been a summons to repair to Walsingham forthwith. John's next letter was to the effect that his austerities, which it was his delight to practise, had made him too feeble to undertake the journey on foot, while the hard-heartedness and irreligion of the countryside, of which the prior had had ample proof (*litteris supradictis satis probatum*), made it unlikely that any attempt to borrow so much as an ass would be successful.

The prior could hardly be expected to put up with this, nor did he. He must have told John that he proposed to visit him in person, for the last letter was as follows:

Quamquam in rebus humus vitae delectari non fas, attamen cum hic viderim oculis meis sanctissimum Priorem una cum duo bus fratribus dilectissimis libenter dicam Domine nunc dimittis servum tuum, etc.
(Although we are forbidden to take pleasure in the things of this life, yet when I have seen here with my eyes the most holy prior together with two of my dearly beloved brethren I shall gladly say, 'Lord, now lettest thou Thy servant depart,' etc.)

'Well,' I said to myself, 'he may have been an impudent rascal if nothing worse. But he seems to have had a sense of humour and to have been pretty sure of his ground. I wonder how the story ended?'

Next moment I gave a violent start, for I heard what sounded like a laugh close behind me. I whipped round in my chair. But there was no one there. The library was a large room and I was some distance from the door. Although the carpet was thick, I did not think anyone could have come in without my knowledge. However, I got up, and went all round the room and even looked behind the window curtains. Of course I found nobody, and sat down again feeling rather ashamed of myself for being so fanciful.

There was only one more paper to be examined. Unfortunately, the top had been torn off and the first words remaining were *nusquan inveniri potuit* (could not be found anywhere).

Then followed an inventory of the contents of the chapel and cell.

The only unusual item was *Duae cerae nigrae* (Two candles of black wax).

I concluded that the prior had paid his visit, but that John's nerve had failed him at the last moment and he had disappeared. He could have made his way to Lynn without much difficulty and got on board a ship bound for the Low Countries.

No doubt the prior was not sorry to be rid of him, and as the inventory was dated *Festo S. Edithae MDXXXII* (16 September 1532) the convent soon had other things to think about.

On my way home I speculated, not for the first time, upon the question whether there is or can be any foundation for any of the stories of compacts between human beings and evil spirits. In the abstract the possibility seems difficult to dispute. The belief is ancient and widely diffused. The real point seems to be whether the game could be worth the candle.

As I had finished all I meant to do at Folkham House I decided that I would spend tomorrow on a visit to the chapel and perhaps sketch it. The day after I would return home.

When I imparted my plan to the landlord, he naturally expressed a civil regret that my stay at Stivinghoe was coming to an end. He seemed doubtful whether the ruins (as I had learned the chapel was called locally) were worth visiting, seeing as it were a dull trudge along the bank to get there. I thought from his manner that that was not his only reason for trying to discourage me. But he was summoned elsewhere before he had time to say more. While I was at dinner, he looked in to see if I had everything I wanted. This was an unusual piece of condescension and I suspected an ulterior motive of some sort. I was not mistaken. After a moment or two he made an obvious effort.

'You'll excuse me, Sir. But the ruins is a queer place. Rare goings on there in those ancient times—by what I've heard.'

This was interesting as it suggested that some reminiscence of John of Costessey lingered on the scene of his activities. But before I could ask for details he went on rapidly, 'Not that I've any call to listen to the fishermen's talk—no more than what you 'ave.'

After this there was obviously no more to be got out of him. But I thought I would try a cast among the company in the parlour later on. After some miscellaneous conversation I mentioned that I thought of spending my last day in walking out along the bank and making a sketch of the ruins. For some reason the company seemed to find this proposal disturbing. No one made any comment but there was an awkward pause. Then two ancients near the fireplace held a short, muttered conversation. The only words I could catch sounded like 'not lately, have he?'

Plainly they knew more than they meant to tell. Presently someone introduced some ordinary topic, and conversation flowed easily as before.

I went to bed about eleven and slept soundly.

Next morning I started soon after breakfast. I had ascertained that the tide would be low between 1 and 2 p.m. so that I should be able to find a position from which to make a sketch. I could hardly do this if I were confined to the bank itself. Also, the day, though fine, was windy; windy enough, I thought, to make the top of the bank a wet place at high water.

I asked for some sandwiches to take with me and said that I should be back in time for dinner as usual, probably for tea. I thought the landlord looked at me rather reproachfully, but he said nothing. When I had gone a few steps on my way I found that I had not filled my tobacco pouch that morning. I turned back to make the omission good and my eye was caught by a horseshoe nailed over the front door. Nothing remarkable in that, you may say, but I wondered that I had not noticed it before, as it now seemed to be unusually conspicuous.

The walk along the bank was pleasant enough. I could see over miles of marsh on either hand. Inland there were groups of red-roofed cottages to be seen, with occasional windmills and church towers. In front of me lay the sea. At the moment no fishing-boats were visible, but the smoke of one or two large ships could be seen on the horizon.

Altogether an exhilarating prospect. But somehow or other I did not feel at all exhilarated. On the contrary I had to admit that I was nervous and depressed.

Certainly, I had had some odd little experiences since I had touched the Stivinghoe papers, First there was the feeling that I was being followed on the way home. Then my uncomfortable and inconclusive dream. Then the laugh which I thought (no, knew) that I had heard in the library; and last of all the obvious conviction of the neighbourhood that the ruins were better left alone. What should I do if I saw a figure emerge from the Chapel and come along the bank to meet me? Should I enter into conversation or should I get down on to the sand and hope that he would pass me by? Or should I run for it? Or could I recall on the spur of the moment any form of exorcism which might prove effective? Fortunately, I did not have to answer any of these questions.

The chapel was a small building, roughly built of grey flint. It measured about twenty-two feet by ten and was lighted by a single lancet in the east wall. There was a door at the west end, I put its date at a little before 1350. Of course, the roof was gone, but the walls looked fairly sound. The altar was still in place. But I noticed that the usual consecration crosses (one in the middle and one at each corner) had been deliberately obliterated. The chisel marks could be seen clearly. Such reforming zeal seemed to be almost excessive.

On the south (that is on the landward) side of the chapel there were some small mounds which presumably indicated the site of the priest's dwelling. The superstructure had disappeared so completely that I wondered whether it had been of wood; also, whether it could possibly be worthwhile to return with a spade.

I sat down on one of the mounds and ate my sandwiches. Then I thought it time to set about my sketch. I went down on to the sand and decided that the best position was a few yards to seaward. (In this part of Norfolk, the coast runs east and west, so that the sea is to the north. The natives are fond of assuring visitors that there is nothing between them and the North Pole. No one who has been there in winter is likely to wish to dispute this statement.) The tide was still ebbing, so I should have plenty of time to do what I wanted.

I settled myself and my sketching materials, but somehow, I did not make very good progress. I had an uncomfortable feeling, as if there was somebody behind me, and caught myself wondering what I should do if a hand (probably a large and bony one) were suddenly laid upon my shoulder. I said aloud 'ridiculous' and as I did so a gull passed very close above my head and gave a derisive squawk, which seemed to indicate his complete concurrence.

The gulls were very many; which was not surprising. But they were so tame (or impudent, whichever you like to call it) that they were a positive nuisance. They flapped their wings almost in my face and one actually perched on my easel. I suppose they had never seen enough of men to be afraid of them. I had a sandwich or two left which I threw as far as I could towards the water's edge. This drew them off for a little, but they were soon as bad as ever.

However, I got a sketch of some sort finished. I thought I would take one more look inside the chapel before I started to walk home in case there were any detail of interest which I had missed. The floor was covered with coarse turf. Probably it had never been paved; if it had, the paving had been covered long since. But just in front of the altar I noticed a patch which somehow looked different from the rest. I had in my knife one of those curious implements said to be intended for taking stones out of horses' feet, and it seemed that at last I had a chance of using it. I scratched at the turf and very soon my hook grated upon a stone. A little scraping disclosed a small rectangular slab about twenty inches long by eight broad. A pentacle had been scratched upon it rather roughly.

It was obviously the lid of something, if it were too small for any kind of coffin. A little more scraping of the earth round its edges and I got it up with less difficulty than I had expected. It was the lid of a coffin of sorts after all and in the coffin were some bones; clearly those of a small monkey. Its forepaws were crossed upon its breast and from some fragments of stuff which lay about I came to the conclusion that it had been buried in some sort of monastic habit.

This discovery explained the stories of the imp. Perhaps John had been really fond of his pet who must have been his only companion. Burial before the altar might perhaps be condoned. But the monastic habit looked like a profane jest. Or was it more than a jest? Taken in conjunction with the pentacle on the lid, the candles of black wax found by the Prior and the erasure of the consecration crosses (which I now began to think was John's handiwork and not the doing of any zealous follower of Dowsing) there was a definite suggestion of serious and sinister purpose. What unhallowed rites had been celebrated there, with what evil intent? And (I could not repress the, further question) in what company?

However, there seemed to be nothing for me to do but to leave things as I had found them. Which I did. The afternoon was wearing on, so I started for home. The tide had probably turned but was still very low. At the seaward end the line of the bank was curved, so I saw that I could shorten my walk considerably if I took to the sands and struck the bank again in about a mile. When I had gone a little way, I turned to take a final look at the chapel. It was a sunny day with big white clouds driving before the wind. As I looked the shadow of one passed across the Chapel, and by some odd trick of light made it seem as if a dark figure had emerged from the door and dropped down the far side of the bank. For a moment I was really startled.

I turned and went on with my walk. I have never considered myself a fanciful person, but it was borne in upon me very forcibly that the sooner I was sitting down to tea at the Fishmongers' Arms the happier I should be.

Presently I reached the point at which I must take to the bank again. Just as I got to the edge of the sand, I saw the print of a naked human foot, pointing towards the bank. It was very recent and could (apparently) only have been made by someone who had passed me quite close, having come across the sand as I had, and gone up the bank before me. This was frankly impossible. Had there been anyone else about I could not have failed to see him. The sand was too wet to hold impressions for long. Most of my own tracks had disappeared already. Yet there was the footprint, unmistakably. I stooped and looked at it (there was only one, which made it odder still) closely.

It struck me as unusually bony, that is to say, the bones showed more plainly than I should have expected. I thought of the shadow which I had seen pass across the end of the chapel. Had it, after all, emerged from the inside? If I went on, should I find someone waiting for me, and with what intent? However, there was nothing for it but to go on. I was within sight of the village now and there were people about who would see if any attack were made upon me, though what help they would be able to give was another matter. So, on I went, and in a few minutes had reached my inn safely.

I turned on the doorstep to take a look over the marshes. Very lonely and solemn they were and very dark was the little chapel. There was no one to be seen; I had not expected that there would be. By this time the wind had freshened and there was a hard brightness on the northeastern horizon which foretold a full gale before morning. There was an old barometer just inside the front door which had fallen so low that I wondered whether it were trustworthy and hoped not. The landlord emerged and appeared ill at ease, and at the same time glad to see me—possibly by reason of the weather; possibly not. He murmured something to the effect of no harm done, as he returned to his occupations. I felt curiously tired, and when I had had tea, after a poor pretence of reading some book (I forget now what) dozed in an armchair by the fire.

I was roused by a clap of thunder and the storm broke with a roar like a train. The thunder was unusual, I thought, for the time of year, especially as the last few days had not been particularly hot. Also, the wind was off the sea, and I knew that there was a belief along the coast that when a thunderstorm comes up from the sea, that will be the beginning of the end of the world.

The Fishmongers' Arms was built to stand weather. But I doubt whether it ever had a worse buffeting than it got that night. There was no more thunder, but the rain came down in sheets and the wind tore at the house till I could almost imagine I felt it swaying to and fro. It was obvious that there would be no customers at the bar, so after dinner I invited the landlord to come to my sitting-room to smoke a cigar and drink a whisky and soda with me. I was really glad of his company, and he seemed to be of mine. We tried to talk of indifferent subjects, but could not do much save listen to the wind. We went to bed about eleven, though there was not much prospect of sleep. I wished that I had not remembered at that moment that Richard Kidder, Bishop of Bath and Wells, had been killed in his bed, together with his wife, by the fall of a chimney-stack through the roof of the palace during the terrible storm of 26-7 November, 1703.

Soon after midnight there was a screech (I can call it nothing else) like that of an animal in pain. I could hardly have believed that the wind could have made such a sound. This seemed to be its last effort, and the storm died away almost as quickly as it had arisen.

When I looked out next morning the Chapel was gone. The whole end of the bank had been washed away. The gale had coincided with a spring tide and I suspect that most of the marsh had been under water for some hours. Of course, the tip of the bank had caught the full force of the sea.

I must confess that I felt relieved. At first, I was glad that I had made a sketch of the chapel. But after a little reflection I burned it. Somehow, I felt safer as I saw it turn to ashes.

The Sundial

The following story came into my hands by pure chance. I had wandered into a second-hand book-shop in the neighbourhood of the Charing Cross Road and was about to leave it empty-handed. On a shelf near the door my eye fell upon a copy of Hacket's *Scrinia Reserata* solidly bound in leather, which I thought well worth the few shillings which the proprietor was willing to accept for it. It is not an easy book to come by, and is of real value to anyone who wants to understand certain aspects of English Church History during the first half of the seventeenth century.

When I opened the book at home a thickish wad of paper fell out. It proved to consist of several sheets of foolscap covered with writing. I have reproduced the contents word for word.

From the look of the paper I judged that it had been there for at least thirty years. The author had not signed it, and there was nothing to indicate to whom the book had belonged. I think I could make a guess at the neighbourhood to which the story relates, and if I am right it should not be difficult to identify the house and discover the name of the tenant. But as he seems to have wished to remain anonymous, he shall do so, as far as I am concerned.

The form of the story suggests that he intended to publish it; probably in some magazine. As far as I know it has not been printed before.

★★★★★★★★★★★★★★★★★

I belong to one of the numerous middle-class English families which for several generations have followed various professions, with credit, but without ever attaining any very special distinction. In our own case India could almost claim us as hereditary bondsmen. For more than a century most of our men had made their way there, and had served John Company or the Crown in various capacities. One of my uncles had risen to be Legal Member of the Viceroy's Council. So, when my own time came, to India I went—in the Civil Service—and there I lived for five and twenty years.

My career was neither more nor less adventurous than the average. The routine of my work was occasionally broken by experiences which would sound incredible to an English reader, and therefore need not be set down here. Just before the time came for my retirement a legacy made me a good deal better off than I had had any reason to expect to be. So, upon my return to England I found that it would be possible for me to adopt the life of a country gentleman, upon a modest scale, but with the prospect of finding sufficient occupation and amusement.

I was never married, and had been too long out of England to have any very strong ties remaining. I was free to establish myself where I pleased, and the advertisements in the *Field and Country Life* offered houses of every description in every part of the kingdom. After much correspondence, and some fruitless journeys, I came upon one which seemed to satisfy my requirements. It lay about sixty miles north of London upon a main line of railway. That was an important point, as I was a Fellow of both the Asiatic and Historical Societies, and had long looked forward to attending their meetings regularly. As a boy I had known the neighbourhood slightly and had liked it, though it is not generally considered beautiful. There were two packs of hounds within reach, which could be followed with such a stable as I should be able to afford.

The house was an old one. It had been a good deal larger, but part had been battered down during the Civil War, when it was besieged by the Parliamentary troops, and never rebuilt. It belonged to one of the largest landowners in the county, whom I will call Lord Rye. It generally served as the dower-house of the family, but as there was at that moment no dowager countess, and as Lord Rye himself was a young man, and both his sisters were married, it was not likely to be wanted for some time to come. It had been unoccupied for nearly two years. The last tenant, a retired doctor, had been found dead on the lawn at the bottom of the steps leading up to the garden door. His heart had been in a bad condition for some time past, so that his sudden death was not surprising; but the neighbouring village viewed the incident with some suspicion. One or two of the older people professed to remember traditions of 'trouble' there in former years.

This had made it difficult to get a caretaker, and as Lord Rye was anxious to let again, he was willing to take an almost nominal rent. In fact, his whole attitude suggested that I was doing him a favour by becoming his tenant. About five hundred acres of shooting generally went with the house, and I was glad to find that I could have them very cheaply.

I moved in at midsummer, and each day made me more and more pleased with my new surroundings.

After my years in India the garden was a particular source of delight to me; but I will not describe it more minutely than is necessary to make what follows intelligible. Behind the house was a good-sized lawn, flanked by shrubbery. On the far side, parallel with the house, ran a splendid yew hedge, nearly fifteen feet high and very thick. It came up to the shrubbery at either end, but was pierced by two archways about thirty yards apart, giving access to the flower-garden beyond. Almost in the middle of the lawn was an old tree stump, or what looked like one, some three feet high. Though covered with ivy it was not picturesque, and I told Lord Rye that I should like to take it up. 'Do by all means,' he said, 'I certainly should if I lived here. I believe poor Riley (the last tenant) intended to put a sundial there. I think it would look rather nice, don't you?'

This struck me as a good idea. I ordered a sundial from a well-known firm of heliological experts in Cockspur Street, and ordered the stump to be grubbed up as soon as it arrived.

One morning towards the end of September I woke unrefreshed after a night of troubled dreams. I could not recall them very distinctly, but I had seemed to be trying to lift a very heavy weight of some kind from the ground. But, before I could raise it, an overwhelming terror had taken hold of me—though I could not remember why—and I woke to find my forehead wet with perspiration. Each time I fell asleep again the dream repeated itself with mechanical regularity, though the details did not become any more distinct. So, I was heartily glad it had become late enough to get up. The day was wet and chilly. I felt tired and unwell, and was, moreover, depressed by a vague sense of impending disaster. This was accentuated by a feeling that it lay within my power to avert the catastrophe, if only I could discover what it was.

In the afternoon the weather cleared, and I thought that a ride would do me good. I rode fairly hard for some distance, and it was past five o'clock before I had reached my own bounds'-ditch on my way home. At that particular place a small wood ran along the edge of my property for about a quarter of a mile. I was riding slowly down the outside, and was perhaps a hundred yards from the angle where I meant to turn it, when I noticed a man standing at the corner. The light was beginning to fail, and he was so close to the edge of the wood that at first, I could not be sure whether it was a human figure, or only an oddly shaped tree-stump which I had never noticed before. But when I got a little nearer, I saw that my first impression had been correct, and that it was a man. He seemed to be dressed like an ordinary agricultural labourer.

He was standing absolutely still and seemed to be looking very intently in my direction. But he was shading his eyes with his hand, so that I could not make out his face. Before I had got close enough to make him out more definitely, he turned suddenly and vanished round the corner of the wood. His movements were rapid: but he somehow gave the impression of being deformed, though in what precise respect I could not tell. Naturally my suspicions were stirred, so I put my horse to a canter. But when we had reached the corner he shied violently, and I had some difficulty in getting him to pass it. When we had got round, the mysterious man was nowhere to be seen. In front and on the left hand lay a very large stubble field, without a vestige of cover of any kind. I could see that he was not crossing it, and unless he had flown, he could not have reached the other side.

On the right hand lay the ditch bounding the wood. As is usual in that country it was both wide and deep, and had some two or three feet of mud and water at the bottom. If the man had gone that way, he had some very pressing reason for wishing to avoid me: and I could detect no trace of his passage at any point.

So, there was nothing to be done but go home, and tell the policeman next day to keep his eyes open for any suspicious strangers. However, no attempts were made upon any of my belongings, and when October came, my pheasants did not seem to have been unlawfully diminished.

October that year was stormy, and one Saturday night about the middle of the month it blew a regular gale. I lay awake long listening to the wind, and to all the confused sounds which fill an old house in stormy weather. Twice I seemed to hear footsteps in the passage. Once I could have almost sworn my door was cautiously opened and closed again. When at last I dropped off I was disturbed by a repetition of my former dream. But this time the details were rather more distinct. Again, I was trying to lift a heavy weight from the ground: but now I knew that there was something hidden under it. What the concealed object might be I could not tell, but as I worked to bring it to light a feeling began to creep over me that I did not want to see it. This soon deepened into horror at the bare idea of seeing it: though I had still no notion what manner of thing it might be. Yet I could not abandon my task. So presently I found myself in the position of working hard to accomplish what I would have given the world to have left undone. At this point I woke, to find myself shaking with fright, and repeating aloud the apparently meaningless sentence—'If you'll pull, I'll push.'

I did not sleep for the rest of that night. Beside the noise of the storm the prospect of a repetition of that dream was quite enough to keep me awake. To add to my discomfort a verse from Ecclesiastes ran in my head with dismal persistence—'*But if a man live many years and rejoice in them all, yet let him remember the days of darkness, for they shall be many.*' Days of darkness seemed to be coming upon me now, and my mind was filled with vague alarm.

The next day was fine, and after Church I thought I would see how my fruit trees had fared during the night. The kitchen-garden was enclosed by a high brick wall. On the side nearest the house there were two doors, which were always kept locked on Sunday. In the wall opposite was a trapdoor, about three feet square, giving on to a rather untidy piece of ground, partly orchard and partly waste. When I had unlocked the door, I saw standing by the opposite wall the figure which I had seen at the corner of the wood. His neck was abnormally long, and so malformed that his head lolled sideways on to his right shoulder in a disgusting and almost inhuman fashion.

He was bent almost double; and I think he was misshapen in some other respect as well. But of that I could not be certain. He raised his hand with what seemed to be a threatening gesture, then turned, and slipped through the trapdoor with remarkable quickness. I was after him immediately, but on reaching the opposite wall received a shock which stopped me like a physical blow. The trapdoor was shut and bolted on the inside. I tried to persuade myself that a violent slam might make the bolts shoot, but I knew that that was really impossible. I had to choose between two explanations. Either my visitor was a complete hallucination, or else he possessed the unusual power of being able to bolt a door upon the side on which he himself was not. The latter was upon the whole the more comforting, and—in view of some of my Indian experiences—the more probable, supposition.

After a little hesitation I opened the trap and, as there was nothing to be seen, got through it and went up to the top of the orchard, where the kennels lay. But neither of my dogs would follow the scent. When brought to the spot where his feet must have touched the ground they whined and showed every symptom of alarm. When I let go of their collars, they hurried home in a way which showed plainly what they thought of the matter.

This seemed to dispose of the idea of hallucination, and, as before, there was nothing else to be done but await developments as patiently as I could. For the next fortnight nothing remarkable took place. I had my usual health and as near an approach to my usual spirits as could reasonably be expected. I had visitors for part of the time, but no one to whom I should have cared to confide the story at this stage. I was not molested further by day, and my dreams, though varied, were not alarming.

On the morning of the 31st I received a letter announcing that my sundial had been despatched, and it duly arrived in the course of the afternoon. It was heavy, so by the time we had got it out of the railway van and on to the lawn it was too late to place it in position that day. The men departed to drink my health, and I turned towards the house. Just as I reached the door I paused. A sensation—familiar to all men who are much alone—had come over me, and I felt as if I were being watched from behind. Usually, the feeling can be dispelled by turning round. I did so, but on this occasion the sense that I was not alone merely increased. Of course, the lawn was deserted, but I stood looking across it for a few moments, telling myself that I must not let my nerves play me tricks.

Then I saw a face detach itself slowly from the darkness of the hedge at one side of the left-hand arch. For a few seconds it hung, horribly poised, in the middle of the opening like a mask suspended by an invisible thread. Then the body to which it belonged slid into the clear space, and I saw my acquaintance of the wood and kitchen-garden, this time sharply outlined against a saffron sky. There could be no mistaking his bowed form and distorted neck, but now his appearance was made additionally abominable by his expression. The yellow sunset light seemed to stream all round him, and showed me features convulsed with fury. He gnashed his teeth and clawed the air with both hands. I have never seen such a picture of impotent rage.

It was more by instinct than by any deliberate courage that I ran straight across the lawn towards him. He was gone in a flash, and when I came through the archway where he had stood, he was hurrying down the side of the hedge towards the other. He moved with an odd shuffling gait, and I made sure that I should soon overtake him. But to my surprise I found that I did not gain much. His limping shuffle took him over the ground as fast as I could cover it. In fact, when I reached the point from which I had started I thought I had actually lost a little. When we came round for the second time there was no doubt about it. This was humiliating, but I persevered, relying now on superior stamina. But during the third circuit it suddenly flashed upon me that our positions had become reversed. I was no longer the pursuer. He—it——whatever the creature was, was now chasing me, and the distance between us was diminishing rapidly.

I am not ashamed to admit that my nerve failed completely. I believe I screamed aloud. I ran on stumblingly, helplessly, as one runs in a dream, knowing now that the creature behind was gaining at every stride. How long the chase lasted I do not know, but presently I could hear his irregular footstep close behind me, and a horrible dank breath played about the back of my neck. We were on the side towards the house when I looked up and saw my butler standing at the garden door, with a note in his hand. The sight of his prosaic form seemed to break the spell which had kept me running blindly round and round the hedge. I was almost exhausted, but I tore across the lawn, and fell in a heap at the bottom of the steps.

Parker was an ex-sergeant of Marines, which amounts to saying that he was incapable of surprise and qualified to cope with any practical emergency which could arise. He picked me up, helped me into the house, gave me a tumbler of brandy diluted with soda-water, and fortified himself with another, without saying a word. How much he saw, or what he thought of it, I could never learn, for all subsequent approaches to the question were parried with the evasive skill which seems to be the birthright of all them that go down to the sea in ships. But his general view of the situation is indicated by the fact that he sent for the rector, not the doctor, and—as I learned afterwards—had a private conference with him before he left the house. Soon afterwards he joined the choir—or in his own phrase 'assisted with the singing in the chancel'—and for many months the village church had no more regular or vocal attendant.

The rector heard my story gravely, and was by no means disposed to make light of it. Something similar had come his way once before, when he had had the charge of a parish on the Northumbrian Border. He was confident, he said, that no harm could come to me that night, if I remained indoors, and departed to look up some of his authorities on such subjects.

That night was noisy with wind, so the insistent knocking which

53

I seemed to hear during the small hours at the garden-door and ground-floor windows, which were secured with outside shutters, may have had no existence outside my imagination. I had asked Parker to occupy a dressing-room opening out of my bedroom for the night. He seemed very ready to do so, but I do not think that he slept very much either. Early next morning the rector reappeared, saying that he thought he had got a clue, though it was impossible to say yet how much it might be worth. He had brought with him the first volume of the parish register, and showed me the following note on the inside of the cover:

'October 31st, 1578. On this day Jn. Croxton a Poore Man hanged himself from a Beame within his House. He was a very stubborn Popish Recusant and ye manner of his Death was in accord with his whole Life. He was buried that evening at ye Cross Roades.'

'It is unfortunate,' continued the rector, 'that we have no sixteenth-century map of the parish. But there is a map of 1759 which marks a hamlet at the cross-roads just outside your gate. The hamlet doesn't exist now—you know that the population hereabouts is much less than it used to be—but it used to be called New Cross. I think that must mean that these particular cross-roads are comparatively recent. Now this house is known to have been built between 1596 and 1602. The straight way from Farley to Abbotsholme would lie nearly across its site. I think, therefore, that the Elizabethan Lord Rye diverted the old road when he laid out his grounds. That would also account for the loop which the present road makes'—here he traced its course with his finger on the map which he had brought.

'Now I strongly suspect that your visitor was Mr. Croxton, and that he is buried somewhere in your grounds. If we could find the place, I think we could keep him quiet for the future. But I am afraid that there is nothing to guide us.'

At this point Parker came in. 'Beg your pardon, Sir, but Hardman is wishful to speak to you. About that there bollard on the quarter-deck, Sir—stump on the lawn, I should have said, Sir—what you told him to put over the side.'

We went out, and found Hardman and the boy looking at a large hole in the lawn. By the side of it lay what we had taken for a tree stump. But it had never struck root there. It was a very solid wooden stake, some nine feet in length over all, with a sharp point. It had been driven some six feet into the ground, passing through a layer of rubble about three feet from the surface. At the bottom the hole widened, forming a large, and plainly artificial, cavity. The earth here looked as if it had been recently disturbed, but the condition of the stake showed that that was impossible. It was obvious to both of us that we had come upon Mr. Croxton's grave, at the original cross-roads, and that what had appeared to be a natural stump was really the stake which had been driven through it to keep him there. We did not, of course, take the gardeners into our confidence, but told them to leave the place for the present as it might contain some interesting antiques—presumably Roman—which we would get out carefully with our own hands.

We soon enlarged the shaft sufficiently to explore the cavity at the bottom. We had naturally expected to find a skeleton, or something of the sort, there, but we were disappointed. We could not discover the slightest vestige of bones or body, or of any dust except that of natural soil. Once while we were working, we were startled by a harsh sound like the cry of a night-jar, apparently very close at hand. But whatever it was passed away very quickly, as if the creature which had made it was on the wing, and it was not repeated.

By the rector's advice we went to the churchyard and brought away sufficient consecrated earth to fill up the cavity. The shaft was filled up, and the sundial securely planted on top of it. The pious mottoes with which it was adorned, according to custom, assumed for the first time a practical significance.

'It not infrequently happens,' said the rector, 'that those who for any reason have not received full Christian Burial are unable, or un-willing, to remain quiet in their graves, particularly if the interment has been at all carelessly carried out in the first instance. They seem to be particularly active on or about the anniversary of their death in any year. The range of their activities is varied, and it would be difficult to define the nature of the power which animates them, or the source from which it is derived.

'But I incline to think that it is less their own personality than some force inherent in the earth itself, of which they become the vehicle. With the exception of Vampires (who are altogether *sui generis* and virtually unknown in this country), they can seldom do much direct physical harm. They operate indirectly by terrifying, but are commonly compelled to stop there. But it is always necessary for them to have free access to their graves. If that is obstructed in any way their power seems to lapse. That is why I think that their vitality is in some way bred of the earth: and I am sure that you won't be troubled with any more visits now.

'Our friend was afraid that your sundial would interfere with his convenience, and I think he was trying to frighten you into leaving the house. Of course, if your heart had been weak, he might have disposed of you as he did of your unfortunate predecessor. His projection of himself into your dreams was part of his general plan: I incline to think, however, that it was an error of judgment, as it might have put you on your guard. But I very much doubt whether he could have inflicted any physical injury on you if he had caught you yesterday afternoon.'

'H'm,' said I, 'you might be right there. But I am very glad that I shall never know.'

Next day Parker asked for leave to go to London. He returned with a large picture representing King Solomon issuing directions to a *corvée* of demons of repellent aspect whom he had (according to a well-known Jewish legend) compelled to labour at the building of the Temple. This he proceeded to affix with drawing-pins to the inside of the pantry door. He called my attention to it particularly, and said that he had got it from a Jew whom he had known in Malta, who had recently opened a branch establishment in the Whitechapel Road. I ventured to make some comment on the singularity of the subject, but Parker was, as usual, impenetrable. 'Beggin' your pardon, Sir,' he said, 'there's some things what a civilian don't never 'ave no chance of learnin', not even if 'e 'ad the brains for it. I done my twenty-one years in the Service—in *puris naturalibus* all the time as the saying is—and' (pointing to the figure of the king) you may lay to it that that there man knew 'is business.'

Between Sunset and Moonrise

During the early part of last year, it fell to me to act as executor for an old friend. We had not seen much of each other of late, as he had been living in the west of England, and my own time had been fully occupied elsewhere. The time of our intimacy had been when he was vicar of a large parish not very far from Cambridge. I will call it Yaxholme, though that is not its name.

The place had seemed to suit him thoroughly. He had been on the best of terms with his parishioners, and with the few gentry of the neighbourhood. The church demanded a custodian of antiquarian knowledge and artistic perception, and in these respects too my friend was particularly well qualified for his position. But a sudden nervous breakdown had compelled him to resign. The cause of it had always been a mystery to his friends, for he was barely middle-aged when it took place, and had been a man of robust health. His parish was neither particularly laborious nor harassing; and, as far as was known, he had no special private anxieties of any kind.

But the collapse came with startling suddenness, and was so severe that, for a time, his reason seemed to be in danger. Two years of rest and travel enabled him to lead a normal life again, but he was never the man he had been. He never revisited his old parish, or any of his friends in the county; and seemed to be ill at ease if conversation turned upon the part of England in which it lay. It was perhaps not unnatural that he should dislike the place which had cost him so much. But his friends could not but regard as childish the length to which he carried his aversion.

He had had a distinguished career at the University, and had kept up his intellectual interests in later life. But, except for an occasional *succès d'estime* in a learned periodical, he had published nothing. I was not without hope of finding something completed among his papers which would secure for him a permanent place in the world of learning. But in this I was disappointed. His literary remains were copious, and a striking testimony to the vigour and range of his intellect. But they were very fragmentary. There was nothing which could be made fit for publication, except one document which I should have preferred to suppress. But he had left particular instructions in his will that it was to be published when he had been dead for a year. Accordingly, I subjoin it exactly as it left his hand. It was dated two years after he had left Yaxholme, and nearly five before his death. For reasons which will be apparent to the reader I make no comment of any kind upon it.

★★★★★★★★★★★★★★★★

The solicitude which my friends have displayed during my illness has placed me under obligations which I cannot hope to repay. But I feel that I owe it to them to explain the real cause of my breakdown. I have never spoken of it to anyone, for, had I done so, it would have been impossible to avoid questions which I should not wish to be able to answer. Though I have only just reached middle-age I am sure that I have not many more years to live. And I am therefore confident that most of my friends will survive me, and be able to hear my explanation after my death. Nothing but a lively sense of what I owe to them could have enabled me to undergo the pain of recalling the experience which I am now about to set down.

Yaxholme lies, as they will remember, upon the extreme edge of the Fen district. In shape it is a long oval, with a main line of railway cutting one end. The church and vicarage were close to the station, and round them lay a village containing nearly five-sixths of the entire population of the parish. On the other side of the line the Fen proper began, and stretched for many miles. Though it is now fertile corn land, much of it had been permanently under water within living memory, and would soon revert to its original condition if it were not for the pumping stations. In spite of these it is not unusual to see several hundred acres flooded in winter.

My own parish ran for nearly six miles, and I had therefore several scattered farms and cottages so far from the village that a visit to one of them took up the whole of a long afternoon. Most of them were not on any road, and could only be reached by means of droves. For the benefit of those who are not acquainted with the Fen I may explain that a drove is a very imperfect sketch of the idea of a road. It is bounded by hedges or dykes, so that the traveller cannot actually lose his way, but it offers no further assistance to his progress. The middle is simply a grass track, and as cattle have to be driven along it the mud is sometimes literally knee-deep in winter. In summer the light peaty soil rises in clouds of sable dust. In fact, I seldom went down one without recalling Hesiod's unpatriotic description of his native village in Boeotia. 'Bad in winter; intolerable in summer; good at no time.'

At the far end of one of these lay a straggling group of half a dozen cottages, of which the most remote was inhabited by an old woman whom I will call Mrs.Vries. In some ways she was the most interesting of all my parishioners, and she was certainly the most perplexing. She was not a native, but had come to live there some twenty years before, and it was hard to see what had tempted a stranger to so unattractive a spot. It was the last house in the parish: her nearest neighbour was a quarter of a mile away, and she was fully three miles from a hard road or a shop.

The house itself was not at all a good one. It had been unoccupied, I was told, for some years before she came to it, and she had found it in a semi-ruinous condition. Yet she had not been driven to seek a very cheap dwelling by poverty, as she had a good supply of furniture of very good quality, and, apparently, as much money as she required. She never gave the slightest hint as to where she had come from, or what her previous history had been. As far as was known she never wrote or received any letters. She must have been between fifty and sixty when she came. Her appearance was striking, as she was tall and thin, with an aquiline nose, and a pair of very brilliant dark eyes, and a quantity of hair—snow-white by the time I knew her.

At one time she must have been handsome; but she had grown rather forbidding, and I used to think that, a couple of centuries before, she might have had some difficulty in proving that she was not a witch. Though her neighbours, not unnaturally, fought rather shy of her, her conversation showed that she was a clever woman who had at some time received a good deal of education, and had lived in culti-vated surroundings. I used to think that she must have been an upper servant—most probably lady's maid—in a good house, and, despite the ring on her finger, suspected that the 'Mrs.' was brevet rank.

One New Year's Eve, I thought it my duty to visit her. I had not seen her for some months, and a few days of frost had made the drove more passable than it had been for several weeks. But, in spite of her interesting personality, I always found that it required a considerable moral effort to call at her cottage. She was always civil, and expressed herself pleased to see me. But I could never get rid of the idea that she regarded civility to me in the light of an insurance, which might be claimed elsewhere. I always told myself that such thoughts were unfounded and unworthy, but I could never repress them altogether, and whenever I left her cottage, it was with a strong feeling that I had no desire to see her again. I used, however, to say to myself that that was really due to personal pique (because I could never discover that she had any religion, nor could I instil any into her), and that the fault was therefore more mine than hers.

On this particular afternoon the prospect of seeing her seemed more than usually distasteful, and my disinclination increased curiously as I made my way along the drove. So strong did it become that if any reasonable excuse for turning back had presented itself I am afraid I should have seized it. However, none did: so, I held on, comforting myself with the thought that I should begin the New Year with a comfortable sense of having discharged the most unpleasant of my regular duties in a conscientious fashion.

When I reached the cottage, I was a little surprised at having to knock three times, and by hearing the sound of bolts cautiously drawn back. Presently the door opened and Mrs. Vries peered out. As soon as she saw who it was, she made me very welcome as usual. But it was impossible not to feel that she had been more or less expecting some other visitor, whom she was not anxious to see. However, she volunteered no statement, and I thought it better to pretend to have noticed nothing unusual. On a table in the middle of the room lay a large book in which she had obviously been reading. I was surprised to see that it was a Bible, and that it lay open at the Book of Tobit. Seeing that I had noticed it Mrs. Vries told me—with a little hesitation, I thought—that she had been reading the story of Sarah and the fiend Asmodeus.

Then—the ice once broken—she plied me almost fiercely with questions. 'To what cause did I attribute Sarah's obsession, in the first instance?' 'Did the efficacy of Tobias' remedy depend upon the fact that it had been prescribed by an angel?' and much more to the same effect. Naturally my answers were rather vague, and her good manners could not conceal her disappointment. She sat silent for a minute or two, while I looked at her—not, I must confess, without some alarm, for her manner had been very strange—and then said abruptly, 'Well, will you have a cup of tea with me?' I assented gladly, for it was nearly half-past four, and it would take me nearly an hour and a half to get home. She took some time over the preparations and during the meal talked with even more fluency than usual. I could not help thinking that she was trying to make it last as long as possible.

Finally, at about half-past five, I got up and said that I must go, as I had a good many odds and ends awaiting me at home. I held out my hand, and as she took it said, 'You must let me wish you a very happy New Year.'

She stared at me for a moment, and then broke into a harsh laugh, and said, 'If wishes were horses beggars might ride. Still, I thank you for your good will. Goodbye.' About thirty yards from her house there was an elbow in the drove. When I reached it, I looked back and saw that she was still standing in her doorway, with her figure sharply silhouetted against the red glow of the kitchen fire. For one instant the play of shadow made it look as if there were another, taller, figure behind her, but the illusion passed directly. I waved my hand to her and turned the corner.

It was a fine, still, starlight night. I reflected that the moon would be up before I reached home, and my walk would not be unpleasant. I had naturally been rather puzzled by Mrs. Vries' behaviour, and decided that I must see her again before long, to ascertain whether, as seemed possible, her mind were giving way.

When I had passed the other cottages of the group I noticed that the stars were disappearing, and a thick white mist was rolling up. This did not trouble me. The drove now ran straight until it joined the high-road, and there was no turn into it on either side. I had therefore no chance of losing my way, and anyone who lives in the Fens is accustomed to fogs. It soon grew very thick, and I was conscious of the slightly creepy feeling which a thick fog very commonly inspires. I had been thinking of a variety of things, in somewhat desultory fashion, when suddenly—almost as if it had been whispered into my ear—a passage from the *Book of Wisdom* came into my mind and refused to be dislodged.

My nerves were good then, and I had often walked up a lonely drove in a fog before; but still just at that moment I should have preferred to have recalled almost anything else. For this was the extract with which my memory was pleased to present me. '*For neither did the dark recesses that held them guard them from fears, but sounds rushing down rang around them; and phantoms appeared, cheerless with unsmiling faces. And no force of fire prevailed to give them light, neither were the brightest flames of the stars strong enough to illumine that gloomy night. And in terror they deemed the things which they saw to be worse than that sight on which they could not gaze. And they lay helpless, made the sport of magic art.'* (*Wisdom* xvii. 4-6).

Suddenly I heard a loud snort, as of a beast, apparently at my elbow. Naturally I jumped and stood still for a moment to avoid blundering into a stray cow, but there was nothing there. The next moment I heard what sounded exactly like a low chuckle. This was more disconcerting: but common sense soon came to my aid. I told myself that the cow must have been on the other side of the hedge and not really so close as it had seemed to be. What I had taken for a chuckle must have been the squelching of her feet in a soft place. But I must confess that I did not find this explanation as convincing as I could have wished.

I plodded on, but soon began to feel unaccountably tired. I say 'unaccountably' because I was a good walker and often covered much more ground than I had done that day.

I slackened my pace, but, as I was not out of breath, that did not relieve me. I felt as if I were wading through water up to my middle, or through very deep soft snow, and at last was fairly compelled to stop. By this time, I was thoroughly uneasy, wondering what could be the matter with me. But as I had still nearly two miles to go there was nothing for it but to push on as best I might.

When I started again, I saw that the fog seemed to be beginning to clear, though I could not feel a breath of air. But instead of thinning in the ordinary way it merely rolled back a little on either hand, producing an effect which I had never seen before. Along the sides of the drove lay two solid banks of white, with a narrow passage clear between them. This passage seemed to stretch for an interminable distance, and at the far end I 'perceived' a number of figures. I say advisedly 'perceived,' rather than 'saw,' for I do not know whether I saw them in the ordinary sense of the word or not. That is to say—I did not know then, and have never been able to determine since, whether it was still dark. I only know that my power of vision seemed to be independent of light or darkness. I perceived the figures, as one sees the creatures of a dream, or the mental pictures which sometimes come when one is neither quite asleep nor awake.

They were advancing rapidly in orderly fashion, almost like a body of troops. The scene recalled very vividly a picture of the Israelites marching across the Red Sea between two perpendicular walls of water, in a set of Bible pictures which I had had as a child. I suppose that I had not thought of that picture for more than thirty years, but now it leapt into my mind, and I found myself saying aloud, 'Yes: of course it must have been exactly like that. How glad I am to have seen it.'

I suppose it was the interest of making the comparison that kept me from feeling the surprise which would otherwise have been occasioned by meeting a large number of people marching down a lonely drove after dark on a raw December evening.

At first, I should have said there were thirty or forty in the party, but when they had drawn a little nearer, they seemed to be not more than ten or a dozen strong. A moment later I saw to my surprise that they were reduced to five or six. The advancing figures seemed to be melting into one another, something after the fashion of dissolving views. Their speed and stature increased as their numbers diminished, suggesting that the survivors had, in some horrible fashion, absorbed the personality of their companions. Now there appeared to be only three, then one solitary figure of gigantic stature rushing down the drove towards me at a fearful pace, without a sound. As he came the mist closed behind him, so that his dark figure was thrown up against a solid background of white: much as mountain climbers are said sometimes to see their own shadows upon a bank of cloud.

On and on he came, until at last he towered above me and I saw his face. It has come to me once or twice since in troubled dreams, and may come again. But I am thankful that I have never had any clear picture of it in my waking moments. If I had I should be afraid for my reason. I know that the impression which it produced upon me was that of intense malignity long baffled, and now at last within reach of its desire. I believe I screamed aloud. Then after a pause, which seemed to last for hours, he broke over me like a wave. There was a rushing and a streaming all round me, and I struck out with my hands as if I were swimming. The sensation was not unlike that of rising from a deep dive: there was the same feeling of pressure and suffocation, but in this case coupled with the most intense physical loathing. The only comparison which I can suggest is that I felt as a man might feel if he were buried under a heap of worms or toads.

Suddenly I seemed to be clear, and fell forward on my face. I am not sure whether I fainted or not, but I must have lain there for some minutes. When I picked myself up I felt a light breeze upon my forehead and the mist was clearing away as quickly as it had come. I saw the rim of the moon above the horizon, and my mysterious fatigue had disappeared. I hurried forward as quickly as I could without venturing to look behind me. I only wanted to get out of that abominable drove on to the high-road, where there were lights and other human beings. For I knew that what I had seen was a creature of darkness and waste places, and that among my fellows I should be safe. When I reached home my housekeeper looked at me oddly. Of course, my clothes were muddy and disarranged, but I suspect that there was something else unusual in my appearance. I merely said that I had had a fall coming up a drove in the dark, and was not feeling particularly well. I avoided the looking-glass when I went to my room to change.

Coming downstairs I heard through the open kitchen door some scraps of conversation—or rather of a monologue delivered by my housekeeper—to the effect that no one ought to be about the droves after dark as much as I was, and that it was a providence that things were no worse. Her own mother's uncle had—it appeared—been down just such another drove on just such another night, forty-two years ago come next Christmas Eve. 'They brought 'im 'ome on a barrow with both 'is eyes drawed down, and every drop of blood in 'is body turned. But 'e never would speak to what 'e see, and wild cats couldn't ha' scratched it out of 'im.'

An inaudible remark from one of the maids was met with a long sniff, and the statement: 'Girls seem to think they know everything nowadays.' I spent the next day in bed, as besides the shock which I had received I had caught a bad cold. When I got up on the second, I was not surprised to hear that Mrs. Vries had been found dead on the previous afternoon. I had hardly finished breakfast when I was told that the policeman, whose name was Winter, would be glad to see me.

It appeared that on New Year's morning a half-witted boy of seventeen, who lived at one of the other cottages down the drove, had come to him and said that Mrs. Vries was dead, and that he must come and enter her house. He declined to explain how he had come by the information: so, at first Mr. Winter contented himself with pointing out that it was the first of January not of April. But the boy was so insistent that finally he went. When repeated knockings at Mrs. Vries' cottage produced no result he had felt justified in forcing the backdoor. She was sitting in a large wooden armchair quite dead. She was leaning forward a little and her hands were clasping the arms so tightly that it proved to be a matter of some difficulty to unloose her fingers.

In front of her was another chair, so close that if anyone had been sitting in it his knees must have touched those of the dead woman. The seat cushions were flattened down as if it had been occupied recently by a solid personage. The tea-things had not been cleared away, but the kitchen was perfectly clean and tidy. There was no suspicion of foul play, as all the doors and windows were securely fastened on the inside. Winter added that her face made him feel 'quite sickish like,' and that the house smelt very bad for all that it was so clean.

A post-mortem examination of the body showed that her heart was in a very bad state, and enabled the coroner's jury to return a verdict of 'Death from Natural Causes.' But the doctor told me privately that she must have had a shock of some kind. 'In fact,' he said, if anyone ever died of fright, she did. But goodness knows what can have frightened her in her own kitchen unless it was her own conscience. But that is more in your line than mine.'

He added that he had found the examination of the body peculiarly trying: though he could not, or would not, say why.

As I was the last person who had seen her alive, I attended the inquest, but gave only formal evidence of an unimportant character. I did not mention that the second armchair had stood in a corner of the room during my visit, and that I had not occupied it.

The boy was of course called and asked how he knew she was dead. But nothing satisfactory could be got from him. He said that there was right houses and there was wrong houses—not to say persons—and that 'they' had been after her for a long time. When asked whom he meant by 'they' he declined to explain, merely adding as a general statement that he could see further into a milestone than what some people could, for all they thought themselves so clever. His own family deposed that he had been absolutely silent, contrary to his usual custom, from tea-time on New Year's Eve to breakfast-time next day. Then he had suddenly announced that Mrs. Vries was dead; and ran out of the house before they could say anything to him. Accordingly, he was dismissed, with a warning to the effect that persons who were disrespectful to Constituted Authorities always came to a bad end.

It naturally fell to me to conduct the funeral, as I could have given no reason for refusing her Christian burial. The coffin was not particularly weighty, but as it was being lowered into the grave the ropes supporting it parted, and it fell several feet with a thud. The shock dislodged a quantity of soil from the sides of the cavity, so that the coffin was completely covered before I had had time to say 'Earth to earth: Ashes to ashes: Dust to dust.'

Afterwards the sexton spoke to me apologetically about the occurrence. 'I'm fair put about, Sir, about them ropes,' he said. 'Nothing o' that sort ever 'appened afore in my time. They was pretty nigh new too, and I thought they'd 'a done us for years. But just look 'ere, Sir.'

Here he showed two extraordinarily ravelled ends. 'I never see a rope part like that afore. Almost looks as if it 'ad been scratted through by a big cat or somethink.'

That night I was taken ill. When I was better my doctor said that rest and change of scene were imperative. I knew that I could never go down a drove alone by night again, so tendered my resignation to my Bishop. I hope that I have still a few years of usefulness before me: but I know that I can never be as if I had not seen what I have seen. Whether I met with my adventure through any fault of my own I cannot tell. But of one thing, I am sure. There are powers of darkness which walk abroad in waste places: and that man is happy who has never had to face them.

If anyone who reads this should ever have a similar experience and should feel tempted to try to investigate it further, I commend to him the counsel of Jesus-ben-Sira.

My son, seek not things that are too hard for thee: and search not out things that are above thy strength.'

The Blank Leaves

Mr. Edward Withington was a gentleman somewhat past middle-age. Deafness had compelled him to give up a considerable practice at the Bar, which his friends hoped would have raised him to the Bench. He was a widower without children, so his existence had become rather solitary.

Fortunately, however, he developed a strong taste for research into pedigrees and family history of all kinds. This led him to make numerous journeys to various parts of the country to make extracts from Parish Registers, copy tombstones and take rubbings of brasses; and so, provided him with exactly the sort of occupation and interest which he needed.

It would be difficult to picture a much more placid pursuit. Indeed, to many people it might appear to be almost dull. But one of these expeditions led to a very curious experience, the history of which is here set down in his own words. He told it to me about three years after it had happened.

****

I was tracing the history of a family named Bolsover which I knew to have settled in Lincolnshire sometime in the reign of Queen Elizabeth. And I had reason to believe that if I went to a little village, which I will call Snettersby, I should stand a good chance of gathering some of the information which I required.

Accordingly, upon a fine afternoon towards the end of October I deposited myself at Scopperland, the nearest railway station, and having engaged a room at the inn for the night began to make some preliminary enquiries. I learned that Snettersby was about three miles off and that it possessed an inn which my landlord did not feel able to recommend. Having ascertained this much I thought I would walk over and have a look at it for myself. Unless the inn were quite impossible it would certainly be more convenient to be actually upon the spot, as otherwise I should have to waste a good deal of time in getting to and fro. (There were no motors in those days.)

My first impressions of Snettersby were favourable. It lay picturesquely enough round a village green—as is common in that part of England. Many of the cottages were of wood, but some were of old red brick which had mellowed to a very attractive tint. The church lay at one end, so screened with trees that only the top of the low square tower could be seen. The rectory lay upon the far side of the churchyard and was not visible from the high-road. An early tea at The Running Man assured me that I should do well enough there for a day or two. So, I engaged a bedroom for the following night and arranged to have my bag sent for in the morning.

On my arrival next day, I went to the rectory and explained the object of my visit. The rector made no difficulty about letting me have the keys of the church and of the safe in the vestry where the parish registers were kept.

I did not spend much time in the church. It was a good-sized perpendicular building dating from about 1440, to which some seventeenth-century additions had been made. It did not differ from scores of others. The painted glass I judged to have been put in about 1850. The artist had held that Biblical characters are best represented in yellow or magenta under-garments with cloaks of apple-green. As it was a bright sunny morning the effect was inexpressibly vivid. There were no interesting monuments; and as soon as I had made sure that the mural tablets contained nothing which I wanted I turned to the safe.

Now those who occupy their business in parochial registers know that they can never foretell their luck. Sometimes the books have been well kept and are in good condition. Sometimes, on the other hand, there are serious gaps in the entries or page after page has become illegible from damp. Sometimes an entire volume may be missing. But the Snettersby registers seemed to be as good as any which I have ever come across. The series was complete from 1558, the books had been carefully kept and were in perfect condition. To add to my satisfaction, I picked up the Bolsovers almost immediately.

I was at work on the Register of Burials and had got past the middle of the seventeenth century when I came upon a page which differed from the rest. The entries did not cover more than two-thirds of it and the remaining space was filled with a number of meaningless marks. Or at any rate of marks which meant nothing to me. Some I recognised as Hebrew letters: one was undoubtedly a Greek *Phi*. Others suggested *Runes*, but I was not sufficiently familiar with Runic lettering to be sure. There were also a number of other marks which I thought stood for the signs of the Zodiac or something of that kind.

In all there were forty-five characters: nine in the top row, eight in the second and so on. The lines were all exactly the same distance apart and the characters in each were carefully spaced. Whatever the purpose of the performance might have been, considerable pains must have been expended on it.

'Well,' I thought, 'someone must have wasted some of his time over this. But as it can't help to fix the dates of the deaths of Tobias and Shelumiel Bolsover, which is what I am after at this moment, I don't see why it should lead me to waste any of mine.'

I turned over but found the next two pages blank. Probably they had stuck together when the book was new and so had been turned over as one by accident. On the third page the entries began again in a different hand.

At this point I thought it time to return to The Running Man for lunch. I left the book open upon the table with the written sheets containing the extracts which I had made beside it.

When I came back, I noticed at once that my papers had been disarranged. I had left them in a neat heap with a sheet half-covered with writing on top. Now they were strewn all over the table and one or two were on the floor. A blank sheet lay beside the open volume as if inviting me to begin upon it.

My first thought was naturally that it had been done by a gust of wind. But the vestry window was shut, as it had been all the morning. I had locked the doors leading into the church and churchyard when I left and had taken the keys with me. But of course, the clerk, or whoever was employed to clean the church, would be likely to have a duplicate set. He or she must have come in while I was away and disarranged my papers by accident.

I soon had them in order again and went on with my pursuit of the Bolsovers. I had found out all I wanted to know, and was just preparing to put away, as the light was beginning to fail, when it struck me that I might as well take a copy of the curious cypher or cryptogram—whichever is the proper name for it. I had a friend at Cambridge who was keenly interested in such things and would be likely to be able to tell me what, if anything, it meant.

I had brought some sheets of tracing-paper, so the copy was quickly made. I was just preparing to shut the book when a voice said very distinctly in my ear: *You ought to copy the blank leaves too.'*

It was low, but of the metallic timbre which even a deaf man can hear. Naturally I jumped. My first idea was of course that someone had come in unheard, as they might easily have done, and I looked round. But there was no one there. I don't think I had really expected that there would be.

I told myself that it was merely imagination, and prepared for the second time to close the book. But as I took it up the voice came again: *You must copy the blank leaves too.'*

Curiously I was not frightened. Of course I had been startled at first, but now I felt quite anxious to carry out my invisible friend's suggestion. But at this point a practical difficulty arose. The leaves undoubtedly were blank. So how could I or anybody else take a copy of them?

After a little consideration I hit upon what I thought a very ingenious device. I laid the book upon the table and spread a sheet of tracing-paper across it. On this I rested my hand with a pencil held lightly between my fingers, shut my eyes and waited.

I did not have to wait long. In a few seconds the pencil began to twitch, much as if someone had taken hold of the end. After a few feeble scratchings it began to travel rapidly over the paper, and I let my hand follow it. It went right round the sheet in a decided if irregular fashion and then stopped.

When I opened my eyes, I had no difficulty in recognising a ground plan of the church. At one point, just outside the north wall, there was a dot where the point of the pencil had nearly gone through the paper.

So far so good. The experiment had proved more interesting than I had expected. But there was still another leaf to be dealt with. So, I took a second sheet of tracing-paper and arranged myself as before.

This time I did not have to wait at all. The pencil wrote something very rapidly and then snapped between my fingers. I opened my eyes and read the following verse from Isaiah. *Their houses shall be full of doleful creatures and owls shall dwell there and satyrs shall dance there.*

The hand was not my own. It was unquestionably identical with one of those in the register: namely, the one which came to an end at the blank leaves.

This, I must admit, disquieted me considerably. For it suggested that I had somehow put myself *en rapport* with some person unknown who might presently force a much closer acquaintance upon me. Still, the mischief, if any, was done now. I collected my papers, put away the book, locked up everything very carefully and returned the keys to the rectory.

It was dark by the time I turned out of the rectory gate, and though I had only a few hundred yards to walk to my inn I was glad when I got there. For on the way I was much annoyed by what seemed to be an unusually large bat, which kept flitting round my head, almost brushing my face with its wings.

My efforts to drive it off were not successful, and though I was pretty sure that bats do not eat cats I did not feel certain that one so audacious as this might not scratch the face or bite the ears of a human being. When I got near the door of the inn it made off, and if I had trusted to appearances, I could have sworn that it flitted straight into the house.

But this seemed so unlikely that I felt sure that my eyes must have been deceived.

Between tea and supper, I occupied myself with going over my notes on the Bolsover family to make sure that I had got them complete. This done, my thoughts naturally turned to the cryptogram and my copy of the blank leaves. But I could make nothing of either. Then I must, I suppose, have fallen asleep. I say 'I suppose' because I can only ascribe my subsequent experience to a dream, though it was at the time, and still remains, as vivid as anything which ever befell me in my waking moments.

First the inn-parlour in which I was sitting seemed to elongate itself until I found myself gazing down a vista of great length. At the far end there was considerable activity of some sort, but I could not discern exactly what was taking place. There appeared to be a number of people gathered round a raised platform of some kind. On this a solitary figure presently appeared. Before I could make out more the whole scene had vanished.

I stared at the darkness for a minute or two. Then a point of light appeared, as if at the end of a long tunnel. It advanced slowly, and there could be no doubt that it was a lamp of some kind which some person unknown was carrying. As it got nearer, I felt that there was something curious and uncanny about it, though I could not have said exactly what. But I felt very unwilling to see it or its bearer at close quarters. I tried hard to make him out, but could see nothing of him at all. Before long this too disappeared and there was nothing but darkness.

I was sitting beside a fire and had two candles on the table beside me. But naturally their light did not extend very far. Beyond it the blackness was impenetrable and gave me a sensation of infinite distance.

Presently I became aware—I say advisedly became 'aware,' because I did not see or hear anything—that the room was full of stealthy movement. Certainly, there was somebody there and he seemed to be pacing softly to and fro, as you may see hungry tigers doing in their cages at the zoo.

Was he preparing for a spring?

Suddenly from the edge of the darkness what looked like an arm was protruded and very quickly withdrawn. I noticed that it was naked, black, and very thin. There was something else unpleasant about it which I did not take in at the moment. But on thinking it over afterwards I realized what it was. The arm had no hand. It ended in a stump at the wrist.

At this point the door burst open and the landlord tumbled into the room with a scared expression on his usually placid countenance.

'Beg pardon, Sir,' he said, 'but is anything the matter? Did you want anything?'

'No,' I replied. 'I didn't ring.'

'No, Sir—I know you didn't. There ain't no bell to begin with. But we thought we 'eard you call out three times, Sir—all on us did. Something 'orrible it sounded, in a manner of speaking, if you'll excuse me saying of it.'

I told him that I had fallen asleep in front of the fire and must have cried out in my sleep. I apologised for the fright I had given to the household and he withdrew apparently reassured.

But I did not believe that I had been asleep, and was quite sure that whoever had called out it was not I.

Happening to look up at the ceiling some play of firelight cast a shadow like the form of a very large bat. But it was only a shadow and disappeared immediately.

The appearance of the room was now entirely normal and the rest of the evening passed uneventfully. So did the night, and by the afternoon of the next day I was back in London.

★★★★★★★★★★★★★★★★

The next part of the story begins with two letters which Mr. Withington received some six weeks after his visit to Snettersby. They explain themselves so I subjoin them in full:

Sandford College, Cambridge.
Dec. 15th, 1912.

Dear Withington,

Many thanks for the cryptogram. It's a curious thing and I never saw one quite like it before. Of the forty-five characters, twelve are the zodiacal signs and seven the planetary symbols. The remaining twenty-six are letters. You were right in thinking that eleven of them are Runes. There is one Greek, and the other fourteen are Hebrew.

I thought that the presence of a solitary Greek letter meant that Greek was the language. I transliterated accordingly and after a little juggling got the following sentence:

(Greek characters displayed in here in the printed book)

(*Let us stand in righteousness, let us stand in fear.*)

The phrase comes in the Greek liturgies and had a great vogue in the west as a charm. I don't suppose most of the people who used it knew what it meant or where it came from.

I don't doubt that is what it is here. It looks as if your friend had dabbled a bit in unlawful arts. But what precisely he thought he was up to I can't say.

Yours ever,   J. L. Masters.

The Rectory,
Snettersby,
Lincolnshire.
Dec. 16th, 1912.

Dear Sir,

I must ask you to forgive me for what may seem to be an impertinent enquiry. But I hope you will recognise that I have good grounds for making it.

When you examined our Registers in October did you notice anything remarkable in them, or did anything in any way odd or unusual befall you? I ask because ever since your visit our quiet village has been troubled in a curious and quite inexplicable manner. The disturbances, which it seems difficult to assign to any natural cause, have increased steadily until life has become almost intolerable.

On the day of your departure a labourer who happened to be passing the churchyard after dark was pelted with stones and clods of earth. After this had happened several times to other people we set a watch—assuming naturally that it was the doing of some mischievous boy. But we could find no one, and our vigilance seemed only to increase the activity of our invisible assailant. On other occasions people have been thrown violently to the ground without being able to see who had attacked them.

Beside this we have been visited by a perfect plague of owls and bats. The hooting of the owls makes sleep difficult at night, and the bats find their way into the houses in a most extraordinary fashion.

Nothing has as yet occurred during the daytime. But with the approach of dark the entire village falls into a state of panic which is evidently shared by the animals. The horses seem to feel it most and in two or three cases have become quite unmanageable.

So far, no serious injury has been inflicted upon anyone: but we cannot tell what the next development may be. As the beginning of the disturbances seems to have coincided with your visit I am writing to you in the hope—I admit a faint one—that you may be able to throw some light upon them.

Yours very faithfully,

James R. Towers.

Two hours after the receipt of these letters Mr. Withington was in the train on his way to Cambridge. A long consultation with Masters resulted in the despatch of a telegram asking whether they could both be put up at the rectory for a day or two. The following afternoon found them at Snettersby, and from this point the story can be most conveniently continued in Mr. Withington's own words.

★★★★★★★★★★★★★★★★

By the time we had finished what we had to tell it was dark, and I think we were all conscious that a slightly creepy feeling had come over us. This was evidently shared by an Airedale who was lying stretched upon the hearth-rug. He made two or three uneasy movements and sniffed the air in a very suspicious fashion. Suddenly he jumped up and ran across the room to the right-hand window—we were in the study, a long room on the ground floor with three windows giving on to the garden. He then gave several short but furious barks, turned tail and went back to his place upon the rug.

Immediately afterwards we heard a drumming sound upon the

74

pane. For a moment we thought it might have been made by a bird's wing. But it was too regular for that. We stole across the room and drew back the curtains. The sound was now more distinct, though considerably muffled by the shutters. It was such as might be made by the palm of a human hand beating steadily against the glass. It reminded me of an episode in *The House by the Churchyard*, by Joseph Sheridan Le Fanu, and I did not like it any the better for that. It certainly suggested that there was someone outside particularly anxious to attract our attention: or possibly to make his way into the house.

We were not at all sure that we were anxious for his company, but after a moment's hesitation we unbarred the shutters. As we did so the sound ceased. Directly afterwards it began at the middle window. But as soon as the shutters were opened it transferred itself to the left-hand end. Pursued there it returned to the middle. We could see nothing, but did not like to open a window for fear of what we might admit. When we separated and each stood at a window the sound ceased altogether. But as soon as a window was left deserted it began again.

None of us liked it at all. But as we had come to Snettersby to see the thing through we felt bound to take a bold line. So, Masters and I decided to go round outside while the rector stayed in the room to observe what he could. The Airedale absolutely declined to accompany us.

It was a dark night, cloudy, with no moon. The door was not upon the same side of the house as the study windows, so we had a corner to turn. We crept round it cautiously. I was armed with an electric torch but had not turned it on for fear of scaring our visitor prematurely.

When we were round the corner, we saw the three broad belts of light coming from the three windows. Mr. Towers was standing at the middle one and his shadow made a dark smudge upon the grass. There was nothing else to be seen and nothing to be heard.

Then as we looked the shadow began to change its shape—though we could see that Mr. Towers had not moved. It contracted to an irregular blotch like a person—or was it an animal?—crouching upon the ground. Then it began to oscillate backwards and forwards—as if preparing for a spring. Then a dark arm or feeler shot out from it and was pressed against the glass. I turned on my torch and as I did so the whole thing disappeared, exactly as a real shadow would have done. There was absolutely nothing there.

When we returned to the house Mr. Towers had not much to add to our story. As soon as we had left the room the drumming ceased. He had remained standing at the window to keep a look-out for anything unusual. But there was nothing to be seen except his own shadow upon the grass. Then he saw as we had done that it was changing its shape. It contracted and thickened until he could make out the form of a person wrapped in a dark cloak of some sort crouching upon the grass. A head protruded, perfectly bald and lolling horribly as if the neck were broken. Then an arm shot out and was pressed against the glass. It had no hand but ended in a black spongy mass which was squeezed against the pane. The effect of this was so indescribably disgusting that it made him feel inclined to be sick.

Then the light of my torch fell upon the creature, and there was nothing there.

We divided the night into watches. Two of us sat up together while the third slept. But nothing unusual occurred.

Next morning we decided that the only thing which could be done was to go to the church to see whether any explanation of our experiences could be found there. We felt pretty sure that nothing further could happen in the daytime.

Naturally we began with the Register of Burials. But when we turned to the place from which I had copied the charm it was no longer there. The entries only covered two-thirds of the page as before. But the remaining third was blank. The rector was positive that no one had touched the volume since I had had it, as he always kept the keys of the safe himself. And Masters' expert eye could detect no trace of any erasure.

On turning over we had surprise number two. The next two pages were no longer blank as I had seen them, but were filled with entries of the usual kind. There was nothing surprising about the sequence of dates. The last before the place from which I had copied the charm was 21 July, 1672: the first after it, in a different hand which continued for several years, was 14 October of the same year.

Our only remaining hope seemed to be in my plan of the church and we could think of no better course than to dig at the point outside the north wall where my pencil had made a deep dot in the paper. If this should involve the illegality of opening a grave that could not be helped. Fortunately, the place was upon the side of the church away from the village. The churchyard was not a thoroughfare and was well screened by trees. So, we were pretty safe from interruption.

We got three spades from the rector's potting-shed and set to work.

Being amateurs our progress was rather slow and it was not until we had got down about three feet that I struck my spade upon something hard. This proved to be a small object some ten inches square by five deep. It was thickly coated with pitch and as it was not heavy, we judged it to be a wooden box.

Here at any rate was a find. We took it to the rectory and got tools to break it open. This took some little time as we had to chip the pitch off with a chisel before we could find the fastening of the lid. But at last, we came upon some screws, which proved easier to turn than we had expected.

The box contained a small and very light package done up in canvas. We unripped this carefully and Masters unrolled it upon the table. We found a dried human hand: a right hand which had been severed at the wrist with a very sharp instrument. The skin was intact but there seemed to be no vestige of fat or gristle between it and the bones. The finger-tips were blackened as if they had been scorched by fire.

Of course, this made us certain that we were on the right track. But as there were still a good many gaps to be filled in, we turned again to the box to see whether it had any more information for us. Sticking to the bottom was a small wad of paper tightly folded. It was not easy to detach this without tearing it. But at last, we got it off in good condition. The inside contained some lines of writing and though the ink was a good deal faded, Masters, who was very expert in such matters, had little difficulty in deciphering it. It was in a late seventeenth-century hand and ran as follows—

'Ye hande of Richd. Partridge sometyme Clerke of this Par-ysshe who was hanged upon September ye Firste in ye yeare of oure Lord 1672. I have done worse and suffer ye rewarde of my misdedes. Lord, have mercy upon me. Wm. Archer.'

'H'm,' I said, 'there's evidently a history here. I wonder what it is? And we seem to be nearly as far as ever from any satisfactory explanation. I suppose it was Partridge who came to the house last night. Are we to offer him his hand if he comes again, or what?'

For the last few minutes Masters had been looking very grave. He now said suddenly and with great emphasis—Burn those tracings of yours. I don't think I'm a superstitious man. But I don't like this one little bit. And so I say burn them.'

We were standing in front of the fire in the study. I took the three sheets from my pocket and without saying anything further threw them on to the blaze. I had been intimate with Masters for many years, and knew that he was not easily moved, and did not say what he did not mean.

They caught at once; a feather of ash whirled up the chimney and was gone.

'Well,' I said, 'that's the end of them. But now what are we to do with the hand?'

We turned to look at it, where we had left it lying upon the table—but it was gone. The box was there, and the canvas wrapper; so was the paper. But of the hand itself there was not the slightest trace. Yet we had not had our backs turned for more than a few seconds. While we stared blankly at one another there came from somewhere outside the melancholy hoot of an owl.

'There are two things I want to do now,' said Masters, 'and if you'll both come with me we can just manage them before the light goes. First, I want to put back the box where it came from, and then I want to have another look at the Register.'

The first task was quickly performed. We had cut the top sods carefully, and when we had put them back felt satisfied that in a few weeks the place would show very few signs of having been disturbed.

Then we adjourned to the vestry. Masters, who had remained silent since we left the house, took the seventeenth-century volume and began to read the entries: while we waited. He had hardly had the book in his hands for more than a minute when he said, half to himself and half to us—'I thought as much.' Then he read aloud 'September 5th, 1673, William Archer. Dyed September 1st. The verdict of the Crowner's Quest was The Visitation of God.'

'Visitation of God,' he went on. 'I fancy we are in a position to correct that verdict. Partridge must have got him all right, on the anniversary of his own execution too! I wonder how he managed it? That's all. Let's go back.'

At a later hour in the evening, he consented to give us his theory of what had occurred.

'I have never been able,' he said, to dismiss witchcraft, *etcetera*, as lightly as some people do. I don't profess to be able to explain it. Perhaps there isn't any explanation. Or perhaps it is really too simple to need one. But anyhow I think it is a force which has to be reckoned with. More perhaps in the past than today. But it isn't dead yet. Partridge must have been up to devilry of some kind—it would be interesting to know whether he was hanged for that or for something commonplace like murder or highway robbery—and he meant something by that charm. He seems to have had a pretty apt pupil in Mr. Archer too.

Did you ever hear of The Hand of Glory? It comes in one of the Ingoldsby Legends, you know. If you could get the right hand of a corpse and turn it into a lamp by fixing a wick steeped in human fat to each finger-tip the highest walks of burglary were open to you at once. On the approach of the hand everyone falls into a sleep from which no noise can wake them, and all locks and bolts fly open of their own accord. If the original proprietor of the hand does happen to have been hanged—so much the better. Well—no doubt that was Archer's game—or one of his games.

Partridge didn't like it, for which I don't blame him myself: and I expect he gave Archer a pretty bad time. Archer got frightened, and as he couldn't get at Partridge's body again for some reason did the best he could by burying the hand.

Well—Partridge got him all right as we know. But he still wanted his hand and didn't know how to come at that. I expect the fact that it was in consecrated ground was what defeated him. When you started digging in his volume of the Registers, which probably hadn't been touched for a couple of centuries—I noticed that the last entry was 1703—he thought he saw a chance. And when you copied his charm you, as it were, wound the machine up and he could get to work. He gave you a clue and a warning—both rather vague I admit—and followed that up with his show at the inn. When you left Snettersby he had got to get you back somehow—and he succeeded at last. Well, he's got his hand now, and I hope he finds it useful wherever he is.'

Here Masters paused for a moment to attend to his whisky-and-soda. When this had been dealt with satisfactorily, he went on—

'Of course, there are several gaps in the story which we can't fill in. I don't know why Partridge, since he could tell you to copy the blank leaves, couldn't go about the rest of the job more directly. All that can be said is that gentlemen of his condition always do adopt what seem to us to be very roundabout methods. Whether that is due to choice or circumstances, I don't know. But I suspect the latter. In fact, their ways—as the Irish orator observed of those of Providence—are indeed unscrupulous! However, I think we are rid of him now.'

A few months later I heard from Mr. Towers that there had been no further disturbances of any kind. He expressed a hope that I would come and pay him a visit. But I have never gone to Snettersby again and as I have learned all I wanted to know about the Bolsover family I don't suppose I ever shall.

The Thirteenth Tree

If, as I incline to think, architecture in general and domestic architecture in particular is the best expression of the characteristics of the
period to which it belongs, there would be a good deal to be said in
favour of having been born soon after the year 1570.

Late Tudor or early Jacobean houses always seem to me to exhibit
the qualities which I admire most. They are dignified and beautiful
without conscious effort. Both inside and out I find them extraordinarily satisfying. 'This,' I say to myself, 'is what a country-house ought
to be.' They look as if they had grown from the soil as naturally as the
trees in their parks. They are as they are because the men who planned
them were solid, dignified and sure of themselves.

Castles speak of violence and cruelty, until they have become an
anachronism. Then they are sights to be seen rather than houses to
live in. Early Tudor houses have something upstart about them; as,
it may be suspected, had their owners. The Palladian palaces of the
eighteenth century are not free from ostentation. They were meant to
display the wealth and taste of their owners, most of whom had probably made the Grand Tour. Despite their dignity and internal comfort,
I can never feel that they belong to the English countryside. But the
type of house which was built about twenty years on either side of the
year 1600 always seems to me to escape all these defects. One of them
was the scene of the story which I am now going to tell.

It is situated in one of the western counties. That is as much as I
shall say about its geographical position, as I do not want to bring the
Society for Spectral Investigations, or any similar body, about my ears or
those of the neighbourhood.

I had known the owner when we were boys. Our paths in life had
diverged and for thirty years or more we never met. We came across
each other accidentally in London, and both welcomed the opportunity of resuming an old friendship. When he asked me to visit him, I

was very glad to accept his invitation. Accordingly, a few weeks later, on a fine day early in October, I caught a train at Paddington for my journey westwards.

I had made acquaintance with the first twenty miles of the Great Western in the year 1890, and for some time after that they had been very familiar to me. But I had not travelled by that route for a good many years and was horrified to see how the Great Wen (as Cobbett rudely called London) had spread over what I remembered as pleasant countryside. One of the few things which did not seem to have altered since I had passed that way last was a building of really exceptional ugliness (a hotel, I believe) close to the station at Slough. For, I think, the first time in my life the sight of it gave me real pleasure.

I had to change three times in the course of my journey and it was nearly five o'clock when I got out at the country station where my host met me. The light was failing when we arrived at the house and I could only see that it was large, and that it promised to be very beautiful.

I was introduced to my hostess and her two daughters, and after tea in the hall in front of a superb log-fire in a large open fireplace my host took me to the smoking-room.

'I had no idea you were such a territorial magnate,' I said to him when we had settled down.

'I never expected to be,' he said. My father was a parson in the north, and I became a solicitor in York—as you know. We lived just outside York for the first fifteen years after I was married. I knew of this place, but never saw it until I succeeded a distant cousin (whom I never saw either) nearly seven years ago. He was unmarried and a queer-tempered old chap by all accounts. Perhaps the fact that he had never seen me influenced his choice of an heir. The place isn't entailed and there were several distant relations beside me.

'It's a curious thing, but this property has never passed in the direct male line since Sir Robert Newton, whose portrait you'll see in the dining-room, bought it and built the house, about the year 1602 I believe. He was Chief Justice of the Queen's Bench. His son was drowned in a pool in the garden. It does not exist now. It was filled in immediately afterwards. No one could ever understand how the boy got into it, or why, having got in, he couldn't get out, as it was quite shallow, I believe, and he was more than a child. There was a daughter who married and brought her family here after her parents' death. But her son was killed at Naseby, leaving several daughters.

'And so, it has gone on. Either there has been no son or he hasn't lived to inherit. My immediate predecessor succeeded a childless uncle, and as we have only two daughters, we keep up the tradition. I'm really almost glad I never had a son, as I am sure my wife would be nervous about bringing him here. Indeed, I don't mind admitting that I think I should be. Of course, the village people say there's a curse on the place, but they don't know why. I can't think that my respected ancestor—he is my ancestor, if by no means in the direct line—was likely to have done anything to provoke one.'

Certainly, when I looked at the portrait an hour or two later, I could detect nothing evil in it. It suggested that Sir Robert had been a shrewd and kindly person, who would probably be as lenient on the Bench as the law allowed him to be. No doubt he had passed many sentences in his time which we should think harsh or even savage. But that would not have been the view of his contemporaries.

After dinner we sat in the library. It was a large room completely lined with well-filled bookcases whose contents looked as if they would repay examination. There is no saying what may not have wandered into such a place; just as any oyster may contain a pearl of price. I asked whether there was a catalogue.

'Not a very good one,' was the answer. 'In fact, I'm not sure that I shan't spend a good part of this winter trying to improve it. You'd like to have a look round it tomorrow, I expect. A good many of the books belonged to Sir Robert. By the way, we've put you in what is said to have been his bedroom. It isn't often used, but we've just had to take up the floors in some of the rooms nearer ours; dry rot, pretty bad too. But I think you'll be quite comfortable there. No; there's no story about it that I ever heard. We don't run to a ghost of any kind.'

We went upstairs soon afterwards, and while I was undressing, I meditated upon the queer fatality which seemed to have pursued the family for three hundred years. Was it more than a series of odd and unfortunate coincidences? Are there, or have there ever been, people who had some malign power which they could direct against their enemies? If it were so, how was this power operative after their lifetime? Did it exhaust itself after a period of time or not?

I had finished undressing before I had arrived at a satisfactory answer to any of these conundrums. When I was ready for bed I went to the window, opened it and drew back the curtains as was my custom. It was a clear night with a good deal of moon. My room was on the first floor at the back of the house, overlooking a part of the garden which I had not seen before. Immediately below me lay a gravelled terrace, bounded on the far side by a stone balustrade. On the other side of this, at a lower level and reached by a flight of steps, lay a small formal garden.

In the middle was a circular stone basin, where I hoped there might be a fountain. Round the edge stood a number of dark clipped trees—yews or cypresses I could not tell which. There were twelve of these: one at each corner and two in between. On the far side was a low stone wall separating the garden from the park beyond. Very white it looked in the moonlight; almost as if it were newly built. About the middle there was a dark patch; ivy or creeper I supposed. It made a clump on the coping and then spread sideways, in a way which almost suggested the head and arms of a person in the act of climbing the wall. I thought it rather ugly and decided that if I were the owner I would have it removed. Then I went to bed.

For some reason sleep did not come as quickly as usual and I was visited with the pictures—half-dreams and half-waking—which belong to the border-line of consciousness. Mine made two scenes. In the first I found myself seated in a large old-fashioned travelling coach. Beside me was a figure very much wrapped up. He turned towards me once as if about to speak, and I recognised the original of the portrait in the dining-room. Presently we were brought to a standstill by a great concourse of people who seemed to be streaming away from some spectacle. I put my head out of the window to see what it was, but drew it in again quickly.

A few yards in front of us was a gallows and there were four bodies dangling from the cross-beam. As I sat down, feeling as if I should be sick, a head was poked in at the window on the other side. It belonged to a young man. The face seemed unnaturally pale. There was something else unusual about it, but I could not take in what it was. The young man said something in a low tone to my companion. I could not catch the words, but they seemed to disconcert him very much. Next moment the face had vanished and we had begun to move again. I woke fully to find myself murmuring, *An eye for an eye and a tooth for a tooth.'*

The second scene was a churchyard by night. A funeral was taking place. I could see the bearers and the men with the torches and the priest. But there appeared to be no mourners, unless I were one. As the coffin was lowered into the grave some bird of the night gave a long and dolorous screech very close overhead. At this I woke. I think there must have been a hunting owl or a night-jar outside my window. As I did not wish for any repetition of such scenes, I got a book and read until I could feel confident that I should sleep soundly.

When I went to my window next morning I received a surprise. There, as was to be expected, was the garden on which I had looked the night before. But there were no trees and no pool, and I could see no growth upon the wall at the bottom. Yet I *knew* that I had seen those things, and that I had not been dreaming at the time. I decided to say nothing about them. When we went out after breakfast, however, I did ask my host whether he knew where the pool in which Sir Robert's son had been drowned had been. But he did not. I noticed that the wall between the garden and park did not look as new as I had thought it the night before. It seemed to be the same age as the rest of the house, as was to be expected. That might, however, be due to the difference between daylight and moonlight. The day was fine and as the neighbourhood was new to me, most of the hours of daylight were passed out-of-doors. After tea, when we were sitting in the library, I asked my host whether he knew why or by whom the curse had been laid upon Sir Robert's descendants.

'Well,' said he, 'there is a bit of a story about it. But all I know is very incomplete and doesn't explain much. It seems that in the old judge's time there was a woman in the village who was reputed to be a witch. Nothing very out of the way about that. In fact, you wouldn't have to look very far to find witches (or reputed ones) in these west-country villages today. Her name was Miriam Urch (Urch is quite a common name in these parts) and they say that she was at the bottom of it. But I don't know why she should have had a down on the Newtons, and as nothing was ever proved against her she was given Christian burial in the churchyard when her time came. You can see what is said to be her grave close to the north door. I expect it is. Village tradition is generally pretty accurate on such points. They aren't quite sure whether she is always in it though, even now. I believe the rector has had something to say to old Job Dixon the sexton about its untidiness more than once. But he says it isn't his fault. There are no other graves anywhere near it, and I don't think there will be as long as there is a scrap of room anywhere else.'

No more was said on the topic that evening and the hours after dinner passed pleasantly with a game of bridge with my host and his two daughters. We were all agreed that games are games, and though due respect must be paid to the rules which govern them they ought not to be transformed into hard and dismal forms of work.

It was near midnight before I found myself in my room, and when I was ready for bed, I admit that I hesitated for a moment before drawing back my curtains. Finally, curiosity prevailed. If there were anything to be seen I might as well see it. It seemed unlikely that any harm could come to me, or to the family through me.

I looked out. The moon shone brilliantly, and there, beyond any possibility of mistake, were the pool and the twelve trees. But were there only twelve? My first impression was that there were more. That was absurd. I counted them again just to make sure, and, as I had thought, there was one at each corner with two in between. But as soon as I looked at them all together, I got the impression that there were more. But I could not have said where the additional one (I felt sure it was only one) was, nor even whether it were always in the same place. And I noticed that the ivy, or whatever it had been on the wall at the bottom, was gone. It might have been cleared away during the day, but I had an uncomfortable feeling that someone or something had come over and was dodging about behind the trees. If so, with what intent?

I began to feel an overpowering desire to go and investigate. Yet I could hardly do that. The door leading to the terrace was doubtless locked and bolted, and I should be sure to disturb someone in getting it open. What could I say if I did? That I thought it a fine night for a stroll and that I always found pyjamas the most comfortable wear for a nocturnal ramble? For I felt quite certain—I don't know why—that the trees and pool would be invisible to anyone except myself. All the same, the desire to investigate more closely grew stronger and stronger. I have never seen or experienced hypnotism, but began to feel as I imagine a hypnotic subject does. It seemed as if I was being dragged out by some force which was overpowering my own will, and that if I could not get the door open, I should have to jump from my first-floor window. This would never do.

As an antidote I began to recite the first thing which came into my head. It happened to be the *Battle of Lake Regillus* from Macaulay's *Days of Ancient Rome* and not for the first time I blessed the wisdom of my mother who had made us all learn quantities of poetry by heart as soon as we could read. This particular poem had been my first major achievement in this line. It had always remained particularly distinct in my memory because the recitation of it had won two new half-crowns from a godfather, and thereby had enabled me to understand (for the first and last time in my life) what is meant by 'the possession of wealth beyond the dreams of avarice.'

(The godfather subsequently became Chief Justice of Trinidad, and was long remembered for his patience with garrulous witnesses, and the fervid eloquence of coloured advocates.)

I am not quite sure whether I declaimed it aloud or not. But I know that I had only got to the end of the first *stanza*:

> But the proud Ides when the squadron rides
> Shall be Rome's whitest day

. . . .when the spell, which I was quite sure had been malevolent, broke and I was completely my own master again. I felt as one does when a motor-car or bicycle has skidded and disaster in a ditch has been escaped by inches. I stopped at the window because I felt sure that something was going to happen. I did not have to wait long. A figure appeared on the terrace; where it had come from, I did not see. When it emerged from the shadow of the house, I saw that it was that of a young man; not much more than a boy. He seemed to be dressed as a young gentleman of quality would have been about the year 1600 or a little later. For some reason this did not surprise me. I wondered whether I was spying upon a lovers' meeting. The moonlight was all that could be desired, if the air were a little chilly.

But there was no second figure to be seen. He went down the stone steps leading from the terrace to the garden below and advanced to the edge of the pool. He stood there for a minute or two looking down into the water. Perhaps he was admiring the reflection of the moon. Then a very horrid thing happened. A vague black shape darted from behind one of the trees and flung itself upon him. It lay on top of him and had obviously forced him into the pool face downwards with intent to drown him. I tried to shout—though what good that could have done I don't know.

But no sound would come. I thought of going to the rescue, but found myself unable to move. Of course, that would have been equally futile could I have got there. The next minute a heavy bank of cloud which had been creeping up from the south-west drove across the moon and I could see no more. There was no sound to be heard. How long I remained looking out of the window into blackness and silence, I cannot say. Presently I found that I could move again, so crept into bed. There was nothing more which I could have done. I think I slept more than might have been expected.

Next morning when we went into the library after breakfast, I decided that I must make an effort and tell my host what I had seen. It did need an effort, for I felt very unwilling to speak about it. I don't know why. I don't think I was afraid of being laughed at and if I were told that I had been dreaming I could only reply that I knew that I had been awake. Somehow that made me the more reluctant. However, I took the plunge.

He listened to my story very attentively, and obviously took it seriously. When I had finished he said—'I think we know now how poor young Newton came by his end. But who do you suppose it was that fell upon him? Mrs. Urch? If so, why?'

Neither of us said anything more for a little while. I could see that, like Odysseus on more than one occasion, he was this way and that dividing his swift mind. Then he said, 'Yes. I think there's sufficient reason. Wait a bit.'

We were sitting beside the fireplace as the morning was chilly. He went to the other end of the room, climbed to the top of a short stepladder and took a smallish tin box from the end of a shelf. I saw that it was tied up with string or tape and that there was a seal over the knot. There was a label attached on which was written, in what looked like an early eighteenth-century hand, *Sir Robert Newton. Secreta. Not to be opened without sufficient reason.*

'Well?' I said.

'Well,' he replied. 'Don't you think there is now?' Of course, I agreed and the string was cut.

The most important part of the contents was a notebook. The handwriting was Elizabethan, and brief inspection satisfied us that the book had belonged to the judge. It was not exactly a diary. By no means were all the entries dated, and there did not seem to have been any attempt to produce a complete record of the period covered, which amounted to several years. There were a number of rather cryptic notes, apparently relating to cases which he had tried. Whether these were meant to direct his summing up or were merely private memoranda was not easy to decide. Neither of us was an expert palaeographer, and to decipher them all would obviously take some time. So, we put the book aside for the moment.

There were several letters from Lady Newton from which it was to be inferred that she had gone down to the west to supervise the completion and furnishing of the new house while her husband was detained by work in London. These told a not unfamiliar tale of dilatory workmen, of things ordered from a distance which were not delivered on the day appointed and so forth. She also feared that when all was done the original estimate would be very much exceeded. (It would have been very interesting had she mentioned the sums, but unfortunately, she did not.) These belonged to the years 1599-1600. As one of them referred to the good effect produced by 'your visit' it would appear that the judge had made an excursion to the scene of action to see whether he could expedite matters and alleviate some of his wife's troubles.

Underneath these was a largish sheet of paper which had been folded more than once. This proved to be a plan of the house and gardens—obviously by a professional hand. You will not be surprised to hear that in the middle of the small garden below the terrace was a circle of considerable size, which obviously indicated a pool. At a distance of some yards were twelve dots at regular intervals forming a square, to show where it was intended to place statues or plant trees or something of the sort. The plan itself did not state what form of ornament the architect had in mind. But I was in a position to say Trees not Statues.

There was only one more paper. This was merely a list of about a hundred names, presumably those of the inhabitants of the village, who were all the judge's tenants. This was dated 7 May, 1603, which my host thought must have been very soon after Sir Robert had come to reside permanently in his new home. It suggested that he had begun to devote himself seriously to the duties of a country gentleman. The name of Miriam Urch appeared among them. It was marked with an X but there was no note relating to her to be found. She must have lived alone, as the names were obviously arranged according to their households and there were no other Urches in the village. Beyond establishing the trustworthiness of tradition—up to a point—this did not get us much farther. Still, it was something to know that, witch or not, she really had existed. And there did seem to have been some special point of contact, however small, between her and the judge.

At this moment lunch was announced, so our investigation was suspended.

When we felt disposed to resume our researches, I suggested that it might be worthwhile to ask the rector for permission to examine the Register of Burials at the church; supposing it to be in existence. So much was destroyed wantonly during the Commonwealth period that it is not uncommon to find no records prior to 1662. Here, however, we were in luck. The registers were complete from 1558 onwards. 7 May, 1603, was our *terminus a quo* and we found the entry of the burial of Miriam Urch on 4 November in that year. She had died on 31 October. There was an asterisk in the margin and at the foot of the page (we thought in another hand but could not be sure)

Under Ye Yew tree by ye north doore.

This was the only note appended to any entry in the volume. It might be presumed that her estate was not sufficient to provide a headstone for the grave and that no one else was prepared to bear the expense. Also, that somebody, whether at the time or afterwards, was anxious that the site should not be forgotten.

We turned on. The entries were few as the population of the village was small. We found the burial of Philip Newton, aged 19 years, on 7 November, 1604. He had died three days before.

I said, 'coincidences do happen. But this seems a little too close not to have been arranged. We know, more or less, how it was done. But I wonder why. There must be a story of some kind behind it.'

Our only remaining source of information was the judge's notebook, so we returned to that. The next day was so wet that there was nothing to distract us and as we became familiar with his hand, we found that we could read most of it without much difficulty. The impression which we had formed on our first cursory inspection was confirmed. There were a number of disconnected memoranda, relating to a variety of matters. Some were dated, but not all. They seemed to cover the last ten or twelve years of his term upon the Bench. Some were concerned with cases which he had heard; others with purely domestic matters. Some were too short to be fully intelligible.

It looked as if it had been Sir Robert's practice to put down from time to time whatever happened to be passing through his mind (not necessarily every day) without attempting to keep a systematic diary. One of the longest entries was a very noble prayer (apparently his own composition) that he might be enabled to do justice 'in the fear of God and with no fear of man.' Shortly after this was another prayer for forgiveness for any failure. It was clear that he had been a conscientious judge and had set himself a high standard. Interesting as much of this was, it was not relevant to our immediate purpose. We had got to almost the last page before we came upon anything which threw any light on the subject of our investigation.

The last case which he heard before his retirement, or at any rate the last of which there was any record, was of four men for highway robbery committed on Hounslow Heath. Their names were given: Roger Hewitson, William Parrett, Edward Backhouse and George Urch. The first three were bracketed together with the words Taken red-handed written against them. But for some reason the case against George Urch seems to have been less clear. His name was followed by a few jottings:

Taken next day. No good alibi. Identified on oath.

Then followed two or three lines which were quite illegible. Below them the words.

Condemned with the others.

The only other entries were purely personal. After this trial, but at what interval it was impossible to say, both his health and his spirits seemed to have been affected. Twice he recorded *Kept my chamber all day*. Once he had sent for the apothecary (to whom he had paid two shillings and sixpence). Another entry showed that he had paid a visit to the rector of S. Margaret's, Westminster. This ended with the word *Comforted*. From which it would appear that whatever his trouble was, it was not entirely physical. At this time his wife and family must have been elsewhere, as he spoke of arranging for his man (whose name was Edward Hilyar) to *'lie in the little chamber next to mine'*—and more than once had *'E. H. to sit with me in the parlour.'*

It is a reasonable guess that George Urch the highwayman was the son of Miriam Urch, and that it was within her knowledge that Sir Robert had sent him to his death. Whether justly or not would not perhaps have concerned her very closely. But the judge's own jottings suggested that there might have been a miscarriage of justice; involuntary on his part. She seems to have had her revenge; if, in the strict sense of the word, she did not live to see it.

We returned to the churchyard. What tradition called her grave could be identified without difficulty as there were no others near it. But there was no vestige of any yew tree. There was, however, a shallow depression, roughly circular and of considerable extent close to it. We had recourse to the rector again, not without apologies. He was able to tell us that he believed that there had been a tree there and that there were one or two old people living in the place who might remember something about it. He promised to ascertain what he could and added that, while he did not wish to appear discourteous, he thought he would be more likely to be successful if he pursued his investigations alone.

He had some information for us next day. There had been a yew tree there, which had been blown down in a terrible storm not long after Victoria became queen. 'It were more than two-under year old, but it were a good riddance.' (No explanation of this was forthcoming.)

'Wold rector had roots grubbed and tooken away and burned. When the men got under there was a gurt twod settin', and he spit at they zo dellish (query devilishly) that they were frit and run for rector. When they come back he were gone. Never zaw he no more. Rector came back wi' 'em and some things were found; bits o' bone and such-like. Rector he wrapped up they and took they away to burn.'

This from a very ancient man whose father had been employed on the work. He had heard his father and mother talking about it once after they thought he was asleep. There had been more said. But that was all he could remember.

(I conjectured that the storm was that of 6-7 January, 1839, which seems to have been little less violent than its better-known forerunner of November 1703. It came from the north-west. *Inter alia* it did considerable damage to Bishop Longley's new palace at Ripon.)

The churchwardens' accounts were available and showed considerable expenditure on repairs to the church and work (nature not specified) in the churchyard in the February and March of that year.

'Well,' I said, 'that's about as much as we are ever likely to know. I doubt whether Mrs. Urch can do any more mischief, if she likes to give a repetition of her original performance now and again. I expect the tree, which would have been quite a small one in her time, was necessary somehow. There seem to be unaccountable but very rigid rules governing these things. Perhaps we shall understand them better someday.'

'You may be right,' said Phillipson. (I don't think I have mentioned his name before.) ' Now I come to think of it, there hasn't been a direct male heir at any time since 1839 for her to try her hand on. All the same I wonder—'

I was not much surprised to hear a few months later that Mr. Phillipson thought the house too expensive and that he was conveying it to the National Trust and going to live elsewhere.

I believe that it is uninhabited now, so that if Mrs. Urch ever returns to it no one will be any the wiser or the worse.

I have also heard that the trustees would like to restore the sunken garden according to the plan found amongst Sir Robert's papers. But Mr. Phillipson is opposed to this, and while they think him rather unreasonable, they feel bound to respect his wishes.

The Coxswain of the Lifeboat

There is upon the coast of Suffolk a church which is locally believed to be haunted. The rector is a friend of mine, and as I do not want to expose him to the attentions of the Phantasmagorical Association or any similar body, I will not describe the place particularly. I will only say that the church is a large building in the Perpendicular style of architecture constructed of grey flint. The neighbourhood is popular with artists. If these details are sufficient to enable anyone to identify it he is entitled to any reward for his ingenuity which he can secure.

The ghost has never, so far as I know, had a name put to him and nobody knows anything of his antecedents. He has never actually been seen. But he may be heard very often. He dances and chuckles, not upon the whole malevolently, but is always careful to keep a pillar or some equally solid object between himself and his audience. He is very agile and no one has ever succeeded in cornering him. It is on record that once when the sexton was locking up, he chased the ghost (who was being noisier than usual) from pillar to pillar all down the nave. Then up the tower staircase as far as the belfry. Still there was nothing to be seen. By this time the sexton was hot and out of breath, so he said rather crossly—'Hey, what are you a sniggerin' at?' A clear voice from amongst the bells replied 'It's not funny enough for two.' The rest, as Hamlet once remarked, is silence.

If the story of what befell me a good many years ago within sight of that church is not interesting enough for two, I must apologise. But I think it sufficiently out of the way to be worth putting on paper.

The church is not particularly rich in monuments. But near the font there is a mural tablet worth attention. It commemorates the crew of the lifeboat from 1850-69. During those years they underwent no change and rescued no less than four hundred and fifty-two shipwrecked mariners. That particular stretch of coast is still, I believe, regarded by seafarers as unusually dangerous. There is no anchorage within thirty miles and about four miles out there is a maze of sand-banks. A sailing ship which gets among them in bad weather is lost and even a steamship finds escape difficult. There has been talk of putting a light there more than once, but nothing has come of it. When there was more coastwise traffic (for the most part in small brigs) than there is now, the calls upon the lifeboat must have been incessant during the winter months.

After nineteen years of beneficent activity (I am quoting from the tablet) disaster came. On 31 October, 1869, the boat was lost with all hands. No bodies were recovered except that of Henry Rigg, the coxswain. I had often wondered what lay behind this. Had they gone on too long and allowed familiarity with danger to blind them to the fact that they had become too old for the work—as is said to be not unknown in the case of Swiss guides? Had the coxswain's nerve and judgment, upon which everything depended, failed at some critical moment? Although it was unlikely that anyone would ever be able to answer these queries, I put them to myself more than once.

For some reason, which I could not explain, I felt sure that there was a story behind this catastrophe which removed it from the category of ordinary hazards of the sea, and I wished very much that I knew what it was. Irrational as I knew the desire to be, it refused to be dislodged. In fact, it became stronger every time I saw the tablet.

One day when I was wandering, rather aimlessly I must admit, in the churchyard, I suddenly found myself opposite Henry Rigg's grave. I don't know why I had never thought of looking for it before. Perhaps I had assumed that in view of his station in life there would be no headstone, or at least a small and inconspicuous one which would be difficult to find. In fact, it was a large and massive slab of the pink granite which was popular for such purposes about the middle of the last century. Personally, I have always thought it one of the ugliest monumental materials known to man, especially when it is polished so highly that it looks wet. There is a striking example in the memorial to the O.W.s who fell in the Crimean War outside Dean's Yard. In 1869 it must have been about the most expensive material which could be procured. The inscription was brief:

In Memory of
Henry Rigg.
For nineteen years coxswain of the Life Boat
Who was drowned with all his crew off the

Anchor Shoal 31 October, 1869, aged 62 years.
When thou passest through the waters I will be with thee.

There was no suggestion that the stone had been erected by public subscription. Had it been, the names of the crew would have been recorded. I concluded that the Rigg family had paid for it, and wondered idly how they had managed to find the money. This led to some reflections on funeral expenditure in general. These might have been prolonged considerably and even have reached a pitch of moral elevation sufficient to justify their committal to paper, had I not had a sudden feeling that there was somebody close behind me. Of course, the churchyard was a public place and anyone might have come up without my hearing his step upon the grass. It might be somebody who had some business with another grave; or an idler like myself who wondered what I was staring at so intently and had allowed his curiosity to get the better of his manners.

Nothing could be more reasonable than either of these hypotheses. But all the same I was conscious of a feeling of discomfort; almost of alarm. I turned round quickly, but there was no one there. I think this disturbed me quite as much as any presence, however malevolent, could have done. I had felt so certain that there was someone. However, as there was nothing to be seen I walked away. When I had gone a little distance, I glanced back. It was between three and four on a November afternoon, so the light was failing. But for a moment I could have sworn that there was an animal of some kind, either a black cat or a black dog, I couldn't see which, sitting on the grave. It was gone in a moment whatever it was. 'Some trick of shadow,' I said aloud, more to reassure myself than because I believed it, and walked on; perhaps a little more briskly. I did not look behind me again and was glad when I was out on the high-road and only a few hundred yards from my inn, The Flood Tide.

I had stayed there often before and was on good terms with the landlord. If business was slack, I would sometimes ask him into my sitting-room after supper. He knew a good deal about the neighbourhood, and was seldom reluctant to impart his knowledge. In perpetuity he might have been a bore. But as an occasional visitor I found him very good company.

I told him that I had come upon Henry Rigg's grave in the churchyard that afternoon.

'Ah,' he said, 'that's a fine stone. Must have cost a deal of money to put that up.'

'Yes, so I thought. Did his family pay for it, or was there a public subscription?'

'No, Sir. It were not his family, for he hadn't none. Never married and kep' himself very much to himself, if you take my meaning. When he die a lawyer chap come over from Saxmundham and say he were executioner for the Will. And he have the stone put and choose the text. No, there were no talk of any subscription, for he were not liked. No, he were not. They couldn't hardly get bearers for the coffin, I believe, and there was some as said he didn't ought to be buried in the churchyard at all. But rector he didn't pay no heed to they. All he say were—Well, he'll be safer there than anywhere else I du suppose. And so, it were done. But no, he were not liked, not even by his own crew, though he were a good seaman—to give the devil his doo—as the sayin' goes' (the last four words seemed to be added hurriedly as an obvious afterthought).

At this point a servant knocked at the door and said that the landlord was wanted in the bar. I have not mentioned that his name was Rust. He went off, not altogether unwillingly I thought, and about half an hour afterwards I went to bed. Sea air always makes me sleepy.

The next two or three days were unusually fine for the time of year and I spent them bicycling about the country. I was taking a belated holiday, having been kept in London all through the summer months by a book which I was writing: an occupation which necessitated frequent and lengthy visits to the library of the British Museum. The manuscript was now in the hands of the printer and I felt that a change of air and scene would equip me to deal with the proof. I took care not to go near the part of the churchyard where Henry Rigg's body reposed. This seemed to me to be a wise precaution, though I must confess that I felt rather ashamed of myself for adopting it. All the same I thought I should like to elicit some more information about him. So, one evening I invited Mr. Rust to join me again. After a little miscellaneous conversation, I came to the point. I think he was expecting me to do so.

'Well, Sir,' he said, 'I don't know as I can tell you much more. I were only a lad at the time.' (You could, but don't mean to, was my unspoken comment.) But by what I've 'eard he was a close-fisted old chap. And then his language. The fishermen aren't so particular as what you or me have to be with a position to keep up. But they du say that the way he went on at his boat's crew was like, well, like nothing—if you take my meaning. They wouldn't ha' stood it, but that he were a good seaman: and you don't find them under gooseberry bushes neither; no nor yet on apple-trees. And he live all alone, with one big black cat what were fierce enough to scrat your eyes out. And nobody knowed what he did to pass the time away, except that he were never seen in church. And then when he die and it come out that he had a mort o' money in the bank at Saxmundham—well, that made more talk. How'd he come by it and why didn't he spend it? That's what people wanted to know. But the lawyer wouldn't tell 'em and the bank wouldn't tell 'em, so they was as wise as they begun.'

'What happened to the money?' I asked.

'Why, he left it all to an old lady somewhere Acle way. But she hadn't hardly got it when the house where she lived all alone got on fire and she were burned dead to a cinder. So, she didn't get no good by it neither. And as she were interstit, what they term, and 'adn't no relations, Queen Victoria took it. There was some as thought she did ought to be warned. But I never 'eard that it done 'er no 'arm. You'd ha' thought she had pretty nigh enough already, wouldn't you, Sir? But there, she had a long family to put out, and a widow-woman too.

'There were an auction of Rigg's bits of things. But nobody wouldn't bid for 'em, not a penny piece. So, the lawyer chap he have them taken away in a cart. And the man what drove the cart slip some-how, and the wheel went over his leg, and broke that in two places. Went lame all his life, he did.

'Then nobody wouldn't take the house till the agent he got some strangers. And they didn't stop no more than a week. So, then Lord S.—what own all this part—he say—"Pull that down." And it were done. There's been nothing of it these many years 'cept a few mounds just outside the village. The old people say it's no place now; specially after dark. But that's as may be, for what I know.'

'Well,' I said, 'he must have been an odd character. Is there anyone left who could tell me any more about him?'

Mr. Rust looked at me for a moment without speaking. Then— 'Odd, well, yes he were. And if I was you, Sir, I'd leave it be so. But there's old Dan Rix what were in the coastguard when that happen. He come up here now and again and if you was to stand him a pot of beer and a screw of tobacco he mought get talkin'. And then again, he moughtn't.'

Luckily, Mr. Rix honoured The Flood Tide with a visit about noon on the following day. I was in as I had happened to have a number of letters to write. An introduction was effected without difficulty and I followed Mr. Rust's advice with good results. I will summarise the story I got in my own words.

Yes. He had known Henry Rigg for several years. Probably as well as anybody. Nobody knew him well. He did not like him. Nobody did. But as coxswain of the lifeboat there was no one to touch him. He (Rix) remembered the day of the disaster very well. He was wakened about dawn by the distress signals of a ship. One of the worst gales he ever remembered. Wind north-east by east; the most dangerous quarter. The lifeboat was launched as quickly as possible, Rigg swearing and cursing more than usual. By the time the boat was away it was quite light, so he watched through his telescope. The ship was a small brig. Foreign certainly: perhaps Russian. She was on the Anchor Shoal and didn't look as if she could last an hour. He could see the men clinging to the rigging.

There was a very nasty sea, but Rigg's steering was wonderful. The devil himself couldn't have bettered it. One funny thing he noticed. More than once, he could have sworn that there was someone sitting beside the coxswain. Must have been the way the old boat-cloak he always wore was blown by the wind. All went well until the lifeboat was nearly up to the distressed ship. Then all of a sudden, the helm was put right over. The boat broached and was gone in a moment. This was before the days of the modern self-righting boats. (I have omitted some maritime technicalities with which the story as told to me was embellished. It will be enough to say that the act amounted to murder and suicide. A shore-going equivalent would be for the driver of a car to turn it off the road at fifty miles an hour.)

The ship went to pieces a few minutes afterwards. There were no survivors, and nothing by which she could be identified ever came ashore.

'Curious,' I said, 'that Rigg himself, who seems to have been entirely responsible for the disaster, was the only one who—well, I can't say "escaped" exactly, but lived (if you can put it that way) to receive Christian burial.' Mr. Rix took a long draught of beer, and put down his empty mug.

'Ar: there's some as the sea can't drown, and others as it won't keep!' With which oracular utterance he stumped off.

After lunch the wind had risen considerably, so I thought that a walk would be pleasanter than a bicycle ride. I would go northwards along the top of the low sandy cliffs and return with the wind behind me along the beach. The tide would not, I knew, be high till six o'clock, so there would be a strip of firm sand available. I walked for a little over an hour, and it was past three o'clock when I turned down to the beach and set my face for home. There was every prospect of a stormy night, and the white water on the Anchor Shoal was very visible under a grey and lowering sky. Naturally my mind ran on the story I had heard. Local opinion evidently held that there was more in it than met the eye.

But what more it seemed unlikely I should find out. It was solitary down there. On my right hand the cliffs were high enough to cut off any view inland. On my left lay the sea. Some three miles in front there was a small projection, you could hardly dignify it by calling it a headland, screening the village for which I was bound. Naturally I had the beach to myself. No one was likely to be about in the gathering dusk and rising storm. On the whole I was glad of that. The company, or even the sight, of another human being might be welcome. But on the other hand, there might be people about whom I should not care to meet. Once I thought of turning up to the top of the cliffs again. But that would be rather silly, and the particular stretch which I was passing then did not look very accessible. I certainly wasn't going to turn back to where I had come down. So, I held on.

Presently I saw a figure some little distance in front of me. He was standing at the very edge of the water. I was surprised that I hadn't noticed him before, and allowed myself to wonder for a moment whether he had just come up from the sea. But of course, that was nonsense. He must have been sheltering, resting perhaps, on the lee side of one of the groynes which crossed the beach at intervals. I could not make out whether he was going in my direction or coming to meet me. After a time, I saw that he was walking up and down; like a man keeping an appointment. An odd and uncomfortable rendezvous, I thought, and no one else in sight. I hope he isn't waiting for me.

I did not like his looks, so decided to strike up along the shingle until I had passed him, though it meant heavy going and climbing the groynes, instead of turning them at the seaward end.

When I got a little nearer, I saw that he was dressed like a seaman of the last (by which I mean the eighteenth) century. In fact, he reminded me of the illustrations in a copy of *Treasure Island* which I had had when I was a schoolboy. He wore a three-cornered hat, a boat-cloak wrapped round him and sea-boots. But for the fact that he had two legs he might have been Long John Silver himself. His hat was pulled down over his forehead and the collar of his cloak turned up: naturally enough as the wind had risen to nearly a gale and was very cold. I could see nothing of his face, for which I was thankful. There was something indescribably sinister, worse than sinister, downright evil about him. However, he took no notice of me. I looked back once or twice when I had passed him to make sure that he was not coming after me. The last I saw of him he was still pacing up and down.

When I got round the little headland there were, as usual, a number of fishing-boats drawn up near the bottom of the slipway which led from the beach to the village. As I made my way through them, I received the impression that there was somebody dodging about among them. But as the light had now failed considerably, I could not see him distinctly. In fact, I could not be sure whether there was anyone there or not. But I thought so; though whenever I looked steadily at the point where I had seen him last there was nothing. Anyhow, whoever he was and whatever he was up to, it was no business of mine and I did not feel called to interfere. Pusillanimous perhaps. But if, as I more than half suspected, he had an appointment to keep in the direction from which I had come, interference on any pretext would not be likely to be very fruitful. I won't pretend that I was not more than ordinarily glad to find myself safely back at The Flood Tide.

After tea I settled down to read that grim, if entertaining, work of Anatole Le Braz—*La légende de la Mort en Basse Bretagne*—which was one of the few books I had brought with me. The inn-library consisted principally of Sunday School prizes acquired from time to time by various members of the house of Rust. From one standpoint the collection was very gratifying, but except for *Little Henry and his Bearer* (which I was delighted to meet again) it was not in the first rank as literature. For the moment at any rate, I preferred the sombre stories of Anatole Le Braz. Now, the reader who gets as far as this may assert, when he has heard the rest of what I have to say, that I fell asleep. I cannot prove that I did not. I can only say that I repudiate the suggestion entirely. I *know* that I did not. Even if I did, my 'dreams' would not be easy to account for.

Quite suddenly I seemed to be looking through the pages of my book at a scene beyond. Every detail was very sharp, though the whole picture was on a small scale. It was exactly like what one used to see in the *camera obscura* when I was a child. Some ingenious arrangement of lenses, and mirrors too I suppose, threw a picture of what was passing outside on to a table in a darkened room. I suppose such a thing hardly exists now. It could not hope to compete with the films; though as a matter of fact I came upon one only about ten years ago in a queer old house in Edinburgh, not far from the Castle. The first thing I saw was a sandy beach. The light was beginning to fail and there were unmistakable signs of gathering storm.

Plainly a reproduction of what I had looked upon not much more than an hour before. And here was the queer sinister-looking seaman whom I had passed. As before, I did not see him come. He was suddenly in the picture, walking up and down. I was intensely interested, as I felt sure that the other party to the appointment would make his appearance before long. I was right. After not more than a minute or two I saw someone coming from the direction of the village. He kept as close as possible to the bottom of the cliffs, which suggested that he was anxious to avoid being seen. That part of the beach consisted of loose shingle, and if there is worse going than loose shingle to be found anywhere in the world I should like to know where and what it is. (I will not dispute the abstract possibility: I merely repeat—I should like to know where and what it is.) He came on slowly, and presently the old seaman saw him and stood still near the seaward end of a groyne.

When the newcomer reached the landward end, he turned and ran down it with surprising speed, bending double. He would have been quite invisible from the far side, and not easy to pick out from the other, or from the top of the cliff. The general effect suggested an animal rather than a human being and was extraordinarily repulsive. He seemed to be dressed like a fisherman, but as he too had a boat-cloak wrapped about him I could make out no details. I could not see his face. He struck me as unusually short, almost a dwarf, and I thought he was slightly hump-backed. When the two men met, they spoke a few words. (Which of course I could not hear.) Then something which looked like a small bag changed hands. The second man stowed it somewhere about his person and started to return as he had come. Then everything became dark and I could see no more.

I felt sure that there was more to come, so waited, looking down at the pages of my book. I did not have to wait long. The next picture was the living-room of a cottage; rather larger and better furnished than the average, but not particularly noteworthy in any way. In the middle of the room was a small round table above which hung an oil lamp. There was a good fire of wood and coal on the hearth and I noticed the little blue flames which old ship-timbers always give off.

(Whether this is due to the salt which they have absorbed, or to the tar, or to both, or neither, I cannot say.) Between the table and the fire, a man was sitting in an easy chair smoking a long clay pipe.

Beside him on the table was a long tumbler nearly half empty from which an inviting steam went up. I had no doubt that this was the second man I had seen on the beach. Now that I could see him plainly, I saw that I had been right in thinking that he was almost a dwarf and, if he were not actually hump-backed, very round-shouldered. He was swarthy, almost as if he had gipsy blood in him, and his face was not a pleasant one. It was mean and sly. At the same time, however, the jaw suggested courage and determination. I could not decide whether I should dislike him more as a friend or as an enemy.

His surroundings were comfortable enough, but it was soon obvious that he was ill at ease. From time to time, he fidgeted in his chair and seemed to mutter something to himself. Once or twice, he looked sharply over his shoulder. The only other occupant of the room was a large black cat which was pacing to and fro in regular quarter-deck fashion on the side of the room farthest from the fire. But for the light catching its eyes from time to time I should not have known that it was there. They glowed very green and very bright. It seemed fairly clear that the man was expecting a visitor—and not a welcome one either. This suspicion was confirmed when he got up, tried the fastenings of the shutters and satisfied himself that the door was locked and bolted. When he sat down, he mixed himself another drink.

Before he had finished it a very strange thing happened. I saw the key in the lock of the door turn and I saw the bolts slide back. I am as certain of that as I have ever been of anything. The door opened slowly and a man came in. Of course, it was the first man I had seen on the beach—and I did not like him any the better at closer quarters. He did not take off his hat or turn down the collar of his boat-cloak. So, I could make no more of his face than I had before. But I was quite sure that two more unpleasant characters can seldom have been found in the same room.

The little man was obviously horribly affected by the entrance of his visitor. But he stood up as if determined to put the best face upon it. (By this time, I think he was at least half-drunk; or, as he might have put it himself, Three sheets in the wind.) The men did not shake hands and no word was spoken. The newcomer drew up a chair to the table and produced a pack of cards. The little man turned himself towards it and they began to play. The cat jumped up upon the table and sat watching with a baleful stare. I do not know what the game was and could not follow it very well. But it became clear that the ace of spades was the master-card, and the visitor held it every time.

As hand succeeded hand the face of the little man became more and more ghastly until it was hardly human. If a cat can laugh, I swear that that cat, which I was coming to dislike as much as either of the men, was laughing to itself. Suddenly the visitor stood up. He seemed to have grown larger and his head almost touched the ceiling. He was between me and the lamp, and his cloak seemed to fly out like the wings of a great bird, so that I could see nothing but blackness. I thought I understood what is meant by *darkness which may be felt* in the account of the ninth of the plagues of Egypt.

When the scene cleared there was a new picture. I was looking at a churchyard, which I had no difficulty in recognising. There was an open grave and a man standing near it; presumably the sexton. One detail struck me as curious. There were several spades lying on the grass beside him as if a whole party of diggers had been at work. Then I saw the funeral procession, headed by the clergyman, approaching from the lych-gate. It came straight towards the grave. The corpse was not to be taken into the church. The coffin was carried by four bearers and there were no mourners following.

As soon as the service was over each of the bearers took a spade and helped the sexton to fill the grave in. All five men worked with immense energy, as if there were not a moment to be lost. The clergyman (this also I thought unusual) stood by and watched them. As soon as the work was finished the party dispersed as rapidly as was consistent with decency. In fact, they might almost be said to have run away. Once or twice while this was going on I thought I saw a figure of some kind just outside the lych-gate. But it was so indistinct, that I could make nothing of it. I could not even be sure whether there was anybody there at all.

When this picture disappeared, I felt sure there was nothing more to come, and soon afterwards the maid came in to lay the table for supper. As this was my last evening, I had Mr. Rust in later to help me pass it. We talked of general matters pleasantly enough and no mention of Henry Rigg was made. But I think we both felt the other was somehow *en garde*. Next morning I returned to London.

Well, there is my story. I could not make it more interesting except by some unwarrantable excursion into the realm of romance. I cannot pretend to say why my adventure (if you can call it that) befell me, nor to explain any of the details. But I think I can guess why Henry Rigg was not popular in his lifetime and why his memory was still odious in the pleasant little village of H—— more than thirty years after his death. And I have sometimes wondered whether the text which the lawyer from Saxmundham had placed on his tombstone had any secret and sinister significance.

The Priest's Brass

The rubbing of monumental brasses in churches is one of the occupations which attract a large number of schoolboys, but are seldom pursued for long after reaching man's estate. The collecting of foreign postage-stamps is another. Some stamp-collectors continue and eventually amass very large and valuable collections. But I think they are exceptional. I never remember to have heard of a brass-rubber who kept on systematically for half a century or more. Yet a complete collection of rubbings of English monumental brasses would be of great interest and value. It would provide a record of costume, ecclesiastical, military, civil and female, such as does not, I think, exist at present, for a period extending from the middle of the thirteenth century until the beginning of the sixteenth.

After about the year 1500 brasses become fewer, but they are still to be found for another couple of centuries. One of the very latest must be that of William Broderip, Vicar-choral and organist of Wells Cathedral, who died in 1726. The matrix is all that remains now.

As stamp-collectors are known as Philatelists, for some reason which I think has never been explained adequately, brass-rubbers might fairly describe themselves as Chalcotribists—should they wish to do so.

Certainly, Chalcotriby can be a pleasant enough occupation during the long days of summer. It meant sallying out with map and bicycle, if part of the journey had sometime to be done by train, and making one's way by little lanes to remote villages, where the appearance of a stranger is (or perhaps was—I am thinking of the golden days which were *regnante Victoria*) an event sufficiently unusual to cause some interest and even excitement. Whatever the present generation may have to say against the bicycle, I maintain that there was no better method of exploring a countryside in the days before the internal combustion engine had, in the emphatic phrase of Lord Grenfell, '*ruined the earth, defiled the sea and made the air dangerous.*' Even now the bicyclist can make use of routes where cars cannot follow him, and probably sees more things worth seeing in a mile than the motorist does in ten. As everybody knows, the part of England in which the *Chalcotribist* will find most to repay him for his trouble is situated to the east of a line drawn from Hull to Bournemouth. Within this area there is no district in which a bicycle cannot be used.

My procedure was always pretty much the same. When I had found my village, which was sometimes not too easy, I began by calling at the Parsonage. Of course, I had always written a few days beforehand, asking leave for what I wanted to do. (This was only refused once, in a letter which I thought very oddly worded. Soon afterwards I heard that the writer had created a considerable sensation by appearing in the pulpit with an umbrella in his hand. He opened this and held it above his head during the whole of his sermon. The day was fine and the roof of the church in good repair. A few weeks later he resigned the benefice, at the instance of the bishop of the diocese, and (I was told) announced his intention of devoting the remainder of his days to the cultivation of parti-coloured roses, and the drilling of ducks. I do not know what success he met with in either undertaking.)

If the incumbent was at home, I always found him friendly and usually hospitable; sometimes almost embarrassingly so. If he had to be out or away, I got a message to the effect that I should find the church open and that the sexton would be about to give me any help I wanted. If possible, I used to lunch off bread and cheese and beer at the inn, as that wasted least time while the light was good. If I was invited to tea I generally accepted, because by that time I had finished my work (if you can call it that) and was prepared to enjoy a little conversation about the place and its people before starting for home or for wherever I had arranged to pass the night.

Not a very hazardous or very exciting way of spending a day, one would think. All the same I did once meet with what may fairly be called an adventure, which might have ended very unpleasantly. I have never understood it thoroughly and up to now only two people beside myself have heard the story. I do not think that any harm can come of putting it on paper after a lapse of more than forty years.

Much Rising will serve as the name of the village concerned, and I need not indicate its situation more particularly than that it is to be found within the boundaries of the old diocese of Lincoln, which anciently extended from the Humber to the Thames.

One fine morning in August, when the last century was nearing its close, I might have been observed (and in fact probably was) ringing the doorbell at the rectory. The rector made me very welcome. He said that my name was familiar and I soon discovered that he had been at Trinity Hall with two of my uncles, and intimate with one of them. Unfortunately, both he and Mrs. Foster (I ought to have mentioned his name before) had to spend a considerable part of the day at the monthly meeting of the hospital committee in the market-town some miles away. As he spoke, I heard the sound of a horse's feet and wheels on the gravel outside the window, as if a trap of some kind were being brought round to the front door.

'However,' he went on, 'you will find the church open and the sexton will be about all day as he has got a grave to dig. I've told him to expect you and give you any help you may want. We ought to be back about four o'clock, and shall be very glad if you will come in to tea before you start for home.' At this point, Mrs. Foster came in, equipped for the expedition. (Roads were often very dusty then.) I will not attempt any details of her costume, which would appear as remarkable now as the get-up of today would have done then. I was introduced, and the invitation to tea was repeated very cordially. Then—'Alfred, my dear, it's high time we were off. You know that if you are late, you'll find that they have made Lord Merton take the chair. And he always goes to sleep after the first ten minutes, and wakes up in a bad temper when we have nearly finished, and wants everything to be discussed all over again. I can't imagine why he doesn't resign; especially as when he is awake, he never hears more than half of what is said.'

As I prepared to take my leave I said, 'By the way, what is the sexton's name? It might be convenient to know and I never like asking people directly, if I can help it.' 'Nicholas Clenchwarton,' replied the rector. 'Odd, isn't it? And not the only odd thing about him either. However, we needn't go into that now. You can tell me what you think of him when we meet this afternoon. We really must be off now.' I thought that the last sentences were added rather hastily. Mrs. Foster's expression suggested that she had a good deal to say about Nicholas Clenchwarton's oddity and was quite prepared to say it, even if it meant finding Lord Merton in the chair at the hospital committee.

When I reached the churchyard, I found that the grave had made so much progress that the digger was invisible. The appearance of spadefuls of earth thrown up from below showed that he was there and hard at work. I advanced towards the place, but was still several yards from it when he climbed out, nimbly enough, and came to meet me. It flitted through my mind that it was a coincidence if he had decided to knock off work at that moment, and if he had heard my step on the grass his ears must be preternaturally sharp. Odd was certainly not an exaggerated description of him. He was very short, almost a dwarf and, as often happens with such people, very broad and deep in the chest. Obviously, he was extremely powerful. His complexion was swarthy and his hair black. Both uncommon in that part of England. He looked as if he might have more than a dash of gipsy blood in him. Had his name been Mace, or Farr, or Lee, I should not have been surprised. He was not wearing a hat, and two tufts of black hair stood out above his ears, almost like horns.

There was something unusual about his face which I did not take in for a moment. Then I saw that his heavy black eyebrows met in the middle; as St. Paul's are said to have done in the Acts of *Paul and Thecla*. He looked as if he might have been a seaman in earlier life and I thought he would not have been out of place as one of the ship's company of the *Hispaniola*. Gunner's mate to 'that brandy-faced rascal Israel Hands' would have suited him very well. (See *Treasure Island*.)

We shook hands, and I mentioned that the day was fine. He assented, but added that the farmers would be glad of some rain. Then—'Be you the gentleman rector told me to look for?' and on receiving an answer in the affirmative, he jerked a thumb in the direction of the church porch, and said 'All ready.' As he seemed to be a man of few words, I left him, and he returned to his grave.

The church was small and, except for a fine Norman arch to the chancel, presented no noteworthy architectural features. There was little coloured glass (of which I was glad) and none of it old. The strips of coco-nut matting which covered the floor had been rolled up so that I could get at what I wanted without delay or difficulty. I decided that this should be worth half a crown to Clenchwarton.

There were five brasses to be seen. None of them of outstanding interest or merit, but worth a visit. The largest and most elaborate was of Thomas Ketton, Lord of the Manor, who died on 9 September, 1513. I wondered whether he had fallen at Flodden, but if he had, the fact was not recorded. At the foot were some lines which I think will bear reproduction.

> *Livest thou, Thomas? Yea, with God on high.*
> *Art thou not dead? Yea, and here I lie.*

I who on earth did live but for to die,
Dyed for to live with Christe eternally.

When I had finished my rubbings, I looked round to see whether there was another brass which I had overlooked. I could not see one, but I had a curious feeling that there was one somewhere. The impression became stronger, and I could almost have sworn that someone had whispered in my ear, 'Look again.' I turned round sharply. But of course, there was no one. How could there be? I went out into the churchyard and told the sexton that I thought I had done all I meant to do and thanked him for his trouble. At this point my half-crown changed hands, and this may have had something to do with the fact that when I asked him to come to the church with me for a minute or two, he raised no objection. When we were inside, I said to him, Now, are there any more brasses beside these five?'

He looked at me rather hard, and then with the air of a man who has made his mind up after a struggle said, 'Yew arsted me, remember that if things come orkard.' Having delivered himself of this enigmatic utterance he turned and stumped up the chancel. Just inside the altar rails he picked up the edge of the sanctuary carpet and disclosed a small brass, which I saw at once to be that of a priest, vested and holding a chalice. There did not seem to be anything unusual about it, except that it was in bad condition.

'Well, there he be. Du yew fare to take his picture?'

'Why, yes. Why not? I shan't do it any harm.'

Again, he paused and looked at me hard. I began to wonder whether he were quite right in his head.

Then very slowly—'I du suppose not. But every seesaw has two ends, as the saying is.' With which he took himself off.

Closer inspection of the brass showed that it was very much worn. The face seemed to be almost entirely obliterated and the inscription round the edge was largely illegible. But as it appeared to be in its original matrix, I concluded that slab and brass must have been moved from some more exposed position: possibly with a view to the preservation of the figure. I knelt down and spread my paper and began to rub. But I must admit that as I did so I began to feel extraordinarily uncomfortable. It was as if I were setting in motion something which had better be left quiet and once started might be beyond control.

Besides this, I kept fancying that someone was watching me from outside, through one of the windows, which were of clear glass. I seemed to get a glimpse of a face (and not a pleasant or friendly one either) out of the tail of my eye. But when I looked full at this window (not always the same one) there was nothing to be seen. Once I got up and went out quickly, but of course there was no one; only the sexton at work on the grave, which was too far away for him to have got to it in time.

I ran round to the other side of the church to make certain that there was no one there and then went back feeling thoroughly ashamed of my attack of nerves. I found that my paper had been moved to a distance of two or three feet and I had some little difficulty in replacing it exactly right. 'Draught from the open door,' I told myself. But I did not really think so.

Altogether I was heartily glad when I had finished and could make my way out into the sunshine of the afternoon. As I passed out of the churchyard I called to the sexton and said, 'I've finished now; you can lock the church as soon as you like.' His reply was indistinct, but I thought I caught something to the effect that there's those as locks and bars won't hold.

On reaching the rectory, which was only about a couple of hundred yards away, I found Mr. Foster and his wife in a somewhat exhausted condition, especially the lady. The committee had been very long and *that* Mrs. Shorton (who appeared to be the archdeacon's wife) even more tiresome than usual. However, tea and some extremely good cakes soon produced a more equable frame of mind.

'Well,' said the rector, 'how did you get on? And what did you make of Clenchwarton?'

'Oh, I found all I wanted, thank you, and I think my rubbings have come out quite well. But I can't say that I took to him particularly.'

'Take to him!' exclaimed the lady, 'I should think not indeed. He gives me the creeps whenever I look at him. I'm sure he's a dreadful man. It would never surprise me to hear that he had committed at least one murder. I don't think he ought to be employed as sexton; and if I've said so once I've said so a hundred times.'

'Yes, my dear, I know you have,' rejoined her husband. 'But, as you know, I didn't appoint him. I found him here when we came, ten years ago, and have no reason for dismissing him. As you saw,' addressing me, 'he keeps the church and churchyard very well. He must have some money of his own (that kind of man often owns a few cottages somewhere), because he does no other work, and he could hardly manage on what we pay him. Of course, in a small place like this the sexton's job is only a part-time one and is paid as such, because it is assumed that he has another. But Clenchwarton really makes it a whole-time one. He does more than he need, and more than we pay him for. I know he isn't liked in the village, but that may be merely because he is a "furriner" and keeps himself very much to himself. I have no idea where he belongs. If he has ever been married, he was a widower without children when he came here. But I don't know even as much as that. There is nothing to be got out of him about his antecedents.'

Mrs. Foster said nothing, but it was clear that she thought his reticence prudent.

'They say that he is out too much at night. But if he were a poacher, he wouldn't be the only one in the parish, so I don't see why they should mind. But I don't think they mean that; in fact, I don't know what they do mean; and I'm not sure that they do. Anyhow the keepers have never caught him and I never heard of him getting drunk or anything of the kind. So, I've nothing against him and he is an extremely useful servant.'

'There's one thing I should like to ask before I go,' I said. 'Why do you suppose he didn't want me to see the brass of the priest in the sanctuary?' and I told what had passed.

When he had heard my story, the rector said nothing for a minute or two. I thought he seemed to be rather disconcerted by it. Then he said, That's very curious. The man's name was William Codd, and when Bishop John Russell held a visitation in 1485, he was accused of practising unlawful arts. Of course, the charges were vague and I don't know how seriously the bishop took them. Bishops often showed plenty of common sense in such matters, more than magistrates. Codd died almost immediately afterwards, so no more was heard of them. There must have been some feeling against him in the parish though, because he wasn't buried in the chancel as the rector had a right to be. They put him at the west end under the tower.'

'I suppose it was then that the brass got so badly worn,' I said, interrupting, perhaps rather rudely.

Yes: I dare say. But anyhow the place didn't suit him and he seems to have made himself troublesome in a variety of ways. Eventually they took him up with the sanction of Bishop William Wickham (about 1590 that was) and put him where he is now. But stories live on in an extraordinary fashion in these villages, and I believe some of the people aren't so sure that he always is there; even today. I wonder how much Clenchwarton knows and what he thinks about it. But I don't suppose that you or I would get much out of him.'

Soon after this I took my leave. I had to bicycle about ten miles to the town where I had taken a room at the inn for a week. There were several churches in the neighbourhood which I wished to visit and the map had showed me that this would be the most convenient centre. I promised myself a pleasant ride in the cool of the late afternoon. There was no summer-time, then, and six o'clock really was six. But I was disappointed. As is usual in that part of England there was a fairly broad strip of grass on each side of the road. Then a wide and deep ditch, dry of course now, with a quick-set hedge beyond it.

As I rode along, I could hear a rustling in the ditch, such as might be made by a small animal. Nothing out of the way in that, you will say. But what was out of the way was that the sound kept up with me, to be exact it kept about two yards behind, never more or never less. I put on speed, but even when I got some help from the ground, I could not shake it off. Twice I dismounted and went to the ditch. But there was nothing to be seen. When I stopped, the rustle stopped. But as soon as I mounted it began again. I did not like it, but there did not seem to be anything to be done. When I got into the street of the town it ceased.

I had company at my supper and afterwards in the shape of a commercial traveller, who was not indisposed for conversation. Ordinarily I might have found this rather tiresome. But that night I must admit that I welcomed it. He gave me a most interesting discourse on the way in which different kinds of soap go in and out of fashion, and how the tastes of different villages vary and change. I gathered that to sell soap successfully in a country district you must have a considerable endowment of prophetic vision and be a close and sympathetic student of human nature. He obviously wanted to know what had brought me there. So, I told him that I was having a holiday, and had spent most of the day at Much Rising.

'A queer place by all accounts,' was his comment, but as it was not on his ground, he had never been there. The town in which we were was the limit of his beat.

I went to bed early, but did not sleep very well. I woke up several times during the night, with an uncomfortable feeling that someone (or something) was moving about the room. Twice I struck a light, but no intruder was visible. The house was an old one and might well harbour rats. As long as they kept behind the wainscot, they could do me no harm. With this reflection, which I did not find quite as comforting as the sterling common sense by which it was inspired ought to have made it, I went to sleep again.

The next morning was very wet. The landlord assured me that it would clear about twelve o'clock. So, I thought I would occupy myself by going over the rubbings I had made yesterday. They had all come out well: Codd's surprisingly so. In fact, I could make out more than I had seen when looking at the original. (This does sometimes happen, just as a photograph of a manuscript, especially of a palimpsest, may be easier to decipher than the manuscript itself.)

The lettering round the edge was very much broken, but I could read as follows:

... ISA AC ... ... NDA MORTE PTVS DIE NOV .... INA CE VERE.

This I reconstructed—

IMPROVISA AC HORRENDA MORTE ABREPTUS XXIX-no DIE NOVEMBRIS SATURNINA LUCE VERE.
He was snatched away by an unforeseen and dreadful death on 29 November, truly a day of ill-omen. (The year was completely obliterated. But the rector had told me that it was 1485.)

My restoration of the day of the month was conjectural. But I remembered that 29 November was the day of St. Saturninus of Toulouse, who was gored to death by a savage bull during the Decian persecution. And I thought that the coining of an adjective from his name, more or less equivalent to our *saturnime*, was not unlikely. I wondered what had happened to William Codd. Probably an accident, which, in view of the suspicions which seem to have been entertained with regard to him, was no doubt looked upon as a divine judgment.

The conventional prayer *CVIS ANIME PPTIETVR DEVS* (*on whose soul may God have mercy*) was not part of the original lettering of this brass. It was incised on the stone slab, rather roughly, and obviously by a later hand. This was out of the common and lent some colour to the idea that the parish discovered that it had not seen the last of him when his funeral was over.

'Well,' I said, half to myself and half to the rubbing on the table before me, 'I wonder what you really were like. Pity there's nothing of your face to be seen.'

And now comes the most remarkable part of my story. As I spoke some lines began to appear. At first, they were very faint. Gradually they became definite, as a photographic negative takes shape in the developing dish. Little by little a face emerged, and it was a face I knew. I had seen it as lately as yesterday. There could be no mistake. There were the eyebrows meeting in the middle, and the horn-like tufts of hair over the ears. I was looking at a portrait of Nicholas Clenchwarton.

For some reason which I cannot quite explain I did not feel frightened. Partly perhaps because surprise left no room for any other emotion; partly perhaps on account of the prosaic nature of my surroundings. The parlour of an inn in a small country-town about eleven o'clock in the morning does not provide a convincing *mise-en-scène* for supernatural experiences.

While I watched, a further change took place. The face became less human; the tufts of hair were now definitely horns and I was looking at a bull's head on a human body.

'Like the Minotaur,' I said to myself. Certainly, the eyes and forehead suggested more than bovine intelligence. In another minute it had faded away and the face was a blank again.

Had I been dreaming? No: I knew I had not. I saw what I have just described as plainly as ever I saw anything in my life. Obviously, I must return to Much Rising as soon as might be and talk matters over with the rector. As the landlord's forecast of the weather proved correct, I put this plan into execution shortly after lunch.

I must admit that I began to feel a little nervous as I left the town. The road was a lonely one and I soon discovered that my companion of the day before was waiting for me in the ditch. However, I must go and I did not see how I could come to any harm. Presently, when I was in sight of the village, the rustle passed me, and about a hundred yards farther on I thought I saw a small animal of some kind leave the ditch and go through the hedge into a field. I only got a fleeting glimpse, and cannot say more of it than that it was of a darkish colour, and about the size of a rabbit. But a rabbit it was not. Nor was it an unusually large rat. A short distance farther on there was a gate into the field.

As I came up to it, a man opened it and said, 'This is your way.' I saw that there was a large meadow with a well-trodden track, quite practicable for a bicycle, running across it. At the far side it disappeared into some bushes and just beyond them I could see the chimneys of the rectory. It was part of the general oddness of the day that I felt no surprise at the fact that the man knew where I was going, any more than, I think, one is ever surprised in a dream. I thanked him, turned through the gate, and began to ride across the field. I only saw him for a moment, and afterwards could not recall him with any clearness. He had a broad-brimmed hat, so that I never really saw his face, and was wearing a long light-coloured garment; at the moment I took it for the smock-frock which was sometimes to be seen on old labourers then. On subsequent reflection, I doubt whether this theory was correct. That was as much as I could say, when I came to tell my story to the rector, and he could not identify my description with that of anyone in the parish. Later, I seemed to remember that the man's voice had been curiously hoarse, as if from long disuse.

When I was about half-way across the field, I heard a noise behind me. I looked over my shoulder and saw a large black bull coming after me; obviously not with any friendly intention. Flight was my only chance, and the shrubbery or plantation, or whatever it might be, for which I was heading might aid my escape. I rode for all I was worth, but the path was narrow and rough, and I judged that the beast was gaining on me. As I entered the plantation, I saw what looked like a small disused quarry straight in front of me. There was only one chance, and that seemed a poor one. I wrenched my front wheel sideways and rolled over amongst the bushes.

As I fell, I heard a bellow and a crash. I picked myself up thankful to be still alive. The bull was nowhere to be seen. I presumed that he had gone into the quarry, and was well content to leave him there. I ran as best I could, staggeringly, blindly, through the bushes, and found myself at the gate leading into the rectory garden. I opened it (thank goodness it was not locked) and ran on a few steps. Then I must have fainted, as the next thing I knew I was in a basket-chair on the lawn with a taste of brandy in my mouth and the rector and Mrs. Foster beside me.

His first remark was very kind and wise. 'Don't try to tell us what has happened until you feel like it.'

But, like many people when they have been badly frightened, but not seriously hurt, I suddenly felt very angry.

'I call it disgraceful,' I said, 'to have a savage bull at large in that field. And that unfenced quarry, or whatever it is in the plantation, is an absolute deathtrap.'

'Bull? Quarry? What are you talking about? All that land belongs to me, it's part of the glebe, always has been. The field is called Bull-Yard; I suspect that goes back to the days when it was part of a rector's duty to provide a bull and a boar for the parish (did you know that, by the way?). But I don't suppose there has been a bull there for years. Certainly not since I've been here. And there's no quarry in the plantation. How should there be? There's a small depression where water collects in winter. It might be nearly up to your knees at times. But of course, it's as dry as a bone now. You could have ridden your bicycle straight across it. I suppose there might have been more of it once. There are a number of small quarries in these parts, and some of them are still worked. But if that was one of them it was filled in, perhaps by nature, long ago.'

During this speech I became more reasonable. I apologised and said, 'Well, will you come and see?'

He would, and we went, and found it as he had said. The only part of my story which seemed to have a word of truth in it was that I had fallen off my bicycle into the bushes. At any rate the bicycle was there, not much the worse, I am glad to say, and my cap and some broken twigs. There was no pit or quarry and no trace of any bull.

'But didn't you hear him bellow?' I asked.

'I thought I heard some distant thunder. But it must have been several miles away,' was the reply.

Wild as my story must have sounded, the rector did not upbraid me or laugh at me. He looked thoughtful and then said, 'I expect you'll have something more to tell me presently,' and led me back into the garden. We met Mrs. Foster coming from the house and she very kindly asked me to stay the night. 'You've had a shock of some sort,' she said, 'you really aren't fit to go. My husband can lend you all you want for the night, or you can have some of Gerald's things.' (Gerald, I learned afterwards, was a soldier son, who naturally left most of his belongings behind him when with his regiment.)

I made some feeble protest, but they both brushed it aside. 'In fact, you must stop,' she went on. 'I have sent a telegram' (telephones hardly were in the country then) 'to the Woolpack—you told me yesterday you were there, and of course I know the people quite well—telling them not to expect you before lunch tomorrow.'

That settled it. I was really grateful to her, as I hardly felt up to bicycling back alone, even less with such company as I might have. At her suggestion I went and lay down on the bed in the room I was to have. I fell asleep and when I was roused about seven o'clock felt much better. After dinner I told the whole story, very much as I have set it out here.

As soon as I had finished, Mrs. Foster exclaimed triumphantly to her husband, 'There, what did I always tell you? You simply must get rid of that horrible man now.'

'You never told me that there was any connection between him and William Codd,' replied the rector, not unreasonably, 'and if you had, I doubt whether I should have believed it. But even now, I don't see that I can dismiss him. What reason could I give? What could I say to him?'

'Say?—why need you say anything?'

And in fact, as you will hear, the necessity did not arise.

On one point we were agreed. The sooner my rubbing of the brass was destroyed, the better. So, we went to the weed-heap in the kitchen-garden, deposited the paper there and applied a match. The flame ran round the edge of the figure in an odd way, and at one moment the blank face was surrounded by a ring of fire. However, it was all over soon, and a puff of wind dispersed the ashes. 'And that's that,' said the rector as we walked back to the house.

I slept more soundly than I had done at the Woolpack the night before, though once or twice I thought the owls seemed to be unusually noisy.

We were finishing breakfast next morning, when the parlourmaid came in and said that the policeman had called and was wishful to see the rector.

'Sorry to disturb you, Sir,' he said as soon as he had been shown in. 'But would you please come down the village? I think there's summat wrong to Clenchwarton's.'

As we went, he told us that no one could recall having seen him since dinner-time the day before. The woman who did for him had gone as usual in the morning, but had been unable to get in. No knocking or calling could elicit any response.

His cottage stood by itself, between the end of the village street and the churchyard. When we arrived, a few people had collected and were standing about. The rector, who was a magistrate, directed that the door should be forced. This was done without much difficulty. The cottage was of the ordinary four-roomed type, living-room and kitchen on the ground floor and two bedrooms above. It was clean, but smelt curiously earthy. We found ourselves in the living-room. At the far corner a steep and narrow staircase gave access to the upper floor. Clenchwarton was lying at the bottom in an attitude which showed plainly enough that he was dead. In view of the narrowness of the staircase, it was thought better not to try to carry him up. The body was laid on an old sofa in the living-room and covered with a counterpane brought down from the bedroom. While this was being done, a certain amount of murmured conversation went on, and I caught 'Saved Jack Ketch a job, I reckon,' from one of the men. This appeared to be the general sense of the meeting.

When the doctor came, he certified that there was a clean fracture between the third and fourth cervical vertebrae. Death must have been instantaneous, and had taken place more than twelve hours previously. Clenchwarton had obviously been killed by falling down the stairs. Whether he had had any kind of fit which had caused him to fall could not be determined without a post-mortem, and as there was no suspicion of foul play it hardly seemed worthwhile to hold one.

I returned to the Woolpack that afternoon, and went home the next day. I did not feel inclined to rub any more brasses just then; especially in that neighbourhood. Afterwards other occupations and interests supervened, so my collection has remained as incomplete as many others.

The verdict of the coroner's jury was of course 'Death by Misadventure' and the body was interred in the churchyard on the south side of the church.

No relations could be discovered. He had owned some house-property somewhere in the west of England. But as he had made no will, and the solicitors who managed it for him and remitted his rents knew no more about him than anybody else, I suppose it passed to the Crown.

The rector paid the funeral expenses out of his own pocket, and had the words *REQUIESCAT IN PACE* inscribed on the tombstone. Some people in the village were inclined to object when the meaning was explained to them, on the ground that the sentiment was Popish. But the general opinion was in favour of them. As far as our knowledge extends, they seem to have been efficacious.

It is easy to frame a number of questions in connection with the episode. But I have never been able to arrive at a satisfactory answer to any of them.

Mystic Voices

Roger Pater

THE AGAPE, or SYMBOLIC SUPPER

A fresco in the catacomb of SS. Peter and Marcellinus, Rome (see p. 119)

Contents

Introduction

The curious experiences collected in this volume were told me by my cousin, an old priest more than forty years my senior, in the course of the two or three years which I spent with him immediately before his death.

I had never met my old relative until this period, because of the estrangement between my father and himself, which had resulted from a quarrel that took place between them many years before I was born. In this quarrel I have always understood that my father was chiefly to blame; indeed, he told me so himself, shortly before he died. But, strange to say, it affected my cousin far more than it did the real offender; and from that date he became more and more of a recluse, usually living alone at Stanton Rivers with a few servants, most of whom had served the family from childhood, and seeing hardly anyone except some five or six intimate friends, chiefly priests, who would come and stay at the old manor house for a few days at a time.

It was not long after the quarrel I have mentioned that my cousin decided to take Holy Orders. The family had kept to the old religion all through the penal times, except once when the squire of the period had conformed to the Established Church. But in no previous case had the head of the family ever become a priest, though there had been a fair sprinkling of vocations among the younger sons, and one—a Benedictine monk—had died for his priesthood on the scaffold at Tyburn.

No small uneasiness therefore seems to have been felt by the servants and tenants on the estate, when the squire announced his intention, and set out for Rome, to make his studies at the College of Noble Ecclesiastics. However, when he returned no changes were made, and except that the squire wore a cassock and said Mass, instead of wearing gaiters and shooting pheasants, the little world of Stanton Rivers rolled on just as it had done before. But gradually, very gradually, the relations between landlord and tenants became modified. The squire's priestly character told upon his people, and their loyal respect deepened into a personal love for him, which grew with the years, until, to one like myself, who came upon it suddenly, it seemed almost the atmosphere of another world.

As I went about the estate, which all too soon was to become my own, I heard on every side of his acts of charity and thoughtfulness; and I cannot help thinking that one cause of his goodness to the tenants was the wish to make some amends for his life-long estrangement from my father, who was his only near relative. During the brief time I spent with him in those last years of his life, I learned to love him much as a saint's disciples love their master. When, with the simplicity of a child, he spoke of things spiritual, he made this world seem as if it were less real to him than the invisible world of the soul. For him, in fact, I am convinced that this was literally the case, and that he looked forward to death as a child looks forward to going home at the end of a long term.

Still, it was only because of a chance phrase, which I did not understand at the moment, that he came to tell me the occurrences with which this volume deals; and, but for my curiosity on the subject, I do not think that he would have made any further reference to them. It may have been merely the reticence of an ultra-sensitive nature, which feared a rebuff, or, worse still, a coldly polite acceptance of the tale, which masks the hearer's patent disbelief in it. But I think the chief reason for his silence was that, for him, such sensible evidence of the supernatural had ceased to be of interest; since, by the time I knew him, he had come to live habitually in a higher state of the spiritual life, where mystical union with God was so real and so direct that these earlier experiences had lost their value for him.

The stories were written down in a kind of diary, and usually on the day on which I heard them; but for some time, I have hesitated about giving them to the public. However, those who have read the original manuscript have urged me to do so, and in any case, I do not see that any harm can come from their publication. If, on the other hand, these pages prove a help to anyone, that fact, I am sure, will reconcile the spirit of my dear old relative to the wider circulation of his strange experiences. In cases where offence might, perhaps, be given by revealing the identity of the characters, I have changed the names, dates, etc., and made any other slight modifications that were necessary to secure anonymity; but apart from this, the stories are exactly as I heard them. In most cases the events described took place many years before they were related to me, but whenever I have been able to check the account by questioning such of the actors as are still living, I have found the squire's memory to be accurate in practically every detail; so, I do not doubt that in all essentials the records which follow are perfectly reliable.

I gladly take this opportunity of thanking the editor of *The Catholic World* for permission to reprint such of the stories as have appeared in its pages; and also, of acknowledging the kindness of Messrs. Houghton Mifflin and Co., in permitting me to reproduce the plate from Lanciani's *Pagan and Christian Rome*, which forms the frontispiece to this volume.

Roger Pater

The Warnings

The library at Stanton Rivers is a long room, facing west, on the ground-floor of the mansion. On a summer evening the last rays of the sun come in at the broad mullioned windows, causing bright gleams of gold and colour on the backs of the long rows of books.

The old squire-priest was sitting by the oriel window with a rug across his knees, and the light on his white hair and thin refined features made him look like one of the portraits that hung in the long gallery. For some time, he had been speaking of the ways in which God's providence had dealt with him, how wonderfully he answers the petitions of his servants, far better than man can foresee when he makes his prayer; and the quiet tone of conviction made his words doubly impressive. After this he remained silent for some minutes while I was thinking over his words. Then abruptly he began again.

"You understand, do you not?" he asked, with a quiet look at me.

"I think so," I answered, "at least all but one point. There was a phrase you used just now I which was new to me. You were speaking of mental prayer and the light God gives you in it; of prayers for guidance in any special difficulty, and how, after a while, light seems to grow upon the mind, and the will becomes clear how to act, as if in obedience to some divine command. And then, all at once, you added, 'But this is quite different to the direct speech that sometimes comes to me.' Now that is what I want you to explain to me; what do you mean exactly by the phrase 'direct speech'?"

The old priest smiled as I stopped speaking, but he kept silence so long that I began to feel uneasy, and started to apologise for my curiosity, fearing lest the question had offended him.

"No, no," said he quickly, "it isn't that at all. I am quite willing to answer your question; the difficulty is to make myself intelligible." After another pause, he began again.

"The phrase which puzzled you is one that I have come to use for a certain kind of experience which happens to me from time to time. Sometimes it takes the form of a sentence, sometimes only of a word or two, sometimes of long-continued sound or speech, but always it appeals to the sense of hearing."

At this I felt more mystified than ever, and I suppose my-face betrayed me, for the old man seemed to see it, and continued. "If you like I will give you some examples of what I mean, but first I must warn you that, although it is many years now since first this kind of thing occurred to me, it still remains without any satisfactory explanation so far as I can see. Moreover, I am quite clear that the sound or voice I hear is not due to merely natural causes, as one might mistake a noise heard in the dark and attribute it to some agency other than the one which really caused it.

"There is one other point as well which makes my experience somewhat unusual. No doubt you have heard of apparitions at the hour of death, cases where the form of a dying man or woman has been seen by someone far away from where the death took place, and who, moreover, did not know his friend was ill. In several instances my voices have warned me of deaths among my friends and relatives, but, instead of this happening at the moment of death, such warnings have always occurred a considerable time afterwards, and only a little while before the news reached me through some ordinary channel."

"May I interrupt a moment?" I asked. "Let me be clear on one point before you give me any instances. 'The voices you hear, are they objective, really sounding in your ears, or are they merely internal, like words spoken in the mind?"

"Sometimes they are undoubtedly subjective," he answered, "but more often they seem to me absolutely external to myself, and, once or twice, it has definitely been my own voice that I heard, my lips and tongue speaking the words aloud without any control on my part, so far as I could tell."

I thanked him and promised not to interrupt again if he would give me some examples of his strange experience, and after a few moments' thought he began once more.

"I am not sure how old I was when this kind of thing first occurred to me, but sometimes I think it must have been when I was quite a child. My old nurse, who remained here as housekeeper for many years, has told me that, quite soon after I learned to talk, I used to come to her and ask what some phrase or other meant. Then, if she questioned me as to who had used the words, all I could answer was just, 'I heard them,' but who had spoken them I could never tell.

"However, if that were the same thing, the faculty passed away for a time, and the first definite instance I remember came soon after I had left school. I was then in my eighteenth year, and the things of God and religion played a smaller part in my life than they have ever done before or since; indeed, the morality of acts interested me less than the question whether they were 'good form' in a young man of my position.

"As you know, I had one brother, four years my senior, of whom I was very fond. My father had recently purchased him a commission in the army, and he was with his regiment in a provincial garrison town at the time of my story.

"For myself I had no very definite ideas about a profession, although, as a boy, I had leanings towards the priesthood. That idea passed away, however, when I was about fifteen, so I fell in readily with my father's proposal, that I should enter the law. I left school soon after my seventeenth birthday, and, after some preliminaries, was duly articled to our solicitors in London, a firm which had a large connection among old Catholic families. Life in town was a novelty to me, and I enjoyed it thoroughly, but the office hours were long, and I seldom got any time to myself before six in the evening. However, that left me free to go to the theatre, and I think I went to see some play or other nearly every week.

"On the night in question the piece I went to was *Hamlet*, with Macready in the title role. It was my favourite among Shakespeare's plays, but I had never seen it acted. After waiting some little time for the doors to open, I got a good place, and sat waiting for the curtain to go up. I think I may say that nothing was further from my mind at the moment than my brother Oswald; indeed, all my thoughts were about the play. Then, suddenly, as if someone were whispering into my ears, I heard quite distinctly the words, 'Oswald is dead.' I gave a start and looked round at my neighbour on the right; there was no one on my left, as I was next the gangway.

But my neighbour was turned away from me, talking to his companion, and obviously had not spoken the words, for, as I looked at him, they came again, 'Oswald is dead.' Now the only Oswald I knew was my brother, and, with a shock, I realised that, if the words meant anything to me at all, they must refer to him. At that moment they came a third time, 'Oswald is dead.' I began to be rather alarmed, although I confess, I felt it must all be some strange illusion, and half thought of leaving the theatre. But just then a bell rang, up went the curtain, and the whole incident was soon forgotten in the absorbing interest of the great drama.

"It was nearly midnight when the play was over, and I walked home to my rooms half intoxicated with the emotions of the tragedy, and without a thought of the strange occurrence that had happened just before the play. Arrived at my rooms, I let myself in with a latch-key, and walked quietly upstairs. To my surprise, on reaching my landing, I saw a bright line of light beneath the door of my sitting-room, and heard someone moving inside. Entering quickly, my surprise was doubled at finding the head of the firm to whom I was articled pacing up and down the room.

He turned on hearing me enter, and, as he did so, I saw that he held a telegram in his hand. Now telegrams were still a novelty in those days, and I guessed at once that something serious was the matter. 'My dear boy,' he said, 'I have been waiting here for hours; your father has sent this telegram, and asked me to break the news to you.' In a flash the words I had heard in the theatre came back to me, but I kept silent as he continued, 'Your brother Oswald, I am grieved to say, died suddenly this morning.' On inquiry afterwards I learned that his death had been caused by an accident a few minutes before midday, about seven hours before I heard the words in the theatre."

"Very strange, very strange indeed," I said, as the old priest remained silent; "and was that the end of the incident?"

"I think I must say it was," he replied, "but, oddly enough, the next occurrence of the kind took place precisely a year later to the day, and I sometimes think the two may be connected. At that date I was due to go in for my first law examination, and, by arrangement with my principal, I stayed away from the office for several weeks before it, so as to give my whole time to reading. By that time, I was fairly sure that I had made a mistake in taking up the law as a profession, and this did not make it easier to work hard at my books. In fact, I found it a real difficulty to keep my attention fixed upon the work, so I sometimes used to read the book out aloud, as that seemed to make it easier.

"I mentioned that the day in question was the anniversary of my brother's death, but the fact had quite slipped my memory, and I did not even notice the coincidence until it was pointed out to me later. Somehow, that morning, I was more stupid than usual, or perhaps my law treatise was exceptionally dry; anyhow, I found it almost impossible to keep awake over my work. I tried reading aloud, and, as that was only a partial success, I put the book upon a tall desk and read aloud standing up. Suddenly at the street door there came the sharp double rap that means a telegram, and, on the moment, I heard my own voice say, 'That telegram is to tell me father is dead,' and then it went on with the sentence of the book just as if the words had been printed on the page.

"A moment before I had been half asleep, but now I was wide awake with every nerve a-tingle. As I stood waiting, I heard the maid pass along the passage to the front-door; it opened and shut again, and her steps came back towards my room. A moment later I had taken the telegram and torn it open. It read, 'Father dangerously ill; come at once,' and was signed by my sister. I hurried home by the first train I could catch, and, on arrival, was told that my father had died at eight o'clock that morning; quite three hours before I received the telegram, which was purposely worded falsely so as to break the shock of his death to me."

The old man stopped speaking and gazed out for a few moments into the gathering darkness, as if lost in the memories his story had awakened. Then he turned to me with a smile of interrogation. "Those were the first occasions on which I heard the voices I call 'direct speech'; what do you make of them?" he asked. The question was a difficult one, for I did not know what to make of them.

"It was a strange experience," I said slowly, "very strange indeed. At first sight it all appears so purposeless. But I will ask you to let me reserve my judgement until I have had some time to think it all over, and another day perhaps you will give me some further instances."

The old man rose slowly from his chair, "That I will do with pleasure," he replied, "if you are sure, it does not bore you to listen to my ramblings."

"Indeed, sir," I began in protest, but his smile reassured me as he took my arm, and walked slowly down the long room towards the door.

The Persecution Chalice

All next morning the old squire-priest was occupied with his es-tate agent, and, except during Mass and breakfast, I did not even see him. However, his work was finished by lunch time, and the agent, who had stayed to that meal, left the house as soon as it was over to catch his train. We both came to the door to see him off, and, when the dog-cart had passed out of the courtyard, the old priest walked, leaning on my arm, to the end of the upper terrace. Here there was an arbour of clipped yew trees, with a seat which looked out across the formal garden and over the lower terrace to the park beyond. The day was warm and bright, and the whole place wore an air of peace and quiet, so restful that we sat in silence for a minute or two enjoying the beauty of the scene.

"I have had your stories of last night in my head ever since," I said at length, "and I have a theory to offer, if you care to hear it."

"Please go on," he said with an air of interest, and, after a moment's thought, I began again.

"You said, I think, that one of the points which seemed to you most unaccountable was the long time that elapsed in both cases be-tween the time of the death and the moment when you heard the voice which warned you of it?"

"Yes," he answered, "that is, to me, one of the strangest features of the whole affair."

"Well, that is the point my theory explains," said I; "of course I don't expect you to agree with it, but this is my idea. If the voice, or message, or whatever we call it, had occurred at the moment of death, you would be inclined to attribute it to the dying man—your brother Oswald in the first case and your father in the second—would you not?"

"Certainly," he answered.

"Very well then," I continued, "I think it follows that, as the occurrence took place so many hours after the moment of death, the motive force which started the telepathic current—which sent the message, if you prefer to put it so—must have been someone else; someone who was intent on communicating with you at the precise moment when you heard the voice."

"That certainly sounds very plausible," he acknowledged, "but who could it have been?"

"In the first instance I think it was your principal, the head of the firm to whom your father had wired, asking him to break the news to you. He received the telegram before leaving his office, and not knowing where you were, was concentrating all his thoughts on how to communicate with you. This concentration of mind, I suggest, produced the words you heard in the theatre."

"That is certainly very ingenious," he admitted, "and I must own I never thought of such an explanation before. But how about the second case Does your theory fit that one as perfectly?"

"Well, no," I acknowledged, "I don't see that it does. Unless by chance the boy who brought the telegram had seen it in the post office, and guessed that the words really understated the truth. But it is foolish of me to theorize so soon; you promised to give me some more examples of the phenomenon, would you care to do so now?"

"By all means," said he, "I will tell you another occurrence of the kind; it happened several years after the cases you have heard already. As you know, I was ordained priest in Rome, and returned here soon afterwards. It was delightful to be home again after spending several years out of England; but one thing I felt dreadfully, and that was the absence of all the externals of Catholicism. Even now it is bad enough in a little country place like this, but forty years ago things were much worse; and after the splendid functions of Rome—Rome before 1870, you recollect—I soon found myself longing to see a High Mass, and hear the liturgy chanted once again. Well, this longing grew upon me so much that I determined to spend Christmas away from home, either abroad or at some religious house in England, and eventually I arranged to go to Faversham.

"I think you told me the other day that you have never been there?" I shook my head, and the old man continued.

"Then I must tell you a little about the place first of all, to make the rest of my story clear. Faversham is a Benedictine Abbey, though it was only a Priory at the date of which I am speaking. The community have only been established in their present home since the

French Revolution. Until then, from the foundation of the monastery somewhere in Queen Elizabeth's reign, the monks were settled at Arras in Flanders. The English Benedictines, as I expect you know, trace their origin back without a break to pre-Reformation times, and the Faversham community always obtained enough vocations from their school to keep the monastery exclusively English, until at last a return to England became possible. Now, during the Reign of Terror the good monks at Arras were arrested and put in prison. They were monks and they were English, which was reason enough I suppose; but, although they remained in prison nearly two years, they were never brought to trial, and when Robespierre fell they were soon set free and allowed to retire to England.

"During their two years in prison the community kept up their regular life as far as possible under the circumstances, and by some means—probably by bribing the guards—they managed to smuggle into prison with them a chalice, altar stone and missal, with a set of vestments and everything absolutely essential for celebrating the divine mysteries. Then on the Sundays and great festivals, through all the period of the Terror, they rose soon after midnight, covered the windows with their straw mattresses, and one of the number said Mass and gave communion to the others. On their retirement to England, they brought the chalice with them; you can see it in their sacristy today.

"To Faversham, then, I travelled a few days before Christmas, and the quiet, peaceful surroundings formed a perfect preparation for the great festival. The country was new to me then, and though the monastery is less than two miles from a small town on the edge of a coalmining district, in the other direction there lie great open moors, where you may wander for hours without meeting a single human being. In those days the beautiful abbey church was only partly built, and I used to say Mass in a little chapel above the north cloister. Nowadays this chapel looks down into the south choir aisle, but at that time the arches were closed with a wooden partition, as the choir had not yet been begun. Indeed, the transepts were the only part of the church that was finished, and my chapel was reached by a spiral staircase in one corner of the south transept, which also communicated with the organ loft.

"I have to give you these details because they affect the story later on; the important point is, first, that my chapel was accessible only by the spiral staircase from the south transept, and, secondly, that its northern wall was pierced with arches closed at that time with a wooden partition, beyond which was the open air, as the choir was not yet built. I hope that is clear. The third day of my stay was the Vigil of Christmas, and when I came in from my walk that afternoon, I found the sacristan busy laying out vestments and making preparations for the feast day.

"'The prior has decided to have midnight Mass this year,' he said to me, as I came into the sacristy to offer my help in his work.

"'But don't you always have it on Christmas night?' I asked with some surprise.

"'Well, we always used to,' he answered, 'but four years ago a Protestant agitator worked up the miners at Bursdon, and the mob announced their intention of coming to wreck the church if we had a Mass at midnight. I don't believe anything would have happened, but the police were anxious about it, and persuaded the prior not to have one, and we have gone without it for three years now. However, the excitement seems quite forgotten by this time, and we are going to begin it again.'

"'I'm glad of that,' I said; 'you know this is my first Christmas as a priest, and I should have been sorry to miss midnight Mass. Am I to say my three Masses in the chapel upstairs as usual?"

"'Oh yes, please,' he answered. 'I have got the bailiff's son to come and serve you; he will be here at seven o'clock. By the way, would you mind laying out your own vestments, as the Brothers have so much to do? I will give you a chalice now, it will be quite safe upstairs; no one will go there before tomorrow morning.'

"Of course, I said I would do what he asked, and he opened the safe and took out a chalice.

"'I thought you might like to use the Persecution Chalice,' said he; 'you know its history, don't you?"

"'I'm afraid I don't,' I answered, 'but from the name I should guess it is one that was used in England during the penal times.'

"'Oh no, not that at all,' he said, 'it was ——,' but just at that moment the bell rang for Vespers, and my good friend hurriedly excused himself, saying, 'I'll tell you the story later.'

"I took the chalice upstairs to my chapel, and made it ready with the three large altar breads. Then, after laying out the vestments, I came down to the church just as Vespers had begun. Supper followed Vespers, and, soon afterwards, I went to my room and lay down, so as to get some sleep before eleven o'clock, when the Matins for Christmas were to begin, the High Mass following at a few minutes after midnight. Neither then, nor later did I give a thought to the chalice, nor to the story I was to hear about it. Indeed, the whole affair was driven out of my mind by the beautiful liturgy of the Christmas Office and Mass.

"After the midnight services I went to bed as usual, and was called by the lay-brother a little after six o'clock. I got up, dressed, made my preparation for Mass, and opened my window wider before going downstairs. As I did so I noticed how perfectly still it was. There had been a little frost in the night, but no snow, and the silence was absolute. I stood at the window for perhaps half a minute; the bleat of a far-away sheep suddenly broke the silence, and then it closed down again, almost oppressive in its stillness. When I got to my chapel, I found the bailiff's boy waiting for me, so I vested at once, and began my first Christmas Mass. Besides the server and myself, there was no one else in the chapel.

"Just after the Offertory, when I had washed my fingers and was bowing down for the prayer before the *Orate fratres*, I noticed a sound far away outside the monastery. It was only a momentary distraction, and I paid no real attention to it, but went on to say the Secret and the Preface. At the *Sanctus* the boy rang the bell as usual, though there was no congregation. As I commenced the Canon I heard the sound again. It was somewhere to the north of the buildings; quite a long distance away, I thought, but certainly nearer and louder than it had been. Try as I might to ignore the distraction, I could not help wondering what it could be.

"As the consecration approached, I forgot all about it, but no sooner had I risen again after the elevation of the chalice than it forced itself on my notice once more. There was no doubt whatever, the sound was much nearer, and now it seemed to me like a number of people shouting. 'Like a crowd at a football match,' I thought to myself, adding mentally, 'It can't be that, whatever it is.' Then, all at once, I remembered what the Father Sacristan had said about the threat of the miners at Bursdon. Perhaps that was the explanation. They had heard about the midnight Mass, and were coming to wreck the church as they had threatened!

"The theory seemed only too probable, for the noise was now quite close at hand, and it was unquestionably the howling of an angry mob. I began to wonder what I ought to do if they did actually break into the church before I had finished the Mass. "If a church catches fire,' I said to myself, 'the *Rubrice generales* order the priest to proceed at once to the communion, and end the Mass directly after that.' I determined to do the same. By this time the noise was almost upon us; it seemed as if the rioters were coming quickly up the road leading from the gatehouse to the church. I could distinguish the different tone and pitch of many voices, some high, some deep, but could not catch any of the words. Even in my anxiety this struck me as odd. 'It is just like a mob in a foreign country,' I thought; 'I can't make out a word they say.'

"However, in spite of my alarm I stuck to my Mass, determined to go straight to the communion if the mob attacked the church. I thought to myself, 'They won't come here at once, for no one would guess there is a chapel up that little spiral stair.' The shouting was almost at the door by now, and I had just said the *Agnus Dei*, when suddenly the whole noise stopped abruptly. I could not imagine what had happened, but the relief was immense. I finished the Mass, and as no further disturbance came, I went on and said the other two Masses: not a sign did my rioters make. I felt thoroughly mystified about the whole affair, and began to doubt if my theory of a Protestant mob could be the true explanation, so I called to my server as he was leaving the chapel after covering up the altar.

"'What did you make of that extraordinary noise during the first Mass?' I asked him.

"'What noise, Father?' he answered, to my utter amazement.

"'Why, that shouting or cheering, or whatever it was,' I said, 'you must have heard it. It began soon after the Offertory, and went on almost up to the communion.'

"'I didn't notice any noise, Father,' said the boy; 'who would be shouting or cheering so early on Christmas morning?'

"'Oh, well,' I said, as carelessly as I could manage, 'perhaps it was my fancy; but thank you very much for coming to serve Mass for me,' and I went to my *prie-dieu*.

"Still wondering what the true explanation could be, I finished my thanksgiving, and went down to the refectory. A number of the community were already seated, and a few minutes later my friend, the Father Sacristan, came in and sat beside me at the guest table.

"'By the way,' he said, after some minutes' conversation, 'I never finished telling you about the Persecution Chalice which you used this morning. Do you know, it never struck me before, but, as you said, the name suggests a chalice used in England during the penal times, while it really refers to something quite different. That chalice is the one which our fathers smuggled into prison with them during the French Revolution; you must remember my telling you how they managed to take in a whole set of things for Mass, and how they celebrated it at intervals during all the Reign of Terror.'

"'Of course I remember it,' I said, for light was beginning to dawn upon me; 'and was that the identical chalice which I used this morning?'

"'That is it,' he answered; 'we don't often use it now, unless someone wishes to do so out of devotion. There cannot be many chalices in existence with so strange a history.'

"'I should think not,' I answered, 'it was a most daring thing to do. I wonder what would have happened to the good monks if they had been caught saying Mass?"

"'No difficulty in guessing that,' he answered, "the guillotine for the whole number. You know the story goes that they were nearly caught on one occasion.'

"'Indeed,' said I, you did not tell me about that; how did it happen?"

"'It was on Christmas morning,' he answered, 'and the Mass was being celebrated by the youngest priest in the community. He had been ordained only a few months before they were sent to prison, and it was his first Christmas Mass. I suppose he took longer than an older priest would have done, and the story goes, too, that the monk whose turn it was to watch and wake the rest had gone to sleep, so that they began much later than had been intended. Anyway, before the Mass was half finished a loud shouting was heard in the distance, which gradually came nearer and nearer to the prison, and finally stopped just at the very gates. Some luckless aristocrat had been caught trying to fly the country, and the howling rabble were bringing him back for execution. 'They say the young priest was seized with fear, and could hardly go on with the Mass, but the saintly old prior came up and said to him, 'Proceed, my son, they will not come in hither; the Lord is mindful of them that serve him.' And in fact, the Mass was finished without discovery, though the mob were howling in the courtyard below the windows before it was over. Little did they guess there was nothing but a straw pallet between themselves and God's most holy sacrifice!'"

In Articulo Mortis

"You must not attach too much importance to my unusual faculty," said the old priest to me some days later, when I was pressing him for other stories of his strange experiences, "There are times, even now, when I think the 'direct speech' is all imagination, a product of my highly strung nature acted upon by circumstances of an unusual kind."

"That doesn't seem to me sufficient explanation," I answered; "besides, in the cases you have told me of, the circumstances were not specially unusual, at any rate not so far as you could tell before the event took place."

"True," said he, "but in a good many instances the circumstances were more out of the common, more calculated to excite the imagination and prepare it for self-deception. But I must own that, although at times I doubt if the whole thing be not subjective, still in the end I always come back to the opinion that such an explanation is quite inadequate. In fact, I only mentioned it because I thought you were inclined to take it all too seriously. For my part I refuse to attach any special meaning or value to the phenomena. I know that my account of them is as truthful and exact as I can make it, and if you ask me for an explanation, all I have to say is that I seem to possess a certain kind of spiritual perception in an unusual degree; but it does not follow that what I hear is of any particular importance, any more than the possession of exceptionally long sight by one man would render a thing important, because he could see it while it was beyond the range of his companions' vision."

He paused for a few moments and I kept silent, hoping he might develop his views on the subject more fully, but instead he proposed to give me another instance of his curious gift.

"Let me tell you another story," he began, "one of the kind I mentioned just now, in which the circumstances themselves were calculated to excite the imagination." I begged him to do so, and he continued:

"While I was in Rome, at the *Accademia*, I became very intimate with one of my fellow-students. He was an Austrian and a member of one of the most ancient families in the empire, but if you do not mind, I will not give you, his name. We chanced to attend the same set of lectures, and the acquaintance thus begun ripened rapidly, so that we were soon on terms of real friendship, and in the vacation time we made several excursions together to various parts of Italy. "He was ordained at the Advent Ordination, and left Rome at once, so as to celebrate his first Mass at his old home, a famous castle in Austria, but before leaving, he made me promise that I would go and stay at his home for a little while on my return journey to England, after my own ordination. That event took place some three months later, on Holy Saturday, and a fortnight afterwards I left the *Accademia* and set my face homewards.

"The journey was a leisurely one, and it must have been the beginning of June when I crossed over the Brenner Pass and entered Austrian territory; but that done I went straight on to the station nearest my friend's home. Even this place was twelve leagues away from the castle, but a diligence ran the rest of the way, and I took a seat in it, glad to be quit of the train. I put up for the night at an inn where the diligence had stopped about an hour before sunset.

"After taking my room and arranging for supper, I walked across the way to see the parish priest and get permission to say Mass next morning. The good man proved to be very unwell, but on learning from his housekeeper that a strange priest wished to say Mass next day, he sent down a message begging me to come upstairs and see him. I found him in bed, apparently suffering from fever, but he assured me that my coming was as good as medicine to him.

"'It is certainly our holy Mother who has sent you,' he exclaimed, 'for tomorrow is a feast day with us, and it would be dreadful if there were no Mass in the church; yet the Herr Doctor has forbidden me to attempt it. Now you are here and will say Mass for my good people, will you not?'

"Of course, I said that I would do anything I could, and he explained that he had special permission from the bishop of the diocese to grant faculties to any priest who came to help him during his illness, so that I could hear confessions if anyone wished to go.

"By the time I left him it was quite dark, and my dinner was waiting for me. Soon after ten o'clock, when I was just thinking of going to bed, a knock came at the door and the landlord entered.

"'Your pardon, Herr Priest,' said he, 'but there is a gentleman below who wishes to speak with you.'

"'Impossible, I exclaimed; 'there must be some mistake; I do not know anyone in the neighbourhood.'

"'But it is true, *mein Herr*,' replied the man, 'the pastor, so he says, told him to come across and ask for you.'

"That is another matter, of course,' said I; 'I will come down with you,' and we went together to the large room on the ground-floor where I had dined.

"At the door the landlord bowed me in before him and then retired, leaving me alone with a tall, distinguished-looking stranger. He was obviously an Austrian noble, but to my surprise he addressed me in excellent English: put shortly, his story was this. He was Count A——, who lived with his younger brother at their family castle, some leagues distant. Neither his brother nor himself were what could be called devout Catholics, and, moreover, they had quarrelled with the local priest. The previous evening his brother had been taken seriously ill, and now wished to see a priest.

"He had, therefore, come to the town himself to beg the pastor to go back with him and see his brother, but as the good man was himself so unwell, this was impossible, and the only alternative seemed to be to come and appeal to me to go instead. He knew it was a very unusual thing to ask of a stranger on a journey, but his brother was dying, of that the doctor left no doubt, and his soul was in danger. I was a priest and, he understood, an English noble. He begged I would not refuse his appeal.

"It was certainly a most inconvenient occurrence, and my first impulse was to refuse, or rather to point out difficulties which made my acquiescence impossible. I was a stranger, had no faculties, was on a journey, and must be off by tomorrow's diligence, had promised to say Mass for the pastor next morning, and anything else I could think of in the way of objections. The count waited until I had finished, and then said quietly, 'My Father, it is a question of saving a soul, surely you cannot refuse?'

"I was silent for a moment, wondering what I ought to do, and then, as if in answer, I heard a voice whispering in my ear say 'Go.' I looked up quickly at the count, wondering if he had spoken, and he began to plead with me once more. 'Go with him,' came the voice again in my ears. It could not be the count, for he was speaking at the moment; and I felt somehow convinced that my duty was to go. Just as he paused the voice came again as if to reassure me, 'Go without doubting, for I am with thee,' and half dazed I said to him, 'Yes, I will go.'

"As we went through the hall to the door of the inn, I chanced to look at the clock. It was just half-past ten, and I remember thinking to myself, 'I shall not get to bed before midnight at the earliest.' At the door stood a carriage, its four horses restlessly pawing the ground, and anxious to be on the move. As the count opened the door and motioned to me to enter, I stopped in surprise. 'Surely,' I said, "you wish me to bring the blessed Sacrament. I must go over to the church and obtain it.'

"'No, no,' said he, somewhat nervously, I thought; 'we must not delay even for that. You understand, it is unlikely my brother will be in a condition to receive Communion.'

"Amazed at this, I began to expostulate with him—what good could I do compared with what our Lord would do in the Holy Viaticum? But even as I spoke the voice came again in my ears, 'Go at once, delay no longer,' and alarmed I stepped into the carriage.

"With a look of relief my companion called out an order to the driver and stepped in after me, the horses at once starting off at a great pace. The carriage was of the old-fashioned, travelling type quite unknown nowadays, with deep comfortable seats, and curtains to the windows. My companion was proceeding to close the windows and draw the curtains, and it was only after some difficulty that I got him to leave the window on my side a little open, with its curtain not drawn. This gave me some fresh air, but the night was very dark, and there was a candle alight in a swinging candlestick within the carriage, so that I could make out nothing of the country through which we were passing.

"I felt some anxiety about the Mass I had promised to say for the pastor next morning, and asked the count how far it was to his castle, and at what time I could get back. 'Several leagues,' was all I got out of him as, ignoring my second question, he lay back in the carriage and closed his eyes as if tired out. Then all at once it struck me that I was behaving very selfishly. The poor man's only brother was dying, and here was I worrying him about needless details; so I too kept silence, and taking my rosary from my pocket, leaned back in my seat and closed my eyes.

"I think I must have fallen into a doze, for I had no idea how long we had been driving, when I was suddenly awakened by the noise of the horses' hoofs striking loudly on a wooden bridge. I sat up abruptly and looked out of the window. The moon must have risen by now, for I could see quite plainly, as we passed under an arched gateway and halted in a stone-paved courtyard.

"The castle loomed up, huge and uncertain in the dim light, the buttresses casting deep shadows across the walls that stood out white in the moonlight. But I had no time to survey the building, for Count A—— quickly alighted and helped me out of the carriage. Before us, at an open door, stood a man-servant holding a lantern, and I was hurried in, through an outer room and across a huge hall, into a smaller one fitted as a library with dark carved bookcases, and a bright log fire in a deep, old-fashioned fireplace. Here the count stopped, begging me to warm myself—though the night was not cold—and to take a glass of wine, while he went to find out if his brother was able and ready to see me.

"As I was uncertain of the time I took no wine, since I had to say Mass in the morning, but stood by the fire, glad to stretch my limbs after the long drive. Not more than two or three minutes elapsed before a servant entered with a message from Count A——, begging me to go with the messenger, who would show the way to his brother's room, where all was ready for me.

"I went at once, preceded by the servant with a light. We went down a long corridor and up some stairs, but I took no special notice of the way, and cannot say if we had ascended one flight or two, when we finally passed through a 'passage-room,' and stopped at a door before which there hung a deep red curtain. Drawing this aside my guide knocked at the door, and a voice within answered clearly in German. The servant then opened the door and stepped back, holding the red *portière* aside for me to enter. As I did so the door was shut behind me, and I heard a dull thud as the weighted curtain fell back into position behind it.

"Now all this, no doubt, sounds very ordinary and natural, but somehow, I had a growing feeling that something was wrong. The non-return of Count A—— to the library, the deserted condition of the whole place, the absence of anything suggesting illness, no sign of doctor, nurse, etc., had surprised me, and my feeling of uneasiness was increased enormously by what I now saw. I found myself in a room, not a bedroom as I had expected, but a large apartment panelled in oak or some dark wood, with a heavily carved cornice and elaborate plaster ceiling decorated in gold and colour.

"Some handsome old-fashioned chairs were ranged stiffly along the walls, which bore several portraits; a wood fire burned in the deep, open fireplace, above which was a lofty overmantel reaching to the ceiling and carved with classic figures. In the centre of the room stood a large table, with a litter of playing-cards and a dice box on it, beside some lighted candles in tall silver candlesticks. Beyond this was seated a young man, not more than twenty-five years old at most, and apparently in perfect health.

"He looked up quickly as I entered, but said nothing, and with some hesitation I began to apologise, as best I could in German, for intruding upon him. The servant must have made some mistake. I was a priest, a stranger, and had been brought in great haste to see the brother of Count A—— who was ill—in fact, was not expected to live till morning. At this the young man rose and came towards me.

"There is no mistake, my Father,' he said, speaking in German, 'it is I whom you were brought to see; I shall be a dead man before sunrise.'

"At this my previous misgivings were increased a hundredfold, and I felt thoroughly alarmed; my fears being oddly coupled with annoyance at the way I had been tricked. Crushing down the angry. words which were rushing up for utterance, I repeated as calmly as I could that there was evidently some mistake. That Count A—— had told me definitely that my services as a priest were needed by his brother, who was very seriously ill and not likely to live till morning; whereas he appeared to be perfectly well. The stranger waited in silence until I had finished.

"'It is not to be wondered at,' said he, 'that you are surprised and annoyed; indeed, the count seems to have misled you in some details, but the main fact is perfectly true. I am his brother, I shall be dead before morning, and it is to hear my confession that we have brought you all this long journey. You will not refuse me, surely, now that you have come?'

"My first inclination was to protest angrily against the way I had been treated, when the recollection of the voice I had heard at the inn came back to my mind. After all it was not the count's story which had brought me, but the strange command, three times repeated, and I was as sure as ever that Count A—— had not spoken the words which impelled me to go with him.

"Taking my silence for consent the young man motioned me to a recess, apparently a window but with shutters drawn, in which there stood a *prie-dieu* with a chair beside it. Almost unconsciously I obeyed his gesture, walking beside him to the *prie-dieu*, where he kneeled down as I seated myself at his side. Even now I am not clear if I did wrong in hearing his confession, and you will understand I had to decide without any time for deliberation. I had been a priest for a few weeks only, and had not heard a dozen confessions in all. The pastor certainly had given me faculties, and Count A—— had mentioned that his castle was in the same diocese when I raised this point as an obstacle to my coming. Then too there was the memory of the voice I had heard, commanding me to go without fear. Automatically I gave the stranger my blessing, and he began his confession.

"What he told me, under the seal, I cannot, of course, repeat to you—indeed, I scarcely understood it all myself, what with the turmoil in my mind and the strange language, for my knowledge of German was, and is, far from perfect. But this I may say, that no sufficient explanation of his position was offered, nor did my questions elicit anything more than that his death before morning was quite certain and utterly unavoidable, and that he desired most earnestly to make his peace with God before he should stand at his judgement seat. In the end I abandoned all efforts to break down his reserve, and with many misgivings imparted absolution.

"As I finished, he rose and thanked me, adding in the most earnest manner, 'Let me beg you, my Father, not to inquire further into this matter. No harm whatever will come to you, and no inquiries you may make will bring you any nearer its solution.' With that he rang a small hand bell, which stood upon the table, and the servant who had brought me to the room appeared almost immediately.

"I tried to speak, but not a word would come; indeed, my one idea was to escape, for I was rapidly becoming unnerved. Accordingly, I allowed myself to be conducted from the room, through the antechamber and down a flight of stairs, where the servant showed me into a room which I had not entered before. Here he left me, saying that Count A—— would be with me very shortly. Left to myself, my mind ran riot as to the meaning of the strange adventure I had just gone through. Doubts if I had done right in hearing the confession and giving absolution, mingled with vague notions of a secret society, and, I must own, no small amount of fear for my own safety. All at once the last prevailed, and I ran quickly to the window and opened it, thinking I might perhaps escape unnoticed.

"The casement opened inwards, and outside were strong iron bars fixed in the masonry, which prevented my leaning out of it, much less climbing through the opening. However, the cool night air revived and calmed me, and I stood looking out into the moonlight. Below was the castle moat, still as glass and reflecting the cold, silvery light, save where the dark shadow of the building fell across it. This shadow stopped in a hard, straight line some few yards to the right of the window, showing me that my room was near a corner of the building; and I found that, by pressing my face against the bars, I could just see the angle of the retaining wall which formed the outer side of the moat as it too turned round the corner.

"I do not suppose I had stood there more than four or five minutes, when I heard the noise of a window being opened somewhere overhead, and apparently round the corner of the building. I listened intently, and could just catch the sound of a voice speaking in a rapid low tone, as if giving some directions; and then, to my amazement, there came a sound like something falling, followed by a loud splash in the moat beneath. My heart was in my mouth, but not another sound came.

"Then, a few seconds later, a series of little waves broke the calm surface of the water, as they flowed round the angle of the wall. Soon they shrank into mere rings, and in a minute or two the moat was a mirror once more. I gazed, fascinated, until the last of the rings disappeared, and then the thirst for safety seized me again. I closed the window and walked quickly to the door. Opening it I found the servant who had brought me there standing, as if listening, at the foot of the stairs. I called to him in German, saying I could wait no longer, but must return at once whence I had come.

"'But surely the Herr Priest will wait and see my master the count?' asked the man in some surprise.

"'No, no,' I said, 'I must get back immediately; I have to say Mass for the people tomorrow morning.'

"'It is *this* morning now, *mein Herr*,' replied the man, 'and indeed if that is so, you will need to start at once, if you wish to get any sleep at all;' and he led the way downstairs, going before me with a light.

"We crossed the same large hall and ante-chamber, and the man opened the door into the courtyard. To my relief the carriage was waiting at the door, so, telling him to make my excuses to his master, I entered it and drove off with a feeling of intense relief. The drive back must have taken a full hour or more, and I was surprised to find the innkeeper waiting for me on my arrival. As I passed upstairs, I looked at the clock again; it was ten minutes to two! Fortunately, the Mass was to be at a fairly late hour, as it was a feast day, but it seemed as if I had scarcely slept at all, when I was awakened and told it was half-past eight.

"After the Mass, when I returned to the inn, I found to my surprise that there was a letter waiting for me. It was from my friend, telling me that he had been called to Vienna, where his mother was lying ill, but begging me to go on to his home all the same, where he would join me as soon as he could leave his mother. Of course I did nothing of the kind, but came straight home to England; and it was some years before we met by chance in Rome, when I told him my strange experience. He made me give him every detail I could remember about the buildings and everything connected with the place, and then said, 'There is one castle in the neighbourhood and one only which fits in with your description,' and he named a place I had never heard of.

"'And its owner,' I asked, 'who is he?' The name was as strange to me as that of the castle, but the answer to my next question was significant.

"'What sort of a man is he?' I asked, and my friend hesitated a little before replying.

"'Well,' said he at length, 'I scarcely know; he is quite a recluse nowadays—in fact, I have only seen him once. People say that he was very wild in his youth, and the story goes that he quarrelled with his younger brother about a beautiful peasant girl who lived in the neighbourhood. He is supposed to have circulated a false report that she was dead, and a few days later his brother was found drowned in the castle moat. The official view was that he had committed suicide, but many people suspected foul play, though no evidence of it was ever forthcoming. It must be ten years now since the affair took place, and it is becoming a mere legend even in the neighbourhood. All the same, if I were you, I should not publish your story in Austria, at any rate so long as the count is living,'"

The Priest's Hiding Place

It was clear that the rain would not stop before nightfall, so after lunch the old squire proposed that we should take our exercise in the long gallery, as the walk which we had planned to an outlying farm was impossible. The gallery is on the second floor, and runs the whole length of the west wing. At each end is a deep oriel window, and smaller windows look out westwards. Opposite these the oak panelling continues without a break the whole length of the wall, except for a door, near either end, where the north and south wings join on. Along this wall hangs a series of portraits, which, though less important from an artistic point of view than those in the reception rooms below, are still full of value for anyone interested in the history of the family. We walked the whole length of the gallery once or twice, and then the old priest stopped in front of one of the pictures.

"Did I ever tell you how I found this portrait?" he asked, pointing to the effigy of an ecclesiastic dressed in black.

"No," I answered; "was it not here when you came into the property?"

"Well, yes," said he, "it was here, but hidden away in a lumber room, almost black with dirt, and without a frame or anything to show whom it represented. I sometimes wondered what the picture was like, so one day I sent it up to London, and had it carefully cleaned on the chance that it might prove of interest. The result surpassed all my hopes, for the cleaning revealed the inscription you see near the top of the painting, to the right of the head; can you decipher it?"

I had not noticed the inscription before, and now tried to read the letters, but could make nothing intelligible of them.

"What is it?" I asked at length. "It looks to me like '*Efigies V. PHIL, de FLUM. M. ob TIB. 1621,*'" and I spelt it out letter by letter.

"Capital!" exclaimed the old man; "and can't you fill in the abbreviations?"

153

"I suppose the '*V.*' stands for '*vera*' to agree with '*effigies*,'" I answered, "but I'm afraid the rest is beyond me."

"It might be that," said he, "but for my part I read it as '*Effigies Venerabilis Philippi de Fluminibus, Martyris, Obiit Tiburnia, 1621.*'"

"*Philippi de Fluminibus*," I cried, my interest now thoroughly aroused; "then it is a portrait of the Venerable Philip Rivers, the martyr priest of the family!"

"Ah, I thought you would be interested in it," said my old cousin, with a smile of satisfaction.

"You can imagine my delight when it came back from being cleaned, and I read the inscription for the first time, for it had been quite invisible under the varnish and dirt."

"And now I understand the carving of the frame," said I, for the design of palms and knives, interlaced with a rope, had puzzled me, "but I wonder who hid it away in the lumber room, and why?"

"I fancy it was my grandfather," said the old squire. "He was your great-grandfather, of course, the one who took the name of Pater. You know that he ceased to practise his religion, and married a Protestant when quite an elderly man. I imagine the mute reproach of his martyred ancestor's portrait was too much for him, so he took it down and put it away out of sight. His wife was many years his junior, but she died when their second child was born. That child was your grandfather, and the elder son was my father. However, they were left orphans while still very young, so they could have known nothing about the picture, though my father would have valued it had he known, as the children were brought up Catholics, thank God."

"What a lucky thing you thought of having the picture cleaned!" I said. "It would have been lamentable if it had been thrown away or burned as worthless. I have always had a devotion to the Venerable Philip Rivers."

"I should think so," interrupted the old priest; "you would not deserve to have such an ancestor in your pedigree if you hadn't a devotion to him; but you haven't heard his Mass as I have!"

"Heard his Mass," I exclaimed in surprise, "what do you mean?"

"Well, I suppose I have let myself in for a story now," he answered with a smile; "come and sit down in the oriel, and you shall hear it." So, we walked to the window seat at the end of the gallery, and after a minute's rest he began.

"In the first years after my ordination I used to give a good number of missions and retreats, especially in Lancashire and the North, and at the time of my story I had undertaken to preach a Mission, at a church in Glasgow, during Advent. I had arranged to get to my destination two days before the Mission was to begin, which proved to be lucky, for, as you will hear, I was delayed on the way. In those days the train service was not nearly so good as it is now, and I had to leave here before dusk, and change twice *en route*, so as to catch the night mail for Scotland at Stafford.

"I was due at Stafford about half-past nine at night, the Scottish mail coming in soon afterwards, but some twenty miles this side of Stafford an accident occurred to my train. If I remember right, it was an axle that broke, but anyhow the coach next to the engine left the rails, and dragged the two adjoining carriages with it. Luckily, we were going slow at the time, as we were quite close to a small station, so the rear part of the train in which I was came to no harm. But the line was blocked by the damaged coaches, and it was impossible for us to get on in time to make the connection at Stafford.

"Fortunately, no one was killed in the accident, but several passengers were injured more or less severely, and these were conveyed to the village inn, which was filled to its utmost limit. I did not feel inclined to spend the night in a railway carriage or in the bare station waiting-room, so I tried various houses in the village in the hope of finding a bed for the night. After two or three unsuccessful attempts a young woman, who appeared in answer to my knock, caught sight of my collar, and asked if I were not a Catholic priest. I answered 'Yes,' and she then advised me to go and apply at the Manor Farm. 'It is not far by the path there,' she said, pointing to a stile in the hedge, 'and the farmer's family are good Catholics, who will be glad to take you in for the night. It is a big house, and they have a spare room furnished.'

"The suggestion seemed a good one, so I thanked her and set off with my handbag along the path in question. There was a bright moon, and I had no difficulty about the path, though the distance proved further than I had expected, for I must have walked quite half a mile before reaching the farm. However, on telling my story I received such a warm welcome from the farmer and his wife that I was very glad I had come.

"The building was quite an imposing one, and had evidently been an old manor house, as its name implied; but my good host could tell me little of its history. It appeared that the owner was an elderly gentleman, a Catholic, who lived at a distance, and dealt with his tenants through an agent. The latter had instructions always to secure Catholic tenants if possible, and, in the case of the Manor Farm, there had not been a Protestant tenant within living memory. The only other detail I gathered was that the old house was said to contain a 'priest's hole,' or secret hiding place.

"However, no one knew where it was, and the farmer himself believed that, if such a thing had ever existed, it must have been in the older wing, which had been pulled down some twenty-five years earlier, as it was in a ruinous state, and the house was more than large enough without it. This much I learned in conversation during supper, which the farmer's wife provided for me, and, as soon as it was over, I asked to be shown to my room, as I could see the good folk were themselves anxious to retire.

"The spare room proved to be an attic chamber on the second floor. It was a long, low room, with oak rafters showing through the plaster ceiling, and panelled along one side and at each end. On the other side the ceiling sloped down almost to the floor level, except where two broad dormer windows cut into the angle of the roof. The door was at one end of the room, and on the long wall opposite the windows was a broad projection, which I took to be the upper part of a chimney stack, standing out some three feet into the room.

"The bed stood at the far end, its head screened off by the projection, and I noticed that, in spite of the convenient chimney stack, there was no fireplace in the room. The bed had been made up for me while I was at supper, so my host and his wife excused themselves and retired. I had said all my Office for the day in the train, and was feeling very tired, so I decided to go to bed at once, and after saying a few prayers I undressed and got into the bed, which proved to be extremely comfortable.

"I must have slept for several hours when I awoke abruptly, convinced that someone had just called me by name, 'Philip—Philip Rivers'; I was sure of it. You have noticed, no doubt, how one's own name will arrest the attention even in the midst of a babel of conversation. Well, it was like that, only, instead of catching my attention among a crowd of talkers, the name had called me back to consciousness out of sleep.

"I sat up in bed and listened, and as I did so the thought struck me, 'How could anyone here know what my Christian name is? I had introduced myself as Father Pater, and though the label on my bag read 'Rev. P. R. Pater,' there was nothing to show that the initials stood for 'Philip Rivers'; so, I determined to wait and see if the call would be repeated before I answered it. I lay back in bed and waited, but nothing happened, and I began to think I had been dreaming. Still the sensation had been wonderfully vivid, and I could hardly believe it was all imagination. Then, as I lay there, I heard a voice speaking in a low tone, almost a whisper. 'There was no doubt about it now, it was in the room not many feet away from me, though I could see nothing.

"I was on the point of calling out to ask who was there, when I caught the word 'Mass' and a moment later 'pursuivants.' At this I felt sure the voices were not those of the farmer and his wife, as I had first supposed, and I lay as still as possible, scarcely breathing, so as to hear anything else that followed. For some minutes all was silent, and I could feel my heart beating strongly as I listened to catch the lightest sound. 'Then quite distinctly, in a low clear voice, came the words, '*In nomine Patris et Filii et Spiritus Sancti, Amen. Introibo ad altare Dei.*'

"The surprise was overwhelming, and, even if I had wished to speak, I was dumb with astonishment; but somehow all sense of fear left me as the voice proceeded calmly with the opening responses of the Mass. One's mind works oddly on occasions of exceptional activity, and I remember a feeling of annoyance that the answers of the server were indistinct and almost inaudible, but half-unconsciously I repeated in my mind the words of the Mass as I heard them.

"All at once came another surprise. The unknown priest was saying the *Confiteor*, and had got to '*Sanctis Apostolis Petro et Paulo*,' and in my mind, I was going on to '*omnibus Sanctis*,' when the voice inserted the extra words, '*beato patri nostro Benedicto*,' which of course are said only by members of St. Benedict's Order.'

"'So you are a Benedictine monk,' I thought to myself; 'that narrows down the possibilities enormously, and ought to help me to identify you,' but I gave no more thought to the point, as I wished to concentrate my whole mind on the task of listening.

"Soon there came a pause, just where the silent prayers would come as the priest advances to the altar, and then again, the voice began, quite distinctly, reading the *Introit*. '*Ad te levavi animam meam: Deus meus, in te confido, non erubescam; neque irrideant me inimici mei*' . . . and I recognised it at once as the Mass for the first Sunday of Advent. ("*To thee, O Lord, have I lifted up my soul: in thee do I put my trust, let me not be put to confusion, neither let my enemies laugh me to scorn. . . .*")

"I need not weary you with details, but as I lay there I heard the whole Mass proceed, every word of the 'proper' full of significance to those who lived under the terrors of the penal laws, for I now felt sure that it was such a Mass that I was hearing.

"At the consecration came the tinkle of a tiny bell, and later on two or three persons received Communion. Then came the Post-communion and the concluding prayer, against the persecutors of the Church: '*O Lord our God, we beseech thee, leave not exposed to the perils of this human life those whom thou hast rejoiced by a share in this divine mystery.*' The Blessing was given in due course, and the first words of the last Gospel followed. But then, suddenly, from below the windows, there came a sharp whistle, thrice repeated, and the last Gospel stopped abruptly. I heard a rapid whispering, but could distinguish nothing of what was said, and in a few moments, there was perfect silence; nor did I hear another sound, though I lay awake until I was called.

"At breakfast I asked the farmer once more about the 'priest's hiding place,' but without result; I did, however, learn one point of interest. I had noticed at the station, the previous night, that the village was named Codsall, and so concluded that the Manor Farm had formerly been Codsall Manor. Inadvertently I referred to it by that name, and the farmer corrected me, explaining that it was in a different parish to Codsall, and had been known as Marston Manor.

"The name seemed curiously familiar somehow, but I could not fix it, and soon after breakfast I left the place to continue my journey north. But before leaving I made a note of the name and address of the agent, meaning to write and ask for any particulars he could give me about the farm, in case they might cast some light on my experience of the night before. The journey to Glasgow was without incident, but all the way I was thinking over the affair, and trying to recollect why the name of Marston Manor was familiar. I felt convinced that what I had heard was, so to speak, the echo of a Mass celebrated in the penal times, perhaps by some priest who was afterwards martyred; and not unnaturally my thoughts turned to my namesake, the Venerable Philip Rivers. Then, in a flash, it occurred to my mind that in his trial the evidence which sealed his fate was that of a servant, who admitted under torture that Rivers had said Mass at Marston Manor, in Staffordshire, the very day he was captured, which was Advent Sunday, 1621.

"When I got to Glasgow I borrowed a copy of Challoner's *Missionary Priests*, and read his account of Father Rivers, where the facts I have just told you are fully set out. One other detail was mentioned that in 1621 Advent Sunday fell on November 29th, the exact date on which I had slept at the Manor Farm.

"I could do nothing more during my stay in Glasgow except write to the agent, and ask if I might be permitted to examine the old house carefully on my return south; giving my connection with Father Rivers as a reason for my interest in the place, but saying nothing of the incident of the Mass. In reply he wrote me a most hospitable letter, begging me to stay with him on my journey home, and adding that, as he was himself keenly interested in the history of the neighbourhood, he would be delighted to give me all the help he could in my researches. I accepted his invitation gladly, and when the Mission was over, once more turned my steps to Codsall. This time the journey proved uneventful, and I reached the agent's house about dusk on a December evening. My host was an elderly man, well read and cultured, with a knowledge of local history which filled me with admiration, and we soon became excellent friends.

"He told me a good deal about the history of Marston Manor, and how it had fallen on evil days and come to be a farm house, and he promised to show me the spot in the neighbouring wood where, according to tradition, Father Philip Rivers had been captured, while trying to effect his escape on the fatal Advent Sunday. I felt very much inclined to tell him about my experience on the night when I had slept at Marston, but eventually decided to keep silent for the moment, and instead expressed my desire to make a thorough examination of the old house on the following day.

"'I was sure you would wish that,' said the agent, very kindly, 'so I have arranged for the estate carpenter to meet us there tomorrow morning. He has done the repairs at Marston for many years now, and if anyone can cast any light on the whereabouts of the priest's hiding place, it will be he.'

"Next morning, soon after breakfast, we set off together to the Manor Farm, and on our arrival found the estate carpenter waiting for us. I talked to him about the building for some time, and was interested in his account of the older wing, on the demolition of which he had himself worked, as a boy, some five-and-twenty years before. He was positive that nothing like a 'priest's hole' had been found in it, and equally certain that he must have heard of it, had such a thing come to light at all. Moreover, he pointed out that the wing which had been destroyed had been built not later than the early Tudor period, while the existing wing dated from 1610, as recorded by a carved inscription over the entrance, and was therefore more likely to contain a hiding place, since it was built in the penal times when such a thing would be almost a necessity.

"With this we entered the house, and made a tour of inspection, floor by floor, and so came at length to the large attic room in which I had slept some ten days earlier. I remarked on the beauty of the old oak panelling, adding that it seemed odd such fine work should have been made for an attic.

"'I can't help thinking it was brought here from somewhere else, sir,' said the carpenter in reply.

"'But what makes you think that?' I asked, with interest.

"'Well, sir,' said he, 'you will notice that the panels of the top row are square, while the rest are all a good deal longer than they are wide. If you look carefully, you will see that some of the square panels have the grain running horizontally, while in the lower rows it is always vertical. Now you said yourself that the panelling was exceptionally good work, and so it is; which makes me think the men who made it would never have spoiled the run of the grain by setting some of the top panels on their sides. But if the whole lot was brought from somewhere else, and the top row cut down to fit a lower room, then, like enough, the people who altered such fine work wouldn't take too much trouble about it, and so might get some of the panels in sideways when they put 'em together after cutting down.

"'Well, that comes of being an expert,' said I; 'even if I had noticed the blemish, I should never have gathered so much from it. But one thing did strike me as odd when I slept here, and that is the absence of any fireplace, when the chimney stack was here at hand sticking out into the room like this,' and I laid my hand on the projection of which I told you before.

"'Perhaps they thought it too near the rafters to be safe,' said the agent; 'but stop a moment, is this the chimney stack? I thought the chimney was in the gable at the end of this room, not here in the middle. Isn't that so, Bateman?' he asked, turning to the carpenter.

"'Yes, sir,' said the man, after a moment's thought; 'there is no chimney stack near this part of the room.'

"'Come, this is interesting,' said I; 'but if this is not a chimney stack, why is there a projection here at all? They wouldn't have brought the panelling out like this unless there were something behind.'

"While I was speaking the carpenter had been looking up at the cornice of the panelling, and then he moved the table up against the projection and climbed upon it, so that he could easily reach the ceiling.

"'Why, sir,' he said a moment later, 'there is quite a space between the top of the woodwork and the ceiling; see, I can put my hand right into the opening.'

"'Can you feel any wall behind the woodwork?' asked the agent.

"'No, sir,' replied the man, 'but wait a moment,' and taking his rule from his pocket he unfolded it to the full length, and inserted the end through the opening, adding with surprise, 'Why, I can't find anything at all behind; there's a space more than two feet deep, at any rate.'

"'Run your hand along the top of the cornice, Bateman,' said the agent, 'and see if the panelling is fastened to the ceiling in any way.'

"The carpenter did as he was ordered, without encountering any obstacle until he reached the angle, where the side of the projection met the front panelling, when his fingers struck against a support.

"'There's something just at the end, sir,' said he; adding, as he withdrew his hand, 'Why, it's iron; look at the rust on my fingers, sir.'

"'Light a match,' said the agent, 'and see if you can make out what it is.' The man did so, and peered into the narrow crevice.

"'It looks like a hook, sir, holding all this front piece of panelling back to the sides. It must be nearly rusted through, I should say. May I break it, sir?'

"'Try if you can do so without injuring the panelling,' said the agent, and the carpenter took a good grip of the cornice, and pulled it forcibly towards him.

"There was a sound of something snapping, and a lot of dust flew out, as the whole panelled front of the projection moved outwards some inches at that end.

"'Stop,' cried the agent, 'it's holding at the other end, Bateman. See if you can get that loose too, without hurting the woodwork.'

"The carpenter jumped down and moved the table opposite the other end. 'There's a hook here, as well,' he reported; and this time he managed to push it back out of the eye in which it was fixed.

"'Just keep a hand on the panelling, sir, while I move the table away,' cried Bateman; and when that was done the three of us lowered the whole panelled front of the projection to the floor, like the front of an old-fashioned *escritoire*.

"The air was full of the dust we had dislodged, and at first it was difficult to see what was behind the opening. But the agent turned to me with a look of victory. 'I think, Father,' he said, 'that we have discovered your ancestor's hiding place!'

"There could be no doubt about it. The place was a typical 'priest's hole,' some eight feet by six. There were airholes in the floor and ceiling, as well as the long slit above the panelling we had let down. At one end was a long wooden seat, which could have been used as a bed, and opposite this was a small cupboard, rather over three feet high, which had evidently been used as an altar, for inside it we found two little wooden candlesticks, some rotten pieces of linen, and a single altar card, broken across.

"Except for these things the place was absolutely empty, and it had evidently not been used for many years. But in one corner, just above the bed, there was a rough drawing of a crucifix; formed by blackening the plaster with the flame of a candle, and then scraping away the background. Beneath the drawing was the one word '*JHESU*,' and the initials '*P.R.*'"

De Profundis

It was some little time before the subject of the old priest's experiences cropped up again, and I did not like to refer to it deliberately for fear of trying his patience, and so making him avoid the matter entirely. One day, however, he mentioned it himself, and that gave me my opportunity.

"I want to ask you something about these events," I told him. "Have you yourself any theory to account for them at all?"

"*Distinguo*," said he, after a short pause; "without committing myself to a theory to fit every case, they do seem to me to fall into several classes.

"In one category I should place those 'voices' which warn me of events that have happened quite recently, or are actually happening at the moment, but a long distance away; such as the ones that told me of the deaths of my father and brother. Cases of this kind may, perhaps, be due to thought transference, or telepathy; as you yourself suggested, if you recollect, when I first told you of those instances.

"A second type are the 'voices' which order me to go to some place or do some special thing, which I should probably have avoided if left to myself; and on these I have my own opinion, but, if you do not mind, I would rather keep it to myself.

"A third class are those experienced in certain places or in connection with certain articles; such as the story I told you of the Persecution Chalice, or of my hearing the last Mass of Father Philip Rivers the martyr. Such as these would fall into line with the cases we often hear of haunted houses. You know the modern theory of the subject, of course?"

"I'm not at all sure that I do," I answered, "but, in any case, I should like you to explain it to me, and how it bears upon your own experiences."

"Oh, well," he replied, "the idea is just this; that a place or a thing, such as a weapon or article of furniture—almost anything, in fact, which has played a part in events that aroused very intense emotional activity on the part of those who enacted them—becomes itself saturated, as it were, with the emotions involved. So much so, in fact, that it can influence people of exceptional sympathetic powers, and enable them to perceive the original events, more or less perfectly, as if they were re-enacted before them. Thus, in some cases, the person will see the occurrence as if taking place before his eyes. In my case, I hear the words or sounds, just as if I were present on the original occasion, possibly some centuries before."

"That is a new idea to me," I said, "but it doesn't seem impossible. Hitherto the only theory of haunting which ever seemed at all plausible to me was the old-fashioned one that the spirit of a guilty person was sometimes compelled, as part of its purgatory, to frequent the scene of its crime, and there re-enact the events which it now detested. Much in the same way as we hear of a murderer being irresistibly drawn to revisit the spot where he slew his victim, in spite of the evident danger he runs of arousing suspicion thereby."

"I see no reason why both theories should not be true," he answered; "some cases would demand one explanation, some another. In fact, if my experiences go to prove anything, they show that the theory you call 'old-fashioned' is at least as likely to be true as the one I outlined for you just now."

"I scent another story," I cried, "for none of those you have told me, as yet, suggested a soul in purgatory as the chief agent in the 'direct speech.'"

"If it comes to that," said he, with a smile, "I suppose I could give you half a dozen instances where such an explanation seems the most obvious and natural one. But, before we leave the question of explanations, is there anything else you would like to ask me about the subject?"

"Well, yes," said I, with some hesitation, "but if you think me impertinent or too inquisitive, please do not hesitate to say so. I would far sooner drop the subject altogether, than run any risk of hurting your feelings."

"My dear boy," said the old priest, with more emotion than I had seen him exhibit hitherto, "please, please do not talk to me like that. God knows I am a poor enough specimen of what a priest should be, but heaven forbid that I should allow my feelings to block the way whereby you, or I, or any man, may come to understand the manner of his dealings with his creatures. I may fail, indeed I must fail to some degree, in making clear the truth in these matters; just as everyone who tries to express himself always fails to convey things to others as perfectly as he himself perceives them. But that is quite another thing from hiding the light that God reveals to me, in order to save my feelings from possible laceration."

"I am sorry, sir," said I, "I spoke foolishly; but I need not assure you that no such suggestion was intended by me, for a moment."

"I know, I know," he answered quickly, "but the point is one on which I feel strongly, more strongly than most men, perhaps; and you will humour an old man in it, will you not? But go on and ask the question which you had in mind."

"Well, sir," I said rather slowly, for his gentle outburst had distracted me from what I meant to say, "the point I wished to put to you was this. With regard to these experiences of yours, does their occurrence, their frequency, or intensity, coincide with any special state, or set of circumstances, in yourself? I mean such things as physical health, spiritual fervour, intellectual activity or their opposites."

"Really, I don't know that I ever analysed them in that way," he answered. "But, speaking generally, I should say that in the great majority of cases I have been in perfect health at the time, and certainly up to my normal standard of intellectual activity. As regards the spiritual atmosphere on such occasions, I have often remarked that events of this kind always seem to take place when my state of soul is absolutely calm and natural, and, consequently, when my sense perception and judgement are least likely to be deceived."

"Thank you, sir," I said, "that seems to me an important point, since for anyone who knows you personally it disposes of the idea that the whole thing may be self-deception. But you spoke just now of an instance, or possibly of half a dozen instances, where the 'voice' you heard seemed to be that of a soul in purgatory. Would you mind telling me of such a case?"

"I will do so with pleasure," said he, "and the story I will tell you has this further interest, that it is free from an objection you made once before; I mean, that so many of these events seem purposeless. In this case, as you will see in the sequel, what I heard was very much to the point.

"You may remember my telling you of an Austrian priest, a great friend of mine, to whose home I was travelling when I was obliged to undertake an extraordinary 'sick call'; and how I next met my friend years later in Rome?" I nodded my acquiescence, and he continued, "Well, it was then that the event took place of which I propose to tell you. By that time my friend had become the head of one of the ecclesiastical colleges in Rome, and, at the personal request of the Austrian Emperor, he had been made a titular archbishop. As he was now a *personaggio distinto*, I felt a little doubtful about intruding on him, but he was so genuinely pleased when I did call that my fears all vanished, and we soon became as intimate as ever.

"One afternoon I had arranged to call for him soon after lunch, so that we might take a long walk together; but on my arrival he met me with apologies.

"'I am sorry to upset our plan,' he said, 'but this morning I received a note from my sister, begging me to go and see her at once. She is a nun in one of the strictly enclosed convents here in Rome, and was solemnly professed only a few weeks ago, just before you came out from England. You have never met her, she is the youngest of the family and a good many years my junior.'

"Of course, I said that the postponement of our excursion did not matter in the least, and proposed that I should walk with him to the convent. 'I will wait in the church, during your interview,' I said, 'and afterwards we can take a stroll on the *Pincio*, if you are not kept too long.' He fell in with the proposal at once, and we set out for the convent, which was quite at the other side of the city, fully half an hour's walk from the college.

"On our arrival the out-sister conducted us both to the parlour, when I explained that I would wait in the church, while the archbishop spoke with his sister. The nun then said that she was the sacristan, and would take me to the church through the sacristy, as that was the shortest way. Accordingly, we left the archbishop, and, crossing the passage, passed through a doorway inscribed '*Sagrestia*'

"'But what a large, handsome sacristy,' I exclaimed in Italian, for I had not expected anything on such a big scale. '*Sì, Signore*,' answered the nun, evidently pleased at my surprise; and she explained how, some years before, the nuns had converted the upper portion of one transept into a new choir for themselves, and the lower half had then become the sacristy. 'See,' she added, 'the old pavement is still here,' and she pointed to a number of incised slabs in the floor which marked the site of old interments. Then she opened another door and I passed into the church, asking her to let me know when the archbishop was ready.

"The building was a typical Roman church of the seventeenth century; a nave with small side chapels off it, but no aisles, a low dome at the crossing of nave and transepts, and a shallow apsidal sanctuary. A short inspection of the interior revealed nothing of special interest, so I soon settled down in a quiet corner of the transept opposite the sacristy door and said a few prayers. After some minutes I rose from my knees and sat down on a bench at the side, chancing as I did so to glance at the windows of the nuns' choir, high up in the opposite transept.

"The windows were filled with glass, frosted in some way to prevent one seeing through, but the strong light behind cast the shadow of a kneeling nun across the window as she prayed with her face towards the Blessed Sacrament, which was reserved on the High Altar of the church below. Vaguely I wondered who she was and for what she was praying, and then the figure rose and moved to one side. The silhouette was in profile now, so evidently, she was kneeling before some shrine or picture which stood in the *choretto* itself, at the side of the window.

"I think I have mentioned that, in some cases, when the 'direct speech' comes to me it is heralded by a kind of premonition in myself. Gradually I become less and less perceptive of the things around me, a feeling of bodily fatigue and a sense of muscular lassitude grows upon me, while my mind becomes unusually alert. Then, out of this— physical insulation, may I call it?—a kind of sympathetic union seems to arise between myself and the unknown person, and, finally, the 'direct speech' is heard. It was so in this case, as I gazed up at the figure of the nun who knelt and prayed before the shrine. Then, as from sheer fatigue I closed my eyes, abruptly in my ears came the voice of someone speaking, speaking rapidly, in Italian, with piteous tense accents, as if in extreme pain and distress.

"'No, no, no—do not ask *me* to pray for you. It is all wrong, I say; terribly wrong. A saint! My God, it is I who need your prayers. Oh, why do not they pray for me, that I may rest in peace? O my God, I am punished indeed. Punished for my folly, my pretences, my hypocrisy. Oh, do not pray to me, pray *for* me. Pray, pray for me, the wretchedest of sinners. Oh, pray for me, that God may grant me rest.'

"This went on for some minutes, the distress of the speaker becoming more intense, as if her protests went unheeded by those to whom she spoke. Then, all at once, came silence, and, opening my eyes, I looked up at the tribune. For a moment the shadow of the nun's figure fell across the window, and then she moved away, her prayers completed, and I heard no more.

"With a sense of great relief, I came back to myself again, and for some minutes sat pondering over what I had heard. What could it all mean? Something was wrong inside the convent, I felt certain, but before I had got my thoughts clear, the Sister Sacristan returned and told me that the archbishop had left the parlour, and was waiting for me in the vestibule.

"I got up at once, and joining my companion, we left the convent together. My mind was still full of the words I had heard, and of speculation about their meaning, and we must have walked a considerable distance without either of us speaking. All at once it struck me that I was neglecting my friend, and I glanced towards him, with some trifle of small talk on my lips. To my surprise his face was set and stern, with tense lips and frowning eyes, and, as I thought, an expression half puzzled and half angry. At this the trifle I had meant to say fled from my mind, and instead of it I blurted out abruptly:

"'Something is wrong, then, in the convent, as I fancied?' With a look of surprise, the archbishop turned his gaze full upon me, and I felt that I had given myself away.

"'Explain yourself, friend Philip,' he said at length.

"'Oh, well!' I answered, as lightly as I was able, "it is easy to see that something has upset you, and in any case your sister would not have sent you such an urgent message, unless she had some reason for it.'

"'That is not good enough, my friend,' he answered gently. 'You spoke as if my expression of annoyance had confirmed a suspicion of your own. There is something behind those words of yours, Philip; something which it may be important for me to know. See now, I will be quite frank with you. I left the convent, disturbed and mystified by something which had just been said to me, and your first words show that you too have been affected in the same way. My dear Philip, you must tell me the cause of your anxiety, and then, in my turn, I will tell you what is troubling me.'

"'Well, if you must know,' I said, 'while you were in the convent, I went into the church, and, after a few prayers, I sat down and fell into a reverie;' and then I told him all I have just told you, and how the words I heard had left me worried and anxious. The archbishop listened to my story in silence, and I was half afraid he would laugh at me, but at its close he seemed more serious than ever.

"'It is a strange experience,' he said, when I had finished, 'I don't know that I envy you your curious faculty. But now I must tell you what is troubling me. When you left me to go to the church I waited in the parlour; a plain bare room with a double grille across the centre, and two or three chairs on either side of it. I sat down, and after a little while my sister came in, accompanied by one of the elder nuns—you know their rule forbids them to see a visitor alone. We talked for some time in Italian, for my sister mentioned that the other did not understand German well, but nothing was mentioned which explained why she had sent for me, and I hesitated to ask her in the presence of her companion. It struck me, however, that she seemed ill at ease, and, luckily, an opportunity arose which gave me a few words with her alone.

"'I had inquired after the Reverend Mother, and the elder nun asked if I would like to see her. I said "Yes," and she rose and went out, saying she would go and call her to the parlour. Immediately we were alone my sister said to me, "Sigismund, for God's sake go to the Holy Father and get permission to make a visitation of the convent." Astonished at her vehemence I answered, "My dear sister, whatever is the matter?" "I cannot tell you," she replied, "for I am sworn to secrecy; but if you make a visitation I think you may find out for yourself."

"'Just at that moment the other nun returned with the Reverend Mother, so I could not ask her any more questions. You will imagine I felt in no mood for further conversation, so I simply told the Superioress that I did not wish to leave without seeing her, and after a few minutes' conversation I gave them my blessing and left. Now my sister is a strong-minded woman, and I am convinced she would not have spoken as she did without good reason; and your curious experience makes me still more determined to look into the matter carefully.'

"He stopped speaking, and we walked on in silence for some little time, and then I asked him, 'How do you propose to proceed in the affair?'

"'Well,' he answered, 'I shall begin by going to the *Vicariate*, where I have a friend who is one of the secretaries to the Cardinal Vicar, and who has charge of the archives. If there is anything out of the common in the past history of the convent, he will be able to tell me. Then I shall ask for an audience with the Cardinal Vicar himself, and tell him the whole story. I have very little doubt that he will empower me to enter the enclosure and inspect the convent as his deputy, or else will appoint some discreet person to do so. If he is not prepared to take any action at all, I shall go to the Holy Father himself, and ask his permission to make a visitation in person. In the interval I will ask you to keep the whole affair a secret. I shall probably know more in a day or two, and then I will tell you how I have got on.' By this time, we had reached the college again, and I said goodbye at the door, as the archbishop was evidently disinclined for further conversation.

"During the next few days, I was busy renewing my acquaintance with various favourite spots in the Eternal City, and in that congenial occupation the incident at the convent was forgotten for the time. In fact, it must have been almost a week later that, on returning to my lodgings one evening, about the hour of the *Ave Maria*, I found one of the archbishop's cards on my table, with the words 'Please come and see me at once,' written on it in English. Accordingly, I put on my hat again, walked round to the college, and asked the porter to let the archbishop know that I had come.

"'But his Excellency is expecting you, my Father,' replied the man; 'he told me to say, when you came, that he would be in his private study, and begged you would come up to him.' I knew the way, so I thanked the porter and went upstairs, where I found the archbishop walking up and down his room as if waiting impatiently.

"'Good,' he exclaimed, as I entered, 'I was getting afraid you might not come at all tonight; and I want your help, Philip.'

"Of course, I said I was entirely at his disposal, and asked how his inquiries had prospered.

"'Sit down, and I will tell you all about it,' he answered, and when we were both seated, he continued,

"'I went to see my friend at the *Vicariate* that very evening, after you had left me, and told him exactly what had happened, including your own experience.' I suppose I changed countenance at this, for he added quickly, 'Don't be annoyed with me, Philip, he is a man of great piety and remarkable discretion, and he will not repeat the story without your express permission.

"'Well, at the time he had nothing to tell me about the convent, but he promised to make a search in the archives, and see if there was anything there which seemed likely to help us; and then, on the Friday following, he sent for me. This time he had quite a dossier of papers, and we went through them together. Some of them dated from years back, and most were merely formal documents relating to the election and approval of superiors, dispensations, appointments of confessors, and other ordinary routine business. I was beginning to despair of finding anything that would help us, when we turned up a document, dated nearly twenty years ago, and headed, "*In the matter of the late Donna Anastasia Fulloni, formerly Superioress, etc., and a Petition for the admission of a Cause of Beatification—Report*."

"'It proved to be a copy of a long formal report prepared for the Congregation of Rites, to whom the nuns had sent in a petition asking for the usual commission of inquiry into the heroic sanctity of their Superioress, then lately dead, which is the first preliminary step in a cause of canonisation.

"'The whole thing was really pitiful reading, for the evidence of the chaplain to the convent and of the medical man who attended the nun on her deathbed all went to show that the poor woman, far from being a saint, was a weak-minded creature, whose vanity had led her to practise a whole series of deceptions in order to create the impression that she was favoured with visions, ecstasies, and other divine privileges. On her deathbed she had confessed the truth, and commissioned her confessor to let the real facts be known, should this become necessary.

"'Unfortunately, he took no action in the matter, and in the interval quite a little cultus began to grow up at her grave in the south transept of the church, attached to the convent. Then, finally, the nuns drew up and sent in the petition of which I told you. Of course, after this report, the Sacred Congregation dismissed the petition, and prohibited any further cultus. The whole incident was considered closed, and in fact it had been quite forgotten, until my visit led to the disinterring of the report I have mentioned.

"'There was nothing else of any importance among the papers, but my friend promised to see the Cardinal Vicar and let me know what he decided; then, early on the Monday, I got a note ordering me to call at the *Vicariate* at noon to see the Cardinal himself.

"'When I got there, I found my friend with His Eminence, who told me that he had heard the whole story, and wished me to make a visitation of the convent as his deputy. Of course, I said that I would gladly undertake the task, and then he asked me to name some discreet priest whom I should like to have with me. I suggested your name, which he accepted at once, saying that he had met you himself; and then, as the third member of the commission, he appointed his secretary the archivist, adding that he knew him to be a friend of my own. Today I received the document of authorization for the three of us to enter the enclosure, and hold a formal visitation of the convent as agents of the Cardinal Vicar; and the nuns have notice to expect us tomorrow about ten o'clock.'

"I was not displeased to have an opportunity of solving the mystery, if there were one, so I promised to join the archbishop and his friend at the college in good time next morning, and soon afterwards went back to my lodgings.

"Next day I reached the college about nine o'clock, and found the archbishop with his friend from the Vicariate, to whom he introduced me. The archivist was an Italian priest, about sixty years old, with white hair, and a wonderful smile that reminded me of the portraits of St Philip Neri. We talked for some little time, and got on together so well that, when the carriage was announced, I felt as if I had known him for years.

"On arriving at the convent, the archbishop produced his mandate, and the three of us were admitted into the enclosure and conducted to the chapter-room which opened off the main cloister. Here we found the whole community waiting for us, some eighteen choir-nuns and nine or ten lay-sisters. On being asked if all were present the Superioress answered that one sick nun was absent in the infirmary, and on further inquiry this one proved to be the sister of the archbishop. The archivist then explained that we had been sent by the Cardinal Vicar to hold a visitation as his deputies; and that the three of us together would interview each of the nuns in turn.

"The community then retired, returning one by one to be interrogated by the archbishop. Most of them declared that everything about the convent was quite satisfactory, though some points of detail were mentioned; but we heard nothing to confirm our suspicion of an illicit cultus. When all had been seen, we had a few minutes' private talk, and agreed to go through the convent first on our tour of inspection, and finally to visit the infirmary and interview the archbishop's sister, whose sickness seemed curiously inopportune.

"The Reverend Mother and four of the nuns then conducted us round the cloister and ground-floor rooms, and afterwards to the choir chapel upstairs. This chapel, you will remember, was really the upper portion of one transept of the church, but the nuns had redecorated the walls in typical Roman style, with great panels of red silk damask, framed in gilded mouldings. All this time, I ought to say, I had felt in perfect health, and no suspicion of what was to happen had crossed my mind. But the moment we entered the chapel the physical oppression which I had felt in the convent church on my previous visit returned with overwhelming force.

"Laying my hand on the archbishop's arm, I told him in a whisper what was the matter, and he hurried me forward to a chair which stood close to the large window that opened into the church. I sank into the chair, for I was almost fainting, but after a minute or so I felt stronger and opened my eyes. Opposite to me there was a *prie-dieu*, placed so that anyone kneeling on it would face not towards the altar in the church beneath, but towards the side wall of the chapel.

"'It was there the nun I saw was kneeling, Sigismund,' I whispered, 'ask the Reverend Mother to take down that red silk panel.'

"The archbishop beckoned the Superioress forward, and made the request I had suggested.

"'But it is not meant to be removed,' the nun expostulated volubly, but with evident nervousness.

How is one to take it down without damaging it?"

"The archbishop turned to the group standing at the entrance of the chapel. 'Which is the sacristan?' he asked, and one of the nuns came forward.

"'Remove this,' he ordered, pointing to the wall beyond the *prie-dieu*. The nun hesitated a moment, but a stern look from the archbishop decided her, and going up to the wall she kneeled down, as if to get at something near the floor. There was a click, as if a lock were turned, and the tall silk panel swung outwards like a door. As it did so a wild shriek of laughter rang through the chapel. It was the Superioress, whose self-control had suddenly failed her, and she burst into violent hysterics.

"The other nuns ran forward quickly, but the archbishop's voice rang out in a tone of command. 'Let the Sub-prioress and sacristan stay here, and the rest of you take your Prioress to her room. I will send for anyone I want, when I am ready.'

"We waited before the open panel, while the shrieks of hysterical laughter grew fainter, and finally died away in the distance, and then the archbishop turned to me.

"'Do you feel equal to moving now, Philip?" he asked.

"'Certainly,' I said, 'the faintness has passed away; and in fact, I felt my normal self once more.

"'Good,' he replied, 'then we will continue our inspection; and turning to the two nuns who were still with us, he bade them go before us through the door revealed in the wall.

"You will have guessed the rest of the story already. Beyond the secret door was a small room fitted up as a chapel. In the centre was a kind of shrine, decorated with a red velvet pall or covering, elaborately embroidered in gold, and surrounded by candles. It contained the remains of the late Superioress, Anastasia Fulloni, which the nuns had exhumed from their grave in the transept beneath, after it had become a sacristy.

"By dint of searching inquiries we found that the foolish women had refused to accept the decision of the Congregation of Rites in the matter of her beatification, and had developed a private cultus of their own; converting what had been a tribune, with a gallery opening into the transept, into the secret chapel which we had discovered so dramatically." The old man paused, as if his story were ended, but I could not let him leave it so incomplete.

"Surely," I asked, "the authorities took a very grave view of the affair, did they not?"

"Yes, indeed," replied he, "for such a thing is a most serious scandal. The archbishop reported the whole matter to the Cardinal Vicar, and a few days later was summoned to the Vatican, where he repeated it to the Holy Father in person. Within a week the convent was suppressed, each nun being sent to a different house of the Order, except the archbishop's sister, who was allowed to choose for herself the convent she preferred. A year or two later the church and conventual buildings were handed over to one of the new religious congregations of men, which had not previously possessed a house in Rome. The newcomers destroyed the nuns' choir, and opened the transept into the church once more, turning the tribune, which had formed the secret chapel, into an organ loft.

"The body of Anastasia Fulloni was reburied in its former grave, where you may still read the original inscription on the slab unchanged, and I doubt if there are now fifty people living who remember the poor creature's name. But, for my part, every time I have been in Rome since then, I have made a point of visiting the church and saying Mass there for the repose of her soul."

★★★★★★★★★★★★★★★★

As one of Father Pater's friends has expressed some doubt whether he would have approved the publication of this story, seeing that he was an ardent supporter of contemplative life, especially in the case of women, it will be of interest to add the following extract from my diary of the date on which he told it to me :

". . . Squire told me true but very curious story of convent in

Rome, where private cultus of a deceased nun was developed in defiance of the authorities. I asked if occurrences of such a kind—*i.e.*, indicating a misconception of religious ideals and contempt for authority—were at all common among enclosed religious. Squire said: 'No; quite the contrary. In fact, the chief interest of the story is that, so far as I know, it is a unique example of such folly among nuns, who, as a class, are people of strong common sense, about the last folk in the world to originate a bizarre and improper novelty, such as a false cultus. If the event had not happened within my own personal experience, I should not have believed it possible, and, even as it is, I cannot understand how it can have developed so as to involve the whole community.

'If we knew the inner history of the convent, I am convinced we should find some quite exceptional influence at work, to throw the good sense of the nuns off its balance so terribly. As a student of psychology—and the psychology of religion in particular—I think the story ought to be put on record, since it manifests such an abnormal development. It may be that, in the light of new psychological laws as yet unknown to us, an explanation of the whole may be forthcoming.

'But I want you to understand clearly that the incident is quite without a parallel, and is no more typical of the normal type of convent than the actions of a maniac are typical of a sane man. But just as the study of lunacy has cast a flood of light upon normal psychology, so a story like this may help to elucidate the laws of religious psychology, and for that reason I am anxious it should not be forgotten.'"—R. P.

"Of Such is the Kingdom of Heaven"

One afternoon I had walked to the village with the squire, as he wished to visit a pensioner of his, an old woman who lay bed-ridden in a cottage close by the little church, which his father had built about the year 1840, for the Catholics of the neighbourhood. I knew the old priest would prefer to be alone with "Aunt Sarah," as she was always called, so I said I would wait in the church during his visit, and he promised to come back there for me as soon as he was ready. Either Aunt Sarah was more garrulous than usual, or else the squire forgot about the lapse of time, for I waited and waited; a quarter of an hour, half an hour, three-quarters of an hour, and my patience was rapidly ebbing away.

I had explored every corner of the church and read the inscriptions on the various memorials, and now I moved out into the churchyard and began to repeat the process outside. I could not have been there more than a minute or two, when I heard a step behind me and there was the old priest, full of apologies.

"I was in hopes you would have gone for your walk and left me," he said. "I am so sorry for keeping you so long, but somehow, we got talking and I never noticed how the time was slipping by. You must have been dreadfully bored, for the study of tombstones is not an exhilarating pastime, though this place has a great charm for me; but then I have known almost every one of those who lie buried here, while to you they are simply so many names with their dates of birth and death. That cross there, for example, marks the grave of my old nurse, Susan Norham; and just beyond it lies old Wilson, who was butler at the hall before I was born, and retained the post for more than fifty years. Just here at our feet lies that dear child, Mary Clayton;" and the old man pointed with his stick to a long horizontal slab incised with a simple Gothic cross.

I looked down at the inscription, which ran as follows:

Pray for the soul of Mary Crayton, Born 1870, Died 1887. *'Jesus called a little child unto him.'*

"Was she not rather old to be called 'a little child,'" I asked thoughtlessly, not noticing how the old priest's eyes had filled with tears, as he stood looking down at the grave in silence.

"Rather old in years, perhaps," he answered gently, "but in purity and simplicity she was a child still. *'Except ye be converted and become as little children, ye cannot enter the kingdom of heaven'*—I never realised how true that was, until Mary Clayton revealed it to me." Then he turned away with a sigh, and passing through the private gate which opened into the park, we walked on in silence for a minute or two.

"Would you care to hear about her?" he asked at length. "It is a simple story, but I think a very beautiful one; and I fancy you would find it interesting too." I accepted the offer eagerly, and as we had reached a seat by the side of the lower lake, the old man sat down upon it and began.

"Mary Clayton was born in the village here on the feast of our blessed Lady's Assumption, that was why she was christened Mary. Her father was the last of a family of Catholic yeomen, who had worked on the estate for generations past; a simple, strong, young fellow, devoted to our family, and as reliable as he could be. Her mother was an orphan girl, who had been brought up by some nuns in their convent, and it may have been largely due to their influence that she was such an exceptionally refined, gentle creature.

"One would have said they were meant for long life and happiness; but the ways of Providence are not our ways, and William Clayton, Mary's father, died from the effects of an accident, two or three years after the child was born. His wife was literally heart-broken at losing him, and the village people used to say that she was like a woman in a dream for the rest of her life. She died when Mary was twelve years old, and on her deathbed, I promised to look after the orphan girl myself.

"At that time Susan Norham, my old nurse, whose grave you saw just now, was still alive and acting as housekeeper for me, so I asked her advice on the best way of fulfilling my promise. I did not want to educate the child above her station in life, but at the same time her exceptional character was even then apparent, and I wished to keep her close at hand so that I could see for myself how she would develop.

"Susan took in the situation at once, and with her strong practical common sense found an obvious solution for me. It appeared that she needed, or thought she needed, another girl to help in the house, and although Mary was only a little over twelve, she volunteered to take her at once.

"'You see, sir,' she explained, 'it is better for me to have a young girl and teach her the work slowly but properly, instead of taking one who thinks she knows all about it before she begins, and so has a lot to unlearn.'

"The scheme seemed a capital one, so Mary came to Stanton Rivers, and was apprenticed, so to speak, to Mrs. Norham. I used to see her at Mass, and occasionally met her about the house; but I was careful not to let the other servants see that I took any special interest in her, and no one but the old housekeeper, who was absolutely trustworthy, had any idea that I was her legal guardian. It was nearly two years before anything occurred to bring the child into personal relations with me at all, and the way it happened was this.

"Then, as now, Avison used to serve my Mass every morning, and all the other servants, of course, attended it. I had never thought of getting anyone else taught to serve Mass, and so, when Avison was suddenly taken rather seriously ill, there was, for all I knew, not one of the men in the place who was able to act as server. I foresaw overnight that this difficulty might occur, so I told Mrs. Norham to inquire in the servants' hall if there was anyone who knew how to answer at Mass. At first it seemed that there was no one, but after a moment little Mary Clayton admitted shyly that she could do so.

"Next morning the child answered for me at Mass, and she did it so well that I sent for her later in the day to say how pleased I was. She was now nearly fourteen, and old for her age, and somehow our talk developed into an intimate spiritual conference, and she told me quite a lot about herself.

"It appeared that her mother had taught her to practise mental prayer from the time of her tenth birthday, and she had kept up the practice ever since. I asked how she managed to find time for it, and she told me that she did so by getting up early, so as to spend half an hour in prayer before beginning work at half-past six. On her mother's advice, too, she had begun to go to Communion every week, and, rather to my surprise, she asked if it would be possible for her to communicate more often in future.

"You must remember that this was many years before the famous *motu proprio* of Pius X on frequent Communion, and I felt a little doubtful on the subject. Not, of course, that there was anything rash in so excellent a desire, but I feared it might attract attention and lead to gossip in the servants' hall. In the end the difficulty solved itself, as such things always do when God wishes it. I found that it was part of Mary's work to dust the chapel and keep it tidy, and that she always did this the first thing in the morning. I arranged, therefore, to give her Communion privately, before she began her work, and the half-hour's mental prayer thus fitted in perfectly as a time of preparation. I told Mrs. Norham of the arrangement and warned her not to let it become known to the other servants; and thanks to her discretion and to the fact that the chapel is somewhat out of the way, I fancy none of them ever discovered that one of their number was a daily communicant, for such Mary soon became.

"From this time on she made me her confessor and spiritual adviser, and I soon realised that she was already far advanced in the way of perfection. Her sense of the presence of God was extraordinarily vivid, and while she had, of course, read nothing of the great mystical writers, she described herself as 'feeling our blessed Lord at her side,' in words which were almost identical with those of St Teresa. Besides the intense personal love of Jesus, of which this sensible presence was the outcome, she cherished a deep devotion to our blessed Lady, whom she had come to regard quite literally as her mother, since the time when she was left an orphan.

"It happened that her fourteenth birthday occurred a month or two after our first conversation, and the next morning, after I had given her Communion, she asked if she might speak to me a moment. I consented, of course, supposing that she had something to ask about her work, but what she told me was this.

"On the previous night she had gone to bed as usual and soon fell asleep. After a few hours she awoke; at least, so it seemed to her at the time, but in the morning, she was doubtful if it were not all a very vivid dream. Whichever it was, however, she seemed to herself to be standing near the end of a long corridor, with a number of doors on one side and a row of windows on the other. Some distance down the corridor was a group of figures, 'like beautiful young ladies,' who were moving slowly towards her. When they had approached quite close, the foremost of them moved aside and she saw in the centre of the group a lady of wonderful beauty and dignity, 'like a great queen,' and she knew in some inexplicable way that it was the blessed Mother of God.

"Her first sensation was one of fear—I felt as if I should like to sink into the ground,' she said; but this passed away immediately, as the Queen of Heaven smiled and held out her hand towards the child. Mary fell on her knees and kissed the outstretched hand, a feeling of intense love and gratitude surged through her heart, and while she remained kneeling, not daring to look up, our blessed Lady spoke to her.

"'You love my Son, little one,' she said. 'Love him ever, more and more. If you do so, you shall join us some day, and shall see him face to face, as do all they who love him truly.'

"With this she turned and passed, with her train of attendants, through one of the doors at the side of the gallery, and Mary was left alone, but with a sense of indescribable joy.

"It was certainly a remarkable experience, and I was not prepared to say if it were a vision or only a dream, but as time passed and the effects on her soul showed themselves to be both good and lasting, I felt that it was a direct grace from God. When months went by, however, and nothing of the kind occurred again, I began to think it was probably a dream, and took occasion to impress upon her that she must not attach importance to such things, as the smallest step forward in perfection was more valuable than any number of visions. She received what I said with perfect submission, and so far from showing any sign of over-valuing the occurrence, I soon found that she was giving far less thought to it than I was.

"Things went on as usual for a year, and Mary made a very definite advance in prayer, entering upon what mystical writers call the 'Prayer of Simplicity' or 'of loving attention to God,' which is often a kind of preliminary to the lower stages of mysticism; then, after twelve months, the feast of the Assumption and the child's fifteenth birthday came round together. For my part I had quite forgotten that it was the anniversary of her experience of the previous year, and she told me herself that this fact had escaped her memory till afterwards; but the next morning, after her Communion, she again asked if she might speak to me.

"'You remember the dream, or whatever it was, which I had last year, Father,' she said, 'about our blessed Lady, I mean? Well, last night she came again.'

"I asked her to tell me exactly what happened, and she repeated precisely the same story as on the previous occasion, until she came to the point where the blessed Mother of God spoke to her.

"'This time she said more to me, Father,' she told me, 'and as far as

I can remember it was this :

"""My child, you have done as I directed, and my Son loves you yet more dearly, because he sees how earnestly you strive to please him. Persevere in this and he will reward you greatly, for you shall be one of my chosen band of virgins and shall join us hereafter.""

"Then, as before, she turned and passed through one of the doors at the side of the corridor, and this time Mary rose from her knees and tried to follow. One of the attendant virgins, however, stopped her, saying gently:

"'Not yet; you must not come with us now, but you shall do so later,' and passing through she closed the door behind her. 'This time, too, Mary noticed that the door through which the blessed Virgin and her suite had passed seemed nearer the end of the gallery than on the previous occasion, and she observed that it was the third door from the end.

"The next twelve months saw a wonderful progress in the soul of the child—for so I still regarded her, though she was far ahead of me in things spiritual. She asked and obtained my consent to make a vow of chastity for a year, and from that time forward began to experience the prayer of quiet. I rather expected, after what had happened, that she would be favoured with further experiences in the way of visions; for I no longer doubted that what she had received was a vision and not merely a dream. Nothing of the kind occurred, however, which was a reassuring fact, as showing that the two previous occurrences were not likely to be subjective or produced by the imagination; but one thing did take place which I think bore upon the situation.

"It must have been shortly before Christmas, and therefore some four months after the second vision, that she told me one day how she had lately felt an intense desire to suffer for Christ's sake. I knew she was not over-strong and very sensitive to pain, so I hesitated to give any sort of approval to the proposal she made, that she should offer herself to our Lord as a victim, in expiation of the evil wrought against him by sinners. I told her that I did not think she ought to do anything of the kind without a very definite inspiration to do so, and forbade her to make any such offering of herself without my permission.

"A week or two later came Christmas Eve, and I said Mass just after midnight and gave Communion to all the servants, Mary among the rest. It chanced that she was the last of all to communicate, and immediately after she had received, I walked back to the altar with the ciborium. My mind was full of the feast and the infant Saviour of the world; nothing, I suppose, was further from my thoughts than Mary's wish to offer herself to Jesus as a victim for the sins of others. I replaced the ciborium in the tabernacle, and, as I did so, chanced to raise my eyes so that they fell upon the crucifix above. At the same moment a voice seemed to whisper in my ears:

"'*For this cause was I born, and for this cause came I into the world.*' . . . '*He that taketh not up his cross and followeth after me, cannot be my disciple.*' . . . '*Suffer the little children to come unto me and forbid them not.*' At once the conviction forced itself upon me that these words had to do with Mary's wish to immolate herself by vicarious suffering. I finished the Mass and unvested, for I meant to say the other two Masses in the morning, and after completing my thanksgiving rose to leave the chapel. By the door I saw Mary, still kneeling, and as I approached, she came forward to meet me.

"'You have something to tell me, Father, have you not?' she said, to my surprise. 'Jesus told me at Communion that you had.'

"'It is true, my child,' I answered, for I could have no doubt now as to the meaning of the words I had heard. 'I withdraw my command; you may offer yourself to Jesus as you wish, and may he accept your service and bless you in all things.' With this I hurried out, for I could not trust myself to say more.

"A couple of weeks later Mrs. Norham came to me one morning and said that she thought Mary ought to see the doctor. I asked why, adding that I had seen the child about her work as usual, and that she appeared to be quite well.

"'So, she does, sir,' answered the old housekeeper, 'but I happened to go into her room this morning without knocking, for I knew she ought to be downstairs at the time. Instead, I found her kneeling at the bedside and groaning. I asked her what was the matter, and she said 'Nothing.' But I told her, people don't kneel all of a heap and groan because nothing is the matter with them, and in the end, she admitted that her back was hurting badly. It's my belief she has strained herself in some way, though neither she nor I can think of what has done it, and I shan't be easy till she has seen the doctor.'

"Of course I had the doctor sent for at once. He came, examined Mary, and agreed that she must have incurred some strain, and recommended her to be kept quiet in bed for a few days; to which prescription Mrs. Norham added a good deal of poulticing, etc., on her own account. I had to be away from home for a fortnight or so just then, and when I returned the girl was up again and about her work as usual. She admitted to me that the pain came on at times, and was often very bad at night; but added that it usually disappeared in the morning, so that she was able to get up for Mass as if nothing were the matter.

"In this way the year slipped by, and Mary's patience and resignation seemed to increase as the pains became more frequent. At length the feast of the Assumption came round again, and I felt pretty sure that it would not pass without some special occurrence. Sure enough, next day, Mary told me that the blessed Mother of God had visited her a third time.

"'It was soon after midnight, Father,' she said, 'and I feel sure it was not a dream this time, for my back had been hurting me terribly all night, and I had not slept for a moment. Everything happened just as it did before, except that, after I had kissed the blessed Mother's hand, she laid it on my head for a few moments, saying as she did so:

"'"Have courage, my child, and do not flinch in your sufferings. You have chosen the best way to the heart of my Son, and Jesus loves you most dearly for doing so. Be brave and persevere a little longer. Next time I come, it will be to take you to him." With that she passed out of the corridor, and I noticed this time that the door through which she went was the last but one in the row.'

"For the first time the significance of the doors occurred to me.

"'It was the third door last time, was it not, my child?' I asked her; 'and the fourth door the time before that?'

"'Yes, Father,' she replied; 'at least I think it was the fourth door through which she went the first time I saw her, but I am sure it was the third one a year ago, and the second one last night.'

"'What do you think it means, this matter of the doors?' I asked, though I had no doubt in my own mind. Her answer showed me that the same idea had occurred to her also, for she replied:

"'I think it means that the next feast of the Assumption will be my last birthday, Father, and that on it, Jesus will take me to himself.' A look of intense happiness came into her face as she said this, and I felt convinced it would prove correct.

"From that day the pains in her back became intensified and scarcely ever left her. I had a great specialist down to examine her, and he told me afterwards that nothing could be done.

"'The girl has evidently received some injury to the spine,' he said. 'It may possibly have occurred several years ago and only become evident very slowly as she grew up. However, there is no doubt about her condition now, and I must tell you at once that her case is a hopeless one. She will live some months for certain, possibly even for a year or more, but human skill can do nothing to save her. Of course she must do no work, and before long she will have to take to her bed permanently, and then the end will not be far off.'

"When he had gone Mary asked me what his opinion was. I hesitated for a little, but finally told her that he said her case was hopeless, but that she might linger for a year or even longer, and that her sufferings would not grow less. I wish you could have seen the look of joy that came over her as she listened.

"'Thanks be to God,' she said gently, when I had finished. 'Pray for me, Father, I beg you, that I may not prove unworthy of so wonderful a grace.'

"The year dragged on and Mary's sufferings were sometimes terrible to witness; but with them came consolations so marvellous that, at times, I longed to change places with her. She advanced rapidly in things spiritual, and her prayer soon began to include short periods of mystical union. Not long after her sixteenth birthday she told me that she had seen in a vision the hands of our blessed Lord, pierced with the sacred stigmata and bleeding, and that at the same moment he had said to her: 'Thus am I wounded in the house of my friends.'

"This was the first 'imaginative vision' of Jesus that she had received, and I had some difficulty in reassuring her, for her first impression on coming to herself had been that it was a delusion. Later she beheld his sacred feet, as if nailed to the cross, and later still the wound in his side. Then on Good Friday, at midday, she passed into a trance, and remained so for fully three hours. On recovering the use of her senses, she told me that she had seen our blessed Lord hanging on the cross before her, and that he had spoken many things to her, but forbade her to repeat them, save this, that of all his creatures he loved those best who strove to follow in his footsteps, and suffered gladly for the sins of others as he himself had done on Calvary.

"From that day, so far as I could judge, Mary entered upon the supreme state of prayer which mystical writers call 'spiritual nuptials.' Her ecstasies were now of almost daily occurrence; so, to keep the state she was in from the knowledge of the servants, I installed two nursing sisters from a well-known convent, the Superioress of which was a personal friend of mine, so that I was able, through her, to bind them to secrecy, so long as Mary lived.

"A week or so before the feast of the Assumption all pain suddenly ceased, and the relief was so great that for some hours the nurses began to hope she might recover. I spoke to her on the subject that evening when I visited her, and she told me this was a mistake.

"'It is our blessed Lord's doing,' she explained to me. 'He does not wish me to lose the opportunities of the next few days, so he has taken away all pain from me, to free me from distraction. From this time on I must attend to him only, so pardon me, Father, if I speak very little, even to you.'

"After that, though I saw her three or four times a day, she seldom spoke more than a few words, and those were simply loving expressions of thanksgiving to God for the graces she was receiving, which, she said, made her feel as if she were almost in heaven already. Her strength grew less every day, and I judged that the time had come for her to receive the last Sacraments; for the doctor had warned me that a collapse might come abruptly at any time now. I told her what I thought, and she at once agreed; so, I anointed her and administered Holy Viaticum on the following morning, which was the 13th of August.

"It happened that I was obliged to be away all that day on business, so I did not see her again until the next morning, when I found her evidently much weaker. She could only speak in a faint whisper now, and I asked the nurse to leave us alone for a little while, as I thought she might wish to speak to me privately; nor was I wrong.

"' Father,' she said, 'I am all alone. Since yesterday morning, when you gave me the last Sacraments, I have lost all sense of the presence. Jesus seems to have left me, as his disciples left him in his passion. His presence has gone from me, as wholly as if I had never known it.'

"I told her she must be brave and accept the deprivation as God's holy will. That he knew what was best for her, and doubtless wished her to suffer in solitude and darkness as he had suffered. She caught at the word 'suffer,' and murmured faintly:

"'It is true, Father; you are right, for I am suffering again terribly.'

"'Then has the pain returned, my child?' I asked her.

"'Oh, yes,' she whispered, 'it has all come back again, only it is far worse than ever before; I feel as if my back had broken. I can scarcely endure to lie still for a moment, but if I try to move, I find I cannot.'

"When the doctor came, I told him how the pain had all returned; and he answered that, in that case, the end could not be far off. After remaining with Mary for some time, he came out and told me that he did not think she would live through the night, and that he intended to give her some morphia to allay the pain she suffered. I insisted that he should ask her permission before doing so, and, as I expected, she gently but quite absolutely refused to take it. About sunset, however, the pain grew less acute, and finally she fell asleep, for she was utterly worn out with the sufferings of the last four-and-twenty hours; and the nurse told me she would probably pass away without waking.

"Somehow, I felt fairly sure that this would not be the case; so, about eleven o'clock I came back to her room and sat by her bedside, saying *Matins* and *Lauds* of the Assumption. Perhaps you will think it was all subjective and due to the circumstances of the moment; but I have never felt the inspiration of the breviary so marvellously as I did that night, as I sat there, saying the office of the blessed Virgin by the bedside of her dying child.

"You remember the gospel of the feast; it is the one which tells how Jesus came to the house of Martha and Mary, and ends with the words 'Mary has chosen the best part, which shall not be taken away from her.' As I repeated them, I glanced at the dying girl who lay there motionless, her face thin and pale with the long months of suffering, which she had endured so bravely for the love of God. In a few hours now it would all be over, and I knew for certain that she had indeed chosen the best part, and would find the same reward as Mary Magdalen.

"When I had finished the office, I looked at my watch—it was well past midnight; the feast of the Assumption, Mary's seventeenth birthday, had dawned. Then I think I must have fallen asleep, for the next thing I remember was hearing a clock in the passage strike three. I roused myself at once and, looking at Mary, found that she too was awake. Her eyes were open, and she gave me a smile of recognition as I bent towards her, asking if there was anything she wished me to do.

"'Pray for me, Father,' she answered, in a whisper so low that I could only just hear it. 'I feel so faint and exhausted that I can scarcely say a prayer myself, but I must live until our holy Mother comes for me.'

"'Do you think she will come soon, now? I asked her.

"'Yes, indeed,' she answered, 'very, very soon; and this time I know she will take me with her.'

"I wish I could give you some idea of the calm conviction of her words; it was as if she were speaking of something about which no doubt could possibly arise, and her worn, pale face was all alight with the joy of expectancy. I told her to lie still and not exhaust herself with speaking, and like an obedient child she closed her eyes and lay silent for an hour or more. 'Then, all at once, her eyes opened and she spoke again in a quick, eager whisper.

"'Hark, Father,' she said, 'do you not hear the music?"

"'What music, my child ?' I answered in surprise.

"'Oh, but you must hear it, Father,' she continued. 'It is faint, and far away; but oh! so clear and lovely, Listen, it is coming nearer every moment.' There was a pause for perhaps a minute and then she spoke again.

"'It must be she, our Mother—she is coming for me—did I not tell you she was coming for me—Ah!'

"With a gasp she ceased speaking, and, to my utter amazement, the dying child, who had been unable to move for many days past, sat up in bed without the slightest sign of pain. Quickly I put out my arm to support her, lest she should fall back, but there was no need. She sat erect, her body rigid and motionless, nor did I feel the slightest pressure on my arm.

"For fully a minute she remained like that, silent and entranced; her eyes gazing straight before her with a fixed intensity, utterly absorbed by the vision that I could not see.

"'O blessed Mother,' she murmured softly, 'Mother of God, and our most gentle Queen and Mother; Mother of Jesus, take me to my Lord.'

"A long pause followed, while Mary sat there motionless, with parted lips, as if listening intently. Then suddenly a wonderful smile lit up her features.

"'Jesus,' she murmured, 'Jesus, Jesus, Jesus,' and then the limp weight of her body fell against me, and I laid it softly back upon the pillow.'"

The Astrologer's Legacy

May 26th, St Philip's feast, is the squire's birthday, and every year he celebrates the day by giving a little dinner party to a few very intimate friends. But, as he says, rather sadly, "I have outlived most of my generation"; and, for some years past, the whole number, including the host and a guest or two who may be staying at the Hall, has seldom reached as many as ten.

On the first birthday for which I was present there were only half a dozen of us in all at the dinner. These were, first, Father Bertrand, an English Dominican Friar, and one of the squire's oldest friends, who usually spent some weeks with him every summer. Second, Sir John Gervase, a local baronet and antiquarian, who, besides being an F.S.A., and one of the greatest living authorities on stained glass, was also one of the few Catholic gentry in the neighbourhood of Stanton Rivers.

The third was Herr Aufrecht, a German professor, who had come to England to study some manuscripts in the British Museum, and had brought a letter of introduction from a common friend in Munich. Fourth, there was the rector of the next parish, who had been a fellow of one of the colleges at Cambridge for most of his life, but had accepted the living, which was in the gift of his college, a few years previously, and had since become very intimate with the old squire, who, with myself, completed the number.

The mansion of Stanton Rivers is built round a little quadrangle, of which the servants' quarters and kitchen occupy the north side, the dining-room being at the north end of the west wing. When we are alone, however, the squire has all meals served in the morning-room; a small, cheerful apartment on the east side of the house, with dull, ivory-coloured walls, hung with exquisite old French pastels, and furnished entirely with Chippendale furniture, designed expressly for the squire's grandfather by the famous cabinet maker; the original contract and bills for which are preserved in the family archives.

The birthday dinner, however, as befits an "institution," is always served in the dining-room proper, which is approached through the beautiful long apartment, stretching the whole length of the west wing, which the squire has made into the library. The dining-room is large and finely proportioned, and has its original Jacobean decoration, the walls being panelled in dark oak, with a carved cornice and plaster ceiling delicately moulded with a strapwork design, in which the cockle shells of the Rivers' escutcheon are repeated again and again in combination with the leopards' heads of Stanton. The broad, deep fireplace has polished steel "dogs" instead of a grate, and above it is a carved overmantel reaching to the ceiling, and emblazoned with all the quarterings the united families can boast, with their two mottoes, which combine so happily, *Sans Dieu rien* and *Garde ta Foy.*

I think the squire would prefer not to use the dining-room even for his birthday dinner, but he hasn't the heart to sadden Avison, the butler, by suggesting this. Indeed, the occasion is Avison's annual opportunity, and he glories in decking out the table with the finest things the house possesses in the way of family plate, glass, and china: while Mrs. Parkin, the cook, and Saunders, the gardener, in their respective capacities, second his efforts with the utmost zeal.

The evening was an exquisite one, and we sat in the library talking and watching the changing effects of the fading lights as they played on the garden before the windows, until Avison threw open the folding doors and announced that dinner was served. Hitherto I had only seen the room in *déshabillé*, and it was quite a surprise to see how beautiful it now looked. The dark panelling, reflecting the warm sunset glow which came in through the broad mullioned windows, formed a perfect background to the dinner-table, with its shaded candles, delicate flowers, and gleams of light from glass and plate: and I felt that Avison's effort was really an artistic triumph. The same thought, I fancy, struck the rest of the guests, for no sooner had Father Bertrand said grace than Sir John burst out in admiration:

"My dear squire, what exquisite things you do possess! Someday I shall come and commit a burglary on you. Your glass and silver are a positive temptation."

The host smiled, but I noticed that his eyes were fixed on the centre of the table, and that the eyelids were slightly drawn down, an expression I had learned to recognise as a sign of annoyance, carefully controlled. Following his gaze, I glanced at the table-centre, but before I could decide what it was, the German professor, who was sitting next me, broke out in a genial roar:

"*Mein Gott,* Herr Pater, but what is this?" and he pointed to the exquisite piece of plate in the centre of the table.

"We call it the Cellini fountain, Herr Aufrecht," answered the squire, "though it is certainly not a fountain, but a rose-water dish, and I can give you very little evidence that it is really Cellini's work."

"Effidence," exclaimed the German—"it has its own effidence. What more want you? None but Benvenuto could broduce such a one. But how did you come to possess it?"

There was no doubt about the eyelids now, and I feared the other guests would notice their host's annoyance, but the squire controlled his voice perfectly as he answered:

"Oh, it has been in the family for more than three centuries; Sir Hubert Rivers, the ancestor whose portrait hangs at the foot of the stairs, is believed to have brought it back from Italy."

I thought I could guess the cause of his annoyance now, for the ancestor in question had possessed a most unenviable reputation, and, by a strange trick of heredity, the squire's features were practically a reproduction of Sir Hubert's—a fact which was a source of no little secret chagrin to the saintly old priest. Fortunately, at this point, the rector turned the conversation down another channel; Herr Aufrecht did not pursue the subject further, and the squire's eyelids soon regained their normal elevation.

As the meal advanced the German came out as quite a brilliant talker, and the conversational ball was kept up so busily between Father Bertrand, the rector, and himself that the other three of us had little to do but listen and be entertained. A good deal of the talk was above my head, however, and during these periods my attention came back to the great rose-water dish which shone and glittered in the centre of the table.

In the first place I had never seen it before, which struck me as a little odd, for Avison had discovered my enthusiasm for old silver, and so had taken me to the pantry and displayed all the plate for my benefit. However, I concluded that so valuable a piece was probably put away in the strong-room, which would account for its not appearing with the rest.

What puzzled me more was the unusual character of the design, for every curve and line of the beautiful piece seemed purposely arranged to concentrate the attention on a large globe of rock crystal, which formed the centre and summit of the whole. The actual basin, filled with rose-water, extended beneath this ball, which was supported by four exquisite silver figures, and the constant play of reflected lights between the water and the crystal was so fascinating that I wondered the idea had never been repeated; yet, so far as my knowledge went, the design was unique.

Seated as I was, at the foot of the table, I faced the squire, and after a while I noticed that he, too, had dropped out of the conversation, and had his gaze fixed on the crystal globe. All at once his eyes dilated and his lips parted quickly, as if in surprise, while his gaze became concentrated with an intensity that startled me. This lasted for fully a minute, and then Avison happened to take away his plate. The distraction evidently broke the spell, whatever it was, for he began to talk again, and, as it seemed to me, kept his eyes carefully away from the crystal during the rest of the meal.

After we had drunk the squire's health, we retired to the library, where Avison brought us coffee, and about ten o'clock Sir John's carriage was announced. He had promised to give the rector a lift home, so the two of them soon departed together, and only the professor and Father Bertrand were left with the squire and myself. I felt a little afraid lest Herr Aufrecht should return to the subject of the Cellini fountain, but to my surprise, as soon as the other two were gone, the squire himself brought up the subject, which I thought he wished to avoid.

"You seemed interested in the rose-water fountain, Herr Aufrecht," he remarked, "would you like to examine it now that the others are gone?"

The German beamed with delight, and accepted the proposal volubly, while the squire rang the bell for Avison, and ordered him to bring the Cellini fountain to the library for Herr Aufrecht to see. The butler looked almost as pleased as the professor, and in a minute the splendid piece of plate was placed on a small table, arranged in the full light of a big shaded lamp.

The professor's flow of talk stopped abruptly as the conversationalist gave place to the connoisseur. Seating himself beside the little table, he produced a pocket lens, and proceeded to examine every part of the fountain with minute care, turning it slowly round as he did so. For fully five minutes he sat in silence, absorbed in his examination, and I noticed that his attention returned continually to the great crystal globe, supported by the four lovely figures, which formed the summit of the whole. Then he leaned back in his chair and delivered his opinion.

"It is undoubtedly by Cellini," he said, "and yet the *schema* is not like him. I think the patron for whom he laboured did compel him thus to fashion it. That great crystal ball at top—no, it is not what Benvenuto would do of himself. Think you not so?" and he turned to the squire with a look of interrogation.

"I will tell you all I know about it in a minute, professor," answered the old priest, "but first please explain to me why you think Cellini was not left free in the design."

"*Ach* so," replied the German, "it is the crystal globe. He is too obvious, too assertive; how is it you say in English, he 'hit you in the eye.' You haf read the *Memoirs* of Benvenuto?" The squire nodded. "*Ach*, then you must see it, yourself. Do you not remember the great morse he make, the cope-clasp for Clemens *septimus*? The Pope show to him his great diamond, and demand a model for a clasp with it set therein. The other artists, all of them, did make the diamond the centre of the whole design.

"But Cellini? No. He put him at the feet of God the Father, so that the lustre of the great gem would set off all the work, but should not dominate the whole, for *ars est celare artem*. Now here," and he laid his hand upon the crystal globe, "here it is otherwise. These statuette, they are perfection, in efery way they are worth far more than is the crystal. Yet, the great ball, he crush them, he kill them. You see him first, last, all the time. No, he is there for a purpose, but the purpose is not that of the design, not an artistic purpose, no. I am sure of it, he is there for use."

As he finished speaking, he turned quickly towards the squire, and looked up at him with an air of conviction. I followed his example, and saw the old priest smiling quietly with an expression of admiration and agreement.

"You are perfectly right, professor," he said quietly, "the crystal was put there with a purpose, at least so I firmly believe; and I expect you can tell us also what the purpose was."

"No, no, Herr Pater," answered the other. "If you know the reason, why make I guesses at it? Better you should tell us all about it, is it not so?"

"Very well," replied the squire, and he seated himself beside the little table. Father Bertrand and myself did the same, and when we were all settled, he turned to the professor and began:

"I mentioned at dinner that this piece of plate was brought from

Italy by Sir Hubert Rivers, and, first of all, I must tell you something about him. He was born about the year 1500, and lived to be over ninety years old, so his life practically coincides with the sixteenth century. His father died soon after Hubert came of age, and he thus became a person of some importance while still quite young. He was knighted by Henry VIII a year or two later, and soon afterwards was sent to Rome in the train of the English Ambassador.

"There his brilliant parts attracted attention, and he soon abandoned his diplomatic position to become a member of the Papal entourage, though without any official position. When the breach between Henry and the Pope took place, he attached himself to the suite of the Imperial Ambassador, thus avoiding any trouble with his own sovereign, who could not afford to quarrel still further with the emperor, as well as any awkward questions as to his religious opinions.

"Of his life in Rome I can tell you practically nothing, but if tradition be true, he was a typical son of the Renaissance. He played with art, literature, and politics; and he more than played with astrology and the black arts, being, in fact, a member of the famous, or infamous, Academy. You may remember how that institution, which was founded in the fifteenth century by the notorious Pomponio Leto, used to hold its meetings in one of the catacombs. Under Paul II the members were arrested and tried for heresy, but nothing could be actually proved against them, and afterwards they were supposed by their contemporaries to have reformed. We know now that in reality things went from bad to worse. The study of paganism led them on to the worship of Satan, and eventually suspicion was again aroused, and a further investigation ordered.

"Sir Hubert got wind of this in time, however, so he availed himself of his position in the household of the Imperial Ambassador, and quietly retired to Naples. There he lived till he was over eighty, and no one in England ever expected him to return. But he did so, bringing with him a great store of books and manuscripts, some pictures, and this piece of plate; and he died and was buried here in the last decade of the sixteenth century.

"His nephew, who came in for the estates on his death, was a devout Catholic, and had been educated at St Omers. He made short work with Sir Hubert's manuscripts, most of which he burned, as being heretical or worse, but he spared one volume, which contains an inventory of the things brought from Naples. Among the items mentioned is this fountain. In fact, it has a whole page to itself, with a little sketch and a note of its attribution to Cellini, besides some other words, which I have never been able to make out. But I think it is clear that the crystal was used for evil purposes, and that is why I dislike seeing it on the table. If Avison had asked me, I should have forbidden him to produce it."

"Then I am ver' glad he did not ask you, *mein Herr*," observed the German, bluntly, "for I should not then have seen him. But this inventory you speak of, is it permitted that I study it?"

"Certainly, Herr Aufrecht," replied the squire, and walking to one of the bookcases, he unlocked the glass doors and took out a small volume, bound in faded red leather with gilt ornaments.

"This is the book," he said; "I will find you the page with the sketch," and a minute later he handed the volume to the professor. I glanced across and saw a little drawing, unquestionably depicting the piece of plate before us, with some lines of writing beneath; the whole in faded ink, almost the colour of rust.

The professor's lens came out again and, with its aid, he read out the description beneath the picture.

"*Item. Vasculum argenteum, crystallo ornatum in quattuor statuas imposito, Opus Benevenuti, aurificis clarissimi. Quo crystallo Rome in ritibus nostris pontifex noster Pomponius olim uti solebat?*"
("Item. A vessel of silver, adorned with a crystal supported on four statuettes. The work of Benvenuto, most famous of goldsmiths. This crystal our Pontiff Pomponius was wont to use in our rites at Rome in days gone by.")

"Well, that sounds conclusive enough," said Father Bertrand, who had been listening intently. "*Opus Benevenuti, aurificis clarissimi*, could only mean Cellini; and the last sentence certainly sounds very suspicious, though it doesn't give one much to go upon as to the use made of the crystal."

"But there is more yet," broke in Herr Aufrecht, "it is in another script and much fainter." He peered into the page with eyes screwed up, and then exclaimed in surprise, "Why, it is Greek!"

"Indeed," said the squire, with interest, "that accounts for my failure to read it. I'm afraid I forgot all the Greek I ever knew as soon as I left school."

Meanwhile the professor had produced his pocket-book, and was jotting down the words as he deciphered them, while Father Bertrand and myself took the opportunity to examine the work on the little

195

plaques which adorned the base of the fountain.

"I haf him all now," announced Herr Aufrecht, triumphantly, after a few minutes. "Listen and I will translate him to you," and after a little hesitation he read out the following:

"In the globe all truth is recorded, of the present, the past and the future.
To him that shall gaze it is shown; whosoever shall seek he shall find,
O Lucifer, star of the morn, give ear to the voice of thy servant,
Enter and dwell in my heart, who adore thee as master and lord."

Fabius Britannicus,

"*Fabius Britannicus*," exclaimed the squire, as the professor ceased reading, "why, those are the words on the base of the pagan altar in the background of Sir Hubert's portrait!"

"I doubt not he was named *Fabius Britannicus* in the *Accademia*," answered the German; "all the members thereof did receive classical names in place of their own."

"It must be that," said the squire; "so he really was a worshipper of Satan. No wonder tradition paints him in such dark colours. But, why—of course," he burst out, "I see it all now, that explains everything."

We all looked up, surprised at his vehemence, but he kept silent, until Father Bertrand said gently:

"I think, Philip, you can tell us something more about all this; will you not do so?"

The old man hesitated for a little while and then answered: "Very well, if you wish it, you shall hear the story; but I must ask you to excuse me giving you the name. Although the principal actor in it has been dead many years now, I would rather keep his identity secret.

"When I was still quite a young man, and before I decided to take orders, I made friends in London with a man who was a spiritualist. He was on terms of intimacy with Home, the medium, and he himself possessed considerable gifts in the same direction. He often pressed me to attend some of their *séances*, which I always refused to do, but our relations remained quite friendly, and at length he came down here on a visit to Stanton Rivers.

"The man was a journalist by profession, a critic and writer on matters artistic, so one evening, although we were quite alone at dinner, I told the butler, Avison's predecessor, to put out the Cellini fountain for him to see. I did not warn him what to expect, as I wanted to get his unbiased opinion, but the moment he set eyes on it, he burst out in admiration, and, like our friend the professor tonight, he pronounced it to be unquestionably by Benvenuto himself.

"I said it was always believed to be his work, but purposely told him nothing about Sir Hubert, or my suspicions as to the original use of the crystal, and he did not question me about its history. As the meal advanced, however, he became curiously silent and self-absorbed. Sometimes I had to repeat what I was saying two or three times before he grasped the point; and I began to feel uncomfortable and anxious, so that it was a real relief when the butler put the decanters on the table and left us to ourselves.

"My friend was sitting on my right, at the side of the table, so that we could talk to each other more easily, and I noticed that he kept his gaze fixed on the fountain in front of him. After all it was a very natural thing for him to do, and at first, I did not connect his silence and distraction with the piece of plate.

"All at once he leaned forward until his eyes were not two feet away from the great crystal globe, into which he gazed with the deepest attention, as if fascinated. It is difficult to convey to you how intense and concentrated his manner became. It was as if he looked right into the heart of the globe not *at* it, if you understand, but at something inside it, something beneath the surface, and that something of a compelling, absorbing nature which engrossed every fibre of his being in one act of profound attention.

"For a minute or two he sat like this in perfect silence, and I noticed the sweat beginning to stand out on his forehead, while his breath came audibly between his lips, under the strain. Then, all at once, I felt I must do something, and without stopping to deliberate I said in a loud tone, 'I command you to tell me what it is you see.'

"As I spoke, a kind of shiver ran through his frame, but his eyes never moved from the crystal ball. Then his lips moved, and after some seconds came a faint whisper, uttered as if with extreme difficulty, and what he said was something like this:

"'There is a low, flat arch, with a kind of slab beneath it, and a picture at the back. There is a cloth on the slab, and on the cloth a tall gold cup, and lying in front of it is a thin white disc. By the side is a monster, like a huge toad,' and he shuddered, 'but it is much too big to be a toad. It glistens, and its eyes have a cruel light in them. Oh, it is horrible!' Then all at once the voice leaped to a shrill note, and he spoke very rapidly, as if the scene were changing quicker than he could describe it.

197

"'The man in front—the one with a cross on the back of his cloak—is holding a dagger in his hand. He raises it and strikes at the white disc. He has pierced it with the dagger. It bleeds! The white cloth beneath it is all red with blood. But the monster—some of the blood has fallen upon it as it spurted out, and the toad is writhing as if in agony. Ah! it leaps down from the slab, it is gone. All present rise up in confusion; there is a tumult. They rush away down the dark passages. Only one remains, the man with the cross on his back. He is lying insensible upon the ground. On the slab still stands the gold cup and white disc with the blood-stained cloth, and the picture be-hind——' and the voice sank to an inaudible whisper, as if the speaker were exhausted."

"Almost without thinking, I put a question to him before the sight should fade entirely. 'The picture, what is it like?' But instead of an-swering he merely whispered '*Irene, da calda,*' and fell back as if ex-hausted in his chair."

There was silence for a few moments.

"And your friend, the spiritualist," began Father Bertrand, "could he tell you nothing more of what he saw?"

"I did not ask him," answered the old priest, "for, when he came to himself, he seemed quite ignorant of what he had told me during his trance. But, some years afterwards, I got some further light on the incident, and that in quite an unexpected way. Just wait a minute, and I will show you what I believe to be the picture he saw at the back of the niche!" And the old man walked to one of the bookcases and selected a large folio volume.

"The picture I am going to show you is an exact copy of one of the frescoes in the catacombs of SS. Peter and Marcellinus, where I came upon it, quite unexpectedly, during my period in Rome as a student; it has been reproduced since by Lanciani in one of his books. Ah, here it is," and he laid the album on the table.

There, before us, was a copy of an undeniable catacomb fresco depicting an "agape" or love-feast; a group of figures symbolical both of the Last Supper and the communion of the elect. Above it were the contemporary inscriptions, "*IRENE DA CALDA*" and "*AGAPE MISCE MI*," while round about were scrawled, in characters evidently much more recent, a number of names: "*POMPONIUS, FABIANUS, RUFFUS, LETUS, VOLSCUS, FABIUS*" and others, all of them members of the notorious Academy. There they had written them in charcoal, and there they still remain today, as evidence how the innermost recesses of a Christian catacomb were profaned, and the cult of Satan practised there, by the neo-pagans of the fifteenth and sixteenth centuries.

We sat looking at the picture in silence for a minute or so, and then Herr Aufrecht turned to the Dominican.

"Fra Bertrand," he said, "you are Master in *Theologia*, what is your opinion of all this?"

The friar hesitated for a moment before he answered.

"Well, Herr Aufrecht? he said at length, "the Church has never ceased to teach the possibility of diabolical possession, and for my part I see no reason why a thing," and he pointed to the crystal, "should not become 'possessed' in much the same way as a person can. But if you ask my opinion on the practical side of the question, I should say that, since Father Philip here cannot legally part with his heirloom, he certainly acts wisely in keeping it under lock and key."

A Porta Inferi

Professor Aufrecht returned to London next day and I went with him as far as the junction, where I had some shopping to do, so I saw nothing of the squire and the old Dominican Father until the evening. After dinner we were talking in the library when Avison came in and removed the coffee cups.

"I'm always a little afraid of Avison," remarked Father Bertrand confidentially, as the butler disappeared with his tray, "he makes me feel as if I must be on my best behaviour, like a schoolboy when the headmaster is present."

"I know what you mean," answered the squire, "I used to feel much the same with old Wilson, Avison's predecessor. But then, you see, Wilson once caught me in the pantry, eating the dessert, when I was supposed to be safely in bed in the nursery; and even after I became a priest and his master, I felt that he half suspected I should be up to the same trick again, if he wasn't on his guard! Now with Avison it is different; you see, he has only been here about thirty years, whereas Wilson was butler before I was born."

"Is it really thirty years since Wilson died?" asked Father Bertrand—"but yes, I suppose it must be. He was a splendid old man. I always used to think of him as a retainer, 'servant' was much too undignified a term for him. On my first visit here, I remember feeling that he was taking stock of me, and that, if I didn't pass muster, he would not allow you to ask me down again. Was it all my imagination, Philip, or did he exercise a veto on your visiting list?"

"Oh no," laughed the squire, "Wilson would never have taken such a liberty, but I must admit he contrived to let me know what he thought of my friends. Don't be afraid, Bertrand, you passed with honours on the very first occasion. 'Quite a gentleman, sir, the young Dominican Father,' was his verdict. Dear old Wilson, I can hear him say it now."

"Doesn't Thackeray say somewhere that to win the approval of a butler is the highest test of good breeding?" I asked.

"I don't remember that," answered the squire, "though I think he says that to look like a butler is the safest thing for a political leader, as it always suggests respectability. All the same, I came to trust Wilson's judgement, and it often stood me in good stead as a young man. But it is strange we should have got upon the subject tonight, for the only time I ever came near a quarrel with him was about his opinion of my friend the spiritualist, whose story I told you yesterday. The old butler took a strong dislike to him during his first visit here, and after he left, we had quite a little scene. Wilson literally begged me not to make an intimate of him, and I remember getting annoyed with the old man and telling him sharply to mind his own business. He took the rebuke like a lamb and begged my pardon for venturing to speak in such a way to me, 'But you can't tell, Mr. Philip,' he added, 'what it means to me to see a man like that among your friends.'"

"I meant to ask you what became of the spiritualist," said Father Bertrand, "but it slipped my memory. Was the incident you told us the only thing of the kind, or did you come across any other examples of his faculty?"

"Well," answered the squire, with a little hesitation, "perhaps you'll laugh at me, but old Wilson's opinion impressed me more than I cared to admit to him, and not long afterwards some facts came to my knowledge which went a long way to confirm it. In consequence I let our intimacy cool, and soon afterwards the man left England altogether, and I only met him once again, quite by accident, many years later." He paused for a moment, and then continued. "If you like I will tell you what happened on that occasion. The whole affair was over in a few hours, but while it lasted it was so startling that I have often thanked God since that I followed Wilson's advice and did not allow our former intimacy to develop.

"The incident I told you last night must have occurred about the year 1858, and the man passed out of my life within a year or so after that. Still, I never saw the Cellini fountain without it bringing him back to my mind, and I often wondered idly what had happened to him. I never heard a word about him, however, and in time I came to think he must be dead.

"More than twenty years later I was supplying at a mission on the outskirts of a large manufacturing town in the North. The place was not more than two or three miles from the heart of the city, but it was practically in the country, and the only exceptional feature about my work was the fact that I had to visit a large lunatic asylum which stood within the parish. The building had originally been the mansion of a county family, but they had died out, and when the property came into the market it was bought by the Corporation, and the mansion itself had been added to and adapted to serve its new purpose.

"There were a few Catholics among the inmates, and I found that one of the doctors was a Catholic too, so we soon became very good friends. One afternoon, as I was leaving the asylum, he asked me to go and have tea in his rooms. These were in a wing of the original building, where I had never been before, and his windows looked out on an old formal garden.

"'Why,' I exclaimed, 'I thought I had seen all the grounds, but this part is quite new to me.'

"'Yes, it would be,' he replied. 'You see, we have to keep the more serious cases separate from the others, and this part of the grounds is in their enclosure. If you like we will go round the old garden after tea; there probably won't be more than one or two patients in it, and it will be all right if I go with you.'

"To tell the truth I was always a little uneasy when I went among the patients, even the harmless ones, but my glimpse of the garden made me long to see it all; so, I accepted the offer, and when tea was over, we walked down on to the terrace beneath. The place had been laid out with great skill in the eighteenth century, and the paved walks with their old stone parapets and vases made an exquisite setting to the beds of bright flowers, relieved here and there by yew trees, clipped into fantastic shapes. There was not a soul about, and I quite forgot my uneasiness until we passed through an opening in a tall hedge at the bottom of the slope and came out on to a lawn beyond. At one end of this was a little pool, and my heart have a great thump as I looked at it, for kneeling by the side, so that his profile was turned towards us, was a man whose face was perfectly familiar.

"It was my former friend the spiritualist, and, except that his shoulders were bent and his hair absolutely white, his appearance had scarcely changed in all the years, so that I recognised him in an instant. But it was not the surprise of meeting him thus unexpectedly which made me catch my breath and held me speechless. What sent the blood back to my heart, and then made it surge to the brain in a great wave of pity, was his occupation; for carefully, with earnest gaze and rapt attention, he knelt there building castles in the mud! The doctor must have noticed that I was upset, for he took my arm, as if to lead me back again, when I stopped him.

"'No, no, Doctor,' I whispered, 'I'm not frightened; it isn't that. But the man kneeling there, I used to know him well, I am certain of it.'

"'Indeed,' he whispered back, 'he is the most curious case we have here—quite a mystery, in fact. I must get you to tell me what you know about him.'

"'Yes, certainly,' I answered, 'but I want to speak to him. He may turn and recognise me at any moment, and I do not want him to think I have come to spy upon him.'

"'You are right,' he replied, 'and if you can only gain his confidence, it may be of great importance, for he is a case of lost identity, and your old friendship may perhaps revive his memory, and reconnect him with the vanished past.' With this he led me up to where the man was kneeling, but he never turned nor seemed to notice our presence, until the doctor addressed him in a loud voice.

"'Come now, Lushington,' he said, 'I've brought an old friend to see you. Look up and see if you don't recognise him.' Very slowly, as if with an effort, the kneeling figure raised its head and turned towards us; but slow as the movement was, it barely gave me time to recover from my surprise, for the doctor had addressed him by a name that was utterly unlike the one he had formerly borne, and yet here he was answering to it, as if it were his own!

"'I wonder if you can recognise me after all these years?' I asked him, when he had gazed at me in silence for some moments without the smallest sign of recognition.

"'Recognise yer? No, I'm shot if I do,' he said at length; and I got another surprise, for the words were spoken in a hard, vulgar voice, totally different from the quiet, refined speech of my former friend.

"'Think again, Lushington,' said the doctor, 'for this gentleman is quite right, he used to know you well many years ago.' With a scowl the man turned upon him angrily:

"'What the blazes do you know about it, you little body-snatcher?' he snarled. 'I'll trouble you to mind your own business. As if you knew anything about me and what I was "many years ago." I wouldn't have spoken to you then, and wouldn't now, but that you've got me locked in this infernal prison of yours.'

"'It must be fully twenty years since last you saw me,' I said gently, for I wanted to calm him down, if possible, 'and I was a layman then, so my dress has changed as well as my appearance; but I hoped you might recollect my face.'

"'I don't, anyhow,' said he, though with less confidence I thought, as if some faint glimmer of memory were returning; 'but you says you're sure you know me, eh? Dick Lushington?"

"Quite sure of it, I answered. 'But I must admit one thing. When I knew you, twenty years ago, you were not called Dick Lushington, but . . . .' and I spoke the man's real name, which I had known him by. The effect was instantaneous and almost terrifying. No sooner had the words passed my lips than he leaped to his feet, shaking with passion. His face became livid with rage, he foamed at the mouth, and I thought he was going to have a fit.

"'Liar, liar, liar!' he shrieked in my face. 'How dare you say it? It isn't true—by Hell, I swear it isn't! He's dead, the blackguard that you say I am—I won't soil my lips by repeating his filthy name—and now you'll be saying I killed him. You devil, why don't you say it? It's a lie, of course, but so's what you said before—lies, lies, lies everywhere!' and the madman dropped to his knees again and drove his fingers deep into the mud. I noticed now that there was a warder standing behind us, and saw the doctor make a sign to him.

"'Come away, Father,' he whispered to me, 'we must give him time to calm down. The warder will look after him, and he will recover more quickly if we go away;' and taking my arm again he led me back towards the mansion. When we had passed through the hedge and were well out of earshot, the doctor began to speak again.

"'I'm afraid the experiment was not a great success, Father,' he said. 'I've never seen Lushington lose his self-control so suddenly, and the worst of it is that his heart is in a terrible state, so an outbreak like this is liable to prove fatal.'

"'It certainly was a terrible thing to witness,' I answered; 'but I'm not so sure we weren't successful in one respect. You are an expert in these matters and I know nothing about them, but surely the fact is clear now that he still knows his real name although he wishes others to be kept in ignorance of it.'

"'Certainly,' answered the doctor; 'but how does that help us, Father?'

"'First let me tell you what I can about his past life, in the days when I knew him,' I answered, 'and then you can say if my idea of his case is a possible one.'

"We had reached the house now, and when we were in the doctor's sitting-room again I told him all I knew. Put shortly it was this.

When I first met Lushington—I will use that name, if you don't mind, as there is no reason for disclosing his identity—he was a young man, well educated, with a comfortable private income of his own, and moving in good society in London, which was only natural, for he came of an excellent family. He was then beginning to dabble in spiritualism, and had been introduced to Home, the famous medium.

"For my part I tried to dissuade him from this, and always refused to attend any of their *séances*, though he often urged me to, but he ignored my advice and became more and more absorbed in his pursuit, as he found that he himself possessed special gifts as a medium; in fact, Home often urged him to devote his whole life to 'the Cause,' as he liked to call it. I also told the doctor the story you heard last night—I mean what happened here, when I brought out the Cellini fountain for him to see—and how, later on, his reputation had become an undesirable one and he had left the country, since when I had heard and seen nothing of him until that afternoon; and then I asked to be told the circumstances which led to his incarceration in the asylum. The doctor hesitated for a little before he answered.

"'Well, Father,' said he, 'you know we are not allowed to let such facts be known outside the staff, but I think you may be considered as one of ourselves. Not that there's much to tell in any case, for, as I told you, Lushington is our enigma. He was brought here about five years ago by the solicitor of a well-known public man, the head of the family to which he belongs; but even the family lawyer could tell us very little. His residence abroad, which you mentioned just now, must have terminated quite ten years ago, for he had been living in Belfast for five years or so before he came here. For a long time before that he had had no personal dealings with his relatives, but they kept in touch with him through the family solicitors, who used to send him a cheque for his half-year's income every six months, which cheques he always acknowledged.

"'The arrangement suited both sides, for Lushington wished to avoid his family, and I gathered that they returned the feeling, though I did not learn why; but what you say about his career as a medium no doubt supplies the explanation. However, shortly before he came here, instead of the customary formal note acknowledging their cheque, the solicitors received a long letter, full of foul language and abuse, with a deliberate accusation of dishonesty on their part, and a threat of legal proceedings for breach of trust and misappropriation of his money. The charge was manifestly absurd, but as the chief trustee was the public man I have mentioned, he could not run the risk of leaving such a charge unanswered, so one of the firm was sent over to Ireland to see Lushington and investigate the affair.

"'He arrived in Belfast to find that his man had been arrested the day before on a criminal charge, but on examination he was found to be hopelessly insane. The solicitor obtained full powers to act on behalf of the family, and he was brought here soon afterwards. But now comes the strange part of the affair. As you know, one element in his case is that of lost identity. The man insists that he is Dick Lushington, and either refuses to admit that he ever bore his real name, or else, as today, maintains that the man who bore it is dead. What makes this feature of his case so odd is that, years ago, a man called Dick Lushington really lived in Belfast.

"'He was a notorious bad lot, cunning and unscrupulous, an habitual criminal, in fact, who served numerous terms in gaol, and, when out of it, was leader of the worst gang of ruffians in the city. Finally, he committed murder, and, failing to escape, took his own life to avoid being arrested and hanged. But the oddest part of it all is this, that the real Dick Lushington killed himself *nearly thirty years ago*, long before our patient ever went to Belfast—in fact, while he was still quite young and respectable; yet one of the senior police officials there, who saw the man before he came here, declares that his voice and manner, his tricks of speech and choice of oaths, are identical with those of the notorious criminal Lushington, whose name this poor wretch has adopted, but whom he never can have seen!'

"'Extraordinary,' I said, 'it sounds like a case of possession;' but as I was speaking a knock came at the door and a warder entered.

"'Beg pardon, sir,' he said, addressing the doctor, "but I came to report about Lushington. After you and the other gentleman left the garden he calmed down, and I got him to come in quietly to his room. When he got there, he threw himself on the bed like one exhausted and began to cry, at the same time talking to himself in his other voice—you know what I mean, sir—like a gentleman. After a bit he called me up and said:

"""Tell him I want to see him."

"""Tell who?" says I.

"""Why, Philip, of course," says he—"the gentleman who was in the garden just now."

"'Well, sir, I didn't want to bother you with his nonsense, so I said I thought the gentleman was gone; but no, he wouldn't have it.

""Go and see," says he, and, try as I would, I couldn't put him off it. At last, I said I'd go and see, so here I am, sir.'

"'And a good thing too,' exclaimed the doctor impatiently. 'I only hope we shall not be too late, and find the quiet mood has passed. Come, Father, this is important. If Lushington is still in this state, you may be able to do something with him.'

"'By all means, let us go at once,' I said, rising, and we hurried off to the poor creature's cell, which the doctor and myself entered, leaving the warder outside, with instructions to come in at once if either of us called. The man was lying on his bed, apparently in a state of extreme exhaustion, but as we entered, he turned his head to see who we were, and a great sigh escaped his lips.

"'Oh, Philip, come to me,' he murmured faintly, and I hastened to the bedside and took both his hands in mine.

"'After all these years, to see you once again,' he said, almost in a whisper. 'Oh, Philip, if I had but taken your advice!' I pressed his fingers in my own, hardly daring to speak, and he lay silent, with eyes closed, for quite a minute. Then, all at once, his eyes opened, and he turned to me with a quick glance of terror.

"'Take me away with you, Philip,' he cried, 'quickly, before the other one comes back!' and he flung his arms round me like a frightened child. Gently I laid him back upon the bed, supporting the poor feeble body in my arms, and tried to reassure him.

"'You're all safe now, old fellow,' I whispered gently. 'He won't come back while I am here, no chance of it.'

"'Oh, do you think so?' he answered eagerly. 'Then—why—then you must never leave me. My God! how I hate him, devil that he is; and oh, to think I let him in so willingly!'

"'Well keep him out together, you and I, never fear of that,' I assured him bravely, though, even as I spoke, I was wondering what in the world it all meant; and then I added foolishly, 'Tell me, who is he?'

"'Who is he?' he almost shrieked, his terror returning more intensely than before. 'Who is he? Why, Dick Lushington, of course—the devil-man, who gets inside and uses me. He uses me, I tell you, like a slave. My hands, my limbs, my brain, my will, he's got it all, all of me, at his mercy. The filthy, hateful devil that he is, and did it by pretending to be my friend.'

"'Hush, hush, be calm,' I said, 'you will exhaust yourself. Be calm, he won't come back while I am here. You see, I am a priest now, did you know it? I promise you, you will be safe with me.'

"'Thank God for that,' he said more calmly, 'but oh, Philip, don't forsake me. I shan't last long now, I shan't keep you long. You were my friend once, be my saviour now. Promise me you'll be with me at the end. Don't leave me here to die, alone with him.'

"'I promise you faithfully that I will do everything in my power to help you,' I answered solemnly; 'but now you must rest yourself, and try to sleep,' and I laid his head back on the pillow, taking his hand in mine again, while he closed his eyes.

"'I will do anything—anything you tell me,' he whispered, 'only forsake me not, or I am lost.' Then he lay still, and in less than five minutes, to my amazement, the grip on my hand relaxed, his fingers fell back, and he was sleeping like a child. The doctor crept to the door and beckoned the warder in.

"'Stay here by the bedside,' he ordered, 'and if he wakes up, say to him at once, "Father Philip is still here and will come if you require him." If he says he does, pull the bell which communicates with my room.' Then he touched my arm and led me away on tiptoe along the gallery.

"'Well, I said, at length, when we had reached the doctor's room, 'I don't know what you think, but to my mind it seems a clear case of possession. I have heard of other similar cases among spiritualists.'

"'it certainly does look like it,' he admitted; 'but I am more concerned as to the immediate treatment than I am to explain the origin of his malady. Do you realise, my dear Father, what you have taken upon yourself?'

"'You mean by promising to do all I can for him?' I asked.

"'I mean by intervening in the case at all,' he answered grimly. 'The man's life is in your hands now, and if you fail him, if you are not at hand whenever he calls for you, I think the consequences will probably be fatal!'

"'I shall certainly not shirk the consequences of my promise,' I answered; 'but did you notice what he said to me? "I shan't last long now, promise me you'll be with me at the end." I may be wrong, but if he is convinced that he is dying, is it not more than probable that he will do so?'

"'Well, yes,' admitted the doctor, 'there is something in that. In fact, if he gets another paroxysm, like you saw in the garden, I do not think he will survive it. But short of that, I shouldn't be surprised if he were to linger on for some time, or even for several weeks.'

"'If he does, I shall have to make some arrangement about the parish work,' I answered, 'but my own belief is that he won't last many hours. I have learned to trust the instincts of a dying man.' We talked for some time longer on the point, each of us maintaining his own view, without convincing the other.

"'Well, I only hope you may be right,' said the doctor, at length; 'for many reasons it will be better so. Still, speaking merely from a professional point of view, I see no reason why——' but his words were cut short by the clash of a bell, ringing violently in the adjoining bedroom. The doctor leaped to his feet, and ran to the door between the two rooms.

"'No. 17!' he exclaimed, 'it is Lushington's cell. Come, Father'— and once more we hurried down the corridor. As we entered the room, I could scarce believe my eyes. The man we had left, not half an hour before, in a state of utter collapse was on the floor kneeling over the prostrate figure of the warder, who was trying to tear away the fingers of the maniac, which were tightly fastened on his throat. The doctor flung himself upon the kneeling man. The weight of the charge knocked him backwards, enabling the warder to rise. The madman's arms shot out, but luckily, I caught one of his wrists, and the warder, a big, powerful man, soon captured the other.

"'The handcuffs, in my pocket—quick, doctor,' he cried, 'get 'em out while we turn him over!'—and in a few seconds we had the poor wretch secured, with his wrists handcuffed behind his back. He went on struggling until the warder had got his ankles fettered with a strap, but the three of us were too much for him, and in a minute or so he was lying, safely pinioned, on the bed. All this while he had never spoken, though his breath came in great gasps that shook his whole frame; now, at length, he seemed calmer, and I thought it time to speak.

"You're all right now, old fellow,' I said gently, 'don't be afraid; it is I, Philip—I am here as I promised.' The man turned his eyes upon me, and the look of hatred in them was appalling.

"'All right, am I? he shrieked savagely. 'If it wasn't for these handcuffs, I'd soon show yer I'm all right. A nice, mean, low sort of priest's trick to play on me. Thought you'd get hold of yer old pal, and pilot him into heaven while number one was out, did yer? Bah!'—and he spat at me— 'you dirty swine!'

"'Ask the warder to wait outside, doctor,' I said, for a sudden inspiration came to me; and the man withdrew at his command.

"'What yer going to do now, curse ye—sing a hymn?' sneered the madman on the bed, as I took my breviary from my pocket. Without answering I turned to the prayers for the dying, and, kneeling down, began to recite them aloud and slowly, while the thing that animated my poor friend's body gave a shriek of malicious hatred.

"The scene that followed was literally indescribable, but I stuck to my task, and, as calmly as I could manage, went through the litanies and all the prayers for a departing soul; while the thing on the bed jerked itself from side to side, so far as the fastenings would allow, and the harsh, strident voice of Dick Lushington, the long-dead murderer, howled oaths, sang filthy songs, hurled curses at my head, and poured forth blasphemies unspeakable.

"As I reached the end of the prayers the question arose in my mind, 'What shall I do now?' when, all at once, a strange phenomenon occurred. It seemed as if some mighty force took hold of me, over-powering my limbs, my will, and all my faculties, so that I no more controlled my soul or body, but simply yielded myself up to serve. I was conscious that I had risen to my feet and was standing beside the bed. Then, in a tone of stern command, I heard my own voice speak the words, '*In the name of the Father and of the Son and of the Holy Ghost, I command thee, thou evil spirit, to go out of him!*'

"The body on the bed gave one tremendous heave, as if to break the bands with which it was fettered, and then fell back with a cry of baffled rage and frenzy, such as I never heard before and never wish to hear again. Then, gradually, before my astonished gaze, the face that was all distorted with anger grew calm, the purple flesh and swollen veins became deadly pale, and the eyes which looked up at me were no longer those of a madman, but the eyes of my long-lost friend. Then the lips moved feebly, and I caught a faint whisper.

"'God bless you, Philip, you have saved me! Jesus, be merciful to me a sinner.'

"The voice died away, one great sigh shook the frame of the dying man, and I quickly gave him the last absolution. There was silence for a minute or so, and then the doctor stepped forward.

"'You may come away now, Father,' he said softly. 'You have kept your promise. He is dead.'"

The Treasure of the Blue Nuns

The afternoon was a hopeless one, with driving rain and a bitter wind, which effectually prevented the old priest from getting out for his daily constitutional; so, after lunch he announced his intention of doing an afternoon's work in the chapel, a favourite expedient of his for rainy days. I volunteered to help him, and we were soon at work.

"I want to have all the relics out of their cupboard," he said, as he unlocked the carved oak doors of a tall aumbry at the north side of the little sanctuary. "Then we will get one of the maids to dust it out thoroughly, while we go over the reliquaries and clean them up a little. It struck me the other day that the place smelt rather fusty, and it must be quite a year since it had a regular cleaning."

The collection of relics at Stanton Rivers is a remarkable one, especially rich in memorials of the English martyrs, to whom the squire cherishes a great devotion, and the task of polishing the glass and silver of the numerous reliquaries kept us busy until it was time for tea. The old priest spoke little during the afternoon's work, but as we were putting the last of the relics into place again, he turned to me with a smile.

"If you will remind me later," he said, "I will tell you another of my stories. It shall be your reward for working so hard this afternoon;" and I noticed, as he spoke, that he took out a long envelope from the drawer in which were kept the papers authenticating the various relics. Then he locked the doors again and we went downstairs together. When tea was over and we had settled down before the fire in the library, I claimed the fulfilment of his promise.

"I don't think you have ever been to Mallerton," he began; "it is a big convent of enclosed nuns in the Midlands."

"No, sir," I said, "but I have heard of it; is it not one of the old foundations which were established abroad during the penal times?"

"Yes, certainly," he replied, "the convent was formerly at Paris. You remember the other day, when we had out the family pedigree, how one or two of the Rivers ladies were marked 'a blue nun at Paris.' Well, that is the same foundation, only the nuns returned to England at the time of the French Revolution and finally settled at Mallerton.

"Some years ago, I used to go there fairly often, to give retreats, attend professions, and so on, and the incident I am going to tell you about happened on one of these occasions. It must have been some time in the eighties. I had been working very hard for many months previously, and really did not feel equal to the task; for the effort of giving three discourses a day for eight days is far more fatiguing than most people would suppose. However, I did not want to disappoint the nuns, and as I was going to have a good holiday as soon as it was over, I began the retreat in spite of my condition.

"Within a couple of days, it was clear that I was really unwell, but I struggled on till the fourth or fifth morning, when I found, on rising, that I could scarcely stand; so I reluctantly abandoned the retreat and sent for the doctor. It happened that he could not get out to see me until the afternoon, by which time I was in a high fever, so he insisted on sending for a trained nurse to attend me. The nuns' chaplain wired to London, and late that evening two nursing sisters came down to Mallerton, the Abbess kindly arranging for them to be put up in the convent when not actually waiting upon me.

"Next morning I was no better. During the day my temperature rose still higher, and the good nuns began to be seriously alarmed about me. Later on, I learned that they arranged to keep up a continual chain of prayer before the Blessed Sacrament for me; taking it in turns to watch for an hour at a time, without a break by day or night. For my part I do not doubt that what happened was due in no small degree to their prayers, for I have known too many cases in which the combined prayers of contemplative religious have worked marvels to doubt about the reality of their power with the Giver of all mercies.

"That evening, when the chaplain came to see me, he brought a message from the Lady Abbess to the effect that she had sent me over 'the pillow,' and begged me to use it, as she had great faith in its efficacy. With this he produced a flattish, oblong cushion, covered with white linen, explaining that the nuns always used to put this under the pillows of any of their number who got ill, and that they firmly believed the convent tradition, which said that a great improvement in the invalid's condition often followed its use.

"I remember that he added some words of apology for bothering me about what he called 'a regular nun's superstition,' but the Abbess had made him promise to bring it over and ask me to use it. I was not in a state to care one way or the other about such a thing, so I merely said, 'Oh yes, if they wish it'; the nurse slipped it gently under my pillow, and in a few moments the matter passed out of my mind completely.

"For the two previous nights I had scarcely slept at all, but that evening I must have fallen asleep soon after ten o'clock. My slumbers, however, were far from unbroken, for I woke up at frequent intervals, and all night long a succession of vivid dreams kept chasing one another through my brain. Naturally enough in such circumstances, some of them were not a little fantastic, but the strange thing was that, without exception, they all concerned themselves with the penal times and with incidents of persecution.

"In one I found myself going about in disguise, so that my priestly character might not be known, sleeping in secret hiding places, and celebrating Mass at midnight, in an attic with thickly curtained windows. In another I kept hurrying from place to place for fear of the pursuivants; now hearing confessions in a stable, now preaching in a tavern with a pipe of tobacco in my hand and a mug of beer at my elbow. In a third my disguise had changed, and I was a travelling tinker, going from house to house encouraging the faithful, smuggling Catholic books about the country beneath the pots and pans in my pack, and administering the Sacraments whenever and wherever I dared, regardless of the law which made it a crime to do so.

"Then suddenly the scene changed, and I found myself on board ship working as one of the crew, so as to escape the difficulty of entering or leaving the country without the official papers, which, as a priest, I could not possibly obtain. In that dream I remember being very much alarmed by the action of one of my fellow sailors, who seemed to be constantly watching me, so that I feared he must suspect my true character; until one of the crew chanced to fall overboard, when both of us simultaneously pronounced the short form of absolution, each thus betraying himself to the other, to our mutual relief.

"In one dream I found myself in prison, arrested on suspicion of being a priest, and it seemed to me that I was kept there for months, expecting to be brought to trial at any moment. Even now, after all these years, I could draw you an exact picture of the bare, narrow cell, with walls, roof, and floor all of stone, and its tiny window heavily barred, so vividly did every detail impress itself upon my brain.

215

From this my mind jerked off and I found myself one of the crowd at Tyburn, assembled to witness the execution of two Catholic priests. There, before me, was the triple gibbet—the famous Tyburn tree—and by its side a great fire of faggots already lighted, to consume the heart and entrails of the martyrs after they had been hanged and quartered.

"Presently a loud shout announced that the sheriff and his victims were approaching. The crowd parted to make room for them, and the hurdles, with the holy men fast bound upon them, were dragged past me so close that I could have touched them with my hand. Then, before my eyes, I saw the whole ghastly tragedy enacted. The two priests were cut loose from the hurdles and lifted into an open cart beneath the gibbet, while the sheriff at their side denounced them to the crowd as traitors to their country and guilty of plotting against the life of His Majesty the King.

"At this one of the holy men gently protested, declaring that they were no traitors, nor did they wish aught but good to His Majesty, whom they prayed God daily to preserve. On hearing this the crowd cheered, but when he went on to add that he was guilty of no crime, unless it were a crime to serve God in the way his ancestors and theirs had done for centuries, the soldiers of the guard and the sheriff's men all shouted out together, so that the crowd should hear no more. When the noise had subsided, the sheriff bade him be brief if he wished to say more, and the condemned man humbly begged all present to pray for him and for his companion.

"'And know ye,' he added, 'it grieveth us not at all to die, if so, be God's most holy will, but rather it rejoiceth us greatly, seeing that he calleth us to him by so sure a road. For as at first the blessed apostles and martyrs by their blood-shedding sowed the seeds of Christ's Church throughout the world, even so, doubt ye not, the blood of us martyrs—albeit unworthy to be ranked with them—will bring forth in God's own time a rare harvest in this our land of England.'

"At this the sheriff angrily bade him be silent. The hangman quickly placed the ropes about their necks. A sharp cut of the whip made the horse plunge forward, leaving the two bodies hanging; and I awoke with a cry, to find myself in a violent perspiration,

"The sound of my voice brought the nurse to my side in a moment.

"'What is the matter, Father?' she asked anxiously. 'Do you want anything?'

"For a few moments I was quite unable to answer. My mind was still full of my dream, and I could scarcely believe it had not all been real, so wonderfully vivid were the images aroused. Gradually, I took in the situation. My eyes recognised the things around me, and I recollected that some time or other, seemingly quite long ago; I had gone to bed in that room feeling wretchedly weak and ill.

"One thing, however, was absolutely clear to me. Whatever had been my condition when I went to bed, I felt perfectly well and strong now, and I told the nurse so, adding that I would get up soon and say Mass; for I noticed that it was broad daylight. Of course, the good sister simply refused to believe me, but when I persistently maintained my point, she took my temperature and found it normal. This, at any rate, bore out my contention, and I persuaded her to go and ask the chaplain to come to me.

"When she was gone, I got out of bed, and though I half expected to be weak on my legs, I found myself perfectly steady and apparently in normal health. The nurse was away some little while, and when she returned with the chaplain I was half dressed, nor could the two of them persuade me to go to bed again. I said Mass without the least difficulty, had breakfast, and was walking in the garden outside the presbytery when the doctor arrived. At first, he was horrified to see me there, but when at length I convinced him that I was quite well again, he said something about a mistake in his diagnosis and went away in an amusingly ungracious manner, as if I had imposed upon him in some way.

"When he had gone, I went to the parlour and asked to see the Lady Abbess, for, of course, the nuns had heard of my astonishing recovery already. She came, accompanied by the prioress, and I told them all I could remember about the affair, adding that it seemed like a miracle, for there could be no doubt that I had been very seriously ill only a few hours earlier.

"'My dear Father Philip,' she said, to my surprise, 'it is simply the effect of our pillow. We have a number of cases on record where it has produced a cure as rapid and miraculous as yours.'

"I had quite forgotten about the pillow, and for a moment or two could not grasp her meaning. Then, all at once, the incident of the previous evening came back to my mind, and I cried abruptly:

"'Do you mean that little flat cushion, which the chaplain brought over last night and put under my head?"

"'Precisely,' she answered, smiling; 'it has often worked such a cure in the case of our own sisters who have been ill. We look upon it as our greatest treasure.'

"'But what is it?' I asked her. 'You cannot possibly attribute miraculous powers to a mere cushion! It would be grossly superstitious.'

"'We believe it to contain relics, Father,' she replied. 'But as to what they are, we have no record. We know that it was brought over from Paris, when our convent returned to England, but it has never been opened so far as we know, and there is a strong tradition in the house against doing so.'

"'Well, I think the tradition is a bad one,' I answered bluntly. 'It seems to me to run very close on superstition. If there are relics in the pillow, you will lose nothing by being certain of it; and if there are not any, then it is far best that the tradition to that effect should die.'

"We talked the matter over for some time, but I could not bring the two nuns round to my way of thinking. In the end, however, the Abbess was so far shaken that she agreed to submit the point to the bishop of the diocese, promising to be guided by his opinion; and both of us wrote to him on the matter that evening. His answer came in a couple of days' time, and the abbess brought it to the parlour for me to read.

"I found that the bishop took the same view as I had done, only rather more strongly; and while he refrained from laying any absolute command upon the nuns in regard to opening the pillow, he stated it as his definite wish that this should be done. He also gave permission for the chaplain and myself to enter the enclosure of the convent, so that we should be present at the examination, and directed us to draw up a formal report for him on the result of our search. I wanted to get away the following morning, so the abbess proposed to have the investigation that afternoon, in the presence of all the community.

"After lunch, therefore, the chaplain and myself were admitted inside the grille and conducted to the chapter-house, where we found the abbess and community awaiting us in their stalls. In the centre of the room, they had placed two chairs for us and a small table, on which were lying a knife, a pair of scissors, and the pillow. First of all, the abbess asked me to tell the whole community what I had experienced on the night when I had been cured, so I related in detail what I have already told you. She then explained how I had urged her to open the pillow, for fear lest any superstition might gather round its mysterious character, and how, when the matter was referred to the bishop of the diocese, he had taken the same view.

"She added that the community must understand that she was not urged by curiosity in thus going against the established tradition of the convent, but was acting in deference to the advice of the bishop. If, however, there were a number opposed to this, she would postpone the investigation until their view had been laid before him. Rather to my surprise not a voice was raised against the proposal, while several of the nuns spoke in favour of it, and finally the abbess asked me to proceed with the search.

"It did not take long to cut through the stitches of the outer cover, beneath which was a second one, also of linen, somewhat yellow and discoloured, and evidently of considerable age. When this too had been removed, we found that the contents were tightly wrapped in a long strip of silk brocade, wound round and round many times. There must have been fully five or six yards of this material, and when I had taken it all off, I handed it over to the Abbess. After a careful examination by a number of the nuns, they agreed that it was of French make, and, judging by the style of the design, was not newer than the end of the seventeenth century at latest. I have a piece of it still among the vestments in the sacristy upstairs.

"The removal of the silk had reduced the bulk of the pillow very considerably, and we were evidently nearing the heart of the mystery, for out of the wrappings had appeared a thickish, oblong package, some eighteen inches by twelve, wrapped round with parchment, the edges being carefully sewn together and sealed in several places. I tried to make out the impression on the wax, for, as you know, the seal is often an important detail in authenticating relics. Unfortunately, the wax had perished a good deal, and even where it was more or less intact the device was too indistinct to give any clue, so we could learn nothing from this source.

"I now cut open the stitches, broke the seals, and opened the parchment cover. Inside was a package wrapped in rough paper, quite yellow with age, on which was written an inscription in ink almost the colour of iron-mould. I made a copy of it later, here it is.' The old priest produced a folded sheet of foolscap from the envelope which he had brought from the relic cupboard and read as follows:

'The reliques herein enclosede, were brought oute of England by mee Wm. Fenwicke, chplaine to ye blue nuns atte Paris, after my escapeing from ye prison of Newe Gate, in the yere of Or. Lord's Incarnacion, 1647. They hadde bene gathered dur-

ing manye yeres by one of those atached to his Excellencie the
Spanish Ambassador's householde, the whiche, seeing his ende
could not be farre off, desyred mee to convey the same to a
place of safety, where jewells so rare mighte be estemed at their
trewe valewe. *Preciosa in cospectu Dni. mors sanctoru ejus.*

'Wm. Fenwicke, chplaine.

'Paris, 1650,'

"Within this cover were some five-and-twenty little packages,
each folded up in a separate paper and carefully tied with silk. Every
package contained relics of one of the English martyrs who had suffered at Tyburn prior to 1647; and I have not the smallest doubt that
the collection was made, probably at great personal risk, by the devout
Catholic layman whom William Fenwicke described as 'one of those
attached to his Excellency the Spanish Ambassador's household.'

"The nuns were naturally overjoyed to find that the pillow contained so remarkable a treasure; and in gratitude to me for bringing it
to light they generously offered to give me a portion of each of the
relics. I accepted the offer gladly, and afterwards had those four silver
reliquaries, like frames, made to take them—the ones which hang on
the inside of the doors of the relic cupboard upstairs. I also copied the
inscriptions on the different packages, here are some of them"—and
he referred again to the foolscap sheet.

'A fynger of Mr. Reynolds, preste, hanged at Tyburn on jan. ye
21st, 1642.
'A hankercher stayned with ye blode of bro. Henry Heath, a
graye fryer, wth some of hys haire. ob. die 174 Aprilis, 1643.
'Ye left thumb of D. Jhon Roberts, preste and monke of St Ben-
ets order. at Tyburn, Dec. 1610. Ye martir's bodie being recoverd
by some of my Lorde's householde, was conveyde over seas to
ye convent of hys order atte Doway.
'Mr. Garnet, Fesuite, accused of complicitie in ye powdre plott.
2 reliques, wth a peece of ye rope wheerwith he was hang'd,
Tyburn, 1608.
'Mysirys Ann Line, gentlewoman, hanged for harboring of
prestes, 1601: a clout wet wth teeres and blodde, wth some
of holy haire: this given to me by her sister's sonne Wyllyam
Brookes.'
'R. P. Thomae Maxfeelde, Mart : two ribs : given mee by the
lady Luisa before that his Excellencie the Count Gondomar did

transferre the martyr's bodie to his palace in Spaine, where it now is with manie other reliques.

★★★★★★★★★★

This is unquestionably the famous Donna Luisa de Carvajal, who lived in London for many years under the protection of the Spanish Ambassador, and devoted her life to alleviating the lot of those English Catholics who were imprisoned for the Faith.

★★★★★★★★★★★

'Mr. Almonde, preste, two fingers of ye lefte hand. Obtd fr ye same source as those of Mr Maxfeelde.

"I will not weary you with the whole list," said the old priest, "but there is one item which I think will be of special interest to you. Besides the primary relics in the package, we found one secondary one. 'This was a tiny silver crucifix, less than three inches long, the figure on it being worn quite smooth in places, as if the owner had carried it on his person for years; indeed, there was a loop of faded silk ribbon still attached to it. The paper which contained it bore no inscription, so I could tell nothing of its history, and handed it to the Abbess, saying: 'We cannot divide this between us, so you must keep it. Unfortunately, there is nothing to show whom it belonged to.' The nun took it from me, examined it carefully for a little, and then exclaimed:

"'There seems to be something engraved on the back of the cross, Father. I will have it cleaned, and then perhaps we may be able to make out what it is.' With this she gave it over to one of the younger sisters, asking her to take it to the pantry and clean it carefully with plate powder. We had just completed our task of opening the remaining packets, when the nun came back with the little crucifix, now quite bright and shining, which she handed to the Lady Abbess.'

"'I thought so,' she said triumphantly; 'there are some words engraved on the back. See if you can read them, Father, they are too small for my eyes to make out.'

"I took the crucifix and turned it over. The inscription was quite clear and easily legible in spite of its tiny lettering. It read *Crux P. Philippi Rivers, Mart*. There was not a doubt about it. The crucifix must have belonged to my ancestor and namesake, the words being added after his martyrdom at Tyburn in 1621. I read the words out aloud, in amazement, and then held out the relic for the abbess to take.

"'No, no, Father,' she said, drawing back. 'We cannot divide it, as you said yourself, so clearly it is you who must keep it. The inscription has told us not only whom it once belonged to, but also whom it should belong to now.'"

The old priest put his hand to his breast, drew forth a silver chain, and kissed the little cross that hung from it.

"This is the crucifix," he said, holding it out for me to look at. "I have worn it round my neck ever since. When I am gone, it will come to you, and I will ask you too to wear it always, in memory of me and of the glorious martyr, Philip Rivers."

The Watchman

One day, while browsing through the library shelves, I chanced to come upon a *Life of Saint Benedict Joseph Labre,* the "beggar saint." The book was unknown to me, and I skimmed rapidly through the amazing story, which seemed to me an extremely repulsive one. In some vague way I felt that it did not ring true to my ideas of Christian principle, which I had always looked upon as an essentially refining influence, and I told the squire so when we met at tea-time.

"To my mind the whole thing seems revolting and impossible," I said. "If the Church taught men to model their lives on such types as this, it would be all up with her mission to elevate mankind."

"*Distinguo*," replied the old priest gently. "Of course, one must admit that a life like that of St Benedict Joseph is a very special vocation and most exceptional; but I do not see how it can be called impossible, seeing that he is but one example of a well-known type, albeit the most extreme one, nor can I admit that it is necessarily revolting. Personally, while acknowledging that it differs enormously from the way of conforming one's life to that of Christ which seems possible for myself, I can quite see that the difference is one of detail and not of principle, and that, once the call to such a life becomes clear, the very elements in it which, humanly speaking, one would call revolting, are just what give it such extraordinary value."

I had not expected such an answer, for I fancied that the old priest's extreme delicacy of feeling would find the squalor and filth of St Benedict Joseph's life even more horrible than I did; and my surprise must have shown itself in some way, for he continued a moment later:

"Let me explain myself a little more fully, and I think you will see that my point of view has something to be said for it. The essential point of sanctity, the one thing really necessary for canonisation, is simply heroic charity. Now heroic charity means, as Benedict XIV puts it, that the servant of God shall have practised those virtues which his state of life, his rank and circumstances demanded, and that in an eminent or heroic degree. Of course, the heroism must not merely be displayed by a few impulsive and extraordinary acts, but must be manifested consistently throughout life, or at any rate from the date of the saint's 'conversion,' by means of varied and frequent acts, so that it is clearly established as a definite virtue or habit of the soul.

"Now in the case of St Benedict Joseph Labre it was many years before the exact nature of his special vocation became clear to him; you will remember that he tried several different religious orders in vain. When it did come, however, it took the form of work among the lowest stratum of the poor, the 'submerged tenth' as we should call it nowadays. I don't know if you have ever been brought into personal relations with these unfortunates, but if you have, you must have felt that the greatest obstacle to helping them is their ingrained distrust of all one's efforts. We are told in the gospel how our Lord himself could not work miracles among certain men 'because of their unbelief.'

"Well, it always seems to me that this deep distrust of one's motives and labours, on the part of these poor wretches, produces a very similar effect. If once a man can break down this attitude of suspicion and gain their confidence, he can do something for them, and for my part I have no doubt that the very elements which you find so revolting in the life of St Benedict Joseph are precisely those which appealed most of all to the people among whom he worked. Their circumstances were his. If they suffered in helpless, hopeless misery, so did he. The result was a power of understanding and a depth of sympathy for them on his side, and a degree of confidence and love on theirs, which could not have been reached in any other way."

"I begin to understand now," I said, "but even so it is very difficult. Perhaps if I had worked among the poor in our slums, as you have, I should better appreciate the heroism of St Benedict Joseph's life. But if his method be the true way to success among the very poor, is it not strange that we should have no other case at all like his among the records of those who have worked in the same sphere?"

"I don't at all admit that his case has no parallel," replied the old priest. "He is certainly the most extreme instance, but there are today, and have been at all times, numbers of holy men and women who have gone down to the depths in their zeal for souls. It is simply because the world does not care to hear about such things that the glory of their lives is hidden." The old priest paused for a minute, looking straight before him as if lost in thought, then he turned to me again.

"I once chanced to meet a man who lived and died utterly unknown beyond the limit of a London slum. Let me tell you the story of his life, and I think you will acknowledge that St Benedict Joseph has not been without one follower, at all events.

"More than twenty years ago I undertook to act for a time as chaplain to a convent of nuns, who work in the East End of London, near the docks. They visit the parish, teach the schools attached to the church, and take in old people who are past work, but whom, for one reason or another, it is thought best to keep out of the workhouse. The man in question was one of these. He was always known as 'Old Andrews,' and though I learned his real name I will not mention it, if you don't mind, as he wished his identity to remain a secret.

"Some of the old people were a sad trial to the good nuns, for they were always grumbling, though they were far better off in the convent than they would have been anywhere else, and my attention was drawn to Old Andrews because he was always so cheerful and contented—the only one, in fact, who seemed to appreciate the kindness and care that he received. I soon found out that he was altogether different from the rest of the old people, we became quite intimate friends, and eventually he told me his story.

"He was the younger son of a west-country squire whose family, though not a very wealthy one, was one of the oldest in that part of England. After passing through a well-known public school, he went up to Oxford, where he eventually won a fellowship at one of the smaller colleges. It was the time when John Henry Newman was in the height of his power, and Andrews was caught into the Tractarian movement. Like his great leader he became a Catholic towards the end of the forties, and in consequence was deprived of his fellowship.

"He was then about thirty years old, a good scholar, though not exceptionally brilliant, and he at once decided to take orders in the Catholic Church. It seemed clear to him, he told me, that he could serve God best as a priest, and being quite aware of his own abilities and the social advantages of his good birth, he decided to enter the secular priesthood, as the sphere in which his individuality and his talents would find most play.

"To Oscott, then, he went; but somehow, he failed to 'find himself' there at all. Everyone was kind and helpful, he said, but from the first he seemed to feel that it was not the life he was meant for, and this conviction became at last too strong to be neglected. On the advice of the President of the college, he made a week's retreat, with the result that he determined to try his vocation as a Jesuit; but here too he could not settle down, and after a few months the novice-master advised him to leave. The poor man was naturally a good deal cast down at this second failure, and his position was not made easier by the fact that his funds were almost exhausted, for his relatives had dropped him completely on his reception into the Church.

"By way of keeping body and soul together and of finding occupation until his path should become clear, he decided to go in for journalism; so, he came to London and took a room in a cheap lodging house near Gray's Inn. Even now the district has some very unsavoury streets in it, and in those days, it was far worse. Before long the combined effects of anxiety, disappointment, poor food, and an insanitary dwelling resulted in a complete breakdown. He became very ill, and the lodging-house keeper had him removed to St Bartholomew's Hospital, Smithfield.

"Here, no doubt, he received proper care, but from the first his chance of recovery seemed a small one. He grew rapidly worse, and one evening, about a week after his admission, he collapsed suddenly and was pronounced to be dead. His body was, in fact, removed to the mortuary of the hospital, and as the next day chanced to be Sunday not a soul came near the place for fully four-and-twenty hours. On the Monday morning, however, the mortuary attendant was astounded to find the body still warm. He drew attention to the fact, restoratives were applied, and after a long while the man came back to himself.

"His convalescence was long and slow; but, as he told me, it seemed quite short to him, so engrossed was he with his own thoughts. For somehow, when his mind began to work again after its long period of unconsciousness, he found that his whole outlook upon life had shifted. The very elements of his character seemed to have changed. His intellectual scale of values had altered. His memory, which seemed largely to have lost its hold on things academic, now dwelt persistently on events in his past life which he had formerly looked upon as trifles, but which now seemed full of significance, and that always from a spiritual point of view.

"Pardon me if I elaborate the matter somewhat, for this strange 'conversion' seemed, both to him and to me, the most remarkable part of his story. You must understand, then, that before it—I mean before the time when he was given up and left for dead—he had been a typical Oxford don, scholarly and intellectual; religious certainly, but interested in religion as satisfying the claims of the understanding, rather than holding on to it as the essential basis of right conduct; viewing it, in short, as an act of mind rather than one of will, as knowledge rather than as love. Now, after his change, he found himself looking upon life much as the *Curé d'Ars* seems to have done. He seemed almost to have lost hold of the intellectual side, so absolutely was he humbled with regard to the share of the mind in religious life. Instead of it, the will and its activities—charity, self-abnegation, living for others, even to the degree of vicarious suffering voluntarily endured or even actively sought for—this was now his idea of what a religious life should be.

"Previously he had been full of schemes for active work: a crusade of preaching, a rapid conversion of England by means of controversial pamphlets, to say nothing of larger literary ventures, which should answer the attacks of unbelievers and carry the war into the enemies' country. Now, such dreams seemed not merely impossible for him, but actually foolish in themselves, as being mostly wasted energy, or at any rate as requiring an expenditure of personal effort altogether beyond the results they could achieve. Instead, he felt himself drawn to a life absolutely hidden in character, where his active work for souls should be as far as possible unknown; using prayers, communions, and Masses for his weapons, preaching by example instead of by word, substituting a crusade of charity for one of controversy, conquering souls by sympathy instead of argument, and this too as a layman, not as a priest.

"He told me all I have said, but in greater detail and far more convincingly than I can convey to you, and then I asked him to tell me, as well as he could, in what way this wonderful change was brought about in him. He answered that the only way in which he could explain it was that, while he lay there unconscious, he felt as if some overwhelming force took possession of his soul and forcibly changed its point of observation; so that henceforth it looked upon life from quite a novel standpoint, and had no power to shift back again to its former angle of vision.

"As he lay there, dead to all appearances—and you must understand that it seemed to him all the time that he had actually died—his soul seemed to escape from the body and rise above it, as if going to God. He thus came to look upon the world as it were from without and from above; from the point of view of heaven, of the saints of God. Looking upon life from this detached and higher standpoint, he found that the relative values of things were changed, for it was no longer the external or objective appearance, but the inward and spiritual worth of things which he perceived.

"Thus, for example, he saw that the worldly prosperity of a man, or of a family, was of trifling moment compared with their internal, spiritual state. In the same way he saw that the value of each individual soul was inestimably great, and moreover that this value never depreciated—I mean that, whether there were many souls or few, it made no difference in their individual value, since the multitude of souls did not make each several one a whit less precious in God's eyes, in the way that increased supply cheapens the objects of worldly commerce. Then, too, the difference of soul from soul in value—by which he meant in lovableness—became clear to him, and he understood that this difference was proportionate to the degree in which each soul reflected the image of him who made it, and to the effort of will which each was making to love and serve God.

"Another element in the process of spiritual enlightenment which he underwent consisted in a kind of revelation of sin. I wish I could give you an adequate idea of the way in which he spoke of sin, its consequences, and the stupendous part it plays in the world. He saw it, he told me, as it really is; stripped of disguise, in utter nakedness, its nature manifest with every hideous feature plain to see. He realised, as he had never done before, its terrible insidiousness, how, once admitted into the mind, it spreads like some fell infection into the heart, paralyzing the will and soiling the secret places of the memory with a track like that of some hideous reptile. Then, too, its power, so subtle, yet so tremendous, was revealed to him, and the utter helplessness of a soul against it, without the help of God and his grace.

"'The soul that plays with sin,' he said to me, "has no more chance of escape by its own power than a man who is entangled in the mechanism of some mighty engine. The thing may be his own invention, but what of that? The power he has called into being is a thousand times mightier than he, and will it spare him merely because he is its maker? I often wonder,' he added, 'why preachers always liken a soul in mortal sin to a body that is dead. If that were all, its lot would be a happy one compared with what it is. To me a soul that has sinned mortally is like a man buried alive.

"'Alive, with every faculty alert and every sense in full activity, but shut in and entombed, like some poor wretch screwed down and locked within a vault; conscious of his awful fate and all it means, yet powerless to escape or even to move. And then, the very one whom he has wronged, the self-same Lord to whom he has been false, comes down and breaks his bonds and sets him free; washing the poor soul with his precious blood, pouring the balm of grace upon its wounds, nursing it gently back to health and strength; yet knowing all the time, perhaps, that it will fall again, nay that it will go on falling to the end, and even, possibly, will die in sin and so be lost to him eternally. My God, what love is thine, what guilt is ours!'

"You will understand that, after such an experience, with his whole outlook on life reversed, he left the hospital another man. Strange to say, an accident intervened to change his identity as well as his character. When the time came for him to leave the hospital, he was taken to the office to sign the register, a large book in which the name and address of each patient is entered on a separate line, with the dates of entry and departure. In the last column on the right, he signs his name on leaving; or, if he die in hospital, the word *dead* is entered in the space.

"The registrar's clerk, who was in a hurry, asked him the official number he had borne in the hospital, turned to the page, and pushed the book towards him. To his amazement in the space opposite his name appeared the word *dead*, while the space below was blank, the only blank left on the page.

"'Here you are,' said the clerk, pointing to the blank and running his finger along the line to the name at the left-hand side. 'James Andrews, is it? Just write it here.'

"'But I can't write that,' exclaimed my friend; meaning, of course, that he could not sign another man's name.

"'What, can't write your own name!' exclaimed the clerk; 'all right, I'll do it for you then.' And the name was written and the ledger put back, before the other could find words with which to explain.

"Then, suddenly, it dawned upon him that there was a purpose in what had happened. He, the man who had been brought there many weeks before, was officially certified as dead in the hospital records; and after all, was it not more or less true? So far as his soul was concerned, so far as character went and everything by which his personality could have been recognised, he had died and risen again, a new man. Doubtless the entry in the register was just a slip—it was James Andrews who should have been marked as *dead*, not he.

"But, after all, why care about the blunder? He meant to begin life again with a new character, a new outlook, new aims and purposes— in a word, with a new soul. Why not accept the accident as providential, and adopt 'James Andrews' as a new name? His relatives, if they inquired, would be told that he had died in hospital. Why undeceive them? The change of name would prevent them from interfering with the new life that he had planned during the long weeks of convalescence; for he had his scheme all ready, and it was this:

"He would go into the humblest part of the great city and lose himself there. Work of some kind he would get, to keep himself alive; and, while earning his living in this humble way, he would be sure to come in touch with those whom he could help. The destitute, the outcasts of society, hiding where no organized effort ever reached them, these were the souls for whom he meant to work; it was for them, he knew, that God had sent him back to life.

"In pursuance of this plan, he left the hospital without drawing notice to the blunder in the register, and made his way eastward into the slums. Fortunately, it was summer time and he had a little money, which had been in the pockets of his clothes when he was taken to St Bartholomew's. For a week or so he tramped the streets in search of work, sleeping at night in a common lodging house; but the days went by, his money was running low, and no means of earning a livelihood presented itself.

"He was almost at his last shilling when he chanced to see a notice on the hoarding round a big unfinished building. 'Night Watchman Wanted', was all it said, but the words seemed to him like a message from heaven. He had not the physical strength to work as a navvy, and, of course, he knew no sort of skilled trade; but here was the very thing for him. As a night watchman he would have long hours to himself, hours which could be given, as he desired, to prayer and contemplation. He believed himself sent to help the lowest of the low; where could he find them so easily as among the poor wretches who tramp the streets all night for want of shelter, and are glad to share the warmth of a watchman's brazier? The whole thing came to him in a flash, and he walked to the foreman's office and applied for the job.

"'They made no difficulty about giving it to me,' he told me, 'which I took to be another proof that it was God's will. That night I entered on my job, and I stayed with the same firm of contractors as a night watchman, until I got past work and came into the convent here, three years ago.'

"From that day until he died, more than thirty years later, his mode of life never changed, but only intensified itself and deepened with the years. He took a tiny room at the top of a lodging house where he slept during the day; for, of course, his work meant a complete reversal of ordinary hours. As a rule he used to come off work about six o'clock in the morning—the hour varied in winter and summer—and at once he made his way to the nearest church to hear Mass and receive Communion. After his thanksgiving he would go home and have something to eat, for he had fasted from midnight; so, he usually got to bed by eight o'clock. He was up and about by four o'clock in the afternoon, and had an hour or two to himself before going to his work again at dusk, which might be as early as five o'clock in winter, while in summer he would often be free till eight o'clock, if the men were working overtime.

"From the first he found, as he had expected, that the long, quiet hours were a perfect opportunity for mental prayer, and he soon began to spend the whole period from midnight in contemplation. This naturally culminated in the Mass and Communion when he went off work, and I remember his saying that he wondered why communities of religious did not adopt such an arrangement. To him it seemed the nearest possible approach to the primitive plan, in which the Lord's supper came in the evening as the climax of a day spent in serving God; and he told me that, until one had tried, it was impossible to realise how the prospect of Communion to come, when the day's work was ended, coloured every minute and linked up every thought with God. He saw quite clearly that the rule of fasting Communion made such a thing impossible for most people, as they could not work all day without food, and he counted it the chief blessing of his inverted way of life that he was compelled to act in the matter as the early Christians did.

"Up to midnight, or thereabouts, the streets were usually too noisy and the flow of human life too turbulent to make recollection possible, but the knowledge of the quiet hours to come made him fully content that it should be so. Indeed, from the first, he looked upon the opportunities of helping others, which his work supplied, as a signal proof that the whole affair was providential. I do not wish to exaggerate the work he did in this way, or make it seem as if his life was occupied wholly with the salvage of human souls. But it is only the bare truth that he gradually developed a real apostolate of his own among the wreckage of men and women, the flotsam and jetsam of humanity, which is always drifting aimlessly about the streets of London.

"Numbers of these poor creatures—harlots, drunkards, men and women half desperate for want of food and work, little children, orphaned or abandoned, unfortunates of every conceivable type—

would come his way, and stop to warm their famished bodies at his glowing brazier. He had a word of sympathy for everyone, and in most cases that alone was enough to break the ice of their reserve, for none of them suspected what he really was.

"In this way his influence came to be very great. He got to know the clergy of the various slum parishes and, by working in conjunction with them, became the means of bringing many a poor wandering soul back to the practice of religion, rescuing others from lives of crime and infamy, and saving some from self-destruction. I doubt if any of the organised agencies for slum work ever even heard of Old Andrews, but I honestly believe that his years of unknown self-devotion did more real good and saved more souls than any of their costly, much advertised schemes.

"In this way, dividing his time between active work for others and long hours of private prayer in the watches of the night, his soul developed wonderfully in wisdom, love, and sympathy, and on the basis of its natural powers God's grace built up a structure of unusual beauty. It was not merely that all natural repugnance to his life of poverty passed away from him; that the squalor, want, and aimless misery of his surroundings ceased to sadden him; but rather that he came to look upon such things themselves as an essential element of true renunciation, realising that only by them and through them can certain souls achieve that perfect liberty of spirit which is the hall-mark of the sons of God.

"'You must not think, Father,' he said to me one day, 'that I do not realise such things are evils in themselves, or that I look on them as being necessary evils; it is not that. On the contrary, I count them among the chief hindrances to the triumph of good and the re-establishment of all things in Christ. My point is this, that all these evil things are the creation of man himself; that they are simply the material results of countless human wills which are not conformed in all things to the will of God. By things such as these the sins of the fathers are visited upon the children, they are the heritage we receive from the past. A *damnosa hereditas* if ever there was one, but one which we cannot escape or get rid of, save by accepting it as part of our lot in life, and striving, each one of us individually, to remedy the evil by our own personal service.

"'Many years ago, I once read the Rule of St Benedict, and I have never forgotten a sentence in it where the Saint bids his disciples to "return by the labour of obedience to Him from whom you have departed by the sloth of disobedience." It seems to me that those words sum up the whole matter for us, I mean that social progress, like the advance of the individual soul in its personal religion, is a matter of working our way back to God along the paths of duty; for after all, to us Christians, duty is simply the will of God.'

"Certainly, in his own case this life-long 'working back' did bring his soul into very close relationship with God. As he advanced in prayer he often found that he would know beforehand what people were about to come his way. Often, too, by some mysterious foreknowledge which he could not explain, he found that their difficulties and needs were all clear to him before they began to tell him about themselves. Sometimes he would find words put into his mouth to speak to them, and while these were usually quite different from what he would have said of himself, they seemed to give help, and to revive hope in a way which mere human wisdom could not do.

"In this hidden, unknown way he lived and worked for thirty years or so, and God alone knows how many poor souls were saved through his gentle, selfless apostolate. Then, when he was more than sixty years old, he was seriously injured in a street accident, while trying to save a little child from being run over. For some time, his life hung in the balance, and though he recovered in the end, it was clear that he could not resume his old way of life, with its long hours of exposure in all weathers. Accordingly, the nuns of the convent which I mentioned arranged to take him in, and there he remained until his death, a year or two after I had ceased to act as chaplain there.

"His one regret in this last period of his life was that he had no longer any opportunity of doing active work for God.

"'I must try and make up for it by praying better,' he said with touching humility; adding, reflectively, 'I suppose, after all, prayer is the best way of working for others, because in active work we make so many blunders, while in prayer we leave everything to God's grace, and he never makes a mistake.'

"When our acquaintance had developed into intimacy, he told me that there was one soul in particular for whom he was praying. 'This was his own nephew, son of his elder brother, and now the head of the family.

"'Since the day that I left hospital, stamped with another man's name,' he said, 'I have never held any communication with my kith and kin, and if they ever inquired about me they must have been told that I had died in St Bartholomew's. But one day, some few years ago, I saw the notice of my brother's death in the paper, and it mentioned that he was succeeded by his only son, an officer in the Army. Ever since then I have been praying for that young man and especially for his conversion to the Faith, and now that I have no active work to do, I make this the chief intention in all my prayers, and offer up my Communion for him once every week.'

"I remembered this a year or two later, when I saw a notice in the *Tablet* that the young squire had been received into the Church, and I wrote to Old Andrews to congratulate him. A week afterwards the letter came back to me, with a note from the Reverend Mother. She told me that the old man had died several days before my letter had reached the convent, and on comparing the dates I found that his death and his nephew's reception had occurred on the same day. Of course, you can say that this was merely a coincidence, but for my part I like to think it was something more."

The old priest ceased speaking and sat silent for a minute or so, looking out with steady gaze into the west, where the last glow of the sunset was slowly fading; then he turned to me with a smile.

"That is the bare outline of my friend's story," he said. "I could fill in many other details, but I hardly think you need them. He was the nearest parallel I have ever met to the type of St Benedict Joseph Labre, and if you yourself had known him as I did, I cannot believe you would have called his life 'revolting and impossible.'"

The Footstep of the Aventine

Like many another English Catholic gentleman, the squire is a conscientious reader of the *Tablet*, going through it week by week from the first page to the last, on the day that the paper arrives. One evening after dinner he was engaged in his weekly task, and Father Bertrand and myself were playing a quiet game of chess, when all at once the silence was broken by a sudden exclamation.

"Oh dear," he cried, "another old friend gone!" adding as he turned towards us, "It is Count Rudolf von Arenberg, Grand Master of the Knights of Malta; the 'Roman Letter' says he was found dead in his bed, on Monday of last week."

"Count Rudolf von Arenberg," repeated Father Bertrand thoughtfully, "I don't seem to recollect his name at all. Have you ever mentioned him to me, Philip? I thought I knew all your old friends, at any rate by name."

"Really, I can't say," replied the squire, "but it is possible I may not have done so, I knew him fairly intimately a good many years ago, and was once his guest for a considerable time, but for some time past I have heard nothing of him. Still, I remember him very well, for a curious incident occurred while I was staying with him, which made the visit stand out vividly in my memory."

"Would it be too much to ask what the incident was, sir?" I asked; for I had learned by now that such a phrase often indicated one of the old priest's experiences.

"I will tell you the story with pleasure," he replied, "but won't you finish your game first?"

"It is finished,' said Father Bertrand with a smile. "My young friend is only one move off being checkmated—that's why he wants the story;" and he swept the pieces back into the box as I acknowledged my defeat. Then we moved up to the fire where the squire was sitting, and he began,

"For five or six years after my ordination I never went back to Rome, but after that I usually spent a month or two there every spring for quite a number of years. As a rule, I used to stay at the Austrian College, the rector of which was a great friend of mine, as we had been fellow students at the *Accademia* years before. It was he who introduced me to Count Rudolf von Arenberg, who was a relation of his and had become Grand Master of the Knights of Malta several years before I first met him. You must remember their house on the Aventine, Bertrand, almost next door to your own Dominican church of Santa Sabina. It is the place where people go to see the famous view of St Peter's. You look through a little hole in the garden door, and there is the great dome right before you, framed by the two walls of clipped box trees that line the sides of the path.

"Nowadays, of course, the Knights of Malta are very few in number and almost all of them are Austrians, for their only remaining houses are in Austria. The Grand Master, however, has to be in Rome for most of the year, so Count Rudolf used to live up on the Aventine almost alone, and, as we soon became intimate, he begged me to make use of the large garden they have there, whenever I cared to do so.

"One afternoon when I was there—I fancy it must have been the second or third year after we had first met—he asked me if I would come and stay with him on the Aventine for some weeks and act as his chaplain. It appeared that the official chaplain had been called home to Austria on business and was not likely to return for a month or more.

"'Your only duty,' he explained, 'will be to say Mass in the chapel every day. You will have the chaplain's suite of rooms all to yourself, and as for meals, you can have them served in your own apartment or with myself, as you prefer. And I assure you,' he added, 'it will be not only a great convenience to me, but a joy as well if you can accommodate yourself to my proposal, and I am sure you will not regret your kindness in coming to my assistance.'

"That year, as it happened, I was not staying at the Austrian College, but in a hotel, which was not very pleasant; so, I gladly availed myself of the offer he had made so gracefully, and next afternoon took possession of the chaplain's rooms. Count Rudolf was out when I arrived, but Baldassare, the old, white-haired steward, who had been in the employ of the Knights for nearly forty years, received me with true Italian courtesy.

"The Roman house of the Knights stands on a corner of the

Aventine hill, one side of which falls away abruptly towards the Tiber, the steep slope being cut back into terraces and laid out as a formal garden. Behind the house, the face of the hill turns almost at right angles with the terraced garden, and in those days the whole of the enclosure was laid out as a vineyard. This part is now the site of the huge international college of San Anselmo, which Leo XIII built a few years ago for students of the Benedictine Order, but at the time of which I am speaking it was still unbuilt on. At the far end, fully three hundred yards from the house, stands a great bastion, part of the fortification begun by Pope Paul IV but never completed, which was meant to command the Porta San Paolo, only a gunshot off.

"It was about an hour before sunset when I arrived, and after unpacking my belongings and settling into my new abode, I took my breviary and said my office in the vineyard, walking up and down the path that ran along the face of the hill and ended at the great bastion. As I finished, the sun was setting, so I turned back to the house and found my host walking on the upper terrace.

"He greeted me very kindly; we arranged about the hour for Mass and settled that I would take my meals with him and not alone, an arrangement which he said he would much prefer; then a bell rang in the little campanile and we adjourned to get ready for dinner. Not unnaturally, the conversation during the meal turned upon the history of the Knights of Malta and their establishment on the Aventine. The Grand Master was a mine of knowledge on the subject, and when the meal was over, he took me upstairs to the *Archivium*, and showed me the splendid collection of documents relating to the history of the Order, kindly giving me permission to examine them as much as I wished during my stay on the Aventine.

"It was nearly midnight when I left my host and retired to my bedroom. Here I undressed and, after putting out the light, kneeled for a while in prayer by the open window. This window faced towards the vineyard, and as I rose from my knees, I heard the sound of footsteps, pacing quietly along the path leading to the bastion. It was too dark to see anything, but I felt a momentary surprise, as the Romans always insist that the night air is unhealthy. Almost at once, however, it occurred to me that Count Rudolf was an Austrian and slightly contemptuous of Italian ideas, so I felt no doubt that it was he himself, taking a little stroll before going to bed.

"Next morning I spent three or four hours in the *Archivium*, and after lunch went for a long walk in the Campagna. The result was that I felt very tired after dinner, so I excused myself to the Grand Master, said my office, and was in bed about ten o'clock. That spring the weather was exceptionally warm, and though I went to sleep very quickly, I woke up after a time feeling hot and restless. I could not get to sleep again, so after a while I got out of bed and walked to the window to get some fresh air. To my surprise, I heard the same faint footfall which I had heard the night before, pacing along the path that led to the bastion. Whoever it was, he was nearing the house, for as I listened the sound grew steadily clearer and eventually the steps came right up to my window; but there was no moon and I could distinguish nothing.

"'Evidently the Grand Master is a bad sleeper,' I said to myself; 'I must have been in bed a couple of hours at least, and here he is still walking in the vineyard.' I felt curious to know the time, but did not want him to think that I was watching, so I waited until the sound was far away again before striking a light. When I judged that he was almost at the farthest distance from the house, I lit a match and looked at my watch. It was twenty minutes to three! You can imagine my surprise; but, after all, it was no business of mine, so I got into bed again and was soon asleep.

"Next morning, when we met at breakfast, I looked curiously at Count Rudolf. He seemed perfectly fresh, and I could hardly believe he had been in bed for less than four hours. I did not like to ask him point blank why he had stayed up half the night, so I said casually:

"'I hope you did not sit up late again last night, searching in the *Archivium* on my account.'

"'Not at all,' said he, to my amazement. 'I was tired last night, though I had not your excuse, since I had not walked three leagues in the Campagna, but I went to bed soon after you did, and must have slept fully eight hours without waking.'

"It was on the tip of my tongue to tell him that I had heard someone in the vineyard on both the previous nights, but it struck me that it would be wiser to speak first to Baldassare. You have both lived in Italy, so you know the amazing way Italians have of being up at all hours of the night and sleeping during the day to make up for it. Possibly, I thought, it may have been Baldassare himself, or some watchman looking after the vineyard. Yes, I would speak to the steward before saying anything to the Grand Master.

"That morning Count Rudolf had to go into Rome on business, which left me to my own devices, and I was soon in conversation with the old steward. I told him how I had heard footsteps but had failed to distinguish anyone in the darkness, and asked if he knew who could be patrolling the vineyard at night. The old man listened intently to what I had to say, and waited without a word until I had finished.

"'Don Filippo,' he said at length, 'you are a priest and you understand many things. I can tell you nothing about the footsteps except this, that when I first came here, forty years ago, the *capellano*, Don Angelo, warned me that such footsteps were often heard, and told me I need have no fear if I chanced to hear them also. I asked him what it was, but he would tell me no more; though I always think he could have told me, had he wished to.'

"'And have you ever heard the footsteps yourself?' I asked him.

"'I used to do so sometimes,' he answered, 'but for many years now I have slept in the little room above the porter's lodge, and the window there looks out eastward, so I have heard nothing.'

"'And has nothing ever been seen?" I asked him.

"'Nothing, *Signor*, so far as I know; but I think Don Angelo may have seen something, for how else would he know who it is that walks?'

"'Did you ever go into the vineyard at night to watch?' I asked.

"'*Madre di Dio*, I should think not,' said the old man, and he crossed himself at the suggestion. 'The Aventine has not a good reputation, Don Filippo. You know what kind of things used to take place here of old. No one wanders about the Aventine at midnight if he can help it.'

"It was clear that I should get nothing more out of Baldassare, so I thanked him and went back to my sitting-room. Here there were a number of portraits depicting past members of the Order, and I noticed for the first time that one of them bore the inscription *Don Angelo de Angelis, Capellano*, 1825-1866. I felt sure that this must be the Don Angelo of whom Baldassare had spoken, and I determined to ask Count Rudolf about him. That evening, therefore, at dinner, I contrived to turn the conversation on to the subject of the portraits in the house, and so to those in the chaplain's rooms, and the Grand Master told me about a number of them.

"'But how stupid of me!' he broke out suddenly, 'I wonder I did not think of it sooner. Do you know that you have a compatriot among the chaplains whose pictures hang in your sitting-room?'

"'Indeed,' I answered in surprise, 'and who is that?'

"'To tell the truth,' he replied, 'I cannot for the life of me remember his surname, but he was Don Giovanni something. His portrait hangs next to that of old Don Angelo, who was the last chaplain here before my friend for whom you are so kindly supplying. Don Angelo was our chaplain for fully forty years, and he insisted on having his portrait hung next to that of the English chaplain, Don Giovanni. Indeed, I remember now that he had got together some materials for writing a life of him.'

"'But how interesting,' I exclaimed. 'I suppose Don Angelo knew him personally. Was he the chaplain immediately before Don Angelo himself?'

"'Oh, dear no,' replied Count Rudolf, 'he died more than two hundred years ago, for he was chaplain in the time of Urban VIII. I really don't know why Don Angelo was so interested in him; but his collections for the biography must be in the *Archivium* upstairs—you shall go through them yourself, if you care to.'

"Of course, I accepted the offer eagerly, and after dinner we went upstairs to find the papers. To my disappointment, the Grand Master was quite uncertain where they were kept, and in spite of a long search we failed to find them.

"'I have seen the *dossier* myself, so it must be here,' he said, 'but it is some years ago, and I really do not remember where they are.'

"For a couple of hours we searched through cupboard after cupboard and my hopes were sinking very low, when all at once Count Rudolf gave a sharp exclamation.

"'Why now, how foolish of me!' he exclaimed. 'I don't believe they are in this room at all. I feel almost sure that they are in your own apartment, in that little cupboard between the bookcases.'

"I did not remember any such cupboard, and said so, but the Grand Master was quite positive.

"'Oh yes,' he said, 'there is such a cupboard, but you might easily overlook it. It is simply a narrow upright space in the angle of the wall where the two bookcases meet. The door looks like a solid pilaster, set across the angle. Let us go down and look there, at any rate.'

"To my sitting-room we went, then, and the theory proved correct. There was a tall narrow cupboard in the angle of the wall, and of course I had never suspected that the carved wooden pilaster was really a door. Count Rudolf opened it with the key that fitted all the cases in the *Archivium*, and to my delight it contained a package of papers, endorsed *Vita di Don Giovanni Fenton, il solo capellano Inglese dei Cavalieri di San Giovanni sul Aventino.* (*Life of Don John Fenton, the only English chaplain of the Knights of St John upon the Aventine hill.*) It was getting late now, so the Grand Master begged me to excuse him and left me, saying:

"'Do not tire yourself by sitting up half the night reading Don Angelo's collection of notes. You can study the papers at leisure in the morning.'

"When he had gone, I arranged the shade of my lamp so that the light fell on the two portraits of Don Giovanni and Don Angelo, and then seated myself before them in one of the big old-fashioned chairs. I must have stayed there, looking dreamily at the two portraits, for a considerable time, when all at once an idea came into my mind. It struck me that I had never heard of Don Angelo until that morning, and that now I had learned two curious facts about him. The first one Baldassare had told me, *viz.*, how interested he had been in the mysterious footsteps, and how apparently, he, and he alone, knew who it was that walked. The second point Count Rudolf had supplied; I mean his deep and unexplained interest in the long-dead Don Giovanni, the only Englishman who had ever been chaplain at the Aventine house before myself, and how he had collected materials to write his life.

"Were these two interests connected? I asked myself; and if so, was it the Englishman, Don John Fenton, whose footstep was heard so often in the vineyard though no one had ever seen him?

"It was midnight now, and, moved by a sudden impulse, I walked through into the bedroom, opened the window wide, and listened. Sure enough, far away down the path to the bastion, I heard the faint sound of footsteps pacing slowly towards the house. I waited in silence as the sound grew closer, and finally seemed to be just beneath the window. Then, silently, I leaned well out of the casement and said quietly in English:

"'If you are Don John, the former English chaplain, tell me what it is you wish; I, too, am English and a priest.'

"The footsteps, till then quite regular, now ceased abruptly and there was perfect silence for a minute or so. Then I repeated my words and paused again for an answer. This time, from beneath the window, there came the faintest sound—I hardly know how to describe it, but it was like a stifled gasp, the kind of sound a man will sometimes make just before he dies, when he is trying to speak and cannot. After a pause I repeated what I had said a third time, very slowly and distinctly, and once more waited breathlessly for an answer.

"This time there was no doubt about the reply. Very faint it was, the merest whisper in fact, like someone speaking along the wall of a long gallery, but the words were unmistakable.

"'*Burn, burn, burn*,' it said; and then there was silence again.

"'Burn what ? I asked quickly; but no answer came.

"'What is it you wish me to burn?' I said. Still there was silence.

"'Can you not tell me what it is I am to burn?' I asked a third time, and waited. The faintest possible murmur—like a smothered sigh— sounded for a moment only, and then absolute silence, not a footfall even. I remained at the window for quite another half-hour but heard nothing more; so, with a feeling of deep disappointment, I went to bed and eventually to sleep.

"Next morning, after breakfast, I set to work on the packet of papers which we had found the night before. I had decided that I would read straight through them first of all, and afterwards copy such as proved to be of interest. Most of the papers were written in the same hand as that on the outside of the packet, which, I had no doubt, was Don Angelo's, and they were evidently copies of documents in the archives and extracts from various sources. Besides these, however, there was a small package carefully fastened up, with a piece of paper folded round the whole and sealed in several places.

"On close examination I found that the wax looked recent and held strongly, while the paper of the wrapper was clearly ancient. I did not want to tear it, in case there might be writing on the inside, so I brought a candle to the marble-topped table by the window at which I was working, lit it, and held the blade of my knife in the flame until it was quite hot. I then passed it under the flap, cut through the seals without injuring the paper, and the wrapper was open.

"Sure enough, the inside of the sheet was written upon, the words being in Latin and written in the hand which I had decided was that of Don Angelo, though the paper of the cover was evidently far older. I cannot tell you the exact words after all these years, but the gist of them was that the writer had found the enclosed papers among some others in the archives, had removed them and sealed them up, since they appeared to be private and of a confidential nature.

"I felt some doubt whether I ought to go through the contents of the package without first asking the Grand Master's permission, but a glance at the uppermost paper dispelled my scruples, for I saw that it began, 'Jhon, my deare sonne,' and was, in fact, a letter written to the long-dead chaplain by his own mother. There were ten or a dozen such letters, all beginning the same way, and I quickly read them through, for they were quite short, I gathered that they had been written early in the seventeenth century, during the penal times, and that Don John was then in England. I guessed, too, that he was even then a priest, though there was nothing to reveal the fact except a reference to 'summe of youre custumers here,' which reminded me that I had seen a similar phrase used to describe Catholics in other documents of the persecution times, when it was important not to reveal to out siders the religion of those referred to.

"After the letters, and apparently of about the same date, came a little notebook, formed by sewing together some half-dozen small sheets of paper. This contained, first, a list of addresses, some twenty or so in number, and I recognised several of them as the names of houses in the northern counties of England, which had belonged to well-known Catholic families, such as Gilling, Sizergh, and Hutton Hall. After most of the names were a few notes, such as a pedlar might have made; '4 yardes Bawdekinne' was one, I recollect, and another read '10 *ditto* for Ladye P. (blakke).' I felt pretty sure from this that Don John had carried on his ministrations in the disguise of a pedlar, and that the addresses were those of houses where he was sure of a safe refuge.

"The entries about silks and 'bawdekinne' were a difficulty, how-ever, since some of them represented quite large amounts of material, and I could hardly suppose that the trade in stuffs was anything more than a blind. At the end of all I found a note in different ink, which suggested an explanation to me. It ran, 'Alle the sayd obligacions have nowe bene satisfyed,' from which I concluded that the entries of '10 yardes,' etc., were really notes of Masses he had undertaken; the '10 *ditto* for Ladye P.' being marked 'blakke' because Lady P. was dead, and the ten Masses were to be *Requiems* for her soul. This curious list and the letters I decided to copy, but before doing so I set to work to de-cipher the one paper still remaining out of the sealed packet.

"This document was in Latin, very difficult to read and full of abbreviations, the persons referred to being indicated by numbers in-stead of by their names. It took me well over an hour to make out the whole, but the time was well spent, for the document was evidently the most important of them all. It proved, in fact, to be nothing less than a long, written confession, made apparently by a priest, who had abjured the Catholic Faith through fear, and had accepted a benefice in the Established Church. It appeared that his anxiety for reconcili-ation was known, or at least suspected, by the authorities, who were watching him very closely in the hope of catching any priests with whom he might hold communication in his efforts to escape from the terrible predicament in which he found himself.

"The paper was not signed, and I gathered that it had been delivered to Don John by some third party, as it ended with an appeal to the reader to find some means of helping the poor wretch who had written it. I had just reached the end of this terrible narration, and was still lost in wonder and pity at the tragedy it contained, when a knock came at the door and Baldassare entered.

"'The Grand Master sends his compliments, *Signor*,' he said, 'and will be grateful if you can come to him for a minute. There are some legal papers which he has to sign, and he begs you will be so kind as to witness the signature of them.'

"Of course, I said I would come at once, and rising, followed the old steward out of the room. I did not expect to be away for more than a minute or two, so I left the papers and everything just as they were on the table by the window where I had been working. As it happened, I stayed with Count Rudolf quite a quarter of an hour; for, after the documents were witnessed, he asked what I had found in Don Angelo's *dossier*, and my description of the papers interested him greatly.

"'It is really a wonderful find,' he said when I had finished, 'and I congratulate you on it most heartily. After luncheon you must show me the originals. I will not keep you now, for these papers must go off this morning, but later on I shall love to see your treasure.'

"Accordingly, I left him to finish his business and went back to my own apartment. As I opened the door, I noticed a strong smell of burning paper, and a glance at the table revealed the cause. The candle I had so foolishly left alight by the window must have been softened by the heat of the sun's rays and had fallen over on to the marble-topped table, where it had set fire to the pile of papers I had left there. I ran across the room and saw with dismay that the whole collection was now no more than a heap of blackened ashes, mixed with a shapeless mass of dirty, congealed wax. My vexation was intense, the knowledge that the accident was due solely to my own carelessness did not lessen it, and on the impulse of the moment I cried out aloud.

"'Ah! Don Giovanni, you have got your wish. The papers are burned, although I never meant to burn them.'

"To my amazement, from below the window there came the faintest possible whisper:

"'*Deo gratias.*'

"Instantly I thrust my head out of the casement and looked down.

Of course, there was no one there. That night, too, I sat up till well past midnight, listening for the sound of footsteps. But I heard nothing, nor did they ever come again through all the weeks I spent upon the Aventine."

The Scapegoat

The postal arrangements at Stanton Rivers are still somewhat primitive, the nearest post town being about six miles away. Thence, every morning except Sunday, on which there is no delivery, His Majesty's mails set out punctually at 6 am. in a small dog-cart. The postman drives round a circuitous route, calling at quite half a dozen villages before he reaches Stanton Rivers, where he usually arrives about nine o'clock, so that the "Hall bag" is brought in during the course of breakfast.

The said bag is a large leather satchel with brass fittings and a lock, of which the squire and the postmaster possess keys; and on the lock-plate is engraved the name *F. RIVERS-PATER, ESQ.*, 1831, in witness of the fact that it was made for the squire's father in the year before his marriage.

I think the circumstance that the bag is older than the squire himself partly accounts for the high respect shown towards it by Avison, the butler. He always brings it in himself on a large silver tray and deposits it solemnly on a side table; after which he announces its arrival to the squire with a never-varying formula, 'The bag, sir.'

Equally changeless is the squire's answer: "Thank you, Avison; would you mind opening it?" a request which, I am sure, the old servant regards as a piece of ritual whose omission would indicate a sad tendency to modernism on the part of his master.

This morning, however, there was an addition to the concluding formula "Your letters, sir," to the squire, "and yours, sir," to myself, which usually ends the little ceremony; for Avison presented a strip of green paper to his master, saying,

"A receipt for the registered letter in the long envelope, sir; shall I sign it for you?"

"Please do so, Avison," answered the old priest; and the butler retired bearing off some letters for the servants with the empty bag, in

247

state, upon the silver tray.

"Now what in the world can this be?" said the squire, a moment later, as he surveyed the long, registered envelope beside his plate. "Look, Roger, it has an American stamp on it and some name or other in the corner," and the old man produced his spectacles, wiped them, and put them on.

"If undelivered, return to Price and Van Hartsinck, 42, West 17th Street, Philadelphia, Penn.," he read slowly, and then stopped and looked at me in mock alarm.

"Price and Van Hartsinck—what a name for a firm! They must be lawyers, I'm convinced of it. Take my word for it, Roger, some American claimant is going to turn up and lay claim to Stanton Rivers. We shall have to flit, my boy, you and I. You'll go back to your journalism, and I shall end my days in the workhouse."

"Oh, come, sir," said I, laughing, "it may not be that at all. On the contrary, I strongly suspect that some forgotten Rivers or Pater has died a millionaire, and left his riches to restore the family fortunes."

"Well, I shan't open it till after breakfast, at any rate," he declared, with an air of determination. "I'm not going to have my digestion interfered with to please Messrs. Price and Van Hartsinck;" and he turned the offending envelope face downwards, as if to make it feel it was in disgrace.

The old squire was a most methodical man, and after breakfast always retired to the 'writing-room,' as he preferred to call his private study, where he cleared off the business of the day before he reappeared; consequently, I was usually left to myself for most of the morning. On this occasion I took a longish walk after breakfast and, on my return, went to the library. To my surprise, I found the old priest there and evidently waiting for me.

"Come in, my dear boy," he cried, as I entered, "I want to tell you something"—and I saw that he held the long, registered envelope in his hand.

"I know, it's the millionaire theory come true," I said lightly, pointing to the envelope.

"No, no," he answered with a smile, but in rather a sad tone; "we were both of us quite wrong. It is more like the last act of a tragedy; or rather it is the last chapter of a story which, so far as I am concerned, was left unfinished thirty years ago. If you are not busy, I should like to tell it you. This unexpected *dénouement* makes me want to put the whole sad business into words."

I took a chair beside the old man, who sat in silence for fully a minute, lost in the memories which the letter had revived. Then he began to speak very quietly, more as if he were talking to himself than to me, and this is the story as he told it. Some details seem a little misty, probably because he forgot that, to one who heard it for the first time, many things would be less clear than they were to himself, who had taken so intimate a part in the actual events.

"It was somewhere in the seventies, about '77 I fancy, and I was in Paris when I first heard of the affair. My agent wrote to me to say that there had been a tragedy at Mason's cottage. The place, a very lonely one, hidden away in a little valley, had somehow caught fire in the night, and in the morning old Mrs. Mason had been found burned to death; while her son, Will Mason, of whom at first no trace was to be seen, had been discovered some hours later, with his skull fractured and one arm broken, lying at the foot of a quarry two hundred yards away from the cottage. He was taken into hospital, where a trepanning operation had been performed which, they hoped would save his life, but he was still unconscious when the agent wrote. They thought he must have fallen over the edge of the quarry in running to get help when the cottage first took fire.

"That was all his first letter told me, but a second one came next day, saying that there were some suspicious circumstances about the case, and that the inquest would be held on the morrow. I telegraphed to him to say I was returning at once, and travelled back that night, reaching Stanton Rivers about noon the following day. Of course, the inquest had been held even before I received the agent's second letter, and when I got home, I found him here waiting to tell me about it.

"It appeared that the medical examination of Mrs. Mason's body had revealed the fact that her death was caused, not by the fire, but by a bullet from a pistol. There were indications, too, that the woman had been dead some time, probably an hour or two, before the fire reached her body. Moreover, the bullet was found to fit a pistol which the Masons used to keep fastened up over the fireplace in the living-room of their cottage, and which had belonged to Mrs. Mason's first husband, one James Bull, formerly a gamekeeper on the estate here. Everything pointed to murder and arson, and the inquest had therefore been adjourned in the hope of Will Mason's recovery. That was all the agent could tell me, but I instructed him to call at the hospital, when he got back, and tell them that I was coming in to see Mason the next morning.

"Next day I drove in to the little market town and called at the hospital. First of all, I interviewed the Matron, and learned that Mason had shown signs of a return to consciousness. He had become restless and delirious, and was raving a good deal. On hearing this I demanded to be allowed to see him. At first the Matron refused point blank, but I argued that, as Mason's employer, I was the person to whom it fell to look after him, as he had no relations living except his half-brother, Jim Bull, who was in the United States, and whose address was quite unknown to me.

"After some little discussion the matron gave way and took me to the room where he was lying, first cautioning me to make no noise and to say nothing to the patient, no matter what his ravings might be. At first sight the man might have been dead, but for his breathing, so still did he lie. Then, suddenly, his eyes opened and he hissed out,

"'Curse 'ee!'

"I gave a start, for his eyes were fixed full upon me as I stood at the foot of the bed, but a moment's reflection told me that he was delirious and quite unconscious of my presence.

"'Curse 'ee!' he cried again, a moment later, ''tis all thy doin'.' Then, after a pause, came a whisper I could scarcely hear, 'Poor old mother . . . never meant to hurt 'ee. . .my God. . .' and the words ran off into unintelligible mutterings. Then the matron led me out of the room, for I had promised only to stay a minute.

"'You see how it is, sir, she said to me, 'we don't want people to know the kind of thing he keeps on saying.'

"'You have not told the police?' I asked her,

"'No, sir,' said she; 'but you know the coroner is one of our doctors, and he has heard Mason talking like this.'

"'That comes to the same thing, practically,' said I; and, after instructing her to do everything that could be done for the poor fellow and send me the bill, I left the hospital and drove home.

"Next day Mason recovered consciousness, and the first thing he did was to make a confession of his guilt, and ask that it should be communicated to the police. After that, of course, the result of the inquest was a foregone conclusion, and as soon as he was well enough to move, Mason was arrested.

"I saw him in prison during the interval before the Assizes and tried to get at the circumstances of his mother's death, but he kept absolutely silent on the subject. All he would say was, 'I did it,' or ''T'was I,' but he would give no suggestion of his motive. Remembering what

I had heard him say in delirium, I felt almost sure there was something behind which would explain the terrible act, and make it appear somewhat less dreadful than the cold-blooded murder it seemed to be; but when I suggested this, it only increased his reticence, and he simply ceased speaking altogether.

"My solicitor fared no better, for when I sent him to the prison to see Mason about his defence all the man would say was, 'Tell t'squire I'm thankfu' to him, verra thankfu', but I did it, so I'll just plead guilty; and in the end he was found guilty on his own confession, and condemned to death.

"The case aroused little interest, even in the neighbourhood, for the Masons had been a silent retiring couple, and no one knew them really intimately. The mother and son had got on well enough together of recent years, but I learned that, before Jim Bull had gone to America some three years earlier, there had been constant quarrels between the two brothers. In these disputes the mother had always sided with her elder son, and many thought that this had embittered Will Mason until, by brooding over the point, it had become a kind of obsession. This explanation certainly seemed at once the most reasonable and most charitable one, and I tried to think that the poor fellow had been scarcely responsible for his terrible act.

"During the three weeks or so that intervened between the sentence and the date fixed for his execution I said Mass for him many times, for the whole affair weighed heavily on me, and I felt that this was the way in which I could help him best. Then, two days before the execution, I received a letter from the Governor of the gaol.

"He wrote that the prison chaplain could make nothing of Mason, who simply ignored all his attempts at spiritual consolation, and refused to answer his questions. I ought to have told you that, although the mother had been a Catholic of a very nominal kind, the father had insisted that their son should be brought up as a Protestant, and Mason himself had never shown any particular interest in religion. Consequently, it came as a surprise when the governor's letter went on to say that Mason had asked to see him that day, and said that he would like to be attended by a Catholic priest, and if possible, by myself.

"I did not exactly welcome the task, but it seemed a clear duty to go, so I drove in to the town the same morning, and, with the willing consent of the chaplain, arranged to attend Mason for the few hours of life which remained to him. I expected that he would wish to be reconciled to the Church and receive absolution; but, on the contrary, he told me quite simply that he had no wish to become a Catholic. Eventually I gathered that he really wanted to be left quite alone during his last hours on earth, but finding this was forbidden by the prison regulations, had sent for me; for, as he said, 'Ye see, squire, ye've allus been a good friend to t'ould mother and I; and I canna 'bide yon parson chap 'at comes a-wortyin'.'

"It was a strange position, and perhaps rather a false one, but I felt it my duty to stay with him, and gradually he thawed a good deal and talked to me more freely. I determined not to repeat my former blunder, so made no attempt to probe into the motive of the murder, and Mason himself made no reference to it. Instead, his talk was all about the things of the soul, and I found that beneath his reticence, was a deep personal devotion to our blessed Lord.

"He was quite untaught with regard to religion, but he had read his Bible, and from it had acquired a wonderfully vivid idea of Christ as a personal Redeemer. During the long silent days in prison, he had prayed constantly and, to my amazement, I found that he had reached a high state of mystical experience. His sense of the presence of God scarcely ever left him, and from time to time he would ask me questions which showed that something very wonderful was happening in his soul.

"Gradually I began to realise that, far from needing my help, he was being directly prepared for death by the hand of God himself; and, with a feeling of deep reverence, I thanked our blessed Lord for permitting me to behold so wonderful an example of his love for men. This conviction only came to me gradually, you will understand, and I did not arrive at it on the first day I spent with him. But, on the second day, the one immediately preceding his execution, the truth of the affair became too plain to admit of further doubt.

"On that day he was more silent, speaking only at long intervals and then more as if he were thinking aloud than actually addressing me in person. I noticed, too, that his words were constantly interwoven with passages from those wonderful chapters of St John's Gospel which contain the discourse of our Lord at the last supper. He seemed, in fact, to know the whole discourse by heart, as well as those chapters of the first Epistle of St John, which almost form a paraphrase of it, and around these two his ideas seemed to revolve continually.

"When it was almost dark, a warder came to conduct me out of the cell, but, at Mason's request, I sent a message to the governor asking if I might be allowed to stay with him all night. Rather to my surprise, the petition was granted, and soon afterwards the warder brought some supper for us both. By this time the sense of Christ's presence in the place was simply overpowering, and during the meal I felt much as if we two were at Emmaus with the risen Lord.

"After supper Mason sat in silence for fully an hour. Then all at once he rose abruptly, as if at a word of command, and lay down on the low bed, covering himself with the blanket.

"'Father,' he said to me—it was the first time he had ever called me Father—'I mun rest a bit. Would 'ee mind sittin' by me and holdin' my han' while I sleep?'

"Of course I assented, and, moving my chair to the bedside, I sat down beside him and took his hand in mine. Almost immediately he fell into a quiet slumber, clasping my hand beneath the blanket; and I remember wondering how he could sleep so calmly knowing what awaited him at dawn.

"How long I sat there, half awake, half dozing, I cannot tell, but I should say it must have been well after midnight when I awoke abruptly, with a conviction that there was someone in the cell besides ourselves. I had turned the gas low when I moved my chair to the bedside, but there was light enough to distinguish everything in the cell, which was quite bare except for the scanty prison furniture. I could see no one, nor was there anything which could have concealed a man, but still the conviction remained that we were not alone. I thought to myself, 'I must not move for fear of waking Mason,' and then, suddenly, it struck me that perhaps I had already done so, by some unconscious movement, as I woke up, so I quickly glanced down at the bed beside me.

"I wish I could put into words for you what I saw. The man's whole visage was transfigured, changed—glorified, I had almost said—so that I scarcely could believe it was the same. It may have been his paleness in the dim light of the cell, but to me it seemed as if his face shone with a kind of radiance, much as a marble statue does in moonlight; but that was the least part of the marvel.

"What made me catch my breath and held me spellbound was the calm glory of his expression. His eyes were open, with the pupils contracted as if focussed on something only a few feet away, and over the whole face was a look of utter joyfulness, as if something long expected had at last come true, someone long waited had at length arrived; as if, in short, while still on earth and living, he were granted the perfect bliss of the beatific vision— hope giving place to sight and faith to fruition.

"I cannot tell you whether he was sleeping or in ecstasy, but this I know, that—condemned felon as he was, with not a dozen hours to live—I would right gladly have changed places with him, if so, I could have gained what he was then enjoying. Then all at once his lips began to move, and, though it was but the faintest whisper which came, I knew by some sympathetic influence exactly what it was that he was saying:

"'He that loveth his brother abideth in the light, and there is none occasion of stumbling in him. Whosoever doeth not righteousness is not of God, neither he that loveth not his brother. We know that we have passed from death to life because we love our brethren. He that loveth not his brother abideth in death. Whosoever hateth his brother is a murderer: and we know that no murderer hath eternal life. Hereby perceive we the love of God, because he laid down his life for us: and we ought to lay down our lives for our brethren. If a man say, I love God, and hateth his brother, he is a liar: for he that loveth not his brother whom he hath seen, how can he love God whom he hath not seen? And this commandment have we from him, that he who loveth God, love his brother also.'

"Then there came a pause while the look in his eyes deepened in intensity, as if he were listening. This lasted for a few minutes, and then the muscles of his face relaxed again, and once more the lips moved.

"'Peace I leave with you, my peace I give unto you; not as the world giveth, give I unto you. Let not your heart be troubled, neither let it be afraid; perfect love casteth out fear. This is my commandment, that ye love one another, as I have loved you. Greater love hath no man than this, that a man lay down his life for his brother.'

"Then quietly his eyes closed, the strange radiance seemed to fade from his features, and I heard no more, though I watched beside him till the dawn.

"I was present at his execution, but there is no need for me to tell you about that—even now I cannot think of it without a thrill of horror. All I need say is that, after he awoke, he scarcely spoke again, except to pray. Not a word of explanation passed his lips, but it was obvious that his mind was quite untroubled by remorse.

"As I drove back here, through the fresh June morning, my own brain was working feverishly, trying to solve the mystery which lay behind the affair, but, try as I might, I could form no satisfactory theory. On the one hand, it seemed clear that his mind was running on his brother, and that, in some unexplained way, he conceived himself to be taking the other's place and dying in his stead. On the other hand, I was quite at a loss for the connection.

"Jim Bull had left England three years before the tragedy, and although, as I told you, some people thought the mother's favouritism had soured Will Mason, he simply could not have convinced himself that Bull was responsible for the murder, unless he were absolutely insane upon the point, which I felt certain was not the case. Eventually I ceased trying to solve the mystery, and thus it has remained until this morning"—and he held up the envelope I had seen at breakfast.

"'This letter proved to be from a firm of lawyers in Philadelphia, and it enclosed a sealed envelope which, they say, was found with the will of their client, the late Mr. James Bull. On the outside of the sealed packet are endorsed instructions that it is to be sent to me, if I survive him, or, in the opposite event, to be destroyed unopened. Let me read it to you:

Philadelphia, Penn.
December 27, 1903

To Rev. P. R. Pater
Stanton Rivers,
England
    Rev. Sir,
"I am Jim Bull, Will Mason's half-brother; you will remember me. I understand you showed yourself a friend to him, attending him in gaol and on the scaffold.

"I want you to know that he was innocent and did not shoot our mother. I did that, I need not tell you why; but before she died, she begged him to save me, for I was always her favourite, and he promised to do so.

"No one in the place knew I was there that night, or even that I was in England; and so, when I made off, Will let the suspicion come on him, and you know how it all ended. Anyway, I guess he was more fit to die than I was, or ever shall be; but I am an old man now and cannot face death without taking some means to let his innocence be known.

Yours respectfully,

James Butt.

P.S.—You will not receive this until I am dead; if you think right, you may make it public.'

The old priest sat silent for some time and tears began to gather in his eyes.

"And shall you publish it?" I asked at length.

For answer he rose from his chair and thrust the letter, envelope and all, into the fire.

"*Cui bono?*" he asked, when the papers had fallen to ashes. "The whole thing is clear now. At his mother's prayer, Will Mason died to save his brother, and I doubt not the sacrifice was accepted by Him who died to save sinners. The Church teaches that an act of perfect charity wipes out all transgressions, and '*greater love hath no man than this, that a man lay down his life for his friend.*' Although Will Mason's body lies in a felon's grave, I believe his soul to be in glory. But I cannot think that he would ever wish me to tell the secret which he kept at such a cost."

Our Lady of the Rock

The chapel at Stanton Rivers has no claims to notice from an architectural point of view, for it is simply a room on the second floor which the old squire-priest fitted up for himself after his ordination. Some of the ornaments and altar furniture, however, are of great beauty, for it has been a fancy of the squire's to have only genuine old vestments, pictures, etc., and in the course of his long life he has got together a collection of great interest and considerable value.

Besides the old paintings, mostly "primitives" of the Italian and Flemish schools, there is one quite modern picture, which hangs above the holy-water stoup at the door. It is a little sketch in water colours, representing a small cave or natural recess in a rocky cliff, at the back of which is seen an image of the Blessed Virgin, standing in a niche above a small altar.

The sketch has an odd, out-of-place look beside the old pictures, for as a work of art it is simply negligible, a fact which I remarked upon to the squire when he first showed me round the chapel. To my horror, he answered with a smile of amusement:

"You are perfectly right. But then, you see, I painted it myself."

"Oh, sir!" I exclaimed, "it wasn't fair of you to set such a trap for me."

"Unfair! not a bit of it," he answered merrily; "you simply walked into it yourself. But the sketch isn't here as a work of art, it is more like a votive offering; someday Ill tell you all about it."

I remembered the promise and always meant to claim its fulfilment, but in the end the story turned up of its own accord. It was the Feast of the Annunciation, and among the squire's letters was a picture post-card, in colours, showing a lovely little Italian church standing beside a road amid a grove of orange trees, with the deep blue Mediterranean beyond. I noticed that it bore the postmark Amari, and was addressed in a quavering, unsteady hand, such as a very old man would write.

"Do you recognise the place?" asked the squire presently, as he noticed me examining the picture.

"No, sir," I answered, for the view was quite unfamiliar to me, "but then I was only once at Amalfi, and that for a single night, when I was walking from Naples to Salerno."

"Well, you passed it on your road, in that case," said he, "but unless someone told you to look inside, it is ten to one you'd never do so, for it looks just like any other wayside chapel. Indeed, I insisted on that when it was built, though my old friend, Don Giuliano, who sent me that picture of it, was very keen to have something smart and modern looking. That's just like a Neapolitan; none of them ever see how hideous their fine new buildings always are and how perfectly the simple, older ones harmonise with the setting of the orange groves and the wonderful natural beauty of the place."

"But I don't understand, sir," I broke in. "Did you build the church yourself?"

"Of course I did," answered he; "didn't I tell you about it? It is the new home of *la Santissima Madonna della Rocca*; surely, I must have mentioned her to you before."

"Really, I don't think you have," I replied; "but that's all the more reason why you should do so now, isn't it?"

"Well, I think you would like the story," said the squire, "though I quite thought I had told it to you already. If you have finished breakfast we will go to the library, and you can smoke a pipe while I talk.

"I think I see now why I felt so sure I had told you the story before," said the old priest, when we had settled down in the big oriel window. "You see, the whole thing is connected with that sketch in the chapel upstairs; I remember promising to explain why it was put there, and I suppose I must have forgotten to do so."

"I remember the promise quite well," I said; "you made it on the day when you first showed me the chapel, and I put my foot in it so hopelessly about the picture by the holy-water stoup. I've often meant to ask you for the story, but somehow the opportunity never came.'

"Well, you shall have it now," he answered; "but first give me my rug, for it is a little chilly in here this morning." I wrapped the big fur rug round the old priest's knees, and after making him comfortable, sat down again.

"I think it must have been in 1863 that I first met Don Giuliano Mattei, the old priest who sent me the postcard," he began thoughtfully, "so he must be well over eighty now; not that his age matters to the story. What does matter is that I was given a letter of introduction to him by the Rector of the *Accademia*, when I went to Amalfi for change of air, after a sharp attack of Roman fever during my first year there as a student. It was in February, I remember, but Amalfi is a good deal warmer than Rome, so the doctor ordered me there for a month's holiday, that I might get my strength back before the hot weather came.

"To Amalfi I went then, armed with my letter to Don Giuliano, who had just been made parish priest of San Severino, a church on the edge of the little town, with a parish consisting mostly of mountainside and orange grove. He was an old *Accademia* student, and received me most kindly, refused to hear of my taking rooms at a hotel, and insisted that I should stay with him in his big rambling house, where an aunt of his acted as his housekeeper, cook, and general servant, assisted by an old gardener called Girolamo, who looked like one of Fra Angelico's apostles, and did remarkably little work.

"You have seen Amalfi yourself, so I need not tell you that, although it ranks as a cathedral city, it is really no bigger than a large village. In a week or so I had seen everything there was to see there, and as my strength returned, I made excursions to Ravello, La Cava, and any other places of interest I could hear of in the neighbourhood.

"Don Giuliano, of course, professed a good-humoured horror at my energy. 'You a sick man!' he would exclaim. 'But there, all you *Inglesia* are possessed by a demon of unrest'—and he would throw out his hands with a gesture of resignation, and then suggest some new place for me to visit; so that I soon got to know the neighbourhood in a manner I could never have done without him. One day, when the supply of places to visit was running dry, we were discussing what there was left for me to see, when all at once he slapped his cassock impatiently.

"'*Per Bacco!*' he exclaimed, 'I don't believe you've ever been to the shrine of *la Madonna della Rocca!*'

"'I certainly don't remember the name,' I answered; 'but tell me where it is, and I shall know if I've seen it.'

"'Where it is!' he exclaimed, 'why, it is here, or rather up there!' and he pointed to the top of the hill that rises cliff-like above the sea to the south of Amalfi, towering up almost perpendicularly to the height of fully three thousand feet.

"'What, is it that ruin?' I asked; for I could see a half-ruined building perched on the very edge of the cliff above us.

"'To be sure it is,' said he, 'at least, that is a part of the hermitage. The church, or what remains of it, stands further back a little, and the cave of the Madonna is right below the altar. You can't see it from here as it is round the corner of the hill.'

"'Do tell me about it,' I begged him. 'Why is the shrine at such an inaccessible spot, and why has it fallen into ruins?'

"'To say the truth,' he answered, 'I don't know very much about it myself, although it is in my parish. But the legend is that the Blessed Mother of God used to appear there to a certain hermit, who lived in the cave some three or four hundred years ago. They say she ordered him to found a monastery there, and that this was the origin of the settlement. The monks were hermits of Camaldoli, and soon the cave became a place of pilgrimage and the Madonna used to work miracles there.'

"'Why *used to work*, only?' I demanded mischievously. 'Don't you believe our Lady can do so still?'

"'But the statue which was the centre of devotion is there no longer, *caro mio*,' he answered, ignoring my suggestion that his lack of faith was the difficulty; 'or rather, I should say, I don't know if it is. When the French came here in Napoleon's time, they turned out the *Camaldolesi*, wrecked the sanctuary, and carried off all the votive offerings. The people here say that the statue was hidden somewhere near its old site; and the interesting part of it is that they have quite a definite legend which, I fancy, must have come from one of the dispossessed hermits. It says that, though she was hidden from strangers, it is by a stranger that she will be found. 'That is the story, is it not, Aunt Anna?' he said, turning to the white-haired old lady, who had entered the room while we were talking.

"'*Sicuro*—to be sure,' she answered, 'and *la Madonna* will appear again when she wishes to, never doubt it. When I was a girl, we used to go up to the grotto on the Feast of the Annunciation and sing hymns in her honour, for that was the day of her *festà*. Often, too, we prayed that she would show us where her image was hidden, but we never got an answer, for none of us were *forestieri*'

"Well, the end of it was that I climbed the hill that afternoon and reached the hermitage in an hour or so. The size of the place surprised me, for it had looked a mere hut from below, but the shelf widened round the curve of the crag and there was quite a good-sized church, roofless and with gaping door and windows, and a tiny cloister with some six or seven little hermitages grouped round it; all more or less in ruins.

"Beyond the buildings was a path cut in the rock, which divided after a few yards. I took the upper fork first and soon came to another little plateau, surrounded by a crumbling wall, which had doubtless been the garden, but was now indistinguishable from the hill-side beyond. Returning to the buildings, I next tried the lower path, which struck downward sharply by the side of the church. Soon it became a rough stairway, took a turn to the right, and ended in a little open space with a low parapet on two sides, and what seemed to be the mouth of a small cave on the third.

"Above was the apse of the church, and I understood now why Don Giuliano had spoken of the shrine as being right beneath the altar, for the cave ran in some yards and must, in fact, have been exactly covered by the sanctuary above. The place looked utterly forlorn and desolate, and a feeling of depression came over me as I passed beneath the low, narrow archway of the entrance and took my first breath of the cold, dank air within.

"'Poor *Madonna della Rocca!*' I said to myself; 'whoever hid you did his work only too well. It is not likely that anyone will come to seek you in this cold, forsaken place, all damp and dark.'

"Even as the words formed themselves in my mind, I noticed that it was not so dark after all. No doubt my eyes were adjusting themselves to the gloom of the cave after the bright sun outside, and I soon found I could distinguish some faint remains of painting on the walls. After a minute or so I could see quite clearly, and the sense of depression gave place to one of interest and pleasure, as the instinct for exploration arose in my mind.

"I found the cave to be some nine or ten yards deep, and although the entrance was low and narrow, it widened and heightened quickly. In the centre it was six full paces across, and as far as I could judge the height must have been fully fifteen feet or more. The floor was of rock, smoothed by cutting it away in places, and at the far end was an altar, with its altar stone broken right across. Above was an empty niche, its sides decorated with battered stucco pilasters, in the hollows of which faint traces of gold and colour still glimmered here and there.

"When I had examined the place as fully as the light permitted, I came out again and noted the position of the sun. It was fairly low in the southwest, and a little calculation showed me that the cave faced south-east, so that it would be quite well lit up until after 10 a.m. Somehow the place interested me strangely, and I determined to return at an early hour on the morrow.

"Accordingly, next morning I started about eight o'clock and was at the grotto shortly before nine. As I expected, the interior was now lit up by the sun, which poured in at the narrow entrance and was reflected from the white limestone floor, so that there was quite a strong light within. I now saw that the painted decoration had been carried round the whole of the walls, and that, in spite of deliberate mutilation, quite a lot of the design remained in the higher levels which were out of reach. Except round the niche and altar, the work was painted in monochrome only, the part which remained consisting chiefly of a series of Scripture texts referring to our Lady, and forming a kind of frieze all round the cave.

"I now set to work to examine the place minutely, beginning at the ruined altar with the pathetic, empty niche above it. In front of the altar itself was a *predella* or step, not cut out of the solid rock like the floor of the cave, but built up of limestone slabs, carefully worked. Like the altar stone above, these slabs had experienced rough treatment, and there were narrow openings between them as if someone had been at work with the intention of displacing them, but had tired of the task and abandoned it. When I stood on the front stone of the *predella*, I found it unsteady, but not wishing to hasten the collapse of the whole, I did not try to move it.

"My next move was to decipher the inscriptions which, as I said, formed a kind of frieze round the whole cave. The series began close to the entrance with the salutation of the Angel Gabriel, and it struck me, as I made out one after another, that they seemed to be the antiphons of the Annunciation, which had been the *festà* of the *Madonna della Rocca*. I had my breviary in my pocket, and on comparing the two, found my guess was correct, the texts were all taken from the office of the Annunciation. Here and there was a gap, where the paint had peeled off or the surface had perished, but I could fill in these *lacunae* quite easily with the aid of the breviary in my hand.

"All at once I came upon a variant reading: *virtus Altissimi in te descendet, Maria; et Spiritus Sanctus obumbrabit mihi.*

"'What a curious blunder!' I said to myself; for naturally I put it down to the carelessness of the painter. 'Of course it should be: *Spiritus Sanctus in te descendet, Maria; et virtus Altissimi obumbrabit tibi*, for I had the words before me in the Breviary; they are the *Magnificat* antiphon at first vespers of the feast.

"I looked up at the wall again; there was not a doubt about it. The subject had been transposed in the two phrases and the first person, *mihi*, substituted for *tibi*, the second person, as if our Lady and not the angel Gabriel were speaking: 'The Holy Spirit shall overshadow me.'

"'It really is very odd,' I said to myself; 'of course, an ignorant workman might have got the words reversed by accident, but to substitute mihi for *tibi* by accident seems almost impossible. If the painter knew enough Latin for that, he must have known enough to see how it changes the whole meaning'—and I stood for some time looking up at the puzzle. All at once it struck me that the words were exceptionally clear and easy to read, distinctly clearer than the texts on either side of them. The inscription was just by one end of the altar, and I climbed up on to the *mensa* to examine it more closely. The words were still some feet away, but I was now on a level with them and could see that the paint of the lettering was not quite the same colour as that of the fainter inscription beside it, and that the whole looked fresher and more recent.

"'This becomes interesting,' I thought, as I climbed down again. 'If the inscription is a newer one, the curious wording must have been put there on purpose, but what in the world can the purpose be? It can't have been done out of devotion to our Lady, for what possible use could it be to paint up "The Holy Spirit shall overshadow me"?'

"Then, in a flash, it struck me that the words might have been changed so as to refer to the hiding place of the missing statue, which tradition declared to be somewhere close to its former shrine. 'The Holy Spirit shall overshadow me.' If the hiding place were marked with some emblem of the Holy Spirit, then the Madonna herself *was* speaking, and speaking very much to the point. The question was, what would the symbol be?

"I stood there lost in thought for some moments, and instinctively I asked our Lady to help me find her image, if the revival of the cultus would be pleasing to her; and moved by a sudden impulse, I promised to build a little chapel in honour of the *Madonna della Rocca*, if she showed her approval by emerging from the place where she was hidden. My prayer was scarcely finished when my eyes fell on the breviary, which was still in my hand, open at the Feast of the Annunciation. I nearly dropped it in surprise, for the words I read were these, from the first lesson at *Matins*, *Pete tibi signum a Domino Deo tuo, in profundum inferni, sive in excelsum supra.* ("Seek for thyself a sign from the Lord, thy God, either in the depth beneath or in the height above.") I gave a great gasp of surprise, but the next moment felt inclined to laugh at myself.

"'Come now, I'm getting superstitious,' I said to myself. 'It's all the effect of this cold, half-lit cave; let's get out into the open again'—and I walked out into the sunshine and looked over the parapet to the calm blue ocean, three thousand feet below.

"I must have stayed there several minutes, drinking in the beauty of the glorious view, when suddenly I heard a voice, soft, but strangely musical and quite distinct, which came apparently from below the parapet.

"'*In profundum inferni,*' it said; and I quickly leaned over the edge and looked down, to see who could be speaking. There was not a soul in sight, but, far below, my eyes fell upon the form of a beautiful white bird. I was beginning to think it had been all imagination, when the same soft voice spoke again, this time above me.

"'*Sive in excelsum supra,*' it said, completing the text of Isaias. I glanced up quickly, though I felt sure there could be no one there, for the rock rose sheer above the cave. There was no one, of course, but a moment later came a noise of beating wings and a pair of doves circled round the apse of the forsaken church.

"'Superstition or no superstition,' I cried aloud, 'I know I'm going to find the Madonna. If *Spiritus Sanctus obumbrabit mihi* means anything, it means that the image is hidden somewhere and the place is marked with the figure of a dove'—and I hurried back into the cave.

"By this time the sun had moved a long way round to the west, and the light inside the cave was fading rapidly. After a while, too, I found I was seeing doves everywhere in the cracks of the limestone walls, and it dawned upon me that I had eaten nothing all day except a couple of little cakes with my cup of coffee at breakfast; so, I gave up my search and walked down the hill to Amalfi. On the way I decided to say nothing to Don Giuliano at present, since I wanted to find the Madonna myself, if she were to be found; and I did not want to be laughed at, if nothing came of my labours.

"Next day was Saturday, and also the Vigil of the Annunciation. As I made my way up to the grotto at an early hour, a curious feeling came over me that the search would not be in vain; but after two hours I must admit my hopes began to fade. I had brought some candles with me, and by their aid I peered into every nook and cranny of the rock. Not a sign of a dove could I see anywhere, nor indeed the smallest indication that the rock surface had ever been disturbed at all. The sun was beginning to move away from the mouth of the cave when I sat down on the *predella* of the altar to rest a little and think things out.

"'If the whole cave, roof, floor and all, is solid rock, which has never been disturbed, then the statue can't be here,' I argued. 'But I've examined every part of it, and every part is solid, *ergo*.'

"'But have I examined every part of it?' I asked myself, after a moment. 'How about the *predella* I am sitting on? Do these stones rest on the solid rock, or no?'

"In a moment I was up again and at work at the big unsteady stone which formed the front of the *predella*. It was too heavy to lift, but I succeeded in working it loose and managed to roll it over sideways, so that it lay two feet or so from its former position. The flagstones behind it were smaller and lighter, and in a few minutes, I had got one of them out. I found that they were laid upon loose earth which had been piled up to give a level surface for them, and, of course, some of this clung to the underside of the flag I had moved. The second flagstone was the central one of the *predella*, and as I was carrying it out from its place, it slipped from my hands and fell on its edge on the floor of the cave. The jerk did not break the stone, but it did detach the earth which was clinging to it, and my heart gave a great thump as I saw, on the underside of the flag, the figure of a dove rudely cut in outline.

"'*Spiritus Sanctus obumbrabit mihi*,' I cried aloud, for I felt convinced now that I was on the right track; and I renewed my destruction of the *predella* with redoubled energy. In a few minutes I had got up the remaining stones and was shovelling away the earth beneath them. This was only a few inches deep, and below it the shovel grated on a hard flat surface. Would it be the solid rock, or the cover of the Madonna's hiding place? I worked with feverish energy to find out.

"Very soon the earth was all shovelled away and I found a long flat slab of marble, like the top of a narrow table, which I was able to prize up with my shovel. Without much difficulty I got it up and, with a lighted candle, peered into the space beneath. It was a long narrow opening, rather like a place for a coffin, and in it lay an object swathed round and round with the remains of rotten coverings, which tore at the slightest touch. Quickly I dragged away enough of them to see what was beneath. It was a carved wooden statue of the Blessed Virgin, bearing the infant Saviour in her arms.

"That evening I told Don Giuliano what I had found, and on the next day he announced it to his people at the end of Mass, saying:

"'My brethen, we will now go in procession and bring *la santissima*

Madonna to San Severino.'

"This was a development I had not expected; indeed, I had been dreaming of restoring the old hermitage and reinstating the Camaldolese. However, the idea was received with enthusiasm, every able-bodied person in the church joined our procession, and we were soon on our way to the grotto.

"There was no lack of labourers now, and the image was lifted out of its hiding place, and carried up into the half-ruined church above the cave. Here Don Giuliano had it placed upon the altar for all to see; while, with true Italian readiness, he poured forth an eloquent little sermon on the blessed Mother of God. When he had finished, the procession started for Amalfi again, and all the town turned out to receive our Lady. The statue was placed in San Severino, and during the octave of the feast the church was thronged with people every day, for the news of the recovery of the lost Madonna spread quickly over all the countryside.

"I went to the bishop and told him of my promise to the Madonna, adding that I would either restore the old shrine, or build a new one in Amalfi, according to what he decided. In the end, he thought it best that the chapel should be built, not on the old inaccessible site, but on the side of the road to Salerno; outside the town itself, and just beneath the ruins of the ancient hermitage.

"The work was put in hand at once, and just a year later, on the Feast of the Annunciation, the image was solemnly translated and installed in its new home. Every year, on the *festà*, a Mass is said there for the founder of the chapel, and Don Giuliano sends some little token to show that he has not forgotten me. He must be well over eighty now, and we shall never meet again in this life, so you will understand what pleasure it gave me to receive his postcard this morning."

The Communion of Saints

Before I went to live with my old cousin at Stanton Rivers, I had no idea how deeply interesting religion becomes, when it is studied in the records of personal experience, or the phenomena displayed in the course of man's relations with God. But I had come to the right place to learn, for religious psychology, or, as he preferred to call it, "the phenomena of personal religion," had long been the absorbing study of the old priest's life; and his mind was a storehouse of knowledge on the subject, gained by a lifetime of reading in hagiology, religious biography, and the self-revealing writings of the mystics.

No section of his large library was so carefully tended as this one, and in it I found, besides the great standard works on the subject, a large number of rare old books whose very existence is known to few, arranged on the shelves close beside the latest modern studies in mysticism and religious philosophy.

At first sight it was somewhat startling to see Denys the Carthusian, Dame Juliana of Norwich, and Blessed Angela of Foligno in close proximity with Starbuck's *Psychology of Religion*, William James's *Varieties of Religious Experience*, and works by Max Nordau, Professor Ribot, or Havelock Ellis. But I knew the squire's methodical character well enough to feel sure that it was my ignorance and not his arrangement that was at fault. Closer acquaintance with the books in question soon revealed the intimate connection between them, and I ceased to wonder why it was that the great folio volumes of the Bollandist *Acta Sanctorum* ran along the bottom shelf of all, like a solid foundation of rock, supporting alike works Catholic and Protestant, Jew and *Infidel*, ancient and modern, Eastern and western.

So far as I remember, the book which first revealed to me the highly uniform character of these personal experiences, no matter to what religious system the individual may belong, was Professor James's deeply interesting volume mentioned above. Though I had often heard it mentioned, I had somehow never come across the book until I found it at Stanton Rivers; and I read it through carefully and slowly, taking a considerable time in doing so. It happened that I had just finished the book and was still smarting under a sense of disappointment with its chilly, tentative conclusions, when the squire chanced to notice the volume in my hand, and asked how I liked it.

"Really, I find it very hard to say," I answered. "The first half of it struck me as quite wonderful, especially the many personal narratives woven into it so skilfully, but the later lectures on 'Saintliness' and 'Mysticism' were less satisfying, and the two concluding ones I thought frankly disappointing. But, of course, it is only fair to remember that he proposes to supplement them in another work to follow."

"That is interesting," answered the old priest, "but I think I understand how you feel about it. As you say, his marshalling of the facts in the earlier chapters is admirably done, but somehow it is a curiously wrong-headed book. I often wonder that a man of William James's extraordinary insight and psychological training did not see how all these 'human documents' of his are written in sympathetic ink, and cannot really be understood aright except by one who is in sympathy with the emotions which prompted, accompanied, and succeeded the actual experience they record. Probably the explanation lies in the fact that James was a philosopher only, whereas he ought to have been a poet and a mystic as well, to make his work satisfactory. I sometimes wonder what Robert Browning would have made out of the same material; but are you a Browning devotee, by the way?"

I pleaded guilty to the charge and the squire continued.

"Good, then in that case you will see what I mean. Think for a moment of Browning's *Men and Women* of the 'Parleyings with certain people,' and especially of *The Ring and the Book*. I believe the reason why these poems are so marvellous is simply because Browning possessed the power of sympathy in a supreme degree. It is a highly imaginative sympathy, of course, but by it he is enabled to get inside the character he is portraying, to feel just as the real man felt, to see and hear as he saw and heard—in fact, to be for the moment the hero of his poem, in the same way that a consummate actor simply *is* the character he is portraying, having temporarily laid aside his own individuality and taken the other's in exchange.

"That, I think, is the secret of Browning's power, as it is of Shakespeare's and of all supreme poets, and if such perfect sympathy is needed anywhere, it is needed by the writer who would understand and depict the emotions of the soul in its most sublime experiences, that is, in its moments of union with God. A man who has never lost all thought of self in the supreme abandonment of love for another, cannot possibly write a perfect love poem; and one who has never really been in love with God, will never understand aright the language of those who have.

"Now William James, while he makes a great deal of the phenomenon called 'conversion,' never seems to me to have grasped the most important thing about it. He points out, of course, that it involves a shifting of the habitual centres of personal energy on the part of the individual who is converted, and that, in consequence of the conversion, certain feelings, ideas and beliefs which before were cold, dead and sterile become hot, living and fruitful. But he does not bring out the point that all this will not produce any ultimate religionising of the soul, unless it involve a complete and permanent change in the man's personal attitude towards God; since true religious life only begins when the soul comes to realise habitually and to act upon the principle that what matters is not so much the relation of everything towards itself, but the position and relation which it personally takes up and maintains towards God, thus making God and not self the central factor of life, the beginning and end of every thought and act.

"Again, while in some cases this change of attitude takes place abruptly at a particular moment—in which event the word 'conversion ' is precisely the right name for it—in many cases, and especially in the case of the great majority of Catholics, who are brought up from infancy to look upon God and our relations with him as the pre-eminent fact of life which matters infinitely more than all other things put together, no abrupt conversion is customary. Instead of it, we find a growing realisation of God and a steady development of the instinct for union with him, by means of which the soul is gradually religionized, so that a deo-centric attitude of mind and heart and will becomes habitual, without the individual man or woman experiencing any abrupt or instantaneous conversion at all.

"No doubt William James understood quite clearly that such a change of centre—which the old English mystics used to call 'self-naughting'— was essential for a fully religious life. But I think he largely failed to grasp the fact that this change or conversion was, after all, only a beginning of that life, and not by any means an end in itself. Probably his early training in Calvinistic theology had a lot to do with this; for in that system, once the soul has accepted Christ, there really remains nothing more for it to do at all, since the merits of Christ henceforth do everything for it automatically.

"I believe, therefore, that, owing to the influence of his early training, William James was not so much interested in the later developments of the soul, and that, in consequence, the phenomena of the religious life, after it had really become a religious life, did not appeal to him like those of the conversion period. So, naturally, his power to sympathize with and to understand those later developments was a very limited one, and his conclusions are necessarily rudimentary and disappointing, because his own personal experience of religion had been nipped in the bud."

"That explains a great deal," I said, when the old priest paused with an apology for the length of his "lecture," as he called it; "and especially it helps to clear up a difficulty I had felt. I mean, why it is that mystical experience seems to be not only rarer, but usually narrower among Lutherans, Calvinists, and the extreme Protestant sects, than it is in almost every other religious system, non-Christian and Christian alike."

"Precisely," answered the old priest, with a look of pleasure. "I see you have caught the point I was trying to make. You are right; it is the theology of Calvin and his fellow reformers which is to blame, not the souls of their followers. Often, indeed, the instincts of heart and mind are too much for the Geneva doctors, and we find their disciples undergoing advanced mystical experiences, which, according to their own theological theory, ought to be needless if not impossible to them."

"Would you say then," I asked, "to change the subject a little, that the phenomena of personal religion, such as conversion, a sense of God's presence or a feeling of desolation, advanced stages of prayer such as ecstasy, union and the rest, are identical in character, whether they appear in a Christian, a Buddhist, or a Moslem, for example?"

"Most certainly," replied the old priest with conviction; "why should it be otherwise? Are not all God's children brothers by nature? Hath not a Jew eyes? doth not a Buddhist pray, or a Moslem yearn after union with God? The Catholic Church teaches that everyone who strives earnestly to follow the dictates of his conscience is in the 'soul of the Church'; and if God feedeth the young ravens that call upon him, will he not do as much for all mankind, seeing that Christ has died for all?

"No doubt the dogmatic beliefs of each individual who is striving after union will affect both his prayer and the way in which he understands God's answer to it, much in the way that a message will undergo a subtle modification each time it is translated into a new language. That must result inevitably from the limitation of our minds. But the message is the same all the time; and even though everyone who receives it may understand it with a slight shade of difference, that fact proves nothing more than this, that we are all personal, individual beings, and that no one of us can stand in precisely the same position towards God as that which is occupied by his brother."

"I think I see," I said thoughtfully; "but what a broad, encouraging outlook on religion such a view gives one. Why, it really looks as if, in these personal experiences, we might find a basis for religious unity after all." The old man clapped his hands delightedly.

"Well done! well done!" he cried with animation; "you have got it. That is *the* point of all. Of course it is a broad view, it wouldn't be worthy of the Church if it were not; and as for encouraging our hope in an ultimate religious unity, it does more than that, it proves conclusively that such a unity does exist already between all those who sincerely love God. Though we may never achieve a formal unity of system in this world, nor bring all men into the visible fold of Christ, still 'actual life comes next,' and with it union, so we shall have all eternity to enjoy it in."

"Well, sir,' I said, "I must thank you most deeply for giving me so much help. I think your view is a most inspiring one, and enormously more encouraging than William James's *Conclusions*."

"Well, I'm glad you agree with it so fully," he answered. "It is many years now since I first came to hold what I have just explained to you; but I still remember how the thought came to me like a revelation, and its helpfulness has increased with the years, instead of growing less."

I caught at the word "revelation" and drew a bow at a venture.

"When you say 'it came like a revelation,' do you mean that you received the light in a mystical experience, sir?" I asked.

"Well," said he, with a little hesitation, "I hardly know that I should call it that exactly; but it did come in a somewhat unexplained way, and without any conscious working out in my mind. I will tell you the circumstances, if you care to hear them.

"Although anything like public controversy has always been distasteful to me, I have often found it impossible to avoid private discussion with non-Catholics who came to hear me preach or lecture; for

I did a good deal of such work in the first years after my ordination. Now and then I made converts, and felt the quiet joy which comes of realising that God is using one as his instrument; but far more often the discussions ended in a deadlock, neither of us being able to follow the other's mental processes any further, which is always a depressing way to finish. However, I used to make a point of parting friends, and if possible, of securing a promise that the others would pray for me, promising to do the same for them in return.

"One of these discussions was with an elderly Quaker, who came to see me one Lent, when I was lecturing in a large industrial centre in the north of England. He was a somewhat stolid-looking man, thick-set, with iron-grey hair and deeply cut features, and, until he began to talk, one never guessed the fire that burned in his heart and soul. He used to speak very slowly, as if waiting to be prompted by some agency outside his own mind; and, knowing as I did the Quaker belief that what a man says on religion is due not to himself, but to the Spirit moving him, his perfect sincerity and deep earnestness made a great impression on me, and I felt that, in his somewhat rigid and limited way, he was a true servant of God.

"He had no notion of becoming a Catholic, nor was he particularly interested in the Church's teaching; what he came to me about was another thing altogether. I had preached a sermon on the power of prayer, and he, seeing the subject advertised, had come to hear it. In my sermon I had spoken of belief in prayer as perhaps the one single doctrine on which every religious system was agreed, and had urged that, as in prayer we all had our one point in common, so it was probably through prayer alone that we could advance to mutual understanding and eventually to union.

"He came to see me several times, but our talks proved disappointing; for the old man was a typical Bible Christian and intolerant of any interpretation of Scripture other than his own, which was always of the ultra-literal type, except when such a method played into the hands of the Church—as in the account of the Last Supper—when he went off to the allegorical method. However, we parted good friends, and he promised to pray for me daily as long as he lived. In particular he said that he would ask God to enlighten my understanding that I might preach his word effectively, and especially might lead men of all religions to union by means of prayer. That was at our last meeting, and I remember that it took place upon Friday in Passion Week; for I left the place next day to preach on Palm Sunday and during Holy

272

Week in another town.

"I think I may say with truth that the old man and his promise passed from my mind completely, for although I make a memento in every Mass, I say for all those who have promised to pray for me, I do not attempt to remember all their names; so, he vanished at once into that strange limbo of memory which forms a large part of the subconscious self. The next few days were exceptionally full of work, for the parish to which I had gone was a very busy one, and I found myself on Good Friday morning without having prepared my sermon for that day at all. I was not nervous, as I had often preached upon the Passion of Christ, so I contented myself with making a short meditation on the mystery before the Mass of the Pre-sanctified, at which I assisted in the choir stalls, as I was not one of the ministers at the altar.

"I have told you, I think, that sometimes, when the 'direct speech' comes to me, it is heralded by a kind of physical collapse, during which my limbs grow weaker and weaker, while my mind becomes extraordinarily alert. Scarcely had the Mass begun when I felt slightly faint, but I put it down to the fact that I was fasting, and tried to pay no attention to it. At the Passion I stood up with the rest, but I soon found the effort beyond me and had to sit down to save myself from fainting. All this time, however, my mind was exceptionally active, and the tragedy of Christ's Passion and death, which was being sung by the three deacons, passed before me like a vision of some tremendous drama.

"I seemed, if I may say so with all reverence, to look upon the whole scene out of the eyes of Christ himself. My fainting limbs were for the moment his. The fierce throbbing pain in my head seemed concentrated at a hundred points, like the wounds of his crown of thorns. When, for a moment, I gripped the arms of the stall, the sudden pressure of the carved wood against the flesh felt, in my overwrought condition, as if sharp nails were piercing through my palms, and I almost cried out with the pain. Then, all at once, every sense of feeling seemed to pass away from me, and, instead, a kind of vision of Christ's mental sufferings engrossed my whole being.

"I seemed to be raised up to an immense height, from which my gaze enveloped all the world. All mankind was there, from every land and every age of history; and in some mysterious way I knew that Christ crucified was linked to each one individually by the bonds of his perfect love. From out his heart the precious blood poured down, and spreading forth, flowed over all the world. Some seemed to welcome it and bathed therein, uprising white and glorious to see. Some seemed not to notice it at all, but passed on heedless, just as if it were not there. Others there were who looked on it with hatred, and 'when they could not help walking in it, they held up their skirts.' But there it was, poured out for one and all, in heedless prodigality of sacrifice, the one sufficient ransom of mankind, infinite cost defrayed by perfect love.

"'They shall look upon him whom they pierced;' and as with those words the Passion wailed itself out in a mournful descending cadence, my strange half-faint, half-trance came to an end. The short Gospel followed, and then the Master of Ceremonies came across to conduct me to the pulpit. To my surprise I rose and followed him without the least difficulty, and I walked up the steep pulpit steps as easily as possible.

"What I said in my sermon I really cannot tell you, though I know that never in my life, before or since, have I preached with such effect. Certainly, the voice was mine, but it seemed to me that nothing else was. Ideas and words suggested themselves, or rather flowed from my lips, as if some external power was using me as a mouthpiece, through which to speak a message in whose composition I had no part. So much was this the case, that I was able to note the effect upon the audience in a way I never do when preaching, lest it should distract me.

"The very first words caught their attention, and, in my strange, detached state, I noted like a spectator how the sentences gripped and held them, until the whole great building seemed full of tense emotion, born of taut nerves that strained to catch each word. 'The sermon was a short one, scarcely twenty minutes in all, and there was a total absence of eloquent phrasing, loud declamation, or carefully contrived delivery; yet somehow it conveyed an impression of absolute authority, as if it came from a source where doubt or hesitation was unknown.

"All at once the flow of words ceased, and I felt a momentary surprise, for really, I did not know whether the discourse had reached its logical conclusion; and then with the same sense of being controlled by an overmastering force, I felt myself turn, leave the pulpit, and walk back to my stall in the chancel. As I went a kind of hushed murmur swept through the building, as the pent-up emotion of the crowded church broke forth. Far down the nave a voice cried out some broken words, a woman burst into loud sobbing, and numbers fell upon their knees instinctively to pray. Then, as I reached my place in the chancel, the priests at the altar proceeded with that wonderful series of prayers for all mankind, which forms so prominent a feature in the morning office of Good Friday.

"In turn we prayed to God for Church and Pope, for bishops, priests and all the sacred ministry, for catechumens—those children of adoption—for the sorrowful and afflicted, for heretics and schismatics, for Jews and pagans; that all might be united by God's grace into one holy Church, to the praise and glory of his name. That was the moment when the vast inclusiveness of God's plan became clear to me. The vision I had seen of all mankind, united to the cross of their Redeemer by the all-conquering torrent of his precious blood, found its interpretation here; as the Church, the Spouse of Christ, poured forth her prayers for all the human race. It was the cry of those who formed his mystic body, rising to heaven for those who as yet were only in the soul of the Church; a mother pleading for her unborn children, hers, though not yet hers, who counts no human soul an alien to her own.

"The supplications ceased, the last *Amen* died away, and a pause followed, while the acolytes made ready for the creeping of the Cross. As I turned and sat down in my stall for a moment's rest, my eyes chanced to fall upon the space in the centre of the chancel, and I nearly cried out with surprise. For there, full in the middle of the gangway, stood the figure of the old Quaker, from whom I had parted just a week before. I rubbed my eyes, but there was not a doubt about it; the figure seemed as material as you do at this moment, and not in the least shadowy or vague. 'The man looked just as he did when I had seen him last, a thick-set figure, with iron-grey hair and deep-cut features, their stolid expression redeemed by the earnestness of his dark eyes.

"For a minute at least, I stared at the apparition, which appeared completely unconscious of its surroundings, and simply stood there motionless, save for the lips, which moved slowly as if in prayer. Then, at a sign from the Master of Ceremonies, the whole congregation rose together, and, distracted by the noise, I glanced round for an instant. When I looked back at the centre of the chancel the figure I had seen had vanished; but in my ears I heard the old man's slow, deliberate voice repeating the words of his parting prayer a week earlier: 'May God enlighten thine understanding, friend, and may his Spirit come mightily upon thee, that thou mayest be powerful in word to speak as he shall give thee, and lead men to union with him by prayer.'

"I never saw or heard of him again, and he must be dead years ago, for he was an old man when I met him. But I do not doubt that he was praying for me on that Good Friday morning as he had promised, and that to his prayers I owed the inpouring of God's Holy Spirit, which wrought in me so wonderfully on that occasion."

LEONAUR

ALSO FROM LEONAUR
AVAILABLE IN SOFTCOVER OR HARDCOVER WITH DUST JACKET

MR MUKERJI'S GHOSTS *by S. Mukerji*—Supernatural tales from the British Raj period by India's Ghost story collector.

KIPLINGS GHOSTS *by Rudyard Kipling*—Twelve stories of Ghosts, Hauntings, Curses, Werewolves & Magic.

THE COLLECTED SUPERNATURAL AND WEIRD FICTION OF WASHINGTON IRVING: VOLUME 1 *by Washington Irving*—Including one novel 'A History of New York', and nine short stories of the Strange and Unusual.

THE COLLECTED SUPERNATURAL AND WEIRD FICTION OF WASHINGTON IRVING: VOLUME 2 *by Washington Irving*—Including three novelettes 'The Legend of the Sleepy Hollow', 'Dolph Heyliger', 'The Adventure of the Black Fisherman' and thirty-two short stories of the Strange and Unusual.

THE COLLECTED SUPERNATURAL AND WEIRD FICTION OF JOHN KENDRICK BANGS: VOLUME 1 *by John Kendrick Bangs*—Including one novel 'Toppleton's Client or A Spirit in Exile', and ten short stories of the Strange and Unusual.

THE COLLECTED SUPERNATURAL AND WEIRD FICTION OF JOHN KENDRICK BANGS: VOLUME 2 *by John Kendrick Bangs*—Including four novellas 'A House-Boat on the Styx', 'The Pursuit of the House-Boat', 'The Enchanted Typewriter' and 'Mr. Munchausen' of the Strange and Unusual.

THE COLLECTED SUPERNATURAL AND WEIRD FICTION OF JOHN KENDRICK BANGS: VOLUME 3 *by John Kendrick Bangs*—Including twor novellas 'Olympian Nights', 'Roger Camerden: A Strange Story', and ten short stories of the Strange and Unusual.

THE COLLECTED SUPERNATURAL AND WEIRD FICTION OF MARY SHELLEY: VOLUME 1 *by Mary Shelley*—Including one novel 'Frankenstein or the Modern Prometheus', and fourteen short stories of the Strange and Unusual.

THE COLLECTED SUPERNATURAL AND WEIRD FICTION OF MARY SHELLEY: VOLUME 2 *by Mary Shelley*—Including one novel 'The Last Man', and three short stories of the Strange and Unusual.

THE COLLECTED SUPERNATURAL AND WEIRD FICTION OF AMELIA B. EDWARDS *by Amelia B. Edwards*—Contains two novelettes 'Monsieur Maurice', and 'The Discovery of the Treasure Isles', one ballad 'A Legend of Boisguilbert' and seventeen short stories to cill the blood.

www.ingramcontent.com/pod-product-compliance
Lightning Source LLC
Chambersburg PA
CBHW060343030726
47497CB00003B/576